HALCYON

Also by Rio Youers and available from Titan Books

The Forgotten Girl (May 2019)

HALCYON

RIO YOUERS

TITAN BOOKS

Halcyon
Print edition ISBN: 9781785659829
E-book edition ISBN: 9781785659836

Published by Titan Books
A division of Titan Publishing Group Ltd
144 Southwark Street, London SE1 0UP
www.titanbooks.com

First Titan edition: October 2018
10 9 8 7 6 5 4 3 2 1

A CIP catalogue record for this title is available from the British Library.

Printed and bound in Great Britain by CPI Group Ltd.

What did you think of this book?
We love to hear from our readers. Please email us at:
readerfeedback@titanemail.com, or write to us at the above address.

To receive advance information, news, competitions, and exclusive offers online, please sign up for the Titan newsletter on our website.

For Christopher Golden
In this boat together...

PART I
PAVOR NOCTURNUS

1

She saw the man with no hands first. He lay screaming in the road, caught in the shimmer of something burning. His skin was blackened and smoke corkscrewed from his hair. It was his wrists, though—the raw stumps of his wrists—that made Edith close her eyes. Not that she could *un*see, of course, or even turn away.

His shirt had been burned from his body.

Edith Lovegrove, ten years old, clapped a hand across her mouth and managed, with colossal effort, not to scream. Her throat ballooned, dark with pressure. Her ears rang and popped. As if in response, the window expanded. It showed more terrible things. The worst she'd ever seen.

Here was a dead woman slumped across a trashcan.

Here was a parking lot—no, it was a *street*—jammed with burning cars.

Edith rose from her bed and stumbled to her work desk, where she usually made friendship bracelets and birthday cards, and as a little kid had written letters to a certain jolly old elf in the North Pole. Now she opened the drawer where she kept her markers (the *grownup* kind, not the washable kind) and grabbed the first one her fingers happened upon: Aquarius Blue. Stepping away from the desk, she heard a dull, crumpling sound like a wall collapsing. Her eyes—also Aquarius Blue—rolled back into her skull and saliva beaded at the corners of her mouth.

"Draw," she mumbled, because that's all she *could* do. "Out."

She would normally reach for Shirley, her sister, but Shirley had slammed that door, burned that bridge. "No more," Shirley had said, and she'd been adamant. "Never again."

Edith saw the front end of a burnt-out vehicle, its wheels blown from their axles and its hood folded like an envelope.

The marker trembled in her hand.

"Shirley . . ."

It was hard not to reach for her sister, like not reaching for a rope when being dragged out to sea. And maybe, Edith thought, she should. This was bigger and more terrible than anything she'd seen before, and she was certain Shirley wouldn't want her to be alone, despite what she'd said. She would—

Edith saw bodies—eight, maybe nine of them—recognizable by their shoes, their postures, but otherwise charred and dripping. She pulled her box of toys to one side, tore down her Rihanna and *Minions* posters, and used the marker to reproduce the images in her mind. They were hurriedly drawn, wild loops and lines, a kind of psychic shorthand.

The red and blue lights of a fire truck pulsed along a city street already lit by flame. Edith expected them to flash across her bedroom walls. She heard a woman screaming and saw a buckled street sign: W. CHIPPEWA ST.

"Out," Edith said again, and scrawled what looked like a *W* on its side with a swirl beneath it. She started on a second symbol and felt an increment of relief, but not enough.

It was all too big. Too much.

"Bottletop," she blurted, and touched her sister's mind.

Shirley, I'm so scared.

Martin Lovegrove reflected that, when he was a kid, the best part of the day was that magical couple of hours between dinner and bedtime. That was when his family gathered in the living room to watch TV, and even though they were individually absorbed in shows like *Quantum Leap* and *Roseanne*, they were still together. They laughed and cheered in all the same places. And sometimes, the TV stayed off and they played board games or listened to music. It was family time. A Lovegrove observance. Martin remembered it with fondness.

He slouched now in his favorite armchair with one leg cocked on the arm, much like the teenager who'd religiously watched *The Wonder Years*, because that's how he always sat; that's how he was comfortable. He had the TV remote in his left hand, scrolling through options on Netflix. Laura lay on the sofa, watching Jimmy Fallon highlights on the iPad. Her headphones blotted out all sound.

"As *if*," Shirley, their oldest daughter, said suddenly. She wasn't even aware she'd spoken out loud, Martin thought. She was brain-deep in her phone, texting one of her girlfriends. "Like, *nooooo.*" Her thumbs tapped the screen without pausing. Martin wondered if they twitched in her sleep.

Fifteen years old. She'd said maybe ten words to him since he'd rolled home from work. Three of them were *Love you, Dad,* which more than made up for the half a dozen or so other monosyllabic grunts.

Family time wasn't what it used to be.

"We'll go to the zoo on Sunday," Martin said. It came from nowhere—*boom*—into his head and out of his mouth.

"What?" Shirley didn't look up from her phone. She didn't even complete the word: *Wha?*

"The zoo," Martin repeated. "You know . . . exotic animals held in captivity for the viewing pleasure of overfed Westerners. We'll go. The four of us. We'll eat ice cream and pretend we have a fulfilling life."

"When?"

"Sunday."

"It's Claudette's birthday this weekend." Shirley's eyes flicked up briefly. "She turns sixteen. I'm *not* missing it."

"What? Her birthday lasts the whole weekend?"

"Her party is Sunday. I totally told you."

Martin rolled his eyes. "Oh, right. I *totally* forgot." He selected *Lost* and hit play. A crappy show, no doubt, but a guilty pleasure. He sometimes liked to imagine he was marooned on an island, hundreds of miles from civilization, with nothing but a mysterious smoke beast and countless plot holes for company.

He heard creaking from upstairs: the sound of small footfalls across the floorboards. His finger jabbed the pause button and he looked at the ceiling. Edith had retired to bed after dinner—which she hadn't eaten—with a mild fever. Nothing to worry about. Martin was more concerned about the possibility of a night terror. Edith had suffered terribly between the ages of five and eight. Their family doctor had assured them that night terrors were not cause for concern, and did not suggest a deeper psychological condition. "Think of them as temporary disruptions while her central nervous system is maturing," she'd said. "Yes, they can appear quite upsetting, but there is no lasting damage, and Edith will have no recollection of them come morning. Just keep her from harming herself, or others, if she's thrashing around."

Edith rarely thrashed. She'd trembled and screamed, and often spoke phrases that should not have been in a child's vocabulary. Martin had written some of them down, underscoring those that appeared most extraneous. "Blunt force trauma," she'd muttered once. She was six years old. On another occasion she wailed, "*He oído disparos y corrió.*" Martin ran this through Google Translate and it came back with, "I heard gunshots and ran." To the best of his knowledge, this was not a phrase she'd picked up watching *Sesame Street.*

Laura suggested that Edith *could* be drawing on events from a previous life, but then Laura was susceptible to spiritual fancy. Martin thought it more likely Edith had heard these things on the evening news, but agreed to take her to a hypnotherapist. He—a wildly bearded man with

Star Wars collectibles dotted around his office—didn't explore the past-life route, but instead introduced Edith to a visualization exercise that brought an end to her night terrors. It didn't happen overnight, of course, and maybe the disruptions would have ceased anyway, but whatever the reason, they were twenty-three months without incident.

Good, yeah. Positively *bueno.* Martin still thought about it, though, whenever he tucked her in at night. And maybe that would never go away. Not completely. She was his baby, after all.

Another creak from upstairs. Edith was definitely up and moving around, obviously feeling better. Martin smiled and turned his attention back to *Lost,* where Hurley was currently bouncing through the jungle. Oh Hurley . . . four and a half seasons without Kentucky Fried Chicken and *still* a goddamn lard-ass.

Laura muttered, "He does Dylan better than Dylan," and Martin snapped out of his show. That was when he noticed the clicking. It wasn't the rhythmic clicking he associated with Shirley's texting. This was constant. A *purr.* He looked up, expecting to see her zoned out. And she was, but not in the usual way. Her head was angled awkwardly and her eyelids fluttered. Her thumbs blurred off the screen.

"Shirley?"

She was having some kind of seizure. Martin drew his leg off the arm and sprang from his chair. He got Laura's attention by waving a hand in front of her eyes, then crossed the room to where Shirley reclined in the other armchair.

He cradled the back of her head in one hand and gently tilted her jaw to keep her airway open. She garbled something. The veins across her throat bulged.

"What's happening to her?" Laura asked, crouching beside the armchair. She tried removing the cell phone from Shirley's hands but Shirley held tight, her thumbs still working.

"Seizure, I think," Martin said. "Maybe she was looking at flashing images."

"Should I call nine-one-one?"

Martin looked from Shirley to Laura, then down at the cell phone's screen as Laura tried to free it from their daughter's clasp. He glimpsed what she'd typed: a string of random letters, symbols, and emojis, but with several full words interspersed in all the nonsense. Martin barely logged them before Laura pried the phone away. He definitely saw *SCARED* and *CHIPPEWA* and perhaps *BOTTLECAP,* or maybe it was *BOTTLETOP.*

"Martin?" Laura snapped. She threw the cell phone on the floor and clutched Shirley's hands. "Nine-one-one?"

"Wait," he said. He eased Shirley onto her side and peeled damp strands of hair from her brow. "It's okay, baby. Mom and Dad are here." Her eyes flashed open and closed. Her mouth moved silently. Martin pressed the cool back of his hand to her cheek and she whimpered. A moment later, she screwed her face up and started to cry. It was like a pressure release. The tightness left her body at once. Her trembling first lessened, then stopped altogether.

"Mom . . . ?"

"Okay, sweetie," Laura said. "It's okay."

Martin wiped her tears away. She blinked, took deep breaths, and looked into her empty hands for her phone. Her expression switched from confusion to fear.

"Edith," she said.

"What about Edith?" Martin asked.

Shirley shook her head and groaned. More tears spilled from her eyes.

"She's screaming inside," she said.

Martin didn't run anymore. A wobbly jog was the best he could manage—wobbly because the muscles he'd displayed in his twenties, and even into his thirties, had softened, and at forty-one he sported what the magazines kindly called a *dad-bod*. He didn't put this down to being a busy family man, or to working fifty-plus hours a week, but to a torn ACL he'd suffered playing racquetball with his brother. He'd played football and basketball through high school, and amateur league baseball for most of his adult life, all without injury. But five minutes on a racquetball court with Jimmy (three years older, thirty pounds heavier) and he felt his left knee go pop. The operation to repair it was straightforward enough, but his work insurance plan didn't cover sporting injuries . . . and even if he could afford to pay for it himself, it wasn't like he had time to go under the knife.

He took the stairs quickly, though, and with his heart clamoring. As he rounded the newel post, he felt the injury fire a warning shot, and managed only three more lumbering steps before his knee gave out. He slumped against the wall—"Ah, *fuck*!"—and limped the rest of the way to Edith's room. Shirley's words accompanied him. *She's screaming inside.* Martin had no idea what he'd find when he opened Edith's door. There was no way Shirley could know what was happening to her sister, but the whole seizure thing was undeniably eerie.

She spooked you, is all, he thought, grasping the doorknob and pushing the door open. *There'll be a solid explanation for this. They were probably watching the same—*

The thought broke. It didn't fade or even simply end. It *broke,* and with a tiny shattering sound, like someone stepping on a microscope slide.

"Edith?"

Another night terror, certainly, but not like any he'd seen before. *Deeper,* was the word that came to mind. Edith stood in the middle of the room, her face a cracked oval, a thread of drool hanging from her lip. She looked at Martin. Her eyes caught the light like sparking flints.

"It's all flashy now," she said. "And loud. Whoop-whoop."

Martin stumbled toward her, meaning to scoop her into his arms and cradle her until the storm had passed and she was dreaming sweetly. The shock in her expression knocked him back a step, though. Whatever was making her scream inside . . . she wasn't just seeing it, she was *living* it.

"Edith . . . honey, it's—"

She clutched a blue marker in her right hand and used it to point at the wall, where the posters had been removed and she'd drawn a series of symbols. They were esoteric, nonsensical, though apparently not without meaning.

"The whoop-whoop," Edith said, pointing to a diamond with sunrays shooting from it. The marker toppled from her hand. "It all went boom, Daddy."

"Edith—"

"*Everything* went boom."

He swept toward Edith and lifted her into his arms. Effortless, with her being so delicate. The muscles across his chest barely flexed. His injured knee reacted otherwise, buckling under him, spilling him to the floor. He never let go of Edith, though, and she looked at him through ribbons of dark blond hair, her mouth a wavering circle, one hand reaching, not to touch his face, as he thought, but to point at another symbol on the wall behind him, this a broken swirl, and she whispered in the frailest, sweetest voice imaginable:

"The man with no hands is crying."

2

On the evening of Saturday April 14, 2018—three days after Edith Lovegrove scrawled numerous symbols across her bedroom wall—a gray Nissan Altima left a storage unit in Rochester, New York, and took the I-90 west to Buffalo. Its first stop was a gas station on Genesee Street, where its eighteen-gallon tank was filled to capacity. Its second stop was the Whole Hog drive-thru on Broadway, where the driver—thirty-four-year-old Garrett Riley—ordered the last meal he would ever eat: an OMG piggy burger, a large curly fries, and an XL cola. The drive-thru attendant's name was Imani Johnson, and Imani would later tell Autumn McKenzie from Fox 29 News that she noticed nothing suspicious about Garrett or the car he was driving, and that when she said "oink-oink" to him—as all Whole Hog employees were required to do—he smiled and said "oink-oink" right back.

Garrett left the drive-thru and headed west on Broadway. He parked behind a music store near the intersection of Elm Street, where he ate his final meal and listened to the radio.

The music and commercials muffled the voice in his mind, but couldn't silence it.

The voice tick-tocked. It *lulled.*

At 11:03 p.m., Garrett turned the radio off and drove to West Chippewa Street.

The older woman held him. Her hands were as soft as freshly laundered towels and her hair smelled of tree bark—an earthy, *good* smell, evoking strength and kindliness. Garrett rested his head against her bosom and his doubts slipped away. They would return, of course—those tenacious, wolfish doubts—but here, now, in this moment of wakefulness and light, they were subdued. The woman stroked his face and her heartbeat had the soothing rhythm of waves. She spoke his name again and again. She sang to him.

There was a small wooden box on the table beside them and inside that box, apparently, was a watch. The only watch, or clock, on the island. "The only people who mark off time are prisoners," she'd said on the day he arrived. "But if you feel the need"—she tapped the top of the box—"come see me and I'll show you what you've been missing." Garrett had never taken her up on the offer, and didn't know anybody who had.

"Would you like to put your hand inside my shirt, Garrett?"

"No."

"Are you sure?"

"I mean yes."

She popped a button on her shirt and he adjusted his

position to slide his hand more easily inside. He felt doughy, wrinkled skin, then the thick material of her bra.

"There," she said. "How does that feel?"

"Good."

"You've the hand of a strong man," she said a moment later. "I remember the shriveled, darkened boy. The broken thing."

"I get stronger every day," Garrett said.

"I'm awed by how far you've come."

"You've been like a mother to me." Her breast felt like a pouch of warm gel. "You truly live up to your name."

She smiled, held him closer, while he considered the paradox: to feel both strong, here, on the island, and childlike, here, in her arms. His old life—a brother, a construction worker, marking weeks and months and years like a prisoner—had never seemed so far away.

"I get scared sometimes."

"I know, sugar."

"But mostly I feel . . . empowered."

"Empowered?" She grinned. "Why?"

"It's quite a feat," he said, "to burn what was weak to the ground, and rebuild with strong materials. That's what I've done with my life. Thanks to you."

She nodded, kissed the top of his head. Her nipple throbbed against his palm.

"You belong here," she said. "We value you."

"Yes."

"You are *giving* and *intelligent* and *resolute.*" She squeezed his upper arm with every compliment. "And certainly you know—and this is perhaps your most agreeable quality—

that these traits, if not utilized, mean nothing at all. They are the pages of a book no one will ever read."

"I'll *make* them read," Garrett said.

She kissed the top of his head again and said in her loving, motherly tone, "That's the quickest way to Glam Moon."

"Sometimes I think I'm already there."

"Oh no, Garrett. You've a long way to go."

She removed his hand, popped two more buttons, then dragged her heavy right breast from inside her shirt. He saw the scars and veins across her chest and had to hide his disgust. "Sugar," she said, and pulled down the front of her bra to reveal a blunt, leathery nipple, broad as a penny.

He averted his eyes. He looked at the box with the watch inside—the watch, replicating an average American life: a complex but ultimately robotic device, ticking off seconds and minutes, doing the same thing 24/7.

She said, "Your legacy will be not determined by who you are, but by what you *do*."

"Yes," he said. And then, "I should go."

"Not yet. Pop this bitter old thing into your mouth." She curled one hand around the back of his head and ushered him close. "You've nowhere else to be."

West Chippewa Street was a circus. Thinly dressed twenty-somethings thronged the sidewalks. They crowded veneered establishments with names like Platform Eleven and Absolution—weekend superstars, one and all, drinking and dancing, uploading their memories to Instagram. This was young America, adorned and exuberant. The night was an oil spill of color.

Garrett parked on the road between two streetlights, mostly in shadow, and watched from behind a darkened windshield.

Around and around their little lives go. Tick-tock. But where's the progress, Garrett? Where's the ambition?

He saw none. He saw waste and taint and indifference.

Ambition relies on moving forward. So tell me . . . how do you turn a circle into a straight line?

Garrett caressed the control box resting in the center console: a homemade device comprised of a toggle switch, a safety cover, and two nine-volt batteries. Two wires—one red, one black—led from the box to the trunk.

"To begin with," he said, "you break the circle."

He'd left the island just after 4 p.m. with his directive sounding in his mind. It had a hypnotic quality not unlike (and yes, he'd noted the irony) a clock ticking. Nolan Thorne had taken him to the mainland, then driven him to Rochester. Nolan—the island's second-in-command—had handled all the final details. The *precision* work, he'd called it. This amounted to gathering and storing the necessary materials, and assembling the IED.

The ninety-minute drive from Fisherman's Point to Rochester had been a blur. Nolan said nothing. It was only when they reached the storage unit in Rochester that he spoke. He handed Garrett the keys to the Altima and told him what was in the trunk. "If you're compromised, the authorities need to believe you were acting alone. This'll only happen if you can detail what you're carrying." He showed Garrett the red and black wires running from the trunk to the control box in the center console. "This is a two-position toggle switch. Off and on. The safety cover will prevent you from flipping the switch before you're ready." Garrett had looked at the control box and nodded, his brain still engaged by that hypnotic ticking sound. "You get into position, lift the cover, flip the switch. Eighteen volts will only a provide a small spark, but that's all you need." Then Nolan did something he'd never done in all the time Garrett had known him: pulled Garrett into a clumsy embrace. It lasted no more than five seconds—long enough for Garrett to smell Nolan's vinegary sweat and feel the moth-like fluttering in his chest. They'd separated to an awkward silence, then Nolan intoned with affected vigor, "I'll see you in the Glam."

They'd said their farewells. Garrett's was lackluster. *Dazed,* almost. What he wanted to say was, *Would you do it, Nolan? For all your loyalty and expertise . . . would* you *flip the switch?* But every time a negative or resistant thought entered his mind, it was suffocated by that ticking sound.

Live music thumped from a bar called the Bottletop. It was huge, glass-fronted, with a rooftop terrace that bled color into the night. Kids howled and danced, hands in the air. Their silhouettes moved sinuously. Garrett focused on the front windows. Four of them, each as high and wide as a city bus. Garrett saw the people inside, like so many fish in an aquarium. They were as beautiful as fish, too. They dipped and winnowed.

It's time, he thought, except *he* didn't think it; the voice was not his own. He wiped a collar of sweat from the back of his neck and took a photograph from his shirt pocket. It was of a handsome young man with a reddish brush cut and kind green eyes. Jefferson, his brother. More than that: his hero—his *world*—after their parents died. Garrett's eyes blurred with tears. It wasn't Jefferson's voice, either.

"I'm so confused, Jeff," Garrett mumbled. "Everything has gone to—"

It's TIME.

Garrett's mouth closed with a dry click. He drew his shoulders inward—could almost *feel* her close to him. If he looked into the rearview, he thought for sure he'd see her there, hovering, her eyes alight.

He slipped the photograph back into his pocket and started the car. One glance at the control box, then he rammed the transmission into drive. He didn't pull away gradually; he stomped on the gas and the Altima jumped forward. The tires whinnied and smoked and the back end dragged just a little—not surprising considering what was in the trunk.

"These two wires," Nolan had said, showing how they snaked beneath the driver's seat, beneath the rear passenger seat, and into the trunk, "are connected to an igniter fashioned from a Christmas tree light. The igniter is inside a thin plastic tube packed with mercury fulminate and potassium chlorate. This is your detonator. The detonator is pushed inside six pounds of a black-market plastic explosive called Kerna-H4. There's a five-gallon jerry can filled with gasoline on either side of the explosive, but make sure you fill up because that'll put another eighteen gallons in the tank. That's quite the fireball, but it doesn't stop there; the cans are secured by two fifty-pound bags of ANFO: a cocktail of ammonium nitrate and fuel oil. This is the payload, Garrett. The shock and the awe. Anyone within a hundred yards is going to get blown into the goddamn stratosphere."

Garrett Riley was born in Indianola, Mississippi in the fall of 1983. The younger of two children, his upbringing was—for the first thirteen years of his life, at least—perfectly normal. His parents were upstanding Americans, former college sweethearts. Daddy was a track superstar who'd missed making the US Olympic team by the narrowest of margins. He went on to start his own adhesive label business, which flourished in the Reagan era. Mama was a reporter for Sunflower County's Rapid News team. She had aspirations of anchoring at one of the bigger stations, but the arrival of Jefferson, then Garrett, derailed those plans. Not with any regret. Friends of the Rileys maintained that Lynda Riley was an unselfish, caring sweetheart of a mother, who raised those boys with open-hearted, Christian love and unwavering American principles.

For all the digging in the dirt, for all the right-wing and antiestablishment ties the media endeavored to make, the worst that could be said of young Garrett Riley was that he tried too hard to please, and that he was easily led. This fueled speculation that he *was* led on the night of April 14, 2018—that somebody else was pulling the strings. There was no evidence to support this, however, and Garrett marched alone into infamy. He wasn't alone once he got there, of course. The *New York Times* likened Garrett's crime to that of Terry Nichols and Timothy McVeigh's, who'd bombed the Alfred P. Murrah Federal Building in Oklahoma City in 1995, killing 168. The *Boston Globe* drew comparisons to Andrew Kehoe and the Bath School disaster of 1927, in which forty-four people—including thirty-eight children—were killed in a series of devastating explosions. A Christian fundamentalist website declared with absolute earnestness that Garrett Riley had been possessed by the "hateful spirit" of Osama bin Laden. Further comparisons were made to Ted Kaczynski, Ramzi Yousef, and the devil.

With no connections to known terror organizations—domestic or foreign—investigators looked to Garrett's mental stability, and here, particularly in later life, the weaknesses were evident. He and Jefferson were orphaned in 1997 when a drunk driver bounced his Chevy Silverado across the median on I-55, slamming head-on into the Lincoln being driven by Hank Riley. He and Lynda—returning home from a friend's birthday party—were killed instantly. The brothers went to live with an uncle in Louisiana. Letters from Jefferson to his girlfriend in Mississippi, revealed that neither boy was happy there, and it went beyond being taken away from everything they knew. *We're not abused, or anything,* Jefferson wrote. *We're just ignored . . . unloved, which is a kind of abuse, when you think about it.* In subsequent correspondence, Jefferson wrote how Garrett begged Jefferson to run away with him. *He's been reading all these books about surviving in the wild. He's got this idea we'd live like bears, maybe speak some secret language and scare away hikers. I told him we'd be more like Yogi and Boo-Boo.*

Jefferson joined the armed forces in 2000, cutting the apron strings tethering him to his little brother. The people who knew Garrett at that time said he was more like a ghost than a person. "He'd just float in the background," Aunt Bea said. "Wouldn't say nothing to nobody. Randy called him Balloon Boy—just bobbing around, waiting to go pop."

This detachment only deepened with Jefferson's deployment to Afghanistan in 2002. Garrett was eighteen at the time. Other kids his age were going to parties, getting drunk, getting laid. Garrett's interests were limited to reading European literature and writing angry poetry. In a 2004 email to Jefferson, he asked why Jefferson—by then on his second deployment—would want to be a part of such a dishonest war. *Because I love my country,* Jefferson replied. *America has taken its share of knocks recently and we need to move some mighty big pieces to get things back the way they were. One person can't do that. It's the work of MANY people, pushing in the same direction. And that's what I am, Garr . . . I'm one man pushing.*

There are no images of Garrett burning the flag. He never sent threatening letters to his congressman or subscribed to hate propaganda. His response to Jefferson's estimable patriotism—*If you get killed over there (KILLED FOR NO GODDAMN REASON!) then I'm going to do some pushing of my own*—was the only indication of a potentially violent temperament. It was jumped on by the media, sensationalized first and analyzed second.

"Here's a man," said Dr. Clyde Brisk, a noted forensic psychiatrist and author of *Murder Nation: A History of Mass Murder in the USA,* "who is clearly depressed and angry, but who is not, at this time, displaying signs of sociopathic behavior. He is on the precipice. With the right help, he can turn his life around and engage agreeably with society. Conversely, with a nudge in the opposite direction, or even in the absence of help, he can lose whatever grip he has and become incredibly dangerous."

Jefferson left the army in 2010 and returned to Louisiana, where he started his own truck repair business. He bought a house in Lafayette and Garrett moved in with him. This was no doubt a happier time for Garrett. He landed a job in construction and even had a string of girlfriends. None were particularly serious, but it was evidence that Garrett had retreated from the precipice. The photographs of him from this time showed a smiling young man who appeared to be enjoying life. His Facebook profile picture was of him and Jefferson, arms slung around one another, clutching bottles of Budweiser. Ninety percent of the photos he posted were of him and Jefferson: fishing on Spanish Lake; riding the Flyin' Tiger at Dixie Landin'; standing shirtless in the rain at some washed-out barbecue. He loved his big brother, no doubt about it. But it was more than that. Jefferson was his stabilizing force. His center of gravity.

Dr. Brisk said, "Any level of dependency is a double-edged sword; what happens when the person you're leaning on is no longer there? Ultimately, Garrett Riley needed to stand on his own two feet, and he was never able to do that."

On October 6, 2016, Jefferson went to the Eezy-Mart on the corner of his street to buy milk and cookies for his pregnant fiancée. Moments later, a man wearing a Ninja Turtles mask entered the store and leveled a double-action revolver at the cashier. Instead of emptying the register, the cashier leveled a gun of her own. Shots were fired. The assailant fled the scene with the cashier in pursuit, while Jefferson lay facedown in a puddle of milk and blood. He'd taken a bullet to the throat and died before his cookies hit the floor.

Garrett disappeared a short time later.

"Gone," Madeline Burns—Jefferson's fiancée—said blankly. "I figured he'd taken a dive off the Horace Wilkinson Bridge and his body was never recovered. Can't say I missed him. He was like a rag after Jeff died, just laying around all gray and limp. I only realized he was AWOL after his boss called my house looking for him."

Garrett spent at least a portion of the next eighteen months in New York City. He'd used his credit card to purchase a Greyhound ticket from Lafayette to Port Authority, and made three sizable cash withdrawals from the First Pioneer Bank in Brooklyn Heights. Other than that, his electronic footprint was nonexistent.

"He removed himself from the system," senior FBI agent James Wilding said. "No online presence. No known address or place of employment. On record, he disappeared. In reality, he was likely working for cash and sleeping on a friend's couch. Suffice to say, Garrett Riley's whereabouts during this period, along with the identities of any known associates, is of great interest to us."

The common theory was that the cash withdrawals (totaling $22,800 of Garrett's inheritance money) went toward securing the bomb-building materials. Garrett's electronic footprint next appeared in March 2018 when he used his credit card to rent a storage unit in Rochester, New York, and again a month later when he rented a Nissan Altima from Meridian Car & Truck, also in Rochester.

Footage from security cameras showed the Altima striking the plate glass windows of the Bottletop bar in downtown Buffalo at 23:48 on Saturday April 14, 2018. Within ninety minutes, authorities had infiltrated the storage unit in Rochester, where they recovered snippets of multi-strand wire, a small amount of scattered ANFO prills, and a USB flash drive. The eighty-three second video on the flash drive showed Garrett standing in front of a plain white wall. The recording was steady and in focus, suggesting use of a tripod or other stabilizing device. Forensic audiologists confirmed no ambient sound to indicate the presence of a third party.

Garrett introduced himself: full name, date, and city of birth. His eyes were glazed and there was a robotic stiffness to his voice. He appeared sedated.

"My brother was a true and valiant American," he said after a moment. His empty gaze wavered and he took an unsteady breath. "He served his country for ten years, including two yearlong deployments to Afghanistan. He didn't die at the hands of Taliban insurgents. His transport helicopter wasn't shot down over Kabul, and he didn't step on a landmine. He was killed in a convenience store in Lafayette, Louisiana, while buying cookies for his pregnant fiancée. That's right . . . *'Murica*: a different kind of warzone, where repetition and lack of progress are the enemy, and everyone's got blood on their hands."

He wiped his eyes and stared at the camera for a full twenty seconds. Here he appeared most haunted, and *haunting.* Of all the photographs of Garrett, it was a still from this portion of the video that was used most widely by media sources.

"He used to bark at me when I'd call him a hero." The slightest of smiles cracked his face, there and gone in a second. "*Garr,* he'd bark. *I ain't no hero. I'm just one man pushing.* That's what he always called himself: one man pushing. Well, that didn't work out too good for him, did it? So maybe the secret is you've got to push a little bit harder."

The blast from Garrett's rolling IED punched a hole the size of a football field into downtown Buffalo. It obliterated the Bottletop and several of its neighbors, with structural damage reaching to within a three-block radius. It wasn't as large in scale as the truck bomb that rocked Oklahoma City in 1995, but had it beat in terms of casualties: 228 killed and 406 injured, making it the second-deadliest terrorist attack within the United States.

It being an act of terrorism was never debated, despite Garrett (apparently) being a lone wolf, declaring no affiliation to known terror organizations, or taking any real political stance. He *did* have an axe to grind: the "repetition and lack of progress" that he held accountable for his brother's death. But this was no act of revenge. As the president himself said: "If your grievance—however vague—is against a system or ideology and you're killing innocent civilians, then make no mistake, you *are* a terrorist."

"It's difficult for people to quantify a disaster of this magnitude with one person," Dr. Clyde Brisk said to Wolf

Blitzer on *The Situation Room.* "We associate terrorism with antiestablishment organizations . . . with resources, money, people. That one man, with his own set of grievances, could have done this is terrifying. As a psychiatrist, I'm interested in *why,* and so we go back to the precipice. How does someone go from being depressed and disillusioned to being one of the most hated figures in American history? The answer lies in the eighteen months that Garrett Riley was absent from society. He encountered something during this period that had a profound effect on him."

"And ultimately caused him to snap," Wolf added.

"It's more sinister than that," Dr. Brisk said. "These aren't the actions of a weak-willed man who was pushed over the edge. Something—or some*body*—got into his head and radically reshaped his way of thinking."

"Are you suggesting he was brainwashed?" Wolf asked.

"Yes," Dr. Brisk replied without hesitation. "That's exactly what I'm suggesting."

3

"We might have stopped it," Laura said.

"Don't say that."

"I think we had enough information. Yes, it was haphazard. Yes, it was—"

"Illogical."

"*Yes*, but we could have—*should* have—put the pieces together." Laura stood up from the kitchen table. She made a frantic gesture with her hands, as if she wanted to grab something but couldn't, then exhaled and shook her head. "Jesus, I haven't slept much these past few nights."

Martin went to her. He circled her waist with one arm, stroked her hair, the same color—honey gold—as the day they'd met, just as full of body and bounce, and not a shimmer of gray. She looked at him with what he called her flashlight expression: illuminating, but searching. It didn't ask, *How can you make this right?* but rather, *How can* we *make this right?* We. Together. Every knot they'd untangled in their seventeen years of marriage, they'd untangled together.

"This isn't ours to carry," Martin said firmly. "It's not like we had credible intel and chose to ignore it. We're talking about an implausible event—a possible psychic occurrence."

"Possible?"

"What can I say? I'm a rational man." Martin tapped one finger off his skull. "I'm still struggling to make sense of this."

"You saw it with your own eyes," Laura said. "Forget the premonition, or *possible* premonition. Something happened between Edith and Shirley. A connection. A communication. And honey, it wasn't normal."

"We thought it was coincidence." He took her hand and steadied it; she was making grabbing motions again. "We thought they'd watched the same shit on YouTube, or wherever, and it caused Shirley to have a seizure, and Edith to have a night terror. We could never have known it was more than that."

"A paranormal event."

"Yeah. Sure. Call it what you want." Martin brought Laura's trembling hand to his lips and kissed her fingers. "It was crazy shit, and it went beyond rational thinking."

"Yes, but—"

"We can't beat ourselves up for what happened, Laura." Martin's expression was more lead blanket than flashlight: serious and unwavering. "That way lies madness."

Laura had gone to Edith's room after making sure that Shirley was okay—that the seizure, or whatever it was, had passed. She'd bolted upstairs like Martin before her and found Martin on his knees with Edith in his arms. Their youngest daughter appeared on the cusp of sleep, mumbling something, drenched with sweat. Martin stroked her brow and soothed her.

"Jesus Christ," Laura gasped. She started across the room, then noticed the wild scrawling on the wall and stopped dead. "What the hell?"

"That's the whoop-whoop," Martin said, gesturing at one of the strange symbols—a diamond with sunrays shooting from it. He looked at her with huge, questioning eyes. "I don't know what's going on here."

They'd dressed Edith in fresh pajamas and put her in their bed for the night. She slept soundly, barely moving. Laura used her phone to take pictures of Edith's bedroom wall. Then they talked to Shirley. "You told us she was screaming inside," Martin said. "How could you know that?" Shirley shrugged and said she couldn't remember, but they knew she wasn't being entirely truthful. They'd pressed, but gently. Shirley admitted that she sometimes got a "feeling" from Edith. "I've read that some identical twins can feel each other's pain," she said, and shrugged again. "Maybe it's like that."

"Do these mean anything to you?" Laura asked, showing Shirley the symbols on her phone. "Something you saw on TV, or online, perhaps?"

"They're kinda creepy," Shirley replied. She shook her head quickly. "No. I've never seen them before."

Later that night, Martin told Laura about the string of letters and emojis that Shirley had tapped into her phone. He might have dismissed it, he said, only the nonsense had been punctuated by several full words.

"Like what?" Laura asked.

"Chippewa," Martin replied. "That's the only one I remember for certain. And bottle-something. Bottle*cap*, maybe?"

Edith remembered very little of the incident, which lent credence to Martin's theory that she'd suffered a night terror after watching something violent online—something that she and Shirley wouldn't admit to having watched. It was a theory that Laura, reluctantly, accepted.

She checked Shirley's phone, looking for the string of nonsense that Martin had told her about (she wasn't a bit surprised to find it had been erased), and then perusing the browsing history. There was nothing of a violent nature. Same with the iPad, the laptop, and the "Recently Watched" list on Netflix.

"So they deleted it," Martin said. "Must've. Or maybe they watched it on a friend's phone. Claudette's, I bet. Her parents are nuts."

Edith wasn't able to explain her impromptu artwork, either. She stared at her bedroom wall with a flavorless expression. "I know *why* I did it," she said. "To get the bad things out of my head. I just don't remember what any of them mean."

Martin scrubbed the wall, but the ghosts of the symbols remained. He rolled over them with a fresh lick of paint and put the posters back up.

"If only we could paint over it in our minds so easily," Laura had said. "Shit, Martin, maybe we need to talk to someone about this."

"Let's not sign up for the family shrink package just yet,"

Martin replied. "We can file this under 'freak coincidence' and move on."

And they tried. For the next two days they acted as if life was just peachy, and then everything spiraled.

2:37 a.m. The ungodly hours of Sunday morning. Laura had given up on sleep. Not even two glasses of wine and some brief, tussle-like lovemaking could help. She got out of bed and went downstairs, made herself an herbal tea, and sat drinking it in the silence of her living room. The iPad was on the arm of the sofa, its screen smeared with greasy finger tracks. Unconsciously—like every twenty-first century automaton—she grabbed it and logged into her social media. She saw the hashtags **#buffalostrong** and **#prayforbuffalo,** scrolled through her feed, saw photographs of burning buildings and cars, of firefighters and police, of victims and body bags.

"Jesus Christ," Laura said. As with every large-scale disaster from the past seventeen years, she envisioned a passenger plane hitting the World Trade Center and her mind punched out two words. Simple words, but filled with fear and pleading: *Not again.*

Western NY Alerts @WestNYAlerts
100s feared dead as car bomb explodes in downtown Buffalo. Entire buildings wiped off the map. Blast was heard up to forty miles away.

Kate Jacobs @kissieroo

Pls #pray for my daughter Queenie Jacobs celebrating job promotion with friends in #Buffalo. Not answering cell. Call me Queenie please call Mommy.

NewsForce New York @newsforceny
W. Chippewa St. "heartbeat" of Buffalo nightlife. Authorities say death toll could reach 500. #prayforbuffalo

---

Laura turned off the iPad. She grabbed the remote control and flicked on the TV. The story had hijacked scheduled programming; BREAKING NEWS adorned the lower third of every station she flipped to. CNN declared the death toll was at 120. CBS News had it at 150. Any degree of tiredness had vacated Laura's system. She watched with massive, unblinking eyes and a loose jaw.

"*—terrible scenes from downtown Buffalo as firefighters struggle to—*"

"*—advising people to stay in their homes—*"

"*—conflicting reports. Some say the vehicle was parked—*"

"*—hallmark of a terrorist attack, but as yet no—*"

Aerial footage showed the scale of the devastation: a burning hole in the city, buildings ablaze, the damage extending several blocks. More intimate camera work offered the efforts of rescue workers digging through smoldering rubble; a triage nurse wiping ash and blood from a young man's forehead; a high-heeled shoe abandoned on the sidewalk.

Laura covered her mouth. Tears pricked her eyes. The

ticker announced *PRESIDENT CALLS BOMBING "COWARDLY AND DESPICABLE."* A shot of a firefighter rolling a flattened hose across Franklin Street switched to footage of an ambulance bolting north on Main. Its lightbar cut through the smoky darkness. Its siren howled.

Laura imagined a diamond with sunrays beaming from it.

"Whoop-whoop," she said.

She stiffened in her seat, a deep chill rising from the small of her back to her skull. With tears rolling down her face, she flipped channels until she found what she was looking for.

The ticker: *POLICE CONFIRM VEHICLE DRIVEN THROUGH FRONT WINDOW OF CROWDED DOWNTOWN BAR BEFORE BOMB WAS DETONATED.* A map of the area filled the screen, with a small red circle drawn around the Bottletop bar on West Chippewa Street, and a larger circle indicating the blast radius.

Chippewa, Martin had said the other night, referring to one of the few legible words that Shirley had keyed into her phone during her seizure. *That's the only one I remember for certain. And bottle-something. Bottle*cap, *maybe?*

"Bottletop," Laura said. She wanted to scream.

Instead she stood up and walked out of the living room, appearing oh-so-calm on the outside, while on the inside she was cold and shrieking. She went upstairs and shook Martin awake.

"Martin, hey . . ." She nudged him gently. She wanted to blast ice into his face and drag him from between the sheets. "Martin—"

"'Sup?" He blinked groggily.

"Get up. You need to see this."

"Huh? What time—"

"You *need* to see this."

He'd risen from bed with his hair erected in quills and his ass-crack popping from the top of his boxers. Moments later he was alert and bug-eyed, clutching Laura's hand as they sat on the sofa and watched the news unfold. "Can't be," he kept saying. "It's wild coincidence. *Has* to be." His denial faltered when the Fox 29 news anchor somberly intoned, "The following report contains scenes of a graphic nature. Viewer discretion is advised," and the screen displayed footage of a young man with no hands being loaded into the back of an ambulance. He was bandaged and sedated—one of the lucky ones, apparently, although the tears rolling down his face suggested he thought otherwise.

"Fuck." Martin sprung off the sofa—nearly taking Laura with him—and glared at the TV. "The man with no hands is crying."

Laura shook her head once and looked at him. She was almost too fractured to respond. Within the hour she would down a jigger of whiskey and go back to bed, sleep until late afternoon. For now she took a breath that rolled all the way to her toes, and on the exhale asked Martin to elaborate.

"Something Edith said." Martin closed his eyes and touched his forehead, honing the memory. "One of her symbols. The man with no hands is crying."

"She said that?"

"Yeah, but I figured it was just, you know... *randomness.*" He shrugged and sighed at the same time. "I'd pretty much forgotten about it. Until now."

"Right," Laura said, looking at the TV—at a photograph of Garrett Riley. *THE FACE OF EVIL*, according to the caption. She jabbed the red button on the remote and the screen went dark. It was heavenly. "And you still think this is all a coincidence?"

"It's just . . . I don't—"

"Martin. Come on, baby. Coffee beans—smell them." She inhaled robustly. Her teeth flashed. "Edith didn't have a night terror. It was a premonition."

"Jesus Christ, Laura."

"A fucking *premonition*." Laura stood up, her hands balled into fists. She looked like she wanted to let loose—to punch the walls and throw shit. Instead she sunk to her knees and lowered her face into her hands, not crying, but exhausted. She didn't move for a long time, and when she did it was to get the whiskey. Martin did nothing—*said* nothing—to comfort her, but she could tell he wanted to; they'd been together twenty years, married for seventeen. She knew his heart as well as her own. He just stood in his own void, though, looking sad and boyish in yesterday's boxers.

"So what do we do?" Laura asked, still with the flashlight expression, although she'd stopped making the grabbing motions with her hands.

"We continue as normal," Martin replied. "We *try*, at least."

"Bullshit," Laura said. "There *is* no normal. I admit that we couldn't have assumed anything supernatural, but we can't just plunge our heads in the sand. We need to talk to someone.

If Edith has a condition—extrasensory or psychological—she needs to find a way to manage it, and that means getting expert help."

"We took her to that hypnotherapist before," Martin said. He removed his arm from around Laura's waist, returned to the kitchen table, and dropped into his seat with a tired thump. "The Star Wars guy. He seemed to help."

"Maybe," Laura said. She crossed to the other counter, slid a half-full bottle of Merlot toward her. "I was thinking of someone more . . . *sensitive* to the paranormal angle." She held up the bottle of wine. "Am I turning into an alcoholic?"

"This would be a good week to start."

"Hmm. You want?"

"Yeah."

Laura plucked two glasses from the cupboard, emptied the bottle into them, and joined Martin at the kitchen table. They drank and licked their lips at the same time, then Martin said:

"Sensitive?"

"What if *all* Edith's night terrors were actually premonitions? It sounds crazy, but given what we know, we should consider it a possibility."

"It would explain all the wild shit she came up with," Martin admitted. "Things she could never know."

"Right."

"But she's never drawn the symbols before."

"True, but the bombing was on a different scale. It might have been too much for her mind to take."

"So the drawings were overflow? Mental spillage?"

"Or some kind of release. She said she had to get the bad things out of her head, right?" Laura drank from her glass—not a sip but a glug, splashing wine on the table. She mopped it up with her sleeve. "Listen, when I was researching my dissertation, I remember reading about this psychiatrist who'd drawn comparisons between psychic ability and mental illness. He claimed that a small percentage of psychiatric patients had been misdiagnosed—that they actually had some form of extrasensory energy they couldn't align with. He called it a paranormal coil or a psychic coil. Something like that."

"A unique take," Martin said. "I'm sure that went down well with the American Psychiatric Association."

"I'm not saying I believe it," Laura added. "But it suggests a gray area—a lack of knowledge. I think we'd be smart to err on the side of caution. This is our daughter. I don't want her analyzed, prodded, and labeled. And I for damn sure don't want her institutionalized just because some shrink can't think outside the box."

"Agreed."

"Good." Laura reached across the table and clasped Martin's hand. "So you don't mind if I make some inquiries—see if I can find someone more . . . sympathetic?"

"Sure," Martin said. "Let's give it a shot."

"Thank you," Laura said, and found a smile. "Something else: I think we should *all* talk to someone. We're going to need help carrying the load."

"Therapy?"

"Let's call it nonjudgmental conversation," Laura said.

"I've already booked an appointment with a spiritual advisor. You can take a more conventional route, of course. As John Lennon said: 'Whatever gets you through the night.'"

"Okay," Martin said. He'd barely touched his wine, but now he lifted the glass and drained two thirds. "Okay. Yeah. I can do that."

"You're a good man."

He winked and tugged Laura's hand, urging her across the table. And she obliged, shimmying on her stomach like a woman half her age, feet off the floor, lips red with wine. He leaned close and they kissed. Her honey-gold hair was the same as the day they'd met, and so was her mouth—her kiss. The love had changed, though. It was sky-broad and still growing. It was entwined with his. Not a *her* thing but a *them* thing.

"We're going to get through this," he said.

And she said, "You bet."

Shirley stood up from the top stair, where she'd sat for the last fifteen minutes listening to her parents' conversation. She didn't have to strain her ears, either; when Mom and Dad had one of their powwows in the kitchen, their voices—even if they whispered—carried into the hallway and swirled around the ceiling above the stairway. A cool acoustic quirk. Her music teacher once told her there was an area inside Grand Central Station where you could whisper into a corner, and no matter how much noise and kerfuffle there was around (and Shirley figured there was always a good deal of noise and kerfuffle at Grand Central Station), the person standing in the opposite corner would hear your voice like you were standing next to them. This was similar to the way Edith sometimes communicated with her—a direct, secret method, bypassing traditional routes. It was fun to begin with, but it wasn't *normal*, and Shirley knew it had to stop.

No good could come from it.

Shirley eavesdropped on her parents until they started smooching—totally gross—then snuck along the landing to Edith's room. She inched the door open and crept inside.

"Edith? You awake?"

The bedclothes shuffled and Edith sat up, her eyes bright and owl-like in the glow of the nightlight. She clutched Paisley Rabbit to her breast. He squeaked companionably. She was too old for Paisley, but he made an appearance every now and then. A comfort thing.

"They're talking about us again," Shirley said, and perched on the edge of Edith's bed. "About you, mostly."

"What are they saying?"

"That thing in Buffalo. The bomb. They think you saw it in your mind before it happened in real life."

"Oh. That doesn't sound good."

"How much do you remember?"

"Nothing really." Several shallow lines crossed Edith's brow. "Just . . . flashes. Like trying to remember a dream."

They sat in silence for a moment, the only sounds coming from the other side of the blinds: the traffic coursing along Melon Road, a radio playing some catchy nerd-rock song, older kids shooting hoops beneath the lights in Oval Park Court. Just another cool spring evening in Flint Wood, New York.

"They're worried about us." Shirley looked at the wall where Edith had scrawled her symbols. Nothing there now but the fresh-paint tracks Dad had made with the roller. "Mom's bringing in help. A specialist."

"The Star Wars guy?"

"Not this time. It'll be someone different." She recalled her mom's description. "Someone *sympathetic.*"

Edith gathered Paisley a little closer. She appeared to take all this on board, and accept it, then her brow furrowed more deeply and her upper lip quivered, and all at once her face scrunched. Tears jumped from her eyes and she used Paisley's floppy ears to smudge them away.

"It's not my fault," she sniveled, trying to keep her voice down. "I didn't ask for this."

Shirley shuffled closer, threw an arm around her little sister, and kissed her clumsily on the cheek. "Shhh . . . hey, I never said it was your fault."

"You're mad at me. I can tell."

"No, it's just . . . I *told* you, Ede, I can't hold your hand anymore. Not up here." Shirley pressed a finger to her forehead. "I thought I was helping you, but I'm not. I'm making things worse."

"I was scared," Edith moaned, mopping more tears away. "I know you said not to, and I *tried,* but it was too big."

"Yeah, but we freaked Mom and Dad the hell out. They're bringing in a specialist. There'll be questions, examinations. I'm worried it'll lead to *more* questions—smelly old men in suits digging through your brain."

Edith's jaw fell. "You think?'

"Maybe," Shirley said. "This thing . . . it's not natural, Ede. It scares people."

"It scares *me.*"

"Right, which is why you need to control it. And I'm going to help you." Shirley touched her forehead again. "Just not up here."

A barking dog joined the evening chorus. It was loud and insistent. Shirley listened for a moment, lost in thought.

"I'm going to take you somewhere over the weekend," she said.

Edith looked at her curiously. "Where?"

"My special place." Shirley leaned closer, lowering her voice. "But don't tell Mom and Dad. We're in enough trouble as it is."

"Okay."

Shirley smiled. Not a full smile, certainly not a happy one, but better than nothing. She kissed her sister on the cheek again, then stood up and started toward the door.

"Shirl?"

She stopped, turned around. Maybe it was the way Edith's eyes shimmered in the nightlight's bluish glow, or the stuffed toy secured faithfully in her arms, but she looked so young. Five years old, not ten.

"This place," Edith said. "Is it bad?"

Shirley bristled. She tried to keep her voice even, but it quavered just a little. "You need to stay out of my mind, Ede."

Edith shook her head. "I didn't, Shirl. I promise. I . . ." The rabbit in her arms squeaked. "I *didn't.*"

"Do you trust me?"

"You know I do." Edith dabbed at her eyes again. "I love you."

The kids on the court whooped and cheered—one of the them must have sunk a three-pointer. A truck boomed as it crossed the railroad tracks near Abraham Heights and one of their neighbors shouted to quit that goddamn dog barking.

4

Shirley told their mom they were going to Claudette's house to watch the new Five Factor video on YouTube, which was true, but what she didn't say was that she and Edith would be taking an alternate route there.

"It feels like lying," Edith said.

"It's not lying," Shirley insisted, starting across Melon Road with Edith half a step behind. "It's just not the whole truth."

"But Mom said to go straight there and come straight back. And to call before we leave."

"We're taking a detour, that's all, and we *will* call before we leave. Now stop bitching. This is important."

They walked until they were out of their house's sightline (had to assume Mom was watching from Edith's bedroom window, which afforded a good view of Melon Road) before beginning their detour. With a quick glance over her shoulder, Shirley cut through Oval Park Court and across the Bargain Tire parking lot. Edith followed, biting her lip, her chest all bunched up. What if someone saw them? Their mom was a teacher at Flint Wood High. *Everybody* knew her. All it would take was one person. *Hey, I saw your girls outside Bargain Tire on Saturday. They looked to be in an awful hurry.* Edith groaned, imagining the punishment. Grounded, for sure. No screen time for a week. Worst of all, Mom and Dad would be ashamed of them—ashamed for lying. Maybe Shirley wasn't fazed by that, but just the *thought* of it broke Edith's heart.

She faltered, then stopped.

"What's the matter?" Shirley asked.

"Are you sure about this?" Edith looked at her older sister, one hand raised to shield the afternoon sunlight. "What if Mom finds out? What if she calls Claudette's house and we're not there?"

"That's a chance we have to take."

"Why? What's so special about this place?"

"It's going to help you."

"How?"

"Enough with the questions. *Ugh.*" Shirley rolled her eyes, hands on her hips. "Listen, even if Mom finds out, even if we're grounded for a year, it'll be worth it. You want the bad things to go away, right?"

Edith nodded.

"Then come on. And no more questions."

Shirley swiveled on her heels, carried on walking. Edith puffed out her cheeks and followed.

They walked along Peter Avenue and through the new subdivision. There was still building going on and in places the ground was muddy. *Evidence,* Edith thought, frowning at the brownish gloop on her very white sneakers. "We have to cross a creek later on," Shirley said, looking at the mud on her own shoes. "The worst of it will come off then." Edith nodded, but wondered where they were going that they had to cross a creek. There *were* no creeks in Flint Wood, not that she knew of. Beacon River rolled through downtown, but that was too deep to cross—unless, of course, they wanted to get more than their sneakers wet. There were numerous creeks and ponds in the deep country beyond the town proper. In this part of upstate New York—eighteen miles south of Syracuse—they wouldn't have to journey far to find fresh water. The direction they were heading—west, toward Barrow Farm and Judd's Gas Stop—they'd hit the edge of town in a mile or so. *Not crazy far,* Edith thought, but perhaps a little *too* far for two girls who'd told their mom they were playing at a friend's house five blocks away.

Makers Bridge spanned the Beacon, which glimmered serenely in the April sunshine. Swan Park was on the other side, where children chased and howled, spilling joy like water. Edith looked at the swings longingly, but Shirley said they didn't have time. Edith compromised with a quick zip down the slide, then caught up with Shirley, who'd kept walking. After crossing Church Street, they skirted the baseball diamonds, and from there passed into the cool shade of Spruce Forest, a part of the broader, often rugged woodland that gave the town its name.

"Your special place is in the *woods*?" Edith asked, snagging Shirley's T-shirt more firmly than she'd intended.

"Relax. It's on the other side." Shirley took a breath and wiped her brow. "We'll get there quicker by cutting through."

The woods were dappled with flecks of olive and bronze, punctuated by spokes of sunlight that angled through the dense canopy. Birdsong rang throughout and the understory rippled with life—chipmunks, mostly, although they saw an alarmingly plump garter snake that slithered into the foliage like a pulled thread. Edith and Shirley trooped on. Only once did they let their sense of adventure overtake them: Shirley made horns out of pinecones and chased Edith through the trees. They circled and squealed, loud as mockingbirds. "I'm the devil," Shirley announced gleefully. "I'm coming for your *soooooooul.*" The girls broke from the forest line breathless and giggling, then descended a shallow bank splashed with dandelions. Here was the creek, narrow and almost blue. They kicked off their sneakers and washed the mud from them, then crossed the water, getting only the cuffs of their jeans wet. They ascended the adjacent bank still barefoot and looked across a rutted field to the outskirts of Barrow Farm.

"We're a long way from home," Edith said, slipping into her sneakers. "Mom's going to find out, you wait and see. And she's going to be *so* mad."

They made their way across the field, then slipped between the rails of a decrepit fence and stood for a moment assessing the scene. Beyond them, an empty barn loomed pale and bonelike, its uneven shadow spewed across a bleak, unwelcoming yard.

Edith reached for Shirley's hand—for real, not in her mind—and held tight.

"Is this it?" she asked.

"No," Shirley said. "But we're close."

When Edith was five she had a feverish dream in which a man named Cobb beat his wife with a broken chair leg and then set fire to his house. He went outside, sat on the tailgate of his truck, and sipped a Bud while his wife and three children suffocated on black smoke and died before the flames reached their bodies. Except it *wasn't* a dream. Edith had been awake, staring into a terrible window that had opened between her bed and the ceiling. She saw the mesmerizing orange flames lick across the sofa and catch the drapes; saw Cobb's wife splutter and hack and die in a kneeling position; heard Cobb's children make similar noises and bounce their small fists off the walls. There wasn't even enough oxygen to scream. Edith screamed, though. She screamed loud enough for everybody, terrified that she would somehow tumble *upward* through the window and land in the middle of the blazing living room, or that the flames would roll like horrible waves into her world and blacken everything she loved. Mom and Dad reached her before either of these nightmarish fates came to pass. "Thomas," Edith gasped. This was one of the children's names. He was three years old and his small lungs had choked out first. "Fire . . . Broom . . . Spinner." The images eventually faded and the window closed. Edith succumbed to sleep with her heart still dashing. Mom slept with her, curled close enough to pair their dreams.

If they'd lived in Alabama instead of upstate New York, Edith's parents would almost certainly have seen it on the news: *FOUR DEAD IN SPINNER HOUSE FIRE.* They'd have heard how Molson Cobb, thirty-seven, faced four counts of manslaughter after setting fire to his house with his family still inside. They would have seen Spinner police chief Ernie Broom burst into tears during his press conference and promise—with a globule of snot hanging off his lip—a swift and godless reprisal. But, one thousand miles away, what they got was the tragic death of a former SU quarterback and the shooting of an Auburn police officer during a routine traffic stop and postseason baseball scores.

Over the next four months, Edith saw a helicopter crash in the icy peaks of Colorado, a propane explosion at a sheet metal factory in Montreal, and an EF4 tornado that turned the town of Reed Valley, Florida, upside down. Edith's parents saw this latter event on the news—it was *big* news, impossible to miss—a week or so later, but didn't associate it with Edith's nightmare-like ramblings.

Their family doctor recommended an established, comfortable bedtime routine, but that was the best she could do in terms of a remedy. With the episodes persisting, Edith's parents spent the next two years seeking second, third, and fourth opinions from specialists, and were continuously assured there was nothing wrong with Edith's brain, that the night terrors were possibly stress-related, and that they'd have to endure some ugly nights until Edith outgrew them. After trying various treatments they found online—all to no avail—they decided to take an alternative approach.

The hypnotherapist's name was Rafe Caine. ("I know, huh?" he'd remarked excitedly to Edith's parents. "It's like a

Galactic Empire name.") During the initial assessment, Rafe asked Edith about home and school, not in a doctorly—or even a teacherly—way, but more like a big brother. He then asked Edith to list the things that made her anxious, followed by the things that made her happy. The assessment concluded with Rafe using his Star Wars figures to depict a galactic battle between Edith's happiness (the Alliance) and her anxiety (the Empire). Edith's happiness won, of course, when Princess Leia shot Darth Vader off the bookshelf with her blaster pistol.

Edith came into her follow-up session completely relaxed, which was good because Rafe put her to sleep right away. It wasn't *real* sleep, with snoring and dreaming. More like a daydream. Edith's eyes were open, but she felt detached. *Floaty* was how she'd described it to her parents later that day. She lay on a comfortable couch and stared at a soft light focused on an otherwise dark ceiling. Rafe's voice was the only sound in the room.

He told Edith—and her mom, who sat silently in the corner—that going to sleep was like a journey through space, made up of different stages. *Pavor nocturnus,* he said, or night terrors, occurred during the third stage of non-REM sleep, when the brain was throwing out delta waves and the body had started recuperating from the rigors of the day. "It was," he added after a dramatic pause, "the perfect time to strike."

In his softer, big-brotherly tone, and to Edith directly, he said, "You are in control of your journey. You are aware of your surroundings. Your breathing and heart rate have slowed all the way down, but at any point you can turn your ship around or hyperspace to another part of the galaxy. You can even radio for backup. That's right, you're not alone. When the threat is near—when you *feel* it within your airspace—you will visualize your alliance. It may be your mom, or Zelda from school, or—"

"Shirley," Edith whispered.

"Or Shirley, yes. Your big sister. The perfect alliance. Visualize her, Edith. Sorry—*Captain* Lovegrove. See her hair and eyes, and the way she smiles. See the shape of her eyebrows and—"

"She's thirteen," Edith said. "That makes her a teenager."

"Yes it does. Good girl. See how tall she is. Hear her voice. See what she's wearing and—"

"Freckles like mine."

"Good. Yes. She's so close you can see her freckles. You can hold her hand. And when you do—when you reach for it—the threat will retreat. This is the power of your alliance. Visualize it. Reach for it. *Use* it."

Edith had three similar hypnotherapy sessions over the course of six weeks, training her mind to become aware of her sleep patterns and either wake up before the night terror landed, or to visualize an emblem of support and reach for it. Of course, nobody suspected the issue might be paranormal in nature, or that Rafe's method was successful only because of Edith's ability to go *beyond* visualization.

She'd first "reached" Shirley a week after her final session. The window had yawned with a mad, rusty sound and Edith saw a silver passenger train with the words CONNECT VALLEY stenciled on every carriage in happy blue letters. The train wasn't happy, though. It clattered and howled. Reflections blurred across the windows: of trees and mossy embankments and a milky strip of river. The air smelled of oil and rain.

She sat up in bed, eyes wide open. Rafe's big-brotherly voice drifted at the edge of her subconscious: *When the threat is near—when you* feel *it within your airspace—you will visualize your alliance.*

Edith looked beyond the window. She looked for Shirley.

See her hair and eyes, and the way she smiles.

Brakes blew with an explosive hiss and smoke frothed from beneath the locomotive. It thundered into a bend that paralleled a natural curve in the landscape, where coniferous trees towered out of sight and jags of rock announced themselves in variants of gray. The locomotive made it through and so did the second carriage. The third, fourth, and fifth carriages derailed in a blink. They skated on their sides and flipped, then met with the rocks and trees and obliterated.

Edith came close to screaming but pushed it back with everything she had. She closed her eyes but the window was still there, a shimmering, flexing screen powered by some exceptional energy in her brain. She could turn away and it would turn with her. She could run from the room and it would follow. Her skull throbbed. Her heart was a relentless gun. She saw pieces like so many broken plates and burning trees and survivors crawling through the wreckage. Some of them screamed and some died as she watched. She saw a severed leg and a shocked, trembling child and a man holding a dead woman like he meant to dance with her.

The thinnest vein of logic occurred to Edith: that she could *draw* the images from her head—that by transposing them to paper, or even to the wall, they would lose their vitality and the window would close. She would have tried it, too, if she hadn't seen the shocked child again and noted the freckles splashed across her cheeks. They were so like her own freckles. So like Shirley's.

Edith felt it then. Something deep inside her brain either connected or *dis*connected—it was difficult to tell—and in the next instant Shirley was there, as clear as the window but a safe distance from it. Shirley, her alliance, with her freckles and blue eyes, her lips of a particular shape and her sisterly hand reaching.

The window displayed a crying infant being pulled from beneath wreckage and an elderly woman howling at the rain. It displayed blood, ruin, and pain. Instead of screaming, Edith reached across an incomprehensible space and clasped her sister's hand.

Am I dreaming? Shirley asked.

Maybe. I don't know.

Edith? What's going—

I need *you.*

And that was all she had to say. Shirley opened her mind, which brimmed with love and warmth, and Edith found shelter.

The visions persisted, however. Occasionally they were vague enough for Edith to handle alone, but when they were too vivid—too *big*—she reached for her alliance. Through the darkness and beyond reason, she found her sister's hand. It was always there.

I'd be lost without you, Shirl. Totally cray-cray.

Or maybe you'd be more like a zombie, all droolly and smelly. Braaaaaaaaiiins.

Edith became so adept at reaching for Shirley that she didn't really *have* to reach; that connection—or disconnection, whichever it was—became so natural that she could do it without thinking. She sometimes touched Shirley's mind when either of them were feeling low, or during one of their parents' stern talks—*It's hard to take Dad seriously while he's wearing his BAZINGA T-shirt*—or just to say hi.

Yo, girl.

Yo.

And then one evening at the dinner table Shirley surprised Edith by snarling at her, *You can* NEVER *tell anybody about this. It's a freak thing. Don't pretend you don't* KNOW *that.* Edith had dropped her fork and looked across the table with hurt, tear-struck eyes—ignoring her mom, who'd asked if she was okay—and Shirley had stared back with an indifferent expression. *They used to burn girls like you at the stake.*

They walked from wiry grass into a yard where trash and pieces of machinery glittered among the weeds. The farmhouse was a derelict silhouette. Small birds dotted the roof and called. Edith wondered if Shirley's special place was *inside* the house. They'd enter through the crumbling front door, or—worse—through the bulkhead and into the cellar. It would be full of old farm tools with long handles and rusty blades, and there'd be shelves crammed with nameless things in dusty jars—

"Not the farmhouse." Edith stopped walking. One of the birds took wing and vanished in the haze. "I'd rather scream through the night than go in there."

"This way," Shirley said, tugging Edith in the opposite direction.

They passed a rusted tractor with a near-architectural spider's web—thick as string—hanging between the steering wheel and the seat. A few steps farther they came to a water trough pitched on its side, overrun by an embroidery of beautiful, flowering weeds. The dead foal was beyond this.

"Oh, gross."

"Don't look at it," Shirley said.

Hard not to look. It had been dead a long time—a small horse shape, little more than a skeleton draped with papery skin and cartilage. Its ears had been chewed off. Its eye sockets were empty. The hole in its stomach was large enough for a rat to crawl into, dry as a pocketful of dust.

"This place is horrible," Edith moaned.

"It's where bad things belong," Shirley said.

They passed through an open gate into another field. The grass was as tall as Shirley and it rattled as the breeze blew. They walked maybe fifty yards but it felt longer, with Shirley frequently stopping to look back at the farmhouse and keep her bearings. Eventually they stepped into a clearing and Shirley gently pulled on Edith's hand, stopping her.

"We're here. Watch your step."

The clearing was no more than twenty feet in diameter, bordered by more tall grass but also a blackberry bush sprinkled with ripe fruit. There was a crumbling brick ring in the center, waist-high, covered by five boards nailed roughly together. Shirley started to push the boards aside while Edith went directly to the berries.

"Don't eat them," Shirley warned. "They're poisonous."

"What?"

"I'm serious, Ede."

Edith had plucked a berry but now she dropped it with a little gasp and wiped her fingers down the front of her T-shirt. They left a purple stain. More evidence, but it didn't matter anymore. No punishment could compare to this place.

"Help me with this," Shirley said.

Edith did, bending at the knee and using both hands to slide the cover off the partially collapsed brick ring. It revealed a dark hole running deep into the earth, wide enough that Edith could fall in and hit the bottom without touching the sides.

"A well," Edith said, taking a considerable step backward. One of the bricks toppled into the hole, disturbed by the movement of the boards. At least three seconds passed before she heard it hit the water at the bottom. "Jeez, a *deep* well."

"I wouldn't drink the water, though," Shirley said. "Like the berries, it's poisonous. Full of wickedness. This well is only good for one thing."

"What's that?" Edith had taken another step backward.

"It's an energy dump," Shirley said. She pressed both forefingers to her temples, then pointed at the deep, dark hole. "It's where all the bad things go."

"You won't remember the time I ran away from home," Shirley said, standing close enough to the well to make Edith nervous. "You were two years old. I'd just started third grade. There were two girls who bullied me every day and my teacher was a jerk. Also, Mom and Dad were giving *you* all their attention. You were super-cute, I guess, but still . . ."

Something heavy—a deer, perhaps—moved through the grass. Edith flinched but Shirley didn't move a muscle.

"I didn't think anybody would miss me." Shirley shrugged, taking a step away from the well, for which Edith was grateful. "That's how you think when you're eight years old. So I threw some clothes into a backpack, stole twenty bucks from Dad's wallet, and ran away."

"That was really dumb," Edith said.

"Yeah, well, I wasn't gone for long. Five or six hours, maybe. And it's not like I joined the circus or hopped on a train to New York City."

"You came here," Edith said.

Shirley nodded. "The barn first. There were some rain barrels and a few hay bales in the loft. I made a cozy little nest, then decided the barn was way too obvious for hiding in. So I took a stroll into the field, into the tall grass." Shirley looked around the clearing, then her gaze settled on the well. "And yeah . . . stumbled across this place."

"You could've fallen in," Edith said. Her nostrils flared. "Nobody would have found you. *Ever.*"

Shirley was silent for a moment. Edith didn't care for the way she regarded the open hole—with a kind of eerie calm, as if she and it had a mutual understanding. Or shared a secret.

"I thought about jumping in."

"Stop it," Edith demanded.

"It has a freaky pull, don't you think?"

"No. I don't."

Shirley's lips twitched. Her eyes flicked between Edith and the well. "In the end I sat in the grass and imagined bringing Louise Fischer out here. She was one of the girls who bullied me—called me dogface and pulled my hair. A real *beeyotch*." Shirley's expression darkened. She made a pushing gesture with her hands. "Down she went. Bye-bye, Louise. Then I imagined pushing Gabby González in—not *as* big a bitch as Louise, but close." Shirley used her forefinger to mimic Gabby's descent to the bottom of the well. "*Adios*, Gabby. See you never."

"Shirley." Edith shook her head. "That's just horrible."

"I would never have done it." Shirley flipped her shoulders indifferently. "It was good to *think* it, though. Not in a harmful way, but as a kind of stress relief, like slamming a door or having a good cry. And it was like the well *wanted* me to think it—like it was feeding on the bad energy in my head."

Edith wiped a light sweat from her forehead. She wanted to say something but there were no words. She shook her head again.

"So I gave it more," Shirley said, and that eerie calm was back in her eyes. "I collected my bad thoughts and feelings—all the things that were getting me down—and I threw them into the well. It felt good, a little bit silly, but *good*. It was only later, walking home, that I noticed the difference."

"You felt happier?" Edith asked.

"Not exactly," Shirley replied. "Well, yeah, but . . . it's hard to explain. It felt like there was more space around me. More air to breathe. Until I got home, at least. Mom and Dad were *pissed*."

"Go figure."

"They'd checked with all our friends and neighbors and called the police a couple of hours before. Long story short: Dad yelled while Mom hugged me, then Mom yelled while Dad hugged me. They wanted to ground me for*ever.* Instead, they took me—us—out for ice cream, and paid me more attention after that."

A large bird took wing from the tall grass, printing itself briefly against the sky. Edith looked at it, wishing she could fly away, too.

"I've been here a lot since then." Shirley took a deep breath, then wrinkled her nose as if the air was sour. "I come here when I'm down. *Really* down. Fights at home. Fights at school. You know the kind of thing."

Edith nodded. Shirley was great most of the time. A real cool sis. But there'd been occasions—more so recently—when she'd been difficult to be around. She became sullen, wouldn't talk to anybody. There were days she refused to eat or go to school. She once set fire to all her stuffed toys in the garden, some of which she'd had since she was a baby. Mom said these behavioral blips were in keeping with Shirley's sensitivities, that she was displaying her "teenage quills," and that they all had to give her space and support. Giving both at the same time, she added, was one of love's many neat tricks.

Edith looked at the well, thinking that space and support were wonderful things to offer, but that they didn't really matter to Shirley. She had her own way of handling things.

"So here it is. My special place." Shirley stepped toward the crumbling brick wall and peered into the blackness. "It's like extreme therapy, I guess. Unload your crap and go home."

"I don't have any crap," Edith said. "And the bad things . . . they're not in my head *all* the time."

"Just often enough to be a problem."

"I'm never coming back here."

"You don't have to." Shirley sneered and pointed at her temples. "You *visualize* it. That's what the hypnotherapist taught you, right? When the bad things come, you visualize something that can help. But instead of jumping into *my* mind, you come here. You *see* the crappy bricks and the poisonous blackberry bush. You *see* the tall grass and the barn in the distance. Most importantly, you see the well . . ."

Tears gathered along Edith's eyelashes. She shook her head and they plinked heavily onto her cheeks.

"You see it all, Ede. Every detail." Shirley spread her arms and turned a slow circle, like a realtor exhibiting a particularly resplendent room. "Then you draw the bad things from your mind, and throw them down the well."

Edith wiped her cheeks. Several damp strands of hair fell across her eyes, obscuring her vision, and that was fine.

"This can work." Shirley walked around the well to Edith's side. She brushed the hair from Edith's eyes and for the next thirty seconds she was very sweet. "I know it's different than what you're used to, and I know it's scary, but you *can* do this. Pretty soon the bad things won't bother you anymore. They might go away altogether."

"Maybe," Edith said, smearing more tears from her cheeks.

"I can't have you inside my head anymore. I have my own life—my own stuff to deal with. You understand that, don't you?"

"Yeah, you told me that. Like a hundred times."

"And I mean it."

Edith sniveled, her wet eyes turned to the sky. "It's horrible here. It's creepy and dark. I don't think it'll work for me. I need warmth and light. I need—"

"Scream through the night, then," Shirley snapped. Her lips wrinkled. Her eyes flared. "Draw all over the fucking walls. Mom and Dad *know* you're not having night terrors. They won't take you to Luke Skywalker next time. You'll end up in some hospital with a bunch of creepy old doctors. They'll poke and prod you, Ede. They'll cut you."

"Don't say that, Shirl, please, it's—"

"I'm *trying* to help you."

Edith's legs wobbled, then gave. She sat down in the grass with a thud that made her teeth rattle. More tears bubbled from her eyes and she wept loudly. Shirley offered no comfort. By the time Edith regained some composure, the boards were back on the well and her sister stood stone-still and featureless, framed by the tall grass.

"I want to go home," Edith croaked.

Shirley led the way.

5

The Buffalo bombing had fallen off news feeds by the first week of May and America had moved on to its newest grief: a mass shooting at a mall in San Diego. This was something Edith *hadn't* predicted, to the best of Laura's knowledge. Likewise, there'd been no telepathic communication with Shirley, and no bizarre drawings on the wall. Were it not for the therapy and paranormal investigators, it'd be easy to believe they had a normal life.

"Do they still have cameras in Edith's room?" Anna asked.

"Camer*a*. Singular," Laura said. "And yes. They want to witness one of Edith's episodes. I guess they need to know what they're dealing with."

Anna sipped her water—from an aluminum flask, not a plastic bottle—and looked at the river. It was wide here, and deep, with a broken yolk of sunlight shimmering across the surface. In many ways, it mirrored Anna herself: quietly beautiful, but with underlying power. She'd been Laura's spiritual advisor for only two weeks, but offered an aura of such comfort that Laura felt they'd known each other for years. This was where the clichés began and ended; Anna was not the spiritual advisor that Laura had been expecting. She was a farmer's daughter, born in North Platte, Nebraska, now living in Syracuse. Her attire was unspectacular, as was her hair—driftwood brown, pulled back from her face with a simple, sleek barrette. Even her name, Anna Wright, was middle-of-the-road American, without even a hint of New Age.

Almost *disappointingly* normal. Laura joked with Martin that she'd have settled for an eyebrow piercing or a waft of patchouli oil. Anna prevailed in her confidence and intuition, though—what Laura thought of as her *deep knowing*.

"So how do *you* feel about the camera?" Anna asked, screwing the lid on her aluminum bottle. "Set aside everything but your own feelings."

"I don't like it," Laura replied at once. "But if it helps Edith . . ."

"This isn't about Edith. Take Edith out of the equation. Think about the camera, that infrared device purring away through the night. It doesn't make coffee. It doesn't iron your shirts. All it does is watch. *Stare.* How does that make you feel?"

"Awful."

"Okay." Anna's eyes flashed. They were russet, flecked with yellow. Beautiful eyes, magnified by her glasses. "It's invasive, Laura, mechanically and energetically. You know that, and you're responding to it."

Laura shrugged, but her sigh—deep and wavering—suggested she knew it very well.

"You know," Anna continued. "Some cultures believe that cameras can steal from the soul, and refuse to have their photographs taken. Make of that what you will."

It was warm for early May and Meredith Park had settled into a sunshiny daze. A clique of teenage girls—Laura recognized some of them from school—sat on the grass nearby, occasionally talking, mostly trapped in their cell phones. Several benches were occupied by old folks playing chess or reading fat Sunday newspapers. A family of ducks bobbed single-file downriver, quacking agreeably.

"You think the camera's a bad idea," Laura said. Not a question. "Wait, you think the whole of Love Paranormal is a bad idea."

"From everything you've told me," Anna said, "it appears they're trying to identify Edith's ability so that they can drive it out. Eliminate it."

"Heal her."

"It sounds like an exorcism. Or maybe they'll use electrotherapy, or go straight for the lobotomy."

"That's not going to happen."

"Obviously. Because you won't let it. But however it shakes out, I'm concerned their methods will create spiritual angst and agitation, not just in Edith, but in—and among—all of you. I'm concerned they'll make things worse."

Laura fetched another sigh, this coming from an oh-so-tired place, and she didn't have to reach deep to find it.

"I don't have the skill set to help Edith," Anna said after

a moment: a deliberate pause that informed Laura she'd carefully considered what she wanted to say. "I can align with her spirit, but not her mind. That's where her power is. And my feeling—with a view to encouraging positive energies—is that she should learn to coexist with it. To harmonize. It's an active part of her brain, after all. Who knows what damage might be caused by removing it? Or *trying* to remove it."

Laura nodded. She looked at the ducks.

"And by the way," Anna added. "There's nothing wrong with Edith. She doesn't need healing. She needs guiding."

Laura felt she'd struck gold with Anna. There was a charged but congenial energy between them, an immediate feeling of ease. This wasn't the case with the few mediums she'd contacted in regard to Edith. The first (his name was Astral Weeks, which prompted a well-deserved eye-roll from Martin) claimed Edith was being haunted by "future ghosts"—the souls of the still-living, harbingers of their own approaching doom. He insisted on sprinkling a concoction of mugwort and cedar shavings around Edith's bed before she went to sleep, which only resulted in Edith getting a splinter in her foot when she got up to use the bathroom. The second medium (Benedicta, a self-professed psychic diva) said that Edith was paying for her transgressions from a previous life. The idea that Edith—so sweet, so perfectly untainted—could be punished for *anything* upset Laura profoundly, and she felt wholly justified in calling the psychic diva a "trout-faced, callous old phony" and showing her the door.

"Bet she didn't see *that* coming," Martin had joked unhelpfully.

The numerous websites Laura visited offered little encouragement. They all appeared to be designed by ten-year-old *Goosebumps* enthusiasts. There was an unabashed use of creepy music, sound effects, and fonts. At last she happened upon Love Paranormal, a two-person team out of Utica. Their website elevated them from the crowd, in that it was understated and professional. They were further elevated by their promise of compassion, open-mindedness, and discretion. She—Paris Love—was a parapsychologist with thirteen years' experience investigating supernatural phenomena. He—Philip Bean—was a renowned medium with a sensitivity to all forms of nonphysical energy.

They arrived the day after Laura called and spoke at length with her and Martin, who gave a thorough account of Edith's latest "night terror"—how she'd transposed it to both her sister and the bedroom wall, and how some of the details were eerily close to what happened in Buffalo. They discussed previous episodes, along with other aspects of Edith's character: Did she suffer from mood swings? Learning difficulties? Did she have an imaginary friend? Paris—elegantly tattooed, a purple streak running through her hair—asked Laura about the pregnancy. Were there any issues? Did she go full term? Was it C-section or natural birth? Both she and Philip made copious notes. They studied the symbols—the *psychography,* they called it—on Laura's phone, looking for any occult or supernatural relevance. They found none, suggesting the characters were more like prehistoric cave drawings: a series of rudimentary illustrations depicting some story or event. Before leaving, Phillip—a hipster type, with a plaid shirt tucked into skinny jeans and a beard Rutherford B. Hayes would have been proud of—took an energy reading in Edith's room. He sat Buddha-like on the floor for twenty minutes before declaring there was no notable aggressive activity.

On their second visit, they spoke briefly with Shirley, who grunted and sighed her way through several questions. Their conversation with Edith was longer, altogether friendlier. They talked about their favorite Vines and TV shows—all cheery stuff—before delving into what Edith called the "bad things."

"Are you afraid to go to sleep at night?" Paris had asked her.

"Yes," Edith replied.

"But the bad things can't harm you."

"I know."

"So why are you afraid?"

Edith took a moment. Her brow wrinkled, then she turned the question around in a way that Laura thought was quite beyond her years.

"What are *you* afraid of, Miss Love?"

Paris shrugged, a bemused expression on her face. "Let's focus on you, shall we? Why are—"

"Spiders? Snakes? Terrorists?"

Paris drummed her fingers on her knee, then nodded and went with it. "Okay. Crows. I don't care for their hard beaks and scaly claws." Her eyes brightened. She leaned toward Edith and said, "Shudder."

Edith leaned forward, too. "What if you knew that, after you fall asleep tonight, a crow was going to fly into your room? It wouldn't harm you. It would just sit on your bedpost, next to your pillow, and watch while you sleep."

Paris smiled and made a "point taken" gesture with her hands.

"That's why I'm afraid," Edith said. "It's like sleeping with a crow."

This second visit concluded with Edith taking a Zener card test. Five distinct cards—a square, a star, a circle, three wavy lines, a cross—in a deck of twenty-five. Philip shuffled the deck, set it facedown on the table, and had Edith try to predict which card would be flipped over next. Given the numbers, a score of 20 percent or higher over numerous runs *could* suggest a clairvoyant influence. Edith did ten runs and got a total of forty-two hits. Not quite seventeen percent. An unremarkable number, according to Paris.

"So she's *not* psychic?" Martin asked later, once the grownups were alone.

"There are different types of psychic sensitivity," Paris replied. "The cards are a guide. They're in no way conclusive, but when collated with other data—"

"Like a premonition," Laura cut in. "Forget the damn cards—how do you explain the fact that my daughter looked into the future?"

"We're still working on that," Paris said. "But hey, maybe it wasn't a premonition. There's a theory that universal energy patterns shift prior to any significant disaster. It's like a cosmic defense mechanism—a feeling in the air. I'm sure you've heard stories. People cancel flights for no reason. They stay home from work. They take a different route to their parents' house. Are you with me?"

Martin nodded. "Happened to my brother Jimmy. He backed out of going to a Yankees–Red Sox game. Said he wasn't in the mood. Which is crazy, because he *breathes* baseball. Anyway, his buddy's shitty little Pontiac flipped on the Interstate. Three in the car. No survivors. Jimmy calls it the time he cheated the reaper. *I* call it freak luck."

"There are any number of those 'freak luck' stories surrounding 9/11," Phillip said. "A lot of people veered from their daily routine and wound up living to talk about it. Gets to a point when you sense a paranormal force at work."

"Let's roll with that," Paris said. "Let's say your brother, and all those people who inexplicably broke their routine on 9/11, experienced—without their knowing—a genuine psychic occurrence. Isn't it possible that Edith tuned into a similar shifting energy, but in a heightened way? A one-off psychic blast? I know you're querying her earlier night terrors, but there's no evidence they were clairvoyant."

"What about the link to Shirley?" Laura asked.

"A side-effect of the phenomena," Paris said. "Again: heightened. Shirley claims she sometimes feels Edith's emotions. I can believe that; sibling telepathy is well documented, most commonly between twins. There's a pseudoscience attached to it. Quantum entanglement. It's how a husband can sometimes feel morning sickness when his wife is pregnant, or how old couples can finish each other's sentences. It's unusual, but not necessarily paranormal."

"Are you saying you can't help her?"

"I'm saying she may not *need* help," Paris said. "But we want to be sure. With your permission, we'd like to place a night vision camera in Edith's room. We need to witness an episode. Determine whether or not it's paranormal. Then we can assess and proceed accordingly."

"And if it *is* paranormal?" Martin asked.

"There are ways of suppressing unwelcome psychic energy," Paris said. "Don't worry, Mr. Lovegrove. We'll fix your little girl."

They installed the camera the following day, positioning it high into a corner overlooking Edith's bed. It was larger than Laura expected, with an unblinking lens and a ring of red lights that looked oddly extraterrestrial.

"I'm not sure about this," Martin said in bed later. Neither of them could sleep, imagining the camera whirring away in the next room. "They could be watching her right now. Our daughter."

"It's not a live feed," Laura said. "They'll whizz through the footage as required. And they're trying to help her. We need to remember that."

"Right. Yeah."

Laura took his hand beneath the covers and squeezed. "Thank you for standing by me on this. I know it's an unconventional approach, but we have to try everything."

They said nothing for a long time, staring into the settled gloom, listening to their own wakeful breaths and the occasional vehicle zipping along Melon Road. Moonlight seeped through and around the blinds.

"Apropos of nothing," Martin said. They were still holding hands. "I googled my new therapist today. She used to be a Hollywood stuntwoman. Worked on *Smokey and the Bandit*."

"Are you serious?"

"True story." Martin held up his free hand as if he were taking an oath. Laura saw its silhouette against the blinds. "And that's how truly fucking bizarre my life has become. I'm living on the set of *Paranormal Activity* and getting coping advice from Sally Field's stunt double."

Laura smiled, in spite of everything. But that was okay because she *felt* Martin smiling, too. Quantum entanglement at work. Then their smiles turned to giggles, which in turn escalated to a quite lovely laughter. They hushed each other. They touched, kissed, and laughed some more, and for those few moments they forgot about the camera in Edith's room. They forgot about everything.

Anna sipped from her aluminum bottle and her russet eyes glazed over. This was an idiosyncrasy that Laura was already familiar with; it appeared that Anna was daydreaming, when in fact she was extremely aware, tuning into either her own or Laura's vibe, seeking a clear signal amid the noise. She called this *sieving*. A little slice of New Age hoodoo from a woman who grew up mucking out cowsheds in the Cornhusker State. Laura, meanwhile, waited with her gaze on the water. The ducks' quacking carried on the breeze, even though they were some distance downriver.

"You need someone who understands Edith," Anna said a moment later. Her eyes snapped back into focus and she looked at Laura. "Someone who shares her sensitivities."

"Therein lies the problem," Laura sighed. "We don't even know what her sensitivities are."

Anna took a meditative breath, her face brushed by an expression Laura had never seen before. It looked, for all the world, like hesitation. Then her lips twitched at the corners and she said, "Do you want to try something wacky?"

"Wacky?" Laura's turn to smile. "Sure. We're already outside the box. Why not take a few more errant steps?"

Anna's purse was on the bench beside her. She opened it and took out her wallet. "This may not work," she said, and then corrected herself. "This almost certainly *won't* work." She flipped through several of the pockets, each jammed with wallet paraphernalia, then pulled out what Laura at first thought was a baseball card. It was about the same size, kept in a protective plastic envelope. When Anna handed it to Laura, she saw it was actually a photograph of a middle-aged woman with thick auburn hair and horn-rimmed glasses. The quality was not good. It was out of focus—layered, like a 3D image before putting the special glasses on.

"The trouble with hiring a psychic," Anna said, "is that ninety-nine percent of them are charlatans. Yes, they're extremely clever and convincing, but they don't have a psychic bone in their bodies. Genuine psychics are hard to come by. They don't advertise their abilities because they're afraid of the consequences—of being misunderstood and vilified. It's what happened to this lady back in the 1960s."

Laura looked at the oddly blurred face in the photograph, tilting it like a hologram to see it more clearly. She had four irises behind only one pair of glasses, like some peculiar species of insect.

"Who is she?"

"Her name is Calm Dumas," Laura replied. "That photo was taken twenty-some years ago, but it still works. Apparently."

Laura frowned at this curious choice of words, but disregarded it in favor of the question preloaded onto her lips: "Carm, as in Carmella?"

"No. Calm, as in peaceful."

"Of course," Laura said. "Silly me."

"She helped police solve a number of cases in the mid-sixties, including the highly publicized Bookworm Murders, which led to the arrest and conviction of Edwin Barclay. Her information was so precise—finding bodies, identifying murder weapons—that she was, perhaps understandably, put under the microscope. She was even considered an accomplice at one point. The FBI got involved. After two months of experiments and cross-examination, they determined that she was not a murderer *or* an alien—yes, there was genuine concern she might be from another planet—and she was allowed to return to her normal life. Needless to say, she kept a low profile from that point forward."

"Jesus," Laura said.

"These days she lives on a small farm in Virginia. She keeps her ability under wraps and helps very few people—only those she feels will truly benefit from psychic intervention."

"And you think she'll be able to help Edith?" Laura kept tilting the photo, trying to see the face clearly.

"I think it's worth a shot," Anna replied. "Miss Dumas should be able to determine whether or not Edith has some clairvoyant ability, and if so, how she can coexist with it."

"Okay." Laura nodded and exhaled heavily. The movement caused some weight to slide from her shoulders. Or so it seemed. "That's exactly what we want. *Exactly.*"

"Well . . ." Anna shrugged. ". . . give her a call."

There was more to it, though. Laura flicked back to Anna's hesitant expression, and her odd choice of words. *That photo was taken twenty-some years ago, but it still works.* She frowned, turning the photograph over, looking for contact info.

"Does she have a website?"

"No," Anna said.

"A telephone number?"

"Not exactly."

Laura looked at Anna with one eyebrow raised. "Okay. You're not telling me something."

"The wacky part," Anna said, throwing up her hands. "I don't know if this will work. I suspect it *won't*, but I don't want it to affect your opinion of me."

"It won't."

"It *may*, but hey, I can't leave you hanging now."

Laura raised her other eyebrow.

"You call to her," Anna said, pointing at the photograph. "You and Martin. Find somewhere quiet, somewhere you can focus. Place the photograph on a flat surface, stare into her eyes, and repeat her name over and over. If she hears you, she'll come."

Laura shook her head. "What? She'll just appear out of thin air—*poof!*—like Candyman?"

"I don't think so," Anna replied. "She lives in Virginia, remember? She'll likely hop on a plane. It might take a couple of days."

"So we *telepathically* call her?"

Anna nodded.

"But we're not psychic."

"You don't need to be. Think of it like a Ouija board. You focus. You open spiritual pathways. You connect. And the best part . . . if it works, you'll know she's the real deal. You'll know you can trust her."

"That's a pretty big *if*."

"What have you got to lose?"

Laura pressed her lips together, looking at Calm Dumas's strangely layered face. Her impulse was to toss the photograph into the river, let it float inside its plastic envelope all the way to Lake Onondaga. Instead, she unclasped her own purse and placed it inside, nice and deep, beneath purse crap, where Martin or the girls were unlikely to discover it.

"Thank you, Anna. I think I'll keep it in my back pocket for now." She looked at Anna and offered a warm but tired smile. "Martin just found out his therapist was a stuntwoman on *Smokey and the Bandit*. This might send him over the edge."

Anna nodded. "Go with your heart."

The river lapped at its banks. Laura closed her eyes and listened to it, and to the birches' placid whispering—a bright harmony, emphasized by the sun on her skin. She opened herself like a window, aware again, although she never really forgot, just how curled and autumnlike she was inside, and how the rain rarely stopped.

6

The Warehouse District had earned the nickname Engine City because—back in the day, when businessmen wore fedoras and drove shiny black DeSotos—it had kept the town of Sternbridge, New Jersey, running. Located on the banks of the Hackensack River, the warehouses and businesses of Engine City had operated at about 30 percent legal—just enough to provide a credible front. The workers and bosses would return to their homes after a day's graft. They would bounce their kids on their knees, eat *spaghetti alla carbonara*, then peel money from their fists and filter it through Sternbridge's law-abiding communities. In the forties and fifties, the pie was sweet and plentiful enough for everybody to have a slice: the mayor, the councilmen, the chief of police. This unscrupulous kinship fragmented in the eighties when the misdeeds switched from prostitution and racketeering to arms and drug trafficking. This triggered a semester of bloodshed that left nary a bad man standing. It was often said that there were more dead bodies in the river behind Engine City than in all of Sternbridge Cemetery.

By the midnineties, many of the corrupt businesses had either folded or been bought out by owners with a more lawful focus. This turnaround continued into the new century and beyond, and if the waterfront development north of Sternbridge was anything to go by, the restructuring would continue for many years to come.

Valerie Kemp had frequented Engine City over the years. She'd seen the changes one at a time, but was reliably struck by how different it looked to when she'd first arrived in 1982. The moniker prevailed, though. As did one—just *one*—of the businesses.

The White Lantern.

Valerie stepped out of a cab three blocks west and walked in a sunshiny air that smelled vaguely of copper. Her skin bristled. Her heart tapped a swift, distracting beat. She passed a string of produce stores with their goods arranged outside. Scents of apple, ginger, and lemongrass mingled with the copper. Her mouth watered, but she was hungry for something else. Within a block she came to the warehouses, where perspiring workers loaded crates into the backs of docked trucks. There was a time when they would have howled at her. Now, they barely glanced. Somewhere, a radio boomed "Hotel California" by The Eagles. She thought of Pace. He used to sing this to her. This and many others, usually while she rested in his broad, powerful arms. Behind the warehouses, the Hackensack rolled like an oiled conveyor belt.

She crossed Commerce Street and the White Lantern came into view, looking exactly as it had in 1982. A fresh lick of paint, of course, but the same colors: red and gold—dragon colors. The eponymous lantern hung above the door, made of fiberglass, more bone-colored than white. There was another in an upstairs room, this softer and quite alluring. The name of the restaurant was stenciled across the windows in English and Mandarin.

She'd paid the cabdriver at just after 10 a.m., according to a wristwatch hanging from the rearview. The White Lantern opened for lunch at 11:30. Beyond the windows, empty tables and chairs sat in darkness. The front door was open, though, to let in staff.

Valerie went inside.

She used to enjoy Chinese cuisine. Not anymore. The smell of food being prepared in the kitchen—hot sesame oils and fresh fish, coconut milk, fried rice, and aniseed—placed a knot in her throat that was tough to swallow. She peeled a napkin from a nearby table and dabbed her brow. Her heart was faster now.

The White Lantern hadn't changed much inside, either. There was a large Buddha ornament surrounded by pots of half burned incense. Beyond the entrance, a Fu dog spouted water into a pond where koi as fat as Valerie's leg swam slowly. The pictures on the walls were of lotus blossoms, mauve sunsets, junks on peaceable waters. Rear doors opened on riverfront seating.

"Oh. You're here."

Valerie jumped and turned around. The owner, Sasha, stood in the shadow of a bamboo screen. Sasha was Chinese but born and raised in Wales. She had acquired the restaurant from her mother, who in turn inherited it from her brother—Sasha's uncle, the original proprietor—after he'd died of a justly deserved brain cancer in 2000.

"Yes, I'm here," Valerie said. "As agreed."

"Sorry, it's been so busy. I lost track of the days."

Sasha had a delicious Welsh accent that seemed unlikely on her eastern lips. Her skin was ivory-smooth and her eyelashes were as long as daisy stems. In another life, Valerie might have tied strings to those eyelashes, flashed them open and closed while having her sing Chinese folk songs in her little Welsh accent.

"Is the room ready?"

"Yes," Sasha said. She ducked away to fetch the key, giving Valerie a moment to compose herself. Or *try*. Her heart mirrored the sounds from the kitchen. Chopping. Clanging. Sizzling. She always felt like this when she met with the Society. A terrible, wonderful anticipation.

Sasha returned with the key. Valerie took it with a weak smile and clutched it too tightly. The teeth impressed on her palm, hard enough to break the skin.

"I'll have company soon," she said.

"I know."

"Send them right up."

"I will."

Valerie nodded and stepped away from Sasha, wending between the tables toward the restaurant's eastern wall. Here she passed a huge painting of a rising sun, a dizzying circle of fiery brushstrokes. There was a stork in the foreground, and this, again, made her think of Pace, with his long legs and elegant body.

You're set apart, he'd said to her once, rocking her in his arms as if she were no larger than a cat. *A gem. An outrageous wonder. Most of all, I see faith in your eyes.*

Valerie walked down a narrow hallway, past the washrooms, to a subtly crooked staircase painted red.

The bamboo wind chimes on the upstairs landing had been there for as long as Valerie could remember, positioned so that you had to step sideways to keep from brushing against them. Valerie had lost count of how many times she'd heard their hollow music. On the other side were three doors. The one to the right opened on an office. It was closed now, but it had stood ajar enough times for her to see inside. The one to the left . . . she wasn't sure. Storage? Cleaning sundries? Boxes of fortune cookies? Valerie wondered if this was where the Society prepared themselves—where they pulled their masks on.

The door straight ahead opened on a room that had been intended for private functions. Valerie unlocked it and stepped inside. A conference table with nine chairs around it dominated the space. This was a recent addition, having replaced a number of threadbare sofas that smelled heavily of nicotine. Two modest windows offered views of the Meadowlands and the Manhattan skyline beyond—a vista that Valerie sometimes saw in her dreams. The pictures were the same: hanging scrolls and lotus blossoms and junks with their dragon sails flying. And the lantern, of course, a moon-white oval floating over the table.

Valerie looked at it for a moment with sweat trickling down her spine. She moistened her lips and sighed.

So hungry.

She took a seat at the table and waited.

His name was Pace—short for Pacifico, which meant peace-loving, and this was one of the first things he'd said to her. He found her huddled in a wet box beneath an overpass in East Rutherford. She was bruised, shivering, and very thin. He wiped the hair from her eyes, told her that he was going to look after her, and swept her into his arms. She looked at his face. Penny-brown eyes. Blond hair that curled beneath his jaw. Darker facial hair. Her hand rested on his chest and it felt as good as anything she'd ever known.

"I'm damaged," she warned. "Throughout."

That was when he told her his name and what it meant.

He took her to his home and to a bed—but not *his* bed—where he nursed her over a dreamlike course of weeks. He fed her soups, proteins, plenty of water and antioxidants. He took her to the bathroom, washed and dressed her. Whenever she woke from a nightmare—which was often—he was there, perched on the side of the bed, usually wiping her brow with a cool cloth. "Hey," he'd say gently. "It's okay, sugargirl. It's all good now." Once she woke to find him playing an acoustic guitar on a chair in the corner. The sunlight streaming through a gap in the drapes made his golden hair burn like a halo.

There was a mirror in the room and she watched herself grow stronger by the day. The color returned to her face. Her hair regained its fullness and shine. Even her scars appeared less conspicuous. She eventually felt strong enough to venture downstairs, following the sound of voices, music, and laughter. She pushed through a bead curtain into a spacious room with copious light. A girl with glistening Jheri curls sprawled across a beanbag smoking. Another girl, blond, dressed in cutoff shorts and a Madonna T-shirt, sat cross-legged on the floor sorting through a selection of vinyl LPs. Pace lounged on a taupe leather sofa with a third girl—maybe seventeen and pixie-faced—sitting on his knee.

"Hey, sugargirl," Pace said, and smiled. "You get one question before I ask you to sit down and take it easy."

Valerie frowned. She looked from one face to the next, then through the wide balcony doors at a vast, swaying meadow. Her heart lunged; she couldn't remember the last time she'd seen so much open space. She wanted to run through it until she spilled from the edge. Instead, she shuffled her feet and asked her question.

"What year is it?"

The other girls looked at her. Their faces were quite different, but each wore identical expressions of curiosity.

"I've been down a long time," Valerie added.

"The year is about as important as the time of day, which is to say: not at all." Pace smiled and regarded her with his sharp brown eyes. "But for the record, it's 1986. August, I think."

"You think?"

"Time's an inhibitive concept," the girl on his knee said. "The hands of a clock are more like prison bars. Once you embrace that, you grow wings. And once you have wings . . ."

"Sky's the limit," the girl with the Jheri curls finished.

"You're not down anymore," Pace assured her.

But she *had* been down. Four years of pain and degradation. Four years of her precious life removed, as if an enormous hand had reached from the darkness and swatted them away. Valerie looked at the swaying meadow again, recalling her urge to run. She still wanted to, but after so long crawling across the floor, she thought wings might be nice, too.

"My turn to ask a question," Pace said, sliding the pixie-faced girl off his knee, getting to his feet. "What's your name?"

"Sugargirl, I guess."

"Cute."

Valerie wore a too-big bathrobe that she drew tighter as Pace stepped toward her. He ran the back of one hand across her cheek, which was clearer and pinker than when he'd found her in East Rutherford.

"It's Valerie," she said, pulling away from him. "It's a terrible name, I know. A goddamn fat housewife's name."

"Not at all."

"It's a powerful name," the girl with the Jheri curls said. She blew a mast of cigarette smoke into the air and zigzagged one finger through it. "Valerie means valiant and strong-willed. It's a survivor's name."

Valerie's nostrils flared and tears pricked at her eyes. She fought them back; it wouldn't do to be called strong-willed, only to start crying. But something about it touched her deeply, because she *was* strong-willed, she *was* a survivor. It felt like recognition.

"Thank you," she said.

"I'm Iris, by the way." Iris stubbed out her cigarette and sat up on the beanbag. "It means rainbow. And I'm very pleased to meet you, Valerie."

"Iris is our resident name expert," Pace said. "Knows all the origins and meanings. She's also a damn fine painter and a published poet."

"Agnes," the pixie-faced girl said, raising her hand. "It means virginal, apparently. I think I need a new name."

"Yes, you *do*," Pace agreed with a pearly grin. He gestured at the girl sorting records. "That's Amy. Means beloved. She doesn't say much but she can sing like heaven. Had a recording contract with Tom Dowd at Atlantic. She broke those corporate chains to be here with us. How do those wings feel, Amy?"

Amy held up a copy of Talking Heads' *Remain in Light* and smiled.

"Then there's me." Pace touched her cheek again and this time she didn't move away. "You remember my name?"

"Pacifico," Valerie replied. "It means peace-loving."

"Right on. Call me Pace." He trailed his fingers down to her throat, then drew his hand back slowly. "Strong memory. What else do you remember?"

"Too much."

"Not all of it good, I'm guessing."

"None of it."

"Well, it can be sweetness and light from here out—if you want it, of course. Consider this your home now. Stay for as long as you like, but the doors are right there anytime you want to leave." Pace threw his arms wide, mimicking the balcony doors and everything beyond them. "That meadow sure looks pretty, but trust me . . . it's all darkness on the other side. It's all tick and tock."

Pace was never exclusive to her, but Valerie couldn't help but think he favored her. Maybe the other girls believed *they* were favorites, too, but it didn't escape Valerie how often he left their beds to get into hers. Not that he hurried. Many weeks passed before they became intimate. He gave her space and healing, until one night he came into her room and asked, "Are you ready?" and Valerie responded by throwing the sheets off her scarred body. There was a gift in the way he touched her, a brilliant confidence, as if she presented no mystery to him. It was nothing so clichéd as knowing where and when to touch; he *wore* her, almost, and moved her body in ways that unnerved and enthralled her.

They went, just the two of them, for long walks in the North Jersey Skylands. They swam in lakes and beneath waterfalls. Often they went into the meadow behind his house, where the flowers were waist-high and sweetly perfumed. Sometimes he played his guitar with the bees and butterflies droning around him. Other times he sat rock-like while Valerie sketched him in pencils. Without fail, their clothes ended up strewn and they made love. He traveled her body.

"I know how pain feels," she said to him once, stroking his narrow abdomen. "I've been down and broken. If this isn't real, Pace . . . if *you're* not real, I think I'm going to break all over again."

"You don't have to worry."

"I don't," she said. "But maybe *you* do."

They watched the sun rise and the moon fade, surrounded by bird and coyote song. They debated art and fulfillment and how they'd change the world. Pace sermonized about essence and decay, and of course he talked about Glam Moon.

"Don't think of it as heaven," he said—almost *snarled*, such was his passion. "Don't *cheapen* it like that. It's closer to what Guatama found under the Bodhi tree: a transcendent experience."

"You mean spiritual enlightenment?"

"That would suggest a heightened awareness. A state of mind. The Glam is more than that. It's a living world formed of the purest energy, where you can breathe the air, drink the water."

Glam Moon was very much a house affair. It drummed throughout every conversation, every act of love, often directly, other times like a distal pulse. Pace said his dream was to find a secluded spot and establish a self-sustaining community—men and women from all walks of life, who'd cast aside their clocks and chains to find a deeper meaning.

"We'll call it Halcyon," he said.

"Named after a bird—a type of kingfisher," Iris said. "In Greek mythology, the halcyon is a seabird that can calm the waves. As an adjective, it means a time of great tranquility and happiness."

"Hence the phrase: halcyon days," Amy said.

"We'll love, we'll meditate," Pace continued. "We'll find what we're looking for, no matter how long it takes."

"Like a cult?" Valerie asked.

"Cult is such an ugly word," Pace said. "It creates negative energy. I prefer to think of it as living in harmony."

On another occasion—the women preparing dinner and discussing Glam Moon—Agnes mentioned a drug that could take you there: direct and rapid access, no meditation required.

"It's a synthetic hallucinogen," she said. "Like LSD. But there are no trippy side effects. Everything you see and feel is beautiful."

"It *simulates* the Glam," Amy clarified, adding sliced cucumber to the salad. "You're not really there."

"But if you *think* you're there—"

"It's called Rhapsody," Pace said, entering the room. "I've also heard it called Jesus, Bliss, and Route One. And Amy is right, it's a simulation. We can do better. We can find the White Skyway."

"What's that?" Valerie asked.

"It's between here and there," Agnes said.

"Between up and down," Iris added.

"Compare it to an Einstein-Rosen bridge," Pace explained. "A throat, or tunnel, connecting two points in space and time."

"A gateway between dimensions," Amy said.

"Right," Pace said. "In essence, a wormhole, but with an exotic matter added, making it stable . . . traversable."

"And where do we find this wormhole?" Valerie asked.

Pace looked at her, and she saw something in his eyes she didn't like. It was cold and hollow—the closest thing to an answer she got for many years.

They lived simply and happily, farming their own produce, making just enough money through art and music to pay for the things they couldn't do without: a home, electricity, clean water, sanitary towels, birth control. There were no clocks, no concerns, only a raw, unbridled love for one another. Sometimes that love was made as a group—the five of them tangled across the living room like wires. Other times it was one on one. Valerie recalled the first time she woke to find Iris's slick curls tickling her inner thighs—Iris's tongue rolling over her anus.

"I can stop, if you like," Iris said a moment later.

"Don't you dare."

The nightmares never went away, but Valerie learned that she didn't have to be afraid. Her new family made her feel whole and beautiful, and she adored them completely. She would kill them all in time—cut their fucking throats like pigs—but in those early days she felt immeasurable love.

Then there was Pace and the moments they shared, where she felt both womanly enough to tower, and small enough to sleep in his palm. And yes, she was his favorite. She knew this with every crumb in her soul. He even said as much.

"You're set apart." He cradled her as a winter sun shone almost blue through the icy windows. Her body was rigid with cold but warm inside. "A gem. An outrageous wonder. Most of all, I see faith in your eyes."

She pressed herself against his chest. She purred.

"The others . . . they believe me, or they *want* to believe." He shook his head. "I don't know. I sometimes feel they're just along for the ride. But with you there's never a moment of doubt."

"Never."

"Is it because I saved you?"

"No." She slipped from his arms and into his lap, gathered there like a part of him. "It's because I've been there. I've seen Glam Moon."

The lantern swayed in an updraft—heat rising from the kitchen below. The restaurant had opened for lunch and Valerie heard the buzz of clientele, the clatter of cookware. She'd been in this upstairs room two hours, by her rough estimation, and still no sign of the Society.

She got to her feet and walked to the rightmost window, pressed her face against the glass. From this ungainly angle, Valerie had a partial view of the parking lot. Three cars occupied spaces facing the river. They looked too old—not grand enough—to belong to Society members. They would drive Audis or Mercedes-Benzes. Maybe the one with young hands—the snake—drove a Porsche. She waited to see if another car pulled in but none did. Valerie paced the room, floorboards creaking. Her nerves had settled but her hunger raged.

They could be downstairs, of course, gorging on Sichuan chicken and crispy fucking noodles. Or maybe they'd been lured to some new catastrophe—a super typhoon in the Philippines, perhaps, or the recent mass-shooting in San Diego. They'd gorge on that, too, those fucking animals—circle-jerking as the body count soared.

Pleasure out of pain. It was what they did.

And why she needed them.

Valerie groaned, suddenly lightheaded. She collapsed to her knees and raked her fingernails across the floor. She wasn't just hungry. She was *jonesing.*

The lantern floated on its redolent updraft. Valerie looked at it. Her eyes were dark green pits.

The light had faded by the time Valerie heard the chimes on the landing. They plinked sweetly, disturbed not by the movement of air currents, but by someone brushing against them.

She was still on her knees, her back to the door. Her instinct was to move but she could not; her lower body was numb and her spine had stiffened. The chimes' hollow song dwindled. She heard footsteps. A pause. Then the sound of the door opening.

A waft of cologne. Something extravagant. Valerie whimpered and stared dead ahead. She heard the floorboards creak as he approached from behind, along with his breathing, muffled through the mask. She shuddered when a bony hand came down on her shoulder. His voice was muffled, too.

"Valerie. You've been a very bad girl."

The rooster came first.

7

Edith had a mild episode ten days after the night vision camera was installed in her room. Video footage showed her waking at 11:03 p.m. She didn't merely *wake*, though; she sat up suddenly—as if spring-loaded—with her head tossed back and her shoulders trembling. She remained in this position for fifty-six seconds, then lifted her right hand and started to "draw" in the air (the symbols were too vague to discern, even when Philip slowed down and enlarged the video). This continued for eighteen seconds, then Edith lowered her hand and spoke two words:

"Concord . . . Black."

She raised her hand again, as if to continue drawing, then slumped to the pillows and resumed a normal sleep pattern. As always, she had no memory of the episode come morning.

"What does 'black concord' mean?" Martin asked the following day, after Philip had run through the footage with them.

"Concord. Black," Paris corrected him, separating the words. "It could mean anything. It's too general to nail down."

"Right. Concord could refer to a business name, a street name. It could be a horse or a boat." Philip gave his beard an affectionate twist. "There are multiple towns and cities called Concord across America. I stopped counting at twenty. And who's to say Edith's premonition—if that's what it was—is confined to the States?"

"And 'Black' is even more generic," Paris said. "We'll follow it up, but we're bound to get hits."

They did. Entering *CONCORD* and *BLACK* into the search parameters on various news alerts, they hooked a total of twenty-three stories over the next four days, including: Officer Brian Black being fatally shot while responding to a domestic dispute in the town of Concord, California; a fire at Black Electronics on Concord Avenue in Cambridge, Massachusetts; a private jet—named *Fortune's Concord*—crashing into the Black Mountains of North Carolina, killing twelve.

"So there's good news and better news," Paris said hopefully. The four of them were sitting around the kitchen table. Two of them—Martin and Laura—were drinking wine. "The good news is that, her night terrors notwithstanding, Edith appears to be a normal, healthy girl. We've found no conclusive evidence of supernatural ability. I should qualify that by saying that we rarely find evidence of supernatural ability. There's a scientific, or logical, explanation for just about everything."

"True mediums, like myself," Philip added, "are the exception rather than the rule, and even *we* operate on a scientific psychic spectrum. It's more about isolating energy signatures than it is about the kind of otherworldly hoodoo you see in movies."

"Okay," Martin said. "I can dig it."

"Which isn't to suggest she *doesn't* have some psychic sensitivity," Paris said. "There are definite gray areas here. This leads us to the better news . . ."

"Go on." Martin and Laura said this in unison, then sipped their wine.

"By being inconclusive, Edith's case has a broader level of intrigue, which in turn translates to interest . . . opportunity."

"What kind of opportunity?" Laura asked.

Paris nodded at Philip, who opened his man bag and took out a file folder, and from this he took six letter pages clasped with a paperclip. "For your consideration," he said, sliding the document across to Martin and Laura. They read the title: *PARASOMNIA.* Beneath this: *A LOVE PARANORMAL PRODUCTION.* Laura frowned. Martin read the first line—*Night terrors or premonitions? Edith Lovegrove is like any other ten-year-old girl, except*—then he sat back in his seat and took a messy glug of wine.

"I don't need to tell you how hot reality TV is right now," Paris said. Her enthusiasm seemed more practiced than genuine—a note of falseness that had been absent from her character until now. "From *Cops* to *Big Brother,* viewers are reliably captivated by real people, real emotions. This is especially true for the paranormal. Shows like *Ghost*

Hunters and *True Mystic* consistently draw solid numbers for their networks."

"Nielson ratings show *My Psychic Mom* at close to a million viewers per week," Philip said. "It's the number three show on Jingle TV."

"This is a pitch." Paris tapped the pages in front of Martin and Laura. "A proposal, if you will, that outlines our plans for season one. We'll get to know your family, with a focus on Edith, of course. We'll see how you live, where you work, where you do your shopping. It sounds mundane, but viewers *relate* to this. It's what draws them in. Then we'll document night terrors. We'll talk to experts and psychoanalysts. We'll obviously show several of Edith's episodes. Then . . . the investigation. The *hook*: Are Edith's night terrors coming true? Are they, in fact, premonitions?"

"TV gold," Philip said.

"With your permission, we'd like to submit this pitch across multiple networks." Paris drummed her finger on the pages once again. "We think it's intriguing enough to earn some serious looks."

"I have a contact at Syfy," Philip said. "Marianne Perry. She's good people."

"We may not *need* her," Paris said. Her eyes danced. "I personally think this will go to auction. We're talking big money. Big production values. A celebrity host."

"Celebrity," Laura echoed. This was all she could pull from the tight chute of her throat, but it was still more than Martin. He drank his wine. A muscle in his jaw jumped rhythmically.

"Obviously, we'll oversee the whole project," Paris said. "We won't do anything you're not one hundred percent comfortable with. Likewise, we won't air a single scene without your approval."

Laura nodded. She managed a polite half-smile. "And there'll be . . ." She made a vague circling gesture with her finger. ". . . cameras. All over. In the house. Right?"

"A production unit," Paris said. "So yes, cameras, sound equipment and engineers, the director, the host—"

"I'm not going to lie," Philip cut in. "It'll seem invasive to begin with. But you *will* adjust to it, and quickly. Just like you adjusted to the camera in Edith's room."

The muscle in Martin's jaw jumped a little quicker.

"The show will air over twelve weeks," Paris said. "Depending on how everything shakes out, the production unit will likely only be here for three or four."

"Right," Laura said. She recalled Anna, her spiritual advisor, telling her how some cultures believe cameras can steal from the soul—a notion that suddenly didn't seem so ludicrous. "And what happened to discretion? That's what you promise on your website: compassion and discretion. How is airing our family crisis to millions of strangers in any way discreet?"

"We also promise open-mindedness," Philip said, giving his beard an anxious tug. "A willingness to adapt to any situation. That's what we're asking of you now: to come at this from a different perspective."

"Cards on the table," Paris said. "We've hit a roadblock with Edith. It may take a while to get around. Our best bet:

we adapt. *Parasomnia* will reach a worldwide audience, including fellow sufferers and renowned experts in the field. There's every chance someone will come forward who truly understands what Edith is going through, and give her the tools she needs to live a normal life. What's more, the money you make should adequately cover any specialist treatments."

"We promised to help," Philip said, his voice splashed with a generous dollop of gravitas. "That's what we're trying to do."

"It'll be a freak show," Laura said. Martin took her hand and clutched tightly. The muscle in his jaw thrummed like the fat string on a double bass. "You may not intend for it to be that way, but that's how the network will sell it."

"Absolutely not," Paris insisted. "We won't let that happen. It'll be a tasteful and sympathetic account. There'll always be cynics, we can't do much about that, but we're confident the overall response will be encouraging and heartwarming."

Laura nodded, looking from Paris to Philip, then down at the six-page pitch. The bones in her hand throbbed where Martin gripped so tightly. He said nothing—hadn't for some time. There were drips of wine on his chin. For a moment the only sound was the refrigerator humming and the purposeful tick of the clock in the hallway. Eventually, Paris exhaled from deep in her chest and Philip drummed his fingers on the table—a nervous response more than an impatient one.

"It's a big decision," Paris said. "Perhaps life-changing. We don't expect you to make it right now. Heck, we don't *want* you to. Sleep on it. Take as long as you need."

"Okay," Laura managed another half-smile, then extracted her hand from her husband's and massaged her knuckles. "Martin?"

He said something. More a grunt than a word.

"What are you thinking?" Laura asked him.

At last the muscle in his jaw stopped pulsing. He took a breath that expanded his entire upper body and his eyes flashed their high-beams—wide and bright. More wine spilled as he took another sloppy glug. He grinned through maroon-stained teeth and appeared, in that moment, quite frightening, quite mad.

"I'm thinking," he said, switching his gaze from Paris to Philip, "that you should collect your shit and get the fuck out of my house. Do it now—like, *right* now—or I'm going to drag you out by your silly fucking beard, and this"—he scrunched the TV pitch into one steady fist and showed it to Paris—"this'll go directly up your fucking ass."

They stared at him, jaws detached.

"You've got five minutes," Martin added.

They did it in four.

Laura poured more wine but Martin took the glass from her hand and drew her into his arms. He did this as much for his comfort as hers. They held each other while the refrigerator hummed and the clock in the hallway ticked. A long, satisfying moment, but peppered with frustration. Laura didn't cry but she could have. Martin touched her hair, trailing his fingers down her spine to a precise spot in the small of her back that, whenever he kissed her there, she groaned and part-melted.

"So what now?" he asked.

She reached for her wine, took a sip, then looked into his eyes—her famous flashlight expression.

"You want to try something wacky?" she said.

Laura took the photograph of Calm Dumas out of its protective envelope and placed it on the kitchen table. Martin found a handful of candles in the junk drawer and set them burning. "For added atmosphere," he insisted. Already Ms. Dumas looked more vital—the candlelight, probably, reflecting off the photo's shiny surface, or perhaps because it had been removed from its plastic sleeve.

"Kids asleep?" Laura asked.

"Yup. Out like lights."

"Then let's do this thing."

They sat beside each other, Laura's right hand curled into Martin's left, the photo on the table in front of them and a tall candle flickering just beyond this. Laura took a deep breath. She looked from Martin to Calm Dumas's insect-like double irises.

"So we just say her name over and over?" Martin asked.

"Right. We channel her. Like a Ouija board."

"And she'll appear?"

"Yeah." Laura said. "Apparently."

They steadied their breathing, then Laura began, "Calm Dumas," pronouncing the name slowly and clearly—*Kaammm-Dooo-Maaassss*—while concentrating on the lady's out-of-focus face. Martin joined in a moment later, using an affected voice, like an actor in a horror movie trying to summon the dead.

"Use your own voice, Martin."

"Okay."

"Calm Dumas . . ."

"Calm Doooomassss . . ."

"Calm Dumas . . ."

Laura blinked and the photograph wavered. For a second the lines came together and Ms. Dumas stared back with sharp, penetrative eyes. Laura's breath snagged in her throat. She blinked again and the illusion passed.

"For the record," Martin said. His voice started out at some distance, then became clearer. "If the doorbell rings while we're doing this, I'm shitting my pants."

"Martin—"

"It could be an insurance salesman or the neighbor looking for his dog. Doesn't matter. It's pants-shitting time."

"Just concentrate. It won't work if you keep cracking wise." She gave his hand an affectionate squeeze. "Asshole."

"Assssss-hoooooooole."

"Martin!"

He smiled, but then focused his attention more seriously. Before long they were in sync; they inhaled through their noses, spoke her name on the exhale—"Calm Du*massss*"—and waited a beat before repeating the process. The candlelight flickered, and again Laura noticed the image sharpen. Ms. Dumas's four irises blended into two, centered with ink-drop pupils that stared intently. Laura kept going—"Calm Du*massss* . . . Calm Du*massss*"—in perfect rhythm with Martin. And maybe her own eyes were swimming out of focus, but she soon picked out details that were not there before: the pouches beneath Calm Dumas's eyes, the texture of her lips, a mole on her left cheek. Even her glasses changed shape. Dimly, Laura remembered Anna saying, *That photo was taken twenty-some years ago, but it still works,* and it occurred to her—crazy but unshakable—that she was seeing Calm Dumas *now.* They were looking through a window between here and Virginia, and the psychic—twenty-some years older, with a mole on her left cheek and different glasses—was looking back.

"Calm Du*massss* . . . Calm Du—"

"Hello," Laura said.

The window—if that's what it was—closed suddenly. The photograph lost its depth and clarity. A blurred, unremarkable image once again.

"What the—" Martin looked at her, frowning. "You broke the spell."

"That was trippy shit." Laura showed Martin the rigid skin on her forearms. "Serious goosies." She stood up, backed away from the table—from the photograph. "Did you notice anything weird?"

"Honey, it's *all* weird."

"I mean with the photograph. Did it . . . change?"

"Maybe," Martin replied after a moment. "It's hard to tell. My eyes were in and out of focus. It reminded me of one of those Magic Eye images that were all the rage in the nineties. You remember them?"

"Yeah," Laura said. "But it was nothing like that. It was like she got *older* . . . like she was looking at us."

"I didn't get that," Martin said, and then, "I thought what we were *saying* changed. Her name, I mean. We kind of lost it."

Laura gave him a questioning expression.

"We weren't saying *Calm Dumas,*" Martin explained. "Okay, we were to begin with, but after a while it changed to *come to us . . . come to us.* Again and again. We just couldn't quite get her name right."

"It sounded okay to me."

"I guess we had different experiences." Martin stood up and walked over to the stove, raking his fingers through his hair. "I don't know if that—" He stopped, frowned, looked at Laura. "What time did we begin this?"

"Somewhere around ten o'clock."

"Right, and how long were we doing it?"

"Ten minutes," Laura said. "Maybe fifteen."

"Try three hours." Martin stepped away from the stove, showing her the glowing green digits of the clock. As Laura watched, 01:07 ticked over to 01:08.

"Impossible," she said. "There must be—" Now it was her turn to stop and frown. She'd noticed the candle on the kitchen table, brand new and seven inches long when they'd started, but now burned down to a waxy knuckle. She looked at the other candles set out around the kitchen. Most had melted to smoldering nubs. Some had burned out completely.

Laura puffed out her cheeks. She showed Martin her forearms again.

Serious goosies.

It was freaky enough that, despite the lateness of the hour, Martin peered persistently between the living room blinds. "I keep expecting to see her standing under the streetlight," he remarked. "Like Max von Sydow in *The Exorcist*." Laura told him that Ms. Dumas wouldn't just drop everything and appear, and besides, she had to travel from Virginia. "Assuming it worked at all," she added. "Which it probably didn't." Although, from the way Ms. Dumas had stared at her from the photograph, she was sure *something* had worked.

This was the pattern for the next couple of days. Every time a car pulled up outside, Martin dashed to the window and nosed through the blinds. Whenever the phone rang or the doorbell chimed, he or Laura answered sheepishly, their hearts thumping a little quicker than normal. It was usually one of the girls' friends or somebody selling something. On one occasion it was a delicate old lady wearing wireframe spectacles and an uncomfortable-looking wig. "Ms. Dumas?" Martin gasped, taking her hand and leading her into the hallway. "I can't believe you're *here*." But no, it was Mrs. Crumble collecting for the River of Life Church, and it cost Martin twenty dollars to get rid of her.

The weirdness of the telepathic "call" faded, as did their expectation of Calm Dumas showing up at the front door. Martin told his therapist about the incident. She called it "understandably desperate." Laura told Anna, who assured her that Ms. Dumas wouldn't come if she didn't think they *needed* help, so maybe the exercise had been valuable, and that they should take encouragement from it.

They dropped into their regular routine and stopped jumping every time someone came to the door. It was all good for a few days; their dysfunction was in keeping with twenty-first-century America, and it felt oddly comforting.

They didn't dismiss their predicament, though. Laura bounced between wanting to try another medium, going back to hypnotherapy, or waiting for Edith's next episode—if, indeed, there *was* one. They couldn't give up on hope, either.

Exactly five weeks after the Buffalo bombing, and five days after Martin and Laura had attempted to contact Calm Dumas, Edith woke from a nightmare. It wasn't a night terror or a premonition, it was a good, old-fashioned bad dream, which, perversely, pleased her parents no end. Edith soon calmed down, but spent the remainder of the night in Martin and Laura's bed. She slept soundly, as did Martin, the pair of them splashed across the mattress like starfish on a rock. Duly displaced, Laura went downstairs to sleep on the sofa.

She woke just before 6 a.m. with a crick in her neck as intrusive as a fencepost. As she did every morning, she checked her social media while the coffee brewed, bracing herself for the latest catastrophe. This time it was God rather than terrorists, with severe flash flooding across Texas. Laura turned off the iPad, took her coffee onto the back stoop, and watched a peach-colored sunrise shimmer on the morning dew.

The sun had fully risen before she noticed the old woman sitting on the deck behind her.

8

Martin walked into the kitchen dressed in boxers and a T-shirt. Glimpsed in his periphery, he assumed the two people sitting at the table were Laura and Shirley, even though his oldest daughter never got up before 9 a.m. on weekends. Edith was still upstairs, though, sleeping in their bed, so it *had* to be Shirley. This was as much logical thought as he could muster this side of his morning brew. He yawned, shambled over to the pot. "Didn't sleep too good," he moaned, pouring coffee into a mug with *WORLD'S OKAYEST DAD* printed on one side. "How can a ten-year-old hog an entire queen bed?" He added a splash of half and half, then turned to face the table, his eyes—and his mind—adjusting to the two people sitting there. Yup, that was Laura. All good there. And that was—

He coughed, spraying his first mouthful of coffee across the kitchen, spilling more from the mug onto his bare toes.

"Wha*fuck?*"

"Go put some pants on, handsome," Calm Dumas said. "We need to talk."

The photograph hadn't been the best quality, but there was no doubt this was the same woman. She was older, yes—doughier in the face, her hair not quite as thick and completely white—but her eyes had lost none of their intensity. In the photo, she had four irises, four dark pupils, but only one pair of glasses. She managed a similar effect in real life, appearing to look at Martin and Laura simultaneously, even though they sat in separate chairs, five feet apart.

It wasn't quite 8 a.m. The girls were still in bed. Martin, Laura, and Calm sat on the rear deck with the slider open. Their voices wouldn't wake the girls, but the open door invited them to join the conversation whenever they were ready to.

Laura had brought Calm up to date before Martin had staggered downstairs for that first mouthful of coffee. She told her everything, from Edith's "night terrors," even as a little girl, through to the events with Love Paranormal. When Martin returned—pants on—he began his part of the conversation by saying:

"I assume Laura's spiritual advisor contacted you?"

Calm smiled. The wrinkles around her mouth lifted adorably. "You're going to start out being skeptical? Whatever happened to good morning?"

"I'm sorry. Good morning." Martin offered a smile, too. "I'm very pleased to meet you. And it's logic, not skepticism. Laura told her spiritual advisor that we'd tried calling you. Now you're here. I'm just putting two and two together."

"It's okay if you don't believe," Calm said. "As long as you stand by your family should they choose to."

"Always," Martin said. "Laura wanted to take an alternative route and I've supported her every step of the way. So far, I haven't seen anything, or met anyone, to challenge my rational thinking. I'm open to you changing that."

"I didn't travel five hundred miles to prove myself to you, or to anybody." Still with that adorable smile. "I'll do my thing. You make your own mind up. Just extend everyone the same courtesy."

"I *adore* you," Laura said, taking Calm's hand.

With Calm up to speed on Edith, they touched on Martin and Laura's part in this—the fear, the sleepless nights, the guilt. "All those young people," Laura said. "Martin says we could never have known, and I'm sure he's right, but it's hard to distance yourself completely." Martin voiced his concern about the potential strain on their work, home life, and marriage. Sure, they were scratching each other's backs now, but would they always be? Calm listened with her hands folded in her lap, saying very little. Every now and then she nodded or made a small sound in her throat. Her eyes never stopped shining.

"It's a surreal—perhaps even *un*real—situation," Martin said. He finished his coffee and sat back in his seat. "We're doing what we can to find a real way through."

"But we need to understand what we're up against," Laura added. "Does Edith have some kind of psychic gift? And if so, how can we help her?"

Calm removed her glasses, inspecting the lenses for grime. She wiped them on her sweater, then slipped them back on. "First of all," she said. "The girl is *charged* with psychic energy. I can feel her crackling away upstairs. Shoot, I felt her when the taxi I arrived in was half a mile away."

"But the cards," Martin said. "The zenith cards, or whatever they're called. Edith scored poorly. The hipster was unimpressed."

"The hipster was a goddamn fraud," Calm said. "He and his girlfriend were looking to get rich or get famous. The whole thing was a ruse. They downplayed the psychic angle to remain credible . . . trustworthy. And the cards—the Zener cards . . . it's a bullshit test. Psychic energy doesn't work that way. If it did, true psychics would be working the poker tables in Vegas instead of huddled in their closets, contemplating suicide because of the voices in their heads."

"I think I adore you, too," Martin said.

"Which brings me to my second point," Calm continued. "It's not a gift, it's a condition. Think of it as you would autism or bipolar disorder. Edith has it, she'll *always* have it. You—that's all of you—need to find a way to live with it."

"Whatever it takes," Laura said.

"I need more coffee," Martin said. He skipped away and recharged his mug. Stepping back onto the rear deck, he saw Calm with one hand outstretched and a brilliant red cardinal sitting in her palm. Laura was on the edge of her seat, struck with a beautiful wonder. She made a "shhhh" gesture as Martin approached. He paused, afraid his movement might scare the bird away. Calm smiled and urged him closer. He got to within two feet—close enough to see the gray sheen of its tail feathers—before Calm lifted her hand and the cardinal flew away, gone in a red blink.

Laura whooped and applauded delightedly. Martin took his seat, grinning. Calm regarded them both with shimmering eyes.

"Bet the hipster couldn't do that," she said.

"Tell us what we need to do," Martin said.

"I'll know more when I've spoken to Edith," Calm said. "But from everything you've told me, I'm ninety-nine percent sure she's a streamer."

"A streamer?" Martin and Laura asked at the same time.

"Books and movies—not to mention all the phonies out there—have skewed the perception of psychic behavior. Clairvoyants and telepaths are usually depicted as receiving their information in clear and critical snapshots. This *can* happen, but it's rare. It's more like analyzing footprints, gauging size and direction, and restructuring events from there."

"Like tracking an animal in the forest?" Martin asked.

"Exactly. You read the clues and put the pieces together. It's also worth noting that the psychic cosmos is vast, powerful, and incredibly active. Most people who connect to it are overwhelmed—swept away."

"Institutionalized," Laura said. "I remember reading a paper in college about how some psychics have struggled to connect with their gift—sorry, their *condition*—and been misdiagnosed with schizophrenia. It's the main reason I didn't want to take Edith to a psychoanalyst."

"The Dominic Lang paper," Calm said, nodding. "Roundly criticized by the American Psychiatric Association, but entirely accurate."

Martin slurped his coffee. "So you're saying that Edith can connect to the psychic universe—or whatever it is—without being swept away?"

"*Is* connected," Calm said. "It's not like turning a TV off and on. It's more like your internet connection. She's always online."

"Always streaming," Laura said.

"Right. She's receiving psychic data around the clock. Most of the time it's mundane: traffic on the Interstate, passengers boarding a train, someone hanging a picture. Occasionally, the premonitions are good: a little girl getting what she wants for her birthday, a wife telling her husband she's pregnant. Likewise, the data can be bad, and sometimes *very* bad—as was the case with the Buffalo bombing."

"Then why *isn't* she institutionalized?" Martin asked. "All that extra crap flying through her head, she should be climbing the walls."

"Her day-to-day life acts as a suppressor." Calm removed her glasses and wiped them on her sweater again. The morning sun glimmered off the thick lenses. "The more engaged she is—reading a book, playing sports, painting a picture—the more the signal is filtered. But she has to sleep sometime, and it's during the later stages of non-REM sleep, when the body is in shutdown mode, that the connection is clearest. Again, the psychic data may be uninteresting and she'll sleep right through. This happens most nights. But sometimes, the things she sees are violent and disturbing."

"Does dreaming suppress the connection?" Laura asked.

"It does. But dreaming is rare during non-REM sleep, so that's when she's most vulnerable."

"It's that one narrow window," Martin said, "when she's not active, and she's not dreaming. Makes a crazy kind of sense."

Calm nodded. "The imagery fades as she wakes up, but it can take a few minutes, depending on how vivid the episode is. That's when she purges. It's common in streamers. They scream, thrash, throw stuff—whatever helps. I've known streamers get out of bed and dance. Some sleep with an easel in their room so they can paint what they're seeing, just to get it out quicker. And it *works*, because it engages the brain."

"It fires up the suppressors," Laura said.

"Exactly."

"And what's Shirley's part in all this?" Martin asked. "Does she really have a telepathic link to Edith?"

"If she does, it's coming exclusively from Edith. Again, I'll know more after I've spoken to her, but I'm pretty sure Edith was hiding in her big sister's mind. It would explain why the episodes calmed down—or appeared to—for a number of years. But then Shirley decided she didn't want Edith in her mind anymore. And who can blame her? She's fifteen years old—a young woman. Her privacy is a serious business."

"She doesn't even like Edith in her *room*," Laura said.

Calm spread her hands. A "there you have it" gesture.

"If it helps," Martin said. "She can hide in my mind."

"Mine, too," Laura said.

"You say that now, but what happens when—as much as you love her—you grow tired of it? And you *will*, just like Shirley did. What happens when, God forbid, you're not there anymore? And did you consider the fact that Edith may not *want* to jump into her parents' minds? Would you jump into yours?"

"Hell, no," Martin said.

"It's a fix, but not a good one," Calm said. "It's temporary and unstable. What she needs is something permanent. A place she can go when the psychic signal is clear and dangerous."

"How does she go about getting that?" Laura asked.

"She has to build it," Calm replied, and tapped her temple. "Up here. One tiny piece at a time. It won't be easy, and you can help her by encouraging artistic endeavor. Reading, writing, playing a musical instrument. All these things reinforce the creative mind. They make the walls stronger."

Both girls were awake before 9:30 a.m. They shuffled downstairs within five minutes of each other, poured their cereal, and were redirected from the TV in the living room to the deck where the adults sat. They were introduced to Calm, and regarded the peculiar old lady with the same indifferent expression. There'd been a string of oddballs through the house recently, and it was all too easy for Martin—no psychic ability necessary—to read their minds: *Here we go again*. They relaxed a little when Calm repeated the bird trick, this time with a female cardinal. It hopped from her palm, all the way up her arm to her shoulder, before flying away.

"Pretty neat," Shirley said.

"I know lots of tricks," Calm said.

Later that morning, Martin took Edith to the Book Bazaar downtown, a sixty-eight-year-old, wonderful-smelling establishment that had kept its doors open when so many indie bookstores had faltered.

"I call this ten-for-twenty," Martin said, leading Edith to the middle grade section. "You get to choose ten books. Whatever you like. But you have to read at least twenty pages a day. Deal?"

Edith's eyes were huge. "Deal."

She loaded Martin up. At the top of her stack was a book called *Diary of a Ten-Year-Old Rock Star.* The cover was adorned with a picture of a young girl wearing a bandanna and biker's jacket, a guitar slung over her shoulder.

"Looking to unleash your inner rock god?" Martin asked her.

"Maybe," Edith replied with a smile.

"Well, you'll need a guitar before you can do that."

"Yeah, but—" Edith looked at her father with a puzzled expression. "Wait, are you saying you're going to buy me a guitar?"

"Sure," Martin said. "On two conditions: you sign up for lessons, and you practice as often as you can."

"Deal," Edith said.

So they went from the Book Bazaar to the Music Man on the next block, where Martin bought Edith an acoustic guitar and a six-week tutorship with the music man himself. He balanced his purchases for Edith with a new laptop computer for Shirley, thus avoiding sibling Armageddon. They returned home (Martin considerably lighter of wallet but happier of heart) to the smell of fresh-baked goodness—another of Calm Dumas's cool tricks: the greatest goddamn muffins known to man. They all sat around the kitchen table and scarfed them down, saying barely a word, leaving barely a crumb.

* * *

Midafternoon. Calm led Edith to the backyard and lay a picnic blanket down in the shade of the willow. They sat facing each other. The light was muted and perfect.

"You had a bad dream last night," Calm said. "Had to sleep with Mom and Dad."

"Yeah." Edith sighed. "Like a baby, right?"

"You were looking for shelter—for protection. It's a natural thing to do." Calm took a deep breath and exhaled slowly, subtly inviting Edith to do the same, which she did, easing out any lingering jitters. "Tell me about the dream."

"It was horrible," Edith said.

Calm nodded. She plucked a leaf from one of the willow's branches and twirled it between her fingers.

"I've had it quite a lot recently," Edith continued. "Most nights. What's it called when you have the same dream over and over?"

"Recurring."

"Right. That's what it is. I'm always in the same place." Edith lowered her eyes. "A bad place."

"The well," Calm said. "By the abandoned farm."

Edith's mouth fell open. She nodded once, her eyes big and round. "But who . . . how did—"

"I just know, sweetie."

Edith's gaze dropped to the leaf in Calm's hand. Twirling. Rhythmic. Soothing. She blinked at tears and swallowed hard. "Shirley took me there. She told me to imagine the well when the window opens, and then throw everything inside. She said bad things belong in bad places."

"I say stay away from bad places altogether."

"Yeah." Edith looked into Calm's bright eyes. "I tried doing what Shirley said, but I couldn't go back there. Not even in my mind. And now I'm dreaming about it. Sometimes I'm looking into the well, then I lose my balance and fall in. Other times the dead horse—the dead *baby* horse—crawls out of the well and follows me home. But the worst dreams are when Shirley is chasing me."

"Because you trust her," Calm said. "You love her."

"On the walk out there, she pretended to be the devil and chased me through Spruce Forest. She used pinecones for horns. It was fun, in a way. But in my dreams, the horns are real—they're like *goat* horns—and she's not playing."

"Shirley is your conduit to the well," Calm said. "You associate her with its darkness. But you need to remember that she was trying to help you."

"I guess."

"It was actually good advice," Calm said, still twirling the leaf. "To imagine a place where the things you see in the window—the bad things—have less power. But it has to be a place you *want* to go, where you feel safe."

Edith wiped her eyes. They were a little damp, but there were no more tears. She took another deep breath and nodded.

"It needs to be *your* place, Edith, and it can be as wild and wonderful as you like, with waterfalls and colorful birds and towering trees. And you need to build it yourself, right here . . ." Calm tapped her temple again, just as she had with Martin and Laura. "Your own place of power."

Edith nodded again but she looked confused.

"Do your parents listen to the radio while they drive?" Calm asked, appearing to switch the conversation from one subject to another.

"Dad does," Edith replied. "Classic rock, usually. *Boring.*"

Calm smiled. The willow leaf danced between her fingers. "And did you ever notice how, on longer journeys, the reception fades? Or maybe another station comes in on top, so you get two lots of music?"

"Dad hates when that happens," Edith said. "Especially when one of his favorite songs is playing. The crossover, he calls it."

"That's where people like me and you are, Edith. On the crossover. We're constantly picking up two receptions, and sometimes the voices are very loud. We can't exactly flip the switch—not unless we want to unplug our brains. So we have to mute the sound. We have to build a shelter."

"Up here?" Edith's turn to tap her temple.

"Yes."

"How?"

Calm stopped spinning the leaf. She placed it on her palm and held it out for Edith to take. Edith did. She first inhaled its green, oily fragrance it, then she twirled it.

"That's one leaf," Calm said. "One leaf on a tree of thousands—of *tens* of thousands. In a garden full of trees. In a neighborhood, a town, full of trees. And yet that was the only leaf you could see. Really, the only leaf in the whole world. Why? Because I drew your attention to it. You *focused* on it."

"Sure, but . . ." Edith shrugged. "So what?"

"When I was younger, we used to say 'far out' when we thought something was outrageously cool. What do you say now?"

"I don't know. Insane, maybe?"

"Okay." Calm winked and made a ball out of her hands, as if she were holding a spider or small bird. "Then *this* is insane."

Edith looked from Calm's eyes to her hands. "What are you doing?"

"I'm opening a window."

"I don't see—" Edith's words fractured. She covered her mouth and watched as Calm slowly drew her hands apart. There was a crackling sound, a smell like summer rain on hot asphalt. Threads of light snapped from Calm's fingers. She eased her palms wider and the space between them began to shimmer, then separate. It was like a torn flag rippling, until the tear expanded and everything on the other side became clear.

"Whoa," Edith said.

"I call it the Jungle," Calm said.

Edith wiped her eyes and looked through the window Calm had created. She saw plants with broad leaves and burning flowers, a tree with purple branches, distant mountains capped with snow. A stream trickled in the foreground. As she watched, an unusual creature—part bird, part porcupine—loped into view and dipped its beak in. It took a long drink before fluttering away on quilled wings.

"It's beautiful," Edith said. She reached, then drew her hand back. "How are you doing that?"

"The same way you jump inside Shirley's mind." Calm's hands trembled but her voice was strong and even. "I use the electricity in my brain to power a connection. Then I project."

"Onto what?"

"Onto the place between." Calm smiled. "The crossover."

"But can *anyone* see it? My parents, my sister . . . if they were to look?"

"No. Only those who live on the crossover—those who can see the thin places."

Another odd creature appeared in the window, a cross between a small dog and a raccoon. It sprawled in the grass and stretched, its tail swishing happily.

"That's a billy-bumbler," Calm said. "Cute little fellow. I have to admit, though, I stole him from a book."

The broad leaves swayed and the trees creaked as a breeze blew through Calm's jungle. The billy-bumbler leaped to his feet and shuffled away, and that was the last Edith saw before Calm closed the window. She brought her hands together with a snap. Edith caught a whiff of something vaguely electric, like a popped fuse.

"That's my place, my refuge." Calm's powerful eyes shone. "I go there when the voices get too loud. I smell the flowers, climb the trees, sleep in the grass. That stream leads to a warm lake filled with beautiful fish. I'll swim there for hours sometimes, then lay on the rocks and let the sun dry my body."

"I like it better than the well," Edith said. Tears pricked her eyes once again.

"It's taken a long time to build," Calm said. "I add to it

every time I visit. A flower here. A rock there. And it all started with just one leaf."

She pointed at the willow leaf still clutched between Edith's fingers. Edith twirled it again, watching it glimmer.

"It's all about focus," Calm continued. She leaned closer to Edith, her face dappled with the soft light edging through the willow's branches. "One leaf. The only leaf in the world. I studied its color, its structure, its smell. When it was set in my mind, I moved on to the next thing: the branch. I gave it character and shape. I imagined the way it would move in a breeze. Then I added more leaves. Within weeks I was sitting beneath my first tree. Then flowers started to spring up around the tree. Before I knew it, I had a garden. Then it was a forest. And from there . . ."

Calm opened her hands, indicating her wild and colorful jungle, although the window had closed, leaving nothing but a vague smudge in the air.

"In*sane*," Edith said, and grinned. "Can you teach me?"

"That's why I'm here. But you have everything you need to get started." Calm pointed at the leaf in Edith's hand. "The only leaf in the world, remember?"

Edith stopped twirling the leaf and looked at it intensely—at the thin veins running through its flesh, the curl of its stem, its pale underside.

"The beauty of a powerful mind," Calm said. She reached across and clasped Edith's wrist. Her gaze was hard and serious. "But it can be dangerous, too. Our power is real, Edith. It's quicksand. As your secret place—your garden—

grows, you may be tempted to spend more and more time there. You don't want to go so deep that you can't find your way home."

"I won't," Edith said.

Calm let go of her wrist and sat back, her face flushed with kindness once again. Edith glanced away as the recurring nightmare brushed across her mind: the dead foal spilling limply from the well, and her sister with splintered goat's horns—*I'm coming for your* soooooooooul—pursuing her through the forest. These terrible images were muted by the promise of a new place: a garden—her own place of power—full of light and wonder. Just thinking about it made everything inside so much calmer.

No more bad things, she thought.

Calm nodded and started to get to her feet. Edith took her hand to help her up, but that wasn't enough.

"Thank you," she said. Tears flashed down her face and she wiped them away, then pulled the old lady into her arms and hugged her.

Calm stayed with the Lovegroves for four days. Martin and Laura offered their bed, but Calm wouldn't hear of it; she crashed in the basement with the enthusiasm of a boy scout—built herself a den stocked with pillows and comforters. Martin checked it out once, when the girls—Calm included—were out shopping for groceries. He meant to lie down to test its comfort, that was all, but woke up two hours later to find Calm poking him with a hockey stick. "Get out of there," she said. "That's *my* damn nest."

It was like having a favorite aunt visit. She helped with the cooking and cleaning, and in the evening the screens went dark and they all sat around the kitchen table playing board games. It was the kind of family time that Martin thirsted for.

"You can stay for as long as you want," he said to her.

"That's sweet, but I've got dogs in Roanoke," she replied. "They're yappin' for me."

Most importantly, Calm spent those four days helping Edith. They often went somewhere quiet together—usually beneath the willow in the backyard, sometimes the basement—where Calm taught Edith how to meditate. "Breathe slowly. In through the nose. Out through the mouth. Allow all exterior influences to fade away." Once there, Edith focused on the leaf. She detailed it in her mind with loving and patient care. By the time Martin drove Calm to the airport, Edith had the beginnings of a branch, mostly bare but intact, that she could look at whenever she wanted.

Edith kept up her end of the deal; she read twenty (usually more) pages a day and practiced on her guitar. She went from slowly plucking the notes on a major scale to strumming intermediate chord progressions, and all the time the garden in her mind expanded. It quickly became spacious enough for her to inhabit. She squeezed in and sat beneath her first tree. It was small but strong, with shimmering leaves and a smooth bark that smelled like flint. Before long, brilliant flowers bloomed in the grass around the tree, and a tall plant with elaborate orange leaves that always swayed. Edith walked from one side of her garden to the other. Seventeen steps. Next time she tried, it was nineteen. There were more flowers.

It soon felt very real to her, and very powerful.

My garden, she thought. *All mine.*

Edith started to believe that she'd never be scared again—that she'd always have shelter from the bad things—and then she saw her mother die.

9

Nolan Thorne was waiting for her at the RTC in Syracuse. She'd emailed her arrival time from the Rutherford Public Library, and here he was, as reliable as ever. He sat on the hood of his pickup (as their executor on the mainland, Nolan was afforded such luxuries as trucks and email), periscoping his head from left to right, looking for her amid the passengers leaving the station. Valerie was almost on top of him before he recognized her.

"Oh!" he said, surprised. And again, but with a different emphasis: "Oh."

Her hair was pulled back, cinched with a rubber band. She was stooped, walked with a limp. Yes, she looked ten years older than when she'd left.

"You're thin," he said.

"I'm ravaged," she replied.

They drove to Fisherman's Point in silence. Valerie sat in the passenger seat but angled her body away from Nolan. She looked out the window the entire way. Not that there was anything to see. Housing tracts and swampland and dull green markers signaling every tenth of a mile. If there was an opposite to Glam Moon, NY 481 might be it. They crossed the river south of Oswego and drove northwest to Fisherman's Point. This small town on the edge of Lake Ontario featured a trailer park, a marina, and a lively bar called The Hull. They zipped through in all of fifteen seconds, taking Salmon Road west, and then Ridge Lane—an unmarked chicken scratch that cut through an acre of dense forest toward the water. There was a derelict summerhouse where the road ended. Weeds and crawlers burst through its broken windows and dirty siding. Its front porch was covered with raccoon shit. Nolan parked in the driveway, helped Valerie out of the truck, carried her bag as they made their way to the lake. At one point he tried taking her hand and she slapped it away.

The boathouse—in decidedly better shape than the property it accompanied—was home to a twenty-three-foot center console, designed as a fishing boat but used mainly to ferry goods and people to and from the island. The boathouse also stored some of their winter supplies: gloves and hats, lightbulbs, medicines, diesel, canned food. Lake Ontario hadn't completely frozen over since 1934. There was often a thin ice sheet latched to the shoreline but that wasn't a problem. It was the snow; lake-effect accumulation frequently made Ridge Lane impassable, even in Nolan's four-wheel-drive. It was smart practice to stock up by mid-November and journey to the mainland only when absolutely necessary.

Valerie regarded the barrels and boxes with a sneer. "It's May. Do we really need all this shit here?" It was the first thing she'd said since Nolan had picked her up.

"It's a head start," Nolan replied. "Twenty-six of us on the island. That number will go down by winter, but even so, we'll need a lot of supplies."

"Twenty-seven," Valerie corrected confidently.

"Twenty-*six*," Nolan insisted. "Garrett's gone, remember?"

Her nostrils flared. She inhaled the weedy aroma of the lake, along with faint notes of hemlock, old rain, and diesel. The waves stroked the boat's hull.

"To the Glam," Nolan added. There was no question in his voice. Sometimes his loyalty broke her heart a little bit.

He helped her onto the boat and this time she let him take her hand. He untied the mooring line, started the engine, and rumbled out of the slip. Valerie sat ahead of the cockpit, hoping the windblast would invigorate her. *Twenty-six,* she thought, and Garrett Riley floated into her mind, with his big eyes and shapeable heart. Yes, she'd almost forgotten about him. The most hated man in America, maybe, but only a smidge to her—a tool, like a screwdriver or a pencil, and she couldn't be expected to remember *every* pencil. Besides, she was mind-weary. Bone-weary, too.

She looked at the lake, broad and deep blue. On clear days she could see the forty miles to Canada. Not today, though; the horizon was blurred with haze. Impossible to tell where the lake ended and the sky began. Even the island was obscured, eleven miles north by northwest, a gray-green knuckle shimmering in the blue.

Home.

Halcyon.

* * *

The wind picked up and the chop was rough. Nolan eased up on the throttle and Valerie joined him at the cockpit. Her face was wet with spray. She pulled a towel from one of the bait lockers and used it to dab herself dry.

"How close are you now?" Nolan asked. Valerie heard his voice trembling, even above the engine.

"Extremely close," Valerie replied, "I sometimes think I could take a step and be there again, among my flowers, breathing the honeyed air."

Nolan covered his face and started to cry. "Beautiful," he said. "Beautiful, beautiful." Then he lowered his hand and looked at her, boy-like and cracked. "I can't wait to see it."

"It won't be long."

Valerie wondered if Nolan had ever really been a boy—if he'd ever been allowed to cry. The fifth son of a US marine, he could gut and skin a deer before he was eight years old, could strip a small-block V8 before he was ten. He followed in his father's footsteps and joined the Marine Corps in 1988. Three years later—aged twenty-one—he was shipped to the Persian Gulf with the 2nd Marine Division. He traded bullets for 100mm shells when Saddam's 3rd Armored Division, riding in Soviet tanks, opened fire on his unit on the outskirts of Khafji. During a four-month deployment, Nolan saw and did things that he only ever revealed to Valerie. He returned stateside with a slate of physical and psychological woes: if he wasn't laid out with fatigue or a crippling headache, he was screaming at the walls or barreling toward suicide. He applied for disability after being diagnosed with PTSD, but the VA denied his claim, attributing his mental health concerns to a "detrimental" upbringing. So, absolutely nothing to do with the nerve-agent pretreatments he'd ingested, then, or the Iraqi Scud—likely armed with sarin—he'd watched explode over the city of Jubail.

He lost everything: family, friends, love. Valerie found him long-haired and pole-thin, defecating between two garbage cans on a sketchy street in Brooklyn. She extended her hand and saved him, just as Pacifico had saved her fourteen years before.

"It won't be long," Valerie said again. She wiped spray from her throat and regarded Nolan with what she hoped was an honest expression. "Don't worry, Nolan, your faith will be rewarded."

He nodded stiffly. "Do you still need the drug?"

"You *know* I do." Her shoulders swayed as the boat tackled the chop. "Rhapsody is a simulation, but it's also a kind of meditation—a mental development. I'm strengthening my mind to see something that nobody else can."

"The White Skyway."

"That's what this has all been for." Some of Valerie's hair had come loose and swirled madly around her skull. "As soon as I find the Skyway, we can *all* go to Glam Moon. We can leave this dirty world and stay there for as long as we please."

Nolan nodded again and smeared the tears from his cheeks.

"Only *then* will I not need the drug anymore. Or the Society." She clasped Nolan's arm to steady herself as the boat rocked. "Do you understand?"

"Yes."

"I'll be free."

"We'll all be free."

"Exactly." Valerie took a deep breath and looked across the water. "Which is why I need another hit. And soon."

Nolan turned to her, frowning. "Buffalo wasn't that long ago, and you need to regain your strength."

"I'll be fine. And Glenn is nearly ready."

Nolan didn't respond for a while. He studied the water through the cockpit's windshield, then said, "He missed you. He's been howling like a dog."

"Good."

They approached the island, now close enough to see the shadows embedded in the granite outcrops, the sedges and wild grasses swishing in the wind. The signs were impossible to miss: PRIVATE LAND and NO TRESPASSING, both hand-painted, aggressive red uppercase on yellow backgrounds. There were similar signs posted around the 270-acre chunk of land—a crude oval, seen from above. Gulls signaled their arrival by swooping, making noise. There was a man-shape on the dock, indiscernible in the sun's glare, but Valerie knew it was Jake Door, posted there to keep unwanted boats from docking.

Nolan slowed down and worked the wheel to approach port-side. Valerie threw him the towel.

"Dry your eyes," she said.

The rooster had said the same thing, handing her a handkerchief with a blue *R* embroidered into one corner. The Society was so seldom given to kindness that she regarded the handkerchief suspiciously, as if he'd laced it with chloroform. But she used it, dabbing her cheeks gently.

"Did you bring it?" she asked.

"The pig has it."

"I went beyond. You must've been . . . satisfied."

The rooster held out his hand. Valerie gave him the handkerchief and he lifted it to his beak and inhaled—trying to smell the salt in her tears, no doubt, although he likely only got a whiff of latex and his own extravagant cologne. He folded the handkerchief, returned it to the pocket of his suit jacket. The ring on his right forefinger flashed in the light. They all wore them—a gold band, heavy as a nugget, set with a green eye and inscribed with a legend borrowed from Joyce: *DEREVAUN SERAUN*, which scholars believed translated to: *The end of pleasure is pain*.

"The others will be here soon," the rooster said.

They arrived one at a time. Along with the rooster, there was the snake, goat, dog, rabbit, pig, ox, and tiger—eight of the twelve animals that represented the Chinese zodiac. They took their seats quietly, except for the tiger, who remained standing. The tiger was the most fascinating of the animals, and by far the most handsome. He was their leader.

"Excellent work, Valerie."

"Thank you."

The dog howled and slapped his palms against the table. The ox followed suit, and within moments the room was a cacophony of animal sounds and drumming fists. The table shook beneath the barrage, inching across the floorboards. Valerie looked at the softly glowing lantern and waited.

All too gradually . . . silence.

She looked at the pig. "Can I have it, please?"

The pig snorted, reached inside his tailored jacket, and produced an ornate silver box. He placed it on the table and pushed it almost the entire length toward Valerie. Her eyes sparked hungrily. She reached, but was denied; the tiger's hand swooped and snatched it up.

"If you don't mind," he purred.

Valerie's lip flared but she said nothing. The tiger opened the box, then angled it to show her the contents: a small pink pill on a velvet bed.

"Not the Skyway you're looking for," he said. "But it's better than nothing."

Valerie stared, her eyes still sparking. She wiped a sleeve across her mouth, then gripped the table to keep from lunging.

The tiger said, "Tell me, Valerie . . . what is pain?"

"This again? I *know* how it's made." Valerie slammed her own fist on the table. "Just give it to me, dammit. I earned it."

"There's nothing wrong with a little refresher course. People are *dying*, for heaven's sake. You need to appreciate the science at work here." The tiger looked around the table and the other animals nodded in agreement. "So, once again: what is pain?"

"It's a spotlight on the soul," Valerie replied. "It shows us what we're capable of, the depth of our spirits."

"And?"

"It's a gateway. The route to enlightenment is clearer in the absence of pleasure."

"Very good." The tiger stepped away from the table. He swiveled on his expensive Italian shoes and pretended to inspect a painting of a lotus blossom, as if he hadn't seen it a thousand times. "It's beautiful when you think about it. And with deeper pain comes a higher level of enlightenment. Take 9/11. All that death and grief . . . the horror on the ground—on every news station, in every household, and at every water cooler in the nation. Meanwhile, our sense of humanness, our emphasis on each other, as opposed to material items, was accelerated. We became spiritually enhanced, if only temporarily."

A tear slipped from Valerie's eye. She ached inside.

"Pain creates a displacement—an energetic shift." The tiger took the pill from the box and looked at it lovingly. "Advancements in quantum physics have enabled us to replicate that displacement. This little pink pill perfectly mimics the end of pleasure."

"Please . . ."

"Some call it Jesus. Others call it Bliss. We, of course, know it as Rhapsody."

He stepped around the table. Valerie smelled his sweat as he approached, even above his cologne. She imagined it dripping off his cruel body. He crouched and whispered in her ear:

"There's always a price to pay."

"I paid it."

"Yes, you did." His mask pressed against her skin. "Open."

She opened her mouth. He placed the pill on her tongue.

Her involvement with the Society began in the eighties. She'd left home (and her touchy-feely fuckwad of a daddy) to seek her fortune in New York City. And why not? She was intelligent, beautiful, and had a knack for persuasion.

Unfortunately, the Big Apple in 1982 was no place for an eighteen-year-old girl on her own. It chewed her up, spat her out. Within weeks she was broke, hooked on coke, and faced with two choices: whore herself out, or go back to Michigan. She fell in with a pro named Raven K. *Stick with me, kid,* Raven K. said, or something like that, and Raven K. was dead within two weeks, OD'd on horse. She'd had a job lined up, though. A *big* job. With high rollers. *Those filthy cunts'll make it rain all night,* she'd said, and had promised to take Valerie along, but with Raven K. toe-tagged, Valerie decided to go alone—to the White Lantern in Engine City, where the Society of Pain waited, masks on, rings glimmering.

Who are you?

Your new girl.

She's too young.

She's perfect.

They taught her the value of pain—a tough lesson for anyone to learn, let alone a kid who should have been finishing high school and watching *Joanie Loves Chachi.* They introduced her to Glam Moon. She saw the ivory trees for the first time, and the flowers—*her* flowers—with their coppery stems and soft polished petals. She journeyed the landscape and became stronger. She discovered her purpose.

For all the Society knew her, she knew little about them. They kept their masks on, even when their bodies were bare. Certainly, they were well-to-do, judging by their attire. They could be doctors, lawyers, politicians. Only one thing was certain: they were drawn to the pain and misfortune of others. It fueled them.

The tiger once told her how they would race to the scenes of car wrecks, gas explosions, and fires. They satisfied their perverted desires while emergency crews pulled corpses from burning buildings and ripped through car wrecks with their cutting equipment. They even staged several such "accidents," deriving a deeper arousal as they witnessed the events unfold. Eventually, Valerie became their go-to girl, utilizing her manipulative prowess to engineer disaster. She proved incredibly effective at this, and her reward was always the same: a simulation of Glam Moon—that little drop of Jesus.

She held it on her tongue for a moment and then swallowed.

"So what's next?" the goat asked. "How about a chemical attack in Times Square? I'm sure you can find some way to rig that. Or a train bomb. We haven't had a train bomb for a long time."

"I don't know," Valerie replied. "We have to be smart." The Rhapsody was swift—usually kicked in within five minutes. Her eyelids fluttered and her heart slammed. Just knowing it was coming flooded her with good vibes. "Buffalo was big. Everybody is still on alert. One careless move and the FBI will be crawling all over the island."

"Smart?" the tiger said, and she knew he was sneering beneath the mask. "Don't oversell yourself. You're just a hopeless fucking addict."

"Maybe I'm . . ." She closed her eyes and swayed. "Maybe I'm using *you*. Did you ever consider that?"

The edges of the room softened. Valerie crawled onto the

table, as if she were fifteen instead of fifty-four, then rolled onto her back and looked up at the lantern.

"You've always been close, Valerie. But you'll never be close enough." The tiger stepped into view and looked down on her. "Not anymore."

She reached for him but he slapped her hand away. Pain flared all the way to her elbow. This was the last thing she would feel for quite some time.

The walls disappeared. The animal faces swam in and out of focus, then they disappeared, too. Soon only the lantern remained, a glowing oval, not unlike a moon, but *more* like a bud, which bloomed suddenly.

Flowers brushed against her skin.

My flowers. Oh, I missed you.

She was gone.

Valerie left the restaurant days later and wandered heartlessly for days more. The world appeared dim and noisy, with too many harsh angles.

She found no sign of the White Skyway, not even in the thinnest places.

Little by little, her sense of self returned. She discovered a ticket stub in her jeans pocket and remembered that she'd stowed a bag at a bus station in Rutherford. It had clean clothes and her wallet inside. After retrieving her bag, she checked into a motel not far from the overpass she used to sleep beneath. She watched TV, ate pepperoni sticks until she vomited, and masturbated thinking about Glam Moon. A week or so later, she checked out of the motel, bought a

Greyhound ticket, and emailed Nolan to let him know that she was coming home.

Nolan tossed the mooring line to Jake Door, then helped Valerie off the boat. She was shaky on her feet to begin with, but shook off Nolan's hand and insisted on walking alone. By the time she made it up the six wooden steps leading from the dock to the pathway, her legs were steadier and her stoop not so pronounced.

The gulls cawed brightly, a sound she would fail to hear within moments. It would fade into the background along with the waves thumping the granite cliffs and those lake winds agitating the trees. Valerie paused to catch her breath, then continued. Here the pathway cut through staghorn sumac and yellow evening-primrose before darting into evergreen woodland that formed a natural screen from the mainland. After a minute or so she came across an islander—Simon Song—loading firewood into a wheelbarrow. When he noticed her, he dropped what he was carrying and lowered his eyes.

"Mother Moon," he said.

Valerie stroked his cheek and smiled. She felt her strength returning.

Out of the woodland, through the orchard and past the storage barn. The pathway forked here: left toward well number one (forty-three feet deep; the water was cold, clear, and delicious), the chicken coops and livestock farms, and the recreation hall (where troublesome Angela Byrne held occasional "faith" sermons, although Valerie was quick to remind her there was no God, and the only heaven was

Glam Moon). Beyond this was marshland fringed to the northwest by forest, the trees rising to the highest point on the island: a granite ridge that dropped seventy-five feet to the rocks and water below. The right-hand path led to everything else: the vegetable gardens, the clinic, the canteen, their small but cozy cabins. A power plant, comprised of a 10.1 kW off-grid solar kit, with eight diesel generators for backup, gave the island its juice. Well number two provided running water to the buildings and the winter weather kept it prosperous. A tributary path weaved through sedges and goldenrod to a sandy cove, sheltered on both sides by towering pines. Between the main paths was a field of luxurious grass known simply as the meadow. This was where the islanders played, where they danced and sang, and where Valerie often regaled them—looking deeply into their broken, believing faces—with stories of the Glam.

Halcyon. A time of great tranquility and happiness, Iris once told her. This was their home. Their community. The name on the deed—and which fell within the jurisdiction of Callow Township, New York—read Gray Peaks Island. Its former owners included John D. Rockefeller and Bernard Platt-Mellor. Valerie had lived there since 1991, alone at times, but also with lovers and ghosts.

She took the right-hand path, her step surer. The wind blew her hair. She pulled the rubber band out and let it flow.

"Mother Moon," Ainsley Moore said, and fell to his knees. Ainsley's boyfriend was killed when a backpack stuffed with C-4 had exploded on a Chicago city bus. Disillusioned, shattered throughout, he'd relocated to

Halcyon. Done with America. Sick of the fear.

"Hello, Ainsley," she said. "Those fiddleheads won't pick themselves."

Ainsley nodded, pounced to his feet, and resumed his work. Valerie smiled and continued on. Walking past the vegetable gardens, she noticed her shoulders were squarer and her limp improved. And here were more broken Americans: Gilda Wynne, whose elderly mother was killed for the eight dollars in her wallet; Alyssa Prince, whose husband was shot by a policeman for no reason whatsoever. Alyssa nodded and raised one hand. Gilda dropped her shovel and fell to her knees.

"Mother Moon."

Fueled by their devotion, their brokenness, Valerie walked past the meadow where more islanders were gathered. Some stared, others waved, a few more bowed their heads or fell to their knees. She heard their voices on the wind. Beautiful whispers: "*Mother Moon, Mother Moon, Mother . . .*"

She strolled toward her cabin. Her eyes were full of life and light. Some would call their color green and others jade.

PART II
HALCYON

10

Glenn Burdock lost faith in his country—shit, in the *universe*—when the RG-31 his son was riding in hit a landmine on the outskirts of Jalalabad. The kid was twenty-four years old. He'd been Glenn's life. His soul.

"Those RG-31s are designed to withstand IEDs," Glenn had told Mother Moon, who'd been such a friend to him, such a *confidante*. "That didn't help my boy, though."

"Sweet baby." Mother Moon kissed the tears from his cheeks.

"He should never have been there to begin with. US troops should've pulled out years ago. Instead they've been playing babysitter, training the Afghan military." His fists had been so tightly clenched that not even Mother Moon could ease them open. "Fuck this government. Fuck this motherfucking country."

He'd arrived on the island desperate and defeated, amazed at how one person's life could hit the shitter so completely. And it wasn't only that his son had been killed, but that he and Corey had been so damn *close*. Perhaps that came with being a young, single dad. Glenn was only twenty-one when Corey's pointless drip of a mom pulled the old "going out for a pack of Camels" disappearing act (*That's a* man's *asshole move*, Glenn remembered thinking), leaving him with a six-week-old bundle of shit and chaos. But heck, Glenn could switch a diaper and mix formula, so figured everything would be okey-doke. And he was right. There were some tight years and no shortage of sleepless nights, but he managed. Corey grew up smart and strong, and with Glenn being a young dad, it meant they could do so much more together. They took crazy road trips and slept beneath the stars with coyotes howling nearby. They bought surfboards without knowing how to surf and spent three weeks in San Clemente learning. They got matching tattoos on Corey's eighteenth birthday (*BURDOCK BROS* calligraphied on their shoulders). Glenn was—by his own admission—a cool fucking dad. He thought of Corey as his greatest achievement, perhaps his *only* achievement. He was a son, a brother, and a best friend all rolled into one. Glenn had at least 80 percent of his soul tied to the kid.

Nolan Thorne had discovered Glenn drinking his life away at some shit-scrub bar on the outskirts of Binghamton. "If I told you," Nolan had said, "that there's a better version of America, not far from here, would you believe me?" And Glenn had believed him, or *wanted* to. Either way, he sold up whatever shit he had left—which wasn't much—and moved to the island.

He was right to believe; Halcyon was everything Nolan

had promised it would be. And Mother Moon . . . oh, with her hypnotic presence, her near-musical voice and encouraging touch. Impossible not to be swept away.

The first thing she said to him: "My God, look at your *eyes*. I could get lost in them, I swear." And she had beamed, tucked a loop of auburn hair behind her left ear. "You haven't spoken a single word and I can tell you've got moxie. I guess this little slice of American Pie just got sweeter."

Glenn embraced his new community, applying the same tenacity and purpose he'd shown as a single dad. He milked goats and reaped crops. He hand-felled trees and took his turn in the canteen. Before long, the strands tethering him to his former life first frayed, then snapped. The nation's weaknesses no longer concerned him. He was a new man, an *un*-American, risen from the ashes like a motherfucking phoenix.

No regrets. No looking back. And then one winter's night—with a fire crackling in the hearth and snow dusting the windows—Mother Moon kissed him for the first time, a deep kiss, full of warmth, wanting, and taste. She took off her clothes and stood naked in front of him. "Count every scar," she said. "Know me." And he did. There were seventy-four of them. "Wrong," she said, and separated her lush hair to reveal eight more on her scalp, including a thick, curved zipper that ran from behind her right ear to the top of her head.

"What happened to you?"

"I was beaten as a young woman. Ritually abused. Then I found Glam Moon. And *then,* honey . . . then I got strong."

"You're still beautiful."

"I love this island. I love the people. But you're the only one I trust." She ran one hand across his jaw and smiled. "Take off your shirt."

He took off his shirt. Then his pants. She fucked him in front of the fire, the hard, breathless sex of a woman rarely satisfied, and she didn't stop until embers filled the grate and a thread of pink morning light touched the snow outside.

"I might need you to do something for me," she said a short time later. They were still gasping, curled together in a nest of their own discarded clothing.

"Name it."

But she didn't. Not right away. She lay with her head on his chest, listening to the rapid thump of his heart, and he found from that point on that Mother Moon was with him even when she *wasn't* with him, coupled with his mind in the same way she'd been with his body. He wondered, were he to slice his forehead open with a box cutter, if she would emerge, damp and beautiful, like a moth from a cocoon.

Her voice filled him.

Know this, baby: the Glam has a special place for martyrs.

Bravery is beautiful. And you, Glenn darling, are beautiful.

He felt her everywhere, day and night. He'd be raking leaves or chopping wood and swear that she was standing behind him, but when he turned there'd be nobody there. One time he woke up to find her sucking his dick and speaking at the same time—speaking in his mind. She told him that America was on fire but it was a slow burn, and sometimes you had to stoke the flames for people to take notice. Glenn agreed wholeheartedly, his hands clasping her dented skull, and said that he would do the stoking if that's what she wanted. Shit, he'd do anything. She could snap her fingers and he'd walk off the cliffs at the northwest edge of the island, shatter on the rocks below.

The last words she said to him, and which he believed absolutely: "The final bullet will be your ride to Glam Moon. Wait for me there. I'll meet you on the saffron."

On the morning of Wednesday June 13, 2018, Nolan Thorne took Glenn across to the mainland.

He'd been away for eighteen months and it was still burning.

Martin woke to the sound of Laura's hairdryer in the en suite bathroom. It roused him from some vaporous dream and he indulged a moment longer among the pillows, thinking nothing in particular, until the hairdryer was switched off and Laura, glossed and airy as a bubble, floated into the bedroom. "Did I wake you?" she asked without looking at him. "I'm sorry; I didn't have time to wash my hair last night." She then began dressing in the practical, unstimulating attire of a high school English teacher, affixing jewelry to her earlobes and a simple chain around her neck, applying color to her cheeks and a spritz of something to her throat that smelled like lavender and was called Curate.

Martin saw little of this, but after seventeen years of marriage, he knew Laura's morning ritual as well as the slope of her neck or the dimples in her thighs. She would step into her slip left leg first. Zip her skirt at the side then swivel it to the back. Button her blouse from the bottom up. The earrings she selected would be tiny diamond studs visible only in certain lights, and the rouge with which she emphasized her cheekbones would be the color of sunburned skin. Before leaving the room, she would kiss his forehead and say, "Have a happy day," then rally the girls into action. All this before 7 a.m. She was a marvel.

Except this morning she would only have to rally one girl; Edith was at the tail-end of some virulent bug that made her look like she could be cast in *The Walking Dead*. There were signs of improvement, though. A few more days and she'd be back at school—see out the last week or so before everything shut down for the summer.

"Are you alert?" Laura asked him. "Able to receive instruction?"

"Barely," he grumbled, wiping his eyes. "What day is it?"

"Wednesday."

"Groan."

Her upper lip tweaked at the edges. "Firstly, it's your mom's birthday. Don't send her one of those crappy e-cards. *Call* her. You know Jimmy will."

"Ah, fuck Jimmy."

Her smile lengthened. She sat on the edge of the bed. "Secondly, Edith will only eat Wolfgang Puck vegetable soup. We're all out. They have it at Steadman's. Aisle three. Pick up some milk while you're there."

"Sure."

"Thirdly, I'll be home late. I have a doctor's appointment, remember? Female business." She pronounced it *bidnezz* and he wanted to kiss her with his smelly morning mouth. "I should be home in time for dinner, but if I'm not there's pizza in the freezer."

Martin took Laura's hand, resisting a sudden and incredibly strong urge to pull her back between the sheets. That smile still played on her lips and he compromised with a kiss, smelly morning mouth be damned.

"That was *awesome*," she said.

"True love needs no mouthwash."

Laura shook her head in an amused way, as she had, with some frequency, for the past twenty years. They'd met at the Carrier Dome, watching the Orangemen put up big numbers against Rutgers. Martin had painted his face and upper body bright orange and slapped the university *U* on his chest. His buddy, Mickey Hill, was supposed to be the Syracuse *S*, but Mickey's old man had suffered a heart attack hours before the game so Martin was flying solo, looking somewhat ridiculous as the lonesome *U*. Laura came to his rescue, though, sitting in the seat behind with her girlfriends and sign-making kit. She whipped up a quick *S*, then leaped into Mickey's vacant seat and spent the remainder of the game at Martin's side. They chanted "*Deeee-FENCE*" and "*Let's go 'Cuse*" at the top of their voices, they high-fived at the end of nearly every play and howled when the Orangemen scored (they posted seventy points that afternoon, so Martin and Laura howled a *lot*). As the players left the field, Martin clasped Laura by the shoulders and announced with stone-cold seriousness, "We make a great fucking team, baby," then switched seats with her, rearranging their letters to spell *US*. He cocked one eyebrow. *How about it?* that eyebrow said, and for the first time—but by no means the last—twenty-year-old Laura Redman shook her head in an amused way.

They were married in 2001, a small, civil ceremony on the Canadian side of Niagara Falls. During their first dance as a married couple (with Chicago singing "If You Leave Me Now"—a melodic, if slightly inappropriate choice), Martin whispered in Laura's ear, "My parents were divorced after eleven years and eight months of marriage. We go beyond that, and we're going to last forever." Laura had smiled and whispered back that he was a hopeless romantic, and that she adored him . . . and they ran into the years ahead, as side-by-side and colorful as they'd been at the Carrier Dome. Laura never forgot that curious milestone, though, and on the night of their eleven-year, nine-month "anniversary," Martin returned home from work to find Laura waiting in the living room dressed in something slight and red, a bottle of wine and two glasses in her hands. The stereo was playing Chicago's "If You Leave Me Now" and the girls were at Jimmy's.

"What's the occasion?" Martin had asked.

"Forever," Laura had replied.

Now Martin looked into the same eyes he'd looked into when he declared, *We make a great fucking team, baby,* and yeah, they still did. It occurred to Martin—as it did most days—that the big things (love, security, trust) made a marriage work, but the small things made it *great.* Like reminding your husband to call his mother on her birthday, and knowing which leg your wife put into her slip first.

Laura was much better at these things. She gave their marriage breadth and depth, and Martin was consistently awestruck by her.

Propped against the pillows with sleep nuggets in the corners of his eyes and smelly morning breath, he felt the need to articulate this. It was too early, though, and the right words wouldn't come. So instead he squeezed her hand and said, "You rock. I love you."

As last words to say to your wife go, they weren't so bad.

Laura smiled and kissed his forehead. "Have a happy day," she said, and left.

There had been two calls to install metal detectors at Flint Wood High in recent years. The first was following the unthinkable events at Sandy Hook. Here school administrators were quick to warn against a knee-jerk reaction from parents and other members of the community. They also expressed concern that their school not be turned into a prison-like institution. The subject fizzled out, then fell off the table altogether. It surfaced again in 2016, when a fifteen-year-old student strolled brazenly through the main doors, into the faculty lounge, and lodged an eight-inch carving knife into his English teacher's back. It wasn't fatal, but there was a lot of blood and screaming, certainly enough to warrant a second call for metal detectors to be installed. Again, district officials extinguished the flames, suggesting the cost was too great for a system that didn't guarantee safety (violent crime could just as easily occur in the faculty parking lot or on a school bus). And it wasn't only the initial setup, but the ongoing cost of maintenance, staffing, and training. They concluded that the best (and most inexpensive) way to prevent violent crime at school was through common sense, vigilance, and regular lockdown drills.

Nolan Thorne knew all this—God bless the internet—and had planned accordingly.

"So I can go through the main doors?" Glenn asked.

"No," Nolan responded. "No metal detectors doesn't mean no security. There are two sets of main doors, ten feet apart. Both are locked after nine o'clock, with video surveillance inside and out. The doors ahead won't open until the doors behind are locked, and you're not buzzing your way through unless your name is on a list at the front office. Which, by the way, it won't be."

"Got it," Glenn said, and he did, although it was hard to focus on what Nolan was saying; the voice in his head was as invasive as a power drill. He found that looking at the gym bag between his feet helped. It had a stimulating effect, like smelling salts. Inside was a loaded Colt M4 assault rifle and a spare magazine holding thirty rounds.

"There are eight more entrances around the main building, not including the fire doors, which can only be opened from inside. These other doors all have surveillance cameras and the buzz-in lock system. Most are in exposed locations." Nolan took a sheet of paper from his shirt pocket, unfolded it, and showed Glenn a rough layout of the school grounds. He pointed to an *X* on the main building's northwest side. "This is your way in. This entrance is screened from the main road by the gymnasium, and from these classrooms by a line of trees. Students exit through this door frequently, usually in ones or twos. But you know kids—they can't just open a door, they have to blow through like Chuck fucking Norris. That'll work for you; the door is on a pneumatic arm. From fully open it takes eight seconds to close and for the lock to engage. Now this"—he tapped a small square to the left of the *X*—"is a maintenance building. At a brisk walk, it's five seconds from the door. You hide behind it. You wait for a student to exit the building. You move."

"Got it," Glenn said again. They were in Nolan's truck, parked behind what used to be Bucky's DVD Shack and was now a dank, cobwebby space with a FOR LEASE sign in the window. It was a ten-minute walk from Flint Wood High. Glenn was dressed in a baseball cap, aviator sunglasses, and workout gear. He looked, with his bag slung over one shoulder, like some dude on his way to the gym.

"Good." Nolan nodded. "Remember, if you're compromised or taken alive, you acted alone. Do *not* incriminate Mother Moon or anyone else on the island."

"I'm not fucking stupid, Nolan." Glenn looked at the bag once again. "And I won't be taken alive."

"No, you probably won't." Nolan took a calm breath and continued, "Expect the school to go into lockdown mode within ten seconds of you either being seen or firing your first shot. The police will be on the scene inside of three minutes. The classrooms will be locked but there will be students inside. Do what you can."

"Yes."

"Mother Moon wants you to make some noise."

"I know what she wants," Glenn said. "I can't get her out of my head."

Calm Dumas could have told Edith that the psychic cosmos was in constant flux, and that no set time separated the premonition from the event occurring. It could be as long as a month or as little as ten seconds. There might even be occasions when Edith witnessed the event shortly after it happened—a kind of psychic video playback. In the case of the Flint Wood High School shooting, she was ahead by twenty-one minutes.

8:42 a.m. Edith dozed with Paisley Rabbit clutched to her chest. She hadn't slept much through the night, despite feeling that she was finally on the mend. There'd been a lot of coughing and blowing her nose. Mom came in several times to stroke her brow and sing to her, and once with a dose of NyQuil in a little plastic measuring cup. "There, baby," Mom had said. "You sleep. Tomorrow will be a little brighter, I promise." Edith told her mom that she loved her, and she *did* sleep, but not deeply. Her dreams were close to the surface, thin as lace.

By 9:10 a.m.—Dad working downstairs, Mom and Shirley at their respective high schools—the exhaustion won out and Edith went from dozing to sleeping. She entered the third stage of non-REM sleep twenty-eight minutes later. Her body and mind went into recharge mode, and given her illness and the restless night she'd had, they had some serious recharging to do.

The window opened at 10:06 a.m. It tore across Edith's

mind like a dagger through a curtain, and displayed a very familiar scene: a school hallway, but not just *any* school hallway. Edith recognized the gray-tiled floor, the cornflower blue lockers and red classroom doors from the few occasions she'd been there. A banner drooped from the ceiling with GO MUSTANGS printed across it in the same blue color as the lockers. The Mustangs were Flint Wood High's football team. This was Mom's school.

She heard the rising-falling wail of a siren followed by a sterile announcement—words she'd been taught to understand, and react to, but that didn't fully register until she saw the blood on the walls.

"SEEK SHELTER IMMEDIATELY. TEACHERS SECURE—"

Edith sat bolt upright. A scream trembled on her lips and she reached for her garden. She glimpsed it, but couldn't get close. Maybe it was the illness clogging her brain, or her connection to the things on the other side of the window. Whatever the reason—and for the first time since she started building it—she couldn't reach the safe place in her mind.

Her throat swelled. Tears leaked from her eyes.

The window expanded. She saw a dead teacher slumped against the wall and his blood was everywhere, from his shoes to his beard. She saw bullet holes punched into lockers and a backpack lying in a puddle of blood.

"Burdock," Edith croaked. The word came out of nowhere, dropping into her mind like a dead leaf. Her hands snatched at thin air and her chest boomed. She heard that rising-falling siren once again, followed by the voice over the intercom:

"SEEK SHELTER IMMEDIATELY. TEACHERS SECURE YOUR ROOMS. THE SCHOOL IS IN LOCKDOWN. REPEAT: THE SCHOOL IS IN LOCKDOWN."

She saw a man skulking past classrooms with closed doors. He wore dark sunglasses and a Nike baseball cap and carried an ugly black rifle in his hands. Edith watched as he raised it, fired three times. The rifle jumped in his hands and the muzzle smoked.

"Burdock," she said again. She wanted to draw him: a jagged line, like a knife wound. Something vicious.

He stepped over a dead kid and kept walking.

The faculty parking lot was bordered to the north by the Flint Wood Public Library, the two separated by a strip of trees and a chain-link fence. A subtly marked section of this fence had been snipped from the bottom to about halfway up, just as Nolan promised it would be. Glenn gave it a tug and it lifted in a neat triangular flap. He passed the gym bag through, then dropped to his knees and followed.

There were more trees on the high school side, the spaces between them heavily shadowed. Glenn walked at a crouch, then crossed a patch of grass to the back of the maintenance building. He caught his breath and waited for an alarm to sound, or for a cop to appear with his sidearm leveled. *State your business, motherfucker,* the cop would scream, and Glenn would tell him to go fuck himself.

He'd take the bullet instead.

That's what the voice in his head would want.

After a slow count of sixty, with no alarm and no cop, Glenn poked his head out and studied his environment. It was exactly how Nolan had drawn it, with the northwest entrance a short distance away and good cover. The only way he'd be seen was if someone happened to be in the parking lot when he sprung from behind the maintenance building. And even then, from a distance, he'd look like a student.

The side door opened a few minutes later. A kid with headphones looped around his neck bounded out. Glenn watched the door. He wanted to make sure he had enough time to make his move. Nolan had told him it took eight seconds to close. Glenn counted six, but then the door hadn't been fully open.

Even six seconds was long enough.

"Next time it opens," he whispered.

He wiped sweat from his face. From nowhere, like a cool gust of wind, he realized he didn't have to do this. He could walk away. To hell with Mother Moon and the island. He had no house, not a penny to scratch his ass with, but he had family in Pennsylvania—a sister, an aunt. He could dump the gym bag and—

The voice in his head—oh, she was *deep*—lashed out: *NO PURPOSEFUL THING COMES WITHOUT PAIN WITHOUT SACRIFICE BE A GODDAMN MAN A DIFFERENCE MAKER NOT JUST ANOTHER BLIND PATHETIC SHEEP.* At the same moment, the side door bounced open again. Two female students emerged, both absorbed in their cell phones.

NOW!

Glenn grabbed the bag and made his move. He caught the door before it closed and stepped into a hallway with a gray-tiled floor and blue lockers. It was empty of people. A few of the classroom doors stood open but most were closed. Glenn dropped the bag at his feet and unzipped it. He pulled out the assault rifle. It was dense and black and smelled like oil. He stood up straight and tucked the spare mag into the waistband of his sweatpants. Mother Moon went from screaming to soothing. She promised her body—her roadmap of pain and sacrifice. She promised Glam Moon. Glenn marched down the hallway and found his first victim: a teacher with a holly-jolly white beard, wearing a ridiculous Hawaiian shirt and chino shorts. *I bet the kids love this guy,* Glenn thought, and shot him twice in the chest.

Two empty shells were flushed from the rifle. They glittered in the fluorescent light and hit the floor with diminutive tinkling sounds.

And I'll meet you on the saffron, Mother Moon said. *We'll make love and the wind will make music*—real *music—and strange but tame creatures will lick our skin.*

"Yes," Glenn whispered, fighting back tears. He gathered the rifle to his chest and continued along the hallway.

Even the rain is a wonder. So warm and perfumed. Oh, and you can breathe underwater. Did I ever tell you that? For hours on end. The fish are beautiful.

Martin was drafting notes for that afternoon's site meeting when he heard Edith scream.

The sound cut through The Who belting out "Won't Get

Fooled Again" (he usually cranked classic rock while working from home, which achieved the neat trick of making him feel both rebellious and somewhat responsible), not to mention the fog in his brain. He'd spent the past four years as part of the design team behind the new Onondaga Mall—over one hundred thousand square meters of iniquity and consumerism off the I-81 west of Flint Wood. For Martin's part, it hadn't been so much architectural design as reactive planning, which amounted to moderating disputes and trying to save money. This was like treading water with weights tied to his ankles. The project was four months from completion and eight million dollars over budget, with everyone pointing the finger at the person standing beside them. The focus of that day's meeting was to kiss each other's butts and get on the same page, at least until the grand opening in November. Then they could go back to hating and blaming each other again.

So much fog, thick with ass-kissery and bullshit: a day in the life of an architect. Edith's scream blew it apart, though. Martin straightened at his desk. The pencil snapped between his fingers and a thick strip of gooseflesh raced up his spine.

"Not again," he said. In the three seconds between one scream ending and another beginning—this Daltrey's, at the end of the track, and eerily similar it was, too—he recalled Calm Dumas telling them that it would take time for Edith to build her shelter, and that the episodes would continue until then. Martin shouldn't have been so taken aback, but he *was*—perhaps because the family had been in such a cool groove since Calm had left. Worst of all, judging by the depth of Edith's scream . . . whatever she was seeing, it was *bad*.

"Coming, baby. Daddy's coming."

He bolted from his office, took the stairs at a blur and—like last time—felt his injured knee mutter in protest, just a twinge to begin with, then a deeper, tighter pull as he flew down the landing toward Edith's room. He all but knocked her door off its hinges, throwing his entire weight into it. There were two loud cracks as the frame split and the door bounced off the wall. It came back at him hard, thumping off his shoulder.

Edith was on the floor, curled into a whimpering ball, a red marker pen clutched in her right hand. Martin went to her. "Babygirl." He touched her shoulder and she flinched. "Ede, it's Dad. I'm here now, it's all—" She looked up. The eyes staring at him were haunted, shocked. Nothing to do with her sickness, everything to do with her condition.

"Burdock," she said.

Martin looked around. Two of her bedroom walls were covered with graffiti. There were dozens—maybe hundreds—of jagged lines and the number 16 scrawled over and over.

"What are you seeing, Ede?"

"Burdock."

Martin stepped toward the wall where Edith had previously depicted the Buffalo bombing. These new markings were simpler and less varied—just those lightning-bolt lines and the number 16. But no, there was a third symbol, almost lost in the confusion: a heart shape, erratically drawn. Martin ran his fingers over it and looked at Edith. She shook her head. Her mouth wavered.

"Mom," she said, and screamed again.

* * *

The first gunshots came while Laura was reading "The Devil and Tom Walker" to her freshman English class. There were two rapid-fire blasts, the sound suppressed by closed doors and narrow hallways. To begin with, she thought it was someone striking a locker with a baseball bat. Some jilted jock, perhaps, dropped from the starting lineup.

All her students looked up, concerned expressions on their faces, but it was prudent, practical Paige Lewis who said what everyone else was thinking: "Were those gunshots?" A ripple of unease moved through the class. Laura closed *The Complete Works of Washington Irving* and raised one hand.

"Just stay calm," she said, thinking they couldn't be gunshots, but knowing full well they *could* be. "I'm sure there's—"

Her words were cut short by a third blast. The entire class shifted nervously and looked at her with trusting eyes.

"Lockdown," she said decisively, preempting the announcement by three seconds. The siren whooped through the intercom—the same intercom that broadcast the Pledge of Allegiance every morning, and these children stood proud and recited their pledge, eyes on the flag. Now the message was *very* different:

"*SEEK SHELTER IMMEDIATELY. TEACHERS SECURE YOUR ROOMS. THE SCHOOL IS IN LOCKDOWN. REPEAT: THE SCHOOL IS IN LOCKDOWN.*"

Most of her class was on its feet and heading toward the safe corner—the one corner in the room that couldn't be seen should the shooter look through the window in the door.

"Stay calm," Laura said, fighting to keep the tremor out of her voice—to *appear* calm herself, even though everything inside had turned to icy water. "No pushing, Alex. Slow and easy. Hey, Morgan, keep it cool. Just like your drills. Let's do this."

More shots, and God they sounded louder—*closer*. She heard children screaming in other classrooms, then yet more shots. A few of her own students were crying shrilly, with others trying to quiet them down. Gemma Baumgartner was locked to her desk, trembling, huge tears rolling from behind her owlish glasses.

"Johnny, help Gemma," Laura said. Johnny was a cool-headed kid. Chief-of-police material. She could trust him to usher Gemma to the safe corner while she locked the door. She grabbed her keys from the top drawer in her desk. Her cell phone was in there, too, and as she looked at it—as if willing it to happen—the window lit up and the word *HOME* appeared. Martin calling. Complete coincidence. Or maybe this was already breaking news and he was calling to make sure she was okay. But no, it only *felt* like forever since she'd heard those first shots. In reality, it had been seconds. The news teams were quick, but not *that* quick.

Five more shots rang out, definitely closer, and definitely not some jilted jock with a baseball bat. They spurred her in the most terrible way. "Sorry, baby," she said. She slammed the drawer and went to the door. She had to do something else before locking it, but couldn't remember what. Her mind scrambled desperately, and it was only the sight of Johnny coolly escorting Gemma to the corner that helped her remember.

Check the hallway. Yes, a quick glance left and right to ensure there were no stranded students. Once clear, she could lock the door, then draw the blinds and sit in the corner with the students—wait this nightmare out.

Laura opened the door just wide enough to poke her head through. She looked right first. All clear. She looked left, and there, maybe ten feet away, was Deena Culpovich, a sophomore, always quiet, without the attitude and confidence of the more popular girls in her year.

"Deena!" Laura snapped. "In here. *Now!*"

But if Deena heard, she showed no sign. Her mouth was slack and her upper body trembled. She was locked to the spot much like Gemma Baumgartner had been locked to her desk.

"Deena! Now!"

No response. She stared dead ahead. *Tharn,* Laura thought, drawing on another favorite from the freshman English curriculum. And what was the protocol here? Should she leave Deena in the hallway, perhaps to be shot to death, and have to live with that on her conscience for the rest of her life? Or should she rush out, grab her, and leave a classroom full of kids behind an unlocked door?

It'll take five seconds, Laura thought. Deena was a small girl, the same age as Shirley but perhaps fifteen pounds lighter. Jesus, Laura could carry her in one arm if she had to.

"Deena!" One last try, but no . . . nothing. She left the keys hanging from the lock and turned around. "Johnny, if I'm not back in ten seconds, you lock this door. Do you understand?"

"Yes, ma'am, but—"

"Do you understand?"

"Yes, ma'am."

She nodded—good ol' Johnny—and poked her head into the hallway again. With the announcement blaring, it was difficult to determine where the shots were coming from. She looked right. Nobody there. She looked left, beyond Deena. Nothing but blue lockers and closed classroom doors. Laura took a deep breath and stepped into the hallway. She made it to Deena in four broad strides and grabbed her wrist. "Come *on.*" But Deena resisted, trying to squirm her wrist free, shaking, pleading under her breath.

"Please no I don't want to die please oh . . ."

"Deena, it's Mrs. Lovegrove. I need you to come with—"

"Please no *please oh please.*" She snatched her wrist free. Her eyes flooded with terror. "No," she whispered. A final, miserable denial, and that was when Laura knew that the shooter had advanced into the hallway behind her. Deena's eyes might as well have been mirrors, reflecting what she saw.

"Oh, God," Laura said.

She turned and there he was. A small man with a big gun. She watched as he stepped closer, taking aim, and did then the only thing she could think of: she pushed Deena clean off her feet, offering herself—if only temporarily—as the open target.

Laura closed her eyes. The last thing she heard was the infinitely satisfying sound of her classroom door being locked.

Good ol' Johnny, she thought, and that was all.

The whole point of a premonition was that it happened *before* the event, but that didn't stop Martin being sick with fear.

He got Edith into bed and stroked her brow until she was dozing, then he staggered to the bathroom and vomited into the sink.

"Oh, Jesus. Oh, God."

He washed his face with a warm cloth and rinsed the sink, then went into the bedroom and picked up the phone on the nightstand. He wanted more than anything to hear Laura's voice. He didn't think she'd answer—she switched her cell to mute during classes—but he was going to try, anyway.

No dice, as expected. Her voicemail response: *"I'm either busy or frantically trying to find my phone. So try me again later, or leave a message and I'll call you back. If this is Martin or the girls . . . dammit, I love you."* He ended the call, tapped the green dial button again, and got the same response. This time he left a message.

"Hey, honey. So yeah, eventful morning: Edith had another episode. A bad one." He paused, thinking but not saying, *It involved you but I don't know how and just the thought of that made me yodel groceries into the goddamn sink.* The room pitched giddily. He sat on the edge of the bed to keep from losing his balance, then ran a hand across his forehead and continued, "She uh . . . *purged,* I guess. Drew all over the walls. Like I said . . . pretty bad. She's sleeping again now but you should probably come home. I'm declaring this a two-parent situation."

Not knowing Laura's timetable, and not satisfied she would get his message anytime soon, he decided to call the school office and have them page her, partly because she'd *want* to know what was happening at home, mostly because he was desperate to hear her voice.

He dialed. The line was busy. He waited two inexorable minutes and tried again. Still busy.

"Aw shit, come *on*."

That was when he heard the first sirens. Not a lone cruiser or ambulance, but an orchestra of wailing, speeding emergency response vehicles.

If he hesitated, it was for just one second. He swept into Edith's bedroom, cursing as his ACL offered another warning throb. "Sorry, babygirl," he said, scooping Edith into his arms. "We're going for a drive." He hobbled downstairs, grabbed his phone and keys on his way out the front door, and reeled across the driveway to his car.

The sirens were a swirling backdrop of sound, impossible to pinpoint where they were heading. He propped Edith on the backseat and buckled her in, then jumped behind the wheel and gunned the ignition. The radio came on loud but didn't envelop the sirens. Martin jabbed the off button, popped the transmission into drive, and roared out of his driveway. He didn't check for oncoming traffic—missed an old Dodge pickup by a matter of inches. The Dodge let rip with the horn and its driver flipped him the bird.

Martin booted the accelerator and screeched down Melon Road, touching sixty by the time he hit the all-way at Juniper Avenue. He slowed down but didn't stop, blew across it aggressively, forcing a Chevy with the right of way to brake hard.

Keep your cool, he thought, but it wasn't easy, and whatever cool he had cracked down the middle when he saw two cop cars bolt west on Main, heading toward Flint Wood

High. He snatched his cell out of the passenger seat and dialed Laura again.

"Come on, baby. Let me hear your voice."

He knew Laura as well as he knew himself. She would've grabbed her phone when she heard the sirens—would've seen the two missed calls. Heck, she was probably texting right now to assure him that she was okay: *Jeez, a lot of noise out there, huh? All fine here. Any idea what's going on?* That imaginary text seemed so real—so *Laura*—that tears spurted from his eyes and he wiped them away as her voicemail message chimed in his ear.

"I'm either busy or frantically trying to find my—"

He thumbed the end call button, then dialed again.

"Please, baby . . . *please.*"

It was a five-minute drive to Flint Wood High. Three if the traffic was good and the lights were kind. Martin got to within three blocks away when he realized that most of the sirens had fallen silent; the town's emergency units had reached their destination.

A chopper—either a news team or police—hovered in the air above the high school.

Martin turned left on New York Avenue, barely able to focus through the tears in his eyes. He might have believed that everything would be fine if not for Edith's premonition—that single love heart almost lost among the lightning jags and 16s. *Mom,* Edith had said when Martin touched it. He thumped the steering wheel with his left hand. His right still clutched the phone.

". . . try me again later, or leave a message and I'll call you . . ."

A hundred yards from the school, he saw the cruisers and ambulances parked haphazardly, lights beating red and blue signals into the air. Crowd control barriers were being set up. A fire truck blocked the road ahead and the traffic had backed up. People flowed along the sidewalk toward the school.

Martin made a right turn and approached from a different direction. The traffic was lighter here. He parked as close as he could. Edith mumbled in the backseat. She said she wanted to go home.

"Soon, baby," Martin said. Sweat glimmered on his face and throat. His shirt was gummed to his back. "I need to . . . go do something. But I'll be right back, okay?"

"Okay, Dad."

Martin got out of the car and lurched toward the school, managing maybe twenty paces before his damaged knee finally popped. He buckled but didn't go down, and flat-out refused to be *slowed* down. Grimacing at the pain, he braced the injury with one hand and limped on. With his other hand, he dialed Laura again.

"Come on, sweetheart. Please, please . . ."

The chopper thundered overhead and sirens whooped intermittently. Martin reached a crowd of onlookers and pushed through. He heard whispers as he made his way to the front: "*. . . don't think it could ever really . . . lone shooter, that's what . . . oh my God, it's just . . .*" Students and teachers, escorted by police, streamed through the main doors and down the front steps. Most of them were crying. Others were too shocked. Martin looked for Laura. Didn't see her. He dialed her number yet again. How many times now? Ten? Fifteen?

"I'm either busy or frantically trying . . ."

He ducked beneath the police tape and took three faltering steps before a cop stood in his path.

"Stay behind the tape, sir. It's there for a reason."

"My wife's a teacher here," Martin said. "Laura Lovegrove. She—"

"I appreciate your concern, but you need to back up. I can take . . ."

She carried on speaking but Martin didn't really hear. He'd spotted Stephen Griffith in the stream of people walking down the front steps. Stephen was a fifty-something geography teacher who'd once drunkenly shared with Martin that he was having an affair with a former student. Now he imparted information of a very different nature. He looked at Martin with pouchy, wet eyes, gave his head a near imperceptible shake, then glanced quickly at his feet and kept walking. And that was when Martin knew. He just knew.

The strength went out of his good leg and he crumpled to the sidewalk. Someone—the cop, perhaps—tried to help him up, but he wasn't ready for that yet. He looked numbly at the cell phone in his hand. At some point, he'd dialed Laura again.

"If this is Martin or the girls . . . dammit, I love you."

11

Sixteen dead—a number that came as no surprise to Martin. Ten students. Four teachers. A school counselor. The sixteenth victim was the shooter, Glenn Burdock. He didn't take his own life and no cop gunned him down. His weak, miserable existence met its conclusion by way of William H. Finch, aka Old Finchy, a sixty-two-year-old science teacher and gun advocate, who also happened to be a former field rep for the New Hampshire Friends of NRA. Old Finchy exercised his constitutional rights by keeping a Beretta 92 in a "secret drawer" in his classroom. Apparently several senior teachers—and the school board, who'd given its written authorization—knew it was there, but ascribed to the belief that a little extra security was no bad thing. Besides, Old Finchy was *responsible*—knew his way around a firearm. And yes, it was possible a student could have found that secret drawer, but unlikely. Principal Moira Keene defended it as a calculated risk.

On this occasion, the risk paid off; Glenn Burdock was closing in on fifteen-year-old Deena Culpovich—who was sprawled across the floor in a state of shock—when Old Finchy crept into the hallway behind him. At a distance of approximately thirty feet, he raised the 92 just like he did at the range, fired once, and blew a hole through the back of the shooter's skull.

For Glenn Burdock, there was no martyrdom, no ride to Glam Moon. He died just like every mass shooter before him: in a frenzy of hate and national disgrace. Old Finchy experienced quite the opposite reaction. He was hailed a hero, a poster boy for the NRA and the "Arm Our Teachers" supporters. He appeared on CNN's *State of the Union* and shook the vice president's hand.

He was at Laura Lovegrove's funeral.

Martin eulogized briefly, brokenly, about love, gentleness, and memory. He touched on—because how could he fully describe?—Laura's eagerness to care, her unwavering inclination to see the good in all people. The funeral home chapel was full, but he spoke primarily to Edith and Shirley, never losing eye contact with them, as if imparting their mother's final and most valuable lessons. A huge photograph of Laura floated on a projection screen to the left of him. Her coffin was improbably close.

He composed himself by taking frequent deep breaths, and whenever he felt like crying he imagined the links in a freighter's anchor chain: solid and strong, able to keep things from drifting away. Finally he reached the last two sentences—"You'll feel her in the wind, see her in the moonlight, hear her in the river. She was everything precious, everything good"—and his voice cracked but he kept it together. He stepped down and walked past Laura's coffin on the way to his seat. He wasn't sure if he was expected to touch it or not, so he didn't.

It was mainly family and close friends in attendance, but there were a few fellow teachers and a couple of Martin's work colleagues, offering their support, which Martin appreciated, even though it felt like a thimbleful of lukewarm water on the hottest day of the year. Hundreds of students had gathered outside. The press, too, with their tongues hanging lower than their camera straps. Flint Wood had provided good material over the past few days. There'd been gun protests and NRA rallies, candlelight vigils and joint funerals. The vice president had visited, solemn-faced, and promised nothing that hadn't been promised by the previous administration, and the administration before that. The high school was still closed. Its front steps were a mountain of flowers, wreaths, and assorted mementos. It had made the front page of every major newspaper in the country.

All this had been white noise to Martin, who'd concerned himself only with his daughters, and with arranging his wife's funeral. And now that it was here, he was determined to get through it—to do so with strength and dignity, to be a role model to Edith and Shirley, the way their mom would have been.

And he almost—so damn *close*—got to the end without crying, but when "If You Leave Me Now" by Chicago piped through the funeral home's speakers, he felt a blurry heat in his head and tears brimmed in his eyes. It was Laura's favorite song, and, of course, the first song they'd danced to as man and wife. Martin recalled the way they'd melted into one another on their wedding night, and how he'd whispered into her ear that if they lasted longer than eleven years and eight months, they'd last forever.

The biggest part of me, he thought, echoing the lyric, and that was it. It didn't help to imagine the links in a freighter's anchor chain; the tears came fast and heavy. They poured down his face. He didn't hide them.

He looked at his wife's coffin and held his girls' hands.

Martin supposed there was always something good to come out of a death, however brutal and unfair that death might be. The silver lining theory rang true most of the time, and for Martin it came in the form of community support. He was genuinely touched by his neighbors' many acts of kindness—small but important things like mowing the lawn, buying groceries, cooking meals. Services were offered at no charge, from haircuts to housecleaning, and "no" was not an acceptable answer. On a larger scale, fundraisers were set up to aid all the victims' families, and the money came not just from the local community, but from all over the world.

His family stepped up, too. Jimmy took the girls when Martin needed some alone-time, and his mom helped him sort through Laura's belongings—her clothes, mainly, deciding what was okay to consign and what should be trashed. She offered a shoulder to cry on, too, and he took it.

"I'm sorting through my dead wife's things," he said to her incredulously, holding up the small purple bottle of

Curate, recalling how Laura would spritz her throat with it every morning before work. "I think every husband imagines doing this at some point, but they don't truly believe they'll ever have to. The guy dies first, right? That's how it works. Because men are selfish bastards. And whenever I *have* imagined doing this, I'm always an old man, mumbling and farting and grateful for the many years I got to spend with my soulmate. Jesus, Mom, I'm young enough to still get carded on occasion."

He sprayed a little Curate into the air and immediately regretted it; the smell was beautiful-painful. Laura could have just breezed through the room. He sat on the edge of the bed and wept.

"Some people never get to know love," his mom said, holding him the way she used to when he'd scraped his knee or broken one of his toys. "Remember how it feels. Hold on to it. That's Laura's gift to you. And those beautiful babies, of course."

The babies, yes, who, at ten and fifteen, were old enough to understand death and heartbreak. The family and community support was a blessing for so many reasons, not least because it gave Martin time with the girls. It was too early for healing, but not for talking . . . for accepting.

Not that they *were* accepting. Shirley often talked about Laura in the present tense, and got pissed at Martin for taking a box of shoes to the thrift store, as if she expected her mom to appear barefoot one day and start looking for them. She amped up her adolescent obnoxiousness (what Laura had called her "teenage quills"), cranking her music to eleven, slamming doors with a little extra vim, smoking marijuana in front of Martin (he didn't respond positively to that particular quill). On one occasion, she disappeared for the day and didn't return home until after dark, challenging Martin with a "what are you going to do about it" expression. He felt powerless. Any reaction would be the wrong one. So he said nothing, just gave her a look of grave disappointment. "Fuck this life," Shirley responded, and went to bed.

Conversely, there were times when only Dad would do, when she held him like she used to when she was two years old. He wiped her tears and stroked her hair and sometimes they cried together. It was something to share, special in its way. Shirley confided a deep guilt to him, that if she'd attended Flint Wood High, instead of the Catholic high school across town, she might have altered the outcome in some way.

"You know, like the butterfly effect," she said. "One small decision changes everything, and maybe—*maybe*—Mom would still be alive, because she would've reacted differently if I was there, too. But I *had* to go to St. Mary's, didn't I, because I thought it was weird to go to a school where your mom was one of the teachers."

"I love you. You're amazing. But you're wrong." Martin held her close as she trembled and cried. Her pain added another layer to his own. "Decisions are made, things happen. Some good, some not so good. You can call it the butterfly effect, or you can call it by its proper name: *life.* Looking for reasons is a dangerous business. The only way to go is forward."

"I miss her, Dad. I could have been a better daughter."

"I miss her, too. And I'll say it again: you're amazing."

Edith didn't often cry, or even talk. She dealt with things

in her own way: by *not* dealing with them. She refused to go into her own room—spent most of her time in the basement, not watching TV or playing videogames, just huddled in blankets, staring into the gloom. Martin brought her food and drink, which she occasionally accepted. He tried engaging with her, but she was lost in her own world.

"Tell me about your garden," he said on one of the rare occasions she emerged. She was playing her guitar on the back stoop—a note-perfect rendition of The Beatles' "Blackbird." Not bad for ten years old.

"It's beautiful," Edith replied.

"How so?"

"Nobody gets killed there. The trees are tall and you can climb them all the way to the top. The flowers never die. The leaves are always green." She played as she spoke, her gaze flicking between Martin and the fretboard. "Mom's there, too. Not *really* there, but I've noticed the river is brighter and warmer. The clouds smell like her."

"That *does* sound beautiful," Martin said. "I wouldn't mind having my own garden to visit."

"You can make one." Edith let a note carry while she tapped her forehead. "You start with one leaf. The only leaf in the world."

"Maybe I'll do that. But hey, listen, this is important." He dropped an arm around her and leaned close. "It's great that you have somewhere to go, and I know it helps with the bad things, but don't lose yourself in there, babygirl. We're out here. We love you, and we need you."

Edith didn't respond for a long time. She just played and

Martin listened, half-remembering the lyrics. Something about broken wings and learning to fly. He played with her hair, the same color as Laura's, watching the way it fell between her narrow shoulder blades.

"It's scary out here," she said.

Martin had talked to Shirley about moving forward, painfully aware of the hypocrisy. His default condition was static, brooding in silent anger and misery, although he was prone to backward steps: he smashed shit up, chopped down a perfectly healthy tree, drove into the country and screamed at the sky. In front of the girls, he endeavored to show progress, to lead by example. It was all rather sad and desperate. He bought new bedding for himself, something modern and horrible and befitting a middle-aged widower. He replaced the Kandinsky print in the living room with a picture of a tiger running through water, the word ATTITUDE emblazoned across the bottom in motivational uppercase. Shirley took one look at it and suggested he find a new therapist.

He painted Edith's room. A month had passed since Laura's death and he finally faced all those red 16s and jagged lines. He tried scrubbing them first with bleach and hot water—he wanted them *off* the walls, not just painted over—but they wouldn't budge, so he used an electric sander and *that* did the trick. It left a lot of ugly bare spots and he rolled over them with a primer, then a shade of blue he thought Edith would like. The only symbol he didn't paint over was that single red love heart. He emphasized it, in fact—painted a cloud around it.

Edith watched him do this from the doorway. He didn't

notice she was there until she sighed and said, "It's a good color, Dad."

He turned with a start. "Oh . . . hey."

"Hey." She smiled, then looked at the heart on the wall. The heart in the cloud.

"How much do you remember?" Martin asked.

"None of it."

"Good."

Her eyes flicked to him and filled with tears, then she ran across the room and threw herself into his arms. "I love you, Dad. I love you so much." And he said that he loved her, too, that she and Shirley were more than the world to him, and they cried together until their chests hurt.

"What do you want, baby?" he asked later, when their tears had dried but their eyes were still puffy. "You want to get out of here? Move somewhere cool and beautiful? Or maybe we can buy a camper van and drive cross-country. No work or school. No rules."

She blinked brightly and smiled.

"Whatever you want. You tell me and I'll make it happen."

"Promise?"

"Promise."

She lay her head against his chest. "I just want to be safe."

The summer evening dimmed. The heart in the cloud was the last thing to fade.

And throughout all of this—the funeral, the community support, the screaming at the sky—Martin was never once aware that he was being watched.

12

Alcohol was a bad idea. Its (temporary) healing properties made it extremely dangerous—an ill-advised remedy that could devolve into habit. For this reason, Martin rarely imbibed, and never in front of the girls. But when he did, he went all out.

Usually, with the girls at Jimmy's, a bottle of bourbon and something loud on the stereo sufficed. Tonight, though, Shirley's friend Claudette Palazzo was sleeping over, which Martin saw as an encouraging sign, and Jimmy's wife, Felicity, was holding the fort.

"I'll be home at a horrible hour," Martin said to her. "And by way of taxicab. That's a promise. Keep an eye on Ede. She might want a hug before bedtime."

"I can do hugs," Felicity said, flapping a hand at him. "Go. Have fun. Be careful."

There were a couple of bars within walking distance, but even now, seven weeks after the shooting, he couldn't get through a single drink without someone offering condolence or advice. They were always well-meaning, and Martin was grateful, but he wasn't in the mood. He wanted a place where nobody knew him, and where he could drink himself senseless.

He wanted to be like everyone else.

No hope of that in Flint Wood, so Martin drove to Clear River, thirteen miles east. The setting sun colored everything behind him, so he didn't see the white pickup truck in the rearview. He focused on the road ahead, mumbled along to the radio, and finally pulled into the parking lot of a bar called Banjo McCoy's.

Moments later, the white pickup followed.

Friday night but it wasn't busy. A few folks were posted around the bar and several tables were occupied. The clientele was predominately male, an even mix of white and blue collars. The banjo theme was realized through the dozens of banjos affixed to the walls. A plaque declared one of them to have been used in the movie *Deliverance*—not one of the main banjos but a stand-in, which Martin decided wasn't as interesting as having Sally Fields's stunt double for a therapist.

He sat at the bar and handed his keys to the bartender. "Don't give them back to me. No matter what I say."

The bartender was thirty-something and pretty, with penciled eyebrows and a tongue piercing that she tapped against her teeth out of habit.

She said, "You sound like a man who needs a drink."

He said, "Like you wouldn't believe."

He ordered a double shot of Jack with a Sam Adams chaser—downed the Jack in one, then drained half the beer. The door behind him opened. Three people walked in: two women, dressed in blue jeans and cowboy boots, who took a booth by the window, and a middle-aged man in slacks and a peach golf shirt. Martin assumed he was with the women, but he walked past their booth and joined Martin at the bar, taking the next stool but one. He ordered a sparkling water with a slice of lime and asked to look at a menu.

Martin went back to his beer, his eyes flicking between the banjos and the clientele. The man in the peach shirt perused the menu and ordered a chicken wrap with the salad. Martin emptied his glass and nodded at the bartender. She brought him another shot, another beer. He emptied these quickly, too.

"You weren't lying," the bartender said.

"Keep 'em coming."

The bar had started to fill. Most of the tables and booths were occupied. Several long-haired dudes carted instruments and speakers to a small stage in back. A young couple looked for seats at the bar and the man in the peach shirt made room by scooching onto the empty stool beside Martin. They nodded at one another. Martin downed his shot and his vision blurred momentarily. Good.

"Those guys look loud," the man said, gesturing at the long-haired dudes and their instruments. "I was hoping for a quiet bite to eat."

"You came to the wrong place," Martin said. "It's Friday night. I think everybody here wants to let off some steam."

"Right." The man nodded. "Take a breath after a week at the grindstone. Chill the hell out."

"Something like that."

"Jesus, everybody's wound so tight these days." He shrugged and sipped his water. "It's funny how all these hi-tech devices—smartphones, tablets, and such—are designed to make life easier, but nobody has a lick of time to spare."

"Welcome to the digital age," Martin said.

"Yeah, well, the digital age can kiss my ass." He chuckled at that and his eyes shone. He had a wide face chiseled with lines, a graying brush cut, and sloping, muscular shoulders. The peach shirt wasn't exactly in keeping. Martin thought he'd look more at home in military fatigues. Maybe a prison warden's uniform.

"Nolan," he said, extending his hand.

"Martin."

They shook. Nolan's hand was dry and characterless. Like the shirt, it didn't match the rest of him. Martin got the impression he was cobbled together—had rebuilt his life but wasn't sure which pieces to use. *Maybe he's a widower, too,* Martin thought, and had to wonder if, in a couple of years, he'd be the same: thrown together with mismatched pieces.

"It's like this," Nolan continued. "The moment you swipe your cell phone's screen, you remove yourself from your environment. You're no longer looking at the scenery or interacting with the people around you. The time you spend in your phone, whether it's ten seconds or ten hours . . . that's dead time, you don't get it back."

"I guess," Martin said. "But they're useful, so . . ."

"Agreed. For important calls and emergencies." Nolan took a glug of water. "But people are *buried* in their phones. Look around—jeez, those two ladies who walked in ahead of me have barely exchanged a word all night."

Martin glanced at the booth by the window, where the two women sat opposite each other, faces bathed in the glow of their cell phones.

"Maybe they're having a good time. Who are we to judge?"

"That's not quality of life, Martin. I read a report in the *Washington Times* that the average American spends a third of their waking day on their smartphone. You and I both know that most of it is nonessential bullcrap. It's social media and pointless texts."

"Again, welcome to the digital age."

"Again, it can kiss my ass." Nolan didn't chuckle this time. His gray eyes were narrow and serious. "I mean, Jesus, go for a walk, breathe the air. This country wouldn't have so many problems if people had a greater appreciation of how beautiful it is."

"Maybe," Martin said. "But you can lose yourself in a good novel—remove yourself from your environment—and it's generally regarded as a good thing. What's the difference?"

"The difference is that books inspire, challenge, and enrich you in a way that social media or videogames never will." Nolan jabbed the bar with one finger, as if adding an exclamation point. "And hey, it's not that I actively dislike devices. It's more that I *love* life. After what I've been through, I want to make the most out of every day."

"Shit, I'll drink to that."

They touched glasses. Martin finished his drink and ordered another. Just a beer this time. Nolan's food arrived. He ate it slowly, savoring every bite, then pushed his empty plate aside and asked, "What do you do for work?"

"Architect," Martin replied. "Mainly residential, although I've been working on the new Onondaga Mall for the past four years."

"Lot of pressure, I bet."

"Too much, sometimes."

"Are you happy?"

"I guess." Martin shrugged. "I don't do as much design as I'd like. Architect is my job title, but my job *description* is trying to get angry people to stop yelling at me."

"Sounds like corporate America," Nolan said. "Everything's peachy until there's a buck on the line."

"Or eight million bucks that you didn't budget for." Martin sipped his beer, then asked, "How about you? What's your line of work?"

"I, uh . . ." The hesitation was brief but Martin caught it. "I'm a recruiter."

"Right on. You recruit for businesses? Like a headhunter?"

"Not exactly," Nolan replied. Another hesitation. His eyes flickered. "I recruit people who are looking for a better life. A *safer* life."

Martin frowned. "What do you mean?"

Nolan appeared to consider the question, then pulled his wallet from the back pocket of his slacks. From it he took a business card, handed it to Martin. The quality was good but the information sparse: four words and a phone number.

HALCYON

A BETTER AMERICA

680-555-4719

"Halcyon," Martin read. He flipped the card over—nothing on the back—then looked at Nolan with a questioning expression.

"A recent poll," Nolan said, "placed 'halcyon' in the top ten most beautiful words in the English language. Number four, I think. You know what it means?"

"It's a bird," Martin said, digging this information from some dusty alcove in his brain. "A kingfisher, right?"

"I knew you were smart." Nolan's eyes brightened. He tucked his wallet away, didn't ask for the card back. "It also means a period of joy and tranquility."

"But what is this?" Martin tapped the card. "A better America. What does that mean?"

"Exactly what you *think* it means."

Martin studied Nolan's chiseled face.

"Halcyon has been my home for eighteen years," Nolan said, meeting Martin's gaze. "It's a self-sustaining community made up of people who are disillusioned by what America has become. They're tired of all the self-interest and corporate greed. They're tired of living in fear. Simply put, Halcyon is a small solution to a big problem. And it works. There's no crime, no poverty, no discrimination. It's a happy place."

Martin imagined a group of hippies dancing in the moonlight and singing "All You Need is Love." It didn't gel, though, not least because mismatched Nolan didn't fit the image.

"How does it work?" he asked.

"With good people," Nolan responded firmly. "We work together for a common goal: to build the America we *want*. And we're extremely particular about who we accept. It's all about protecting what has taken years to establish."

"Makes sense," Martin said.

"We have twenty-three people right now. That's on the light side. There's usually thirty-plus. But some of our friends have returned to their old lives, and that's fine. We'd never dream of stopping them. Once you leave, though . . . there's no coming back."

"It's a onetime deal?"

"Exactly. We can't have people coming and going. Things would get out of hand in a hurry." Nolan made an exploding gesture with his hands. "Careful management is the key to Halcyon's success."

"Right."

"We also ask that, should you leave, you don't tell anybody about us. That's happened in the past and we've had random people knocking at the door. It upsets the balance of things. Most former residents are good at keeping silent."

"So it's a secret thing?"

"No. If it was a secret, I wouldn't have told you about it, and I certainly wouldn't have had business cards printed." Nolan displayed an uneven grin. "It's a *selective* thing, Martin. There's a difference."

The band finished setting up. They played a few bars of something punky to test their levels. The vocalist announced they were going to start in about twenty, and that shit was going to get loud. Martin wrinkled his brow. He'd been in the mood for something loud at the beginning of the evening, but now he wasn't so sure.

"So you all live and work together," he said. "Farming the land, milking cows, like the Amish?"

"We work hard, but everything is relaxed. And there's no religion, as such." Nolan paused, his eyes momentarily glazed and distant, then he snapped back to the present. "You know, I talk about Halcyon and people always assume one of two things: hippies or Jesus freaks."

"I assumed *both* of those things."

"We're neither." Nolan said, and shook his head firmly. "We're a community of goodhearted Americans who have found strength and healing through a new—but in many ways *old*—way of life. And yes, we're off the grid, but it's not like we live in caves and wear bearskins. We have homes with running water, heating, electricity—"

"Solar power?"

"Right, with gennies for backup. Our infrastructure is set up so that nobody goes without, although everybody is resourceful *and* respectful. We shut off lights, we don't waste food or water. We share and care."

Martin drained his beer and winced—he'd gone off the taste. *All beered out,* Jimmy would say. He considered another shot of Jack, but ordered a water instead.

"You're not getting your keys back," the bartender said.

"It's all good," Martin said.

"We have builders and electricians," Nolan continued a moment later, counting off on his fingers. "We have three tutors, one of whom follows national curriculum standards. We have a chef, a landscaper, a dental nurse, and a board-certified physician. He can handle most of our medical concerns, although anything serious has to be dealt with off-community."

"Medicine?"

"Got it covered," Nolan said. "I said we're self-sustaining, but there are obviously some things we can't make ourselves. Medicine is one of those things. Diesel for the gennies is another. Then you've got batteries, light bulbs, feminine hygiene products, contraceptives. We used to have this guy who made toothpaste out of bentonite clay and baking soda—worked okay but it tasted like shit. Better for everyone if I bulk-buy Aquafresh at Costco."

"Where do you get the money?"

"We sell what we make," Nolan replied, then pointed at himself. "More specifically, *I* sell it. I take care of everything off-community. And believe me, selling quality, organic produce is a piece of cake. Of course, we also accept donations, but they're in no way obligatory."

"It's quite the setup," Martin said.

"It's idyllic," Nolan said, leaning closer. "But it's not for everybody. Halcyon is in many ways a regressed community. There are no tablets or phones, no internet, no TVs. You can't binge-watch your favorite Netflix shows or email your Aunt Fanny on Christmas morning. It's back to basics: clean, simple, and human. And that's exactly what we love about it."

"No beer?" Martin asked, smiling.

"No beer," Nolan said. He gestured at the bottles glistening behind the bar. "No alcohol at all. It has a tendency to make people either maudlin or violent. We don't want either. Likewise, there are no drugs. *Certainly* no guns. And get this . . . there are no clocks or watches on Halcyon."

"What? Really?"

Nolan's eyes gleamed. This was obviously a point of pride. "Time of day is not important. We all have jobs to do, but providing they get done, it doesn't matter when we do them or how long it takes. It's all part of the liberating lifestyle."

Martin sipped his water. It was cold and refreshing. *I could've done without the booze,* he thought. *Hell, I could probably do without lots of things.* He wondered what even a week in Nolan's community could do for him. Detox for the soul.

"Actually," Nolan continued, holding up one finger. "There *is* one clock on Halcyon—a wristwatch, in fact. Mother Moon keeps it locked in a box. It's a reminder, if needed, of the way things operate out here. She says the only people who mark off time are prisoners."

"Mother Moon?" Martin narrowed his eyes. "Okay, now you've got me thinking cult, and when I think cult, I think Jonestown."

"Oh, Jesus Christ, no." Nolan belly-laughed, rolling back on his stool. "Mother Moon is a sweet, *sweet* lady. She has her beliefs, but they're more . . . spiritual in nature." His eyes took on that distant, glazed quality again, if only for a second. "They're beautiful, too."

"Is she the leader?"

"I guess, in as much as we have a leader, but that's not a word Mother Moon uses." Nolan finished his water, wiped his mouth with the back of his hand. "She founded Halcyon back in 2000. It started as an experiment but has become a way of life. We jumped from four people to thirty in the two months after 9/11."

"Jesus."

"Most people stay for a couple of years, then return to their old lives. They use Halcyon as a kind of reset, and that's fine. There are others who've been with us for fifteen years. It's home for them and always will be. And why? Because they feel safe. And valued. America can't offer those things, Martin. We *think* we're valued, but it's like I said earlier . . . everything's peachy until there's a buck on the line."

The bartender asked Nolan if he wanted another water. He shook his head, requested the check. She rang it up and handed it to him.

"You want to talk about value," he continued, flaring his upper lip. "I'm a former Marine, a Gulf War veteran. I saw and did things—was *made* to do things—you wouldn't believe. All for the flag. I returned stateside hollowed out and suicidal, but when I applied for disability, which would entitle me to healthcare benefits, the VA turned me down. That's as big a fuck-you as any person will ever get."

Martin shook his head, whistled through his teeth.

"Things got worse. I lost my job, my family. I was homeless for six years, and then Mother Moon found me. She took me to Halcyon, gave me a purpose—gave me *value*. And here I am today, happy and healthy, with none of those old, ugly symptoms." He took his wallet from his back pocket again, slapped a twenty on the bar. "Halcyon can do that to you, Martin. It's a healing place."

"That's one hell of a story," Martin said. "I'm glad you found your way."

"It's that quality of life I was talking about," Nolan said. "It's a beauty you can't find in your cell phone, your TV, or any material possession. Most Americans think what they *want* is more important than what they've *got*, and as long as that's the case, there'll be problems."

"My wife was killed," Martin said suddenly. It jumped out of his mouth before he could stop it. "She was a teacher at Flint Wood High. One of the victims."

"Jesus Christ," Nolan said. He exhaled heavily, one hand on his chest. "That's just terrible. I'm sorry as hell to hear that."

"I miss her so much, but the grief is just a part of it. I'm lost . . . broken. My daughters look to me for answers I don't have. I feel like a failure." He closed his eyes. Took a second. The tears threatened. "I keep thinking that, if my kids were going to be left with one parent, it shouldn't have been me."

Nolan squeezed his arm affectionately, then handed him one of the napkins that came with his food. Martin smeared it across his eyes and sighed.

"Shit, I came here tonight to forget about it for a while. Drink it away."

"I see this kind of brokenness all the time," Nolan said. "We have victims of hate on Halcyon. Victims of terrorism, betrayal, the state, the system. You're not alone. There are a lot of disillusioned Americans out there."

"What the hell happened to this country?"

"The people pulling the strings aren't good people, and we've been brainwashed into their way of thinking. We need to cut the strings. All of us—three hundred and twenty-five million of us. Then we all fall down. Then we pick ourselves up."

"That's never going to happen."

"Never," Nolan agreed. "Not on a national scale, at least."

"But maybe on a Halcyon-sized scale."

Nolan winked. "It's still a beautiful country, Martin. You've just got to know where to look."

The band started with an electric crunch. Nolan jumped, pressed his fingers to his ears, shouted over the music:

"And that's my cue to exit."

"I'll walk out with you," Martin yelled back. *"I could use some fresh air."*

He signaled to the bartender that he'd be back and followed Nolan out of the bar, into a warm night with mosquitoes buzzing around the lights and the ground wet with a brief, recent rain. Nolan strode across the parking lot to a white Silverado with a bluish neon banjo reflected off the hood.

"Is it on an island?" Martin asked.

"What makes you say that?"

"You use the word 'on' . . . *on* Halcyon." Martin shrugged. "Makes me thinks it's an island."

"I can tell you this much: it's not far from here, it's full of natural beauty—towering trees, wild flowers, granite cliffs—and yes, it has views of the water." Nolan opened the door to his pickup and climbed behind the wheel. "Are you interested, Martin?"

"Intrigued," Martin replied, and then thought of Shirley snarling *Fuck this life,* and Edith with her head resting against his chest, telling him that she just wanted to be safe. He looked at Nolan through the open door and sighed. "Okay. Maybe I'm interested."

"Keep hold of my card. Think it over. Talk to your daughters."

"And if we want to pursue it—"

"Call me. There are no phones on Halcyon, but I keep a burner in my truck and check my messages when I'm off-community, usually every couple of weeks."

"Could we take a look around? Is that how it's normally done?"

"Not anymore," Nolan said. "It used to be that way, but people coming and going . . . it was too unsettling. Some of our residents said they felt like zoo animals. It didn't exactly fulfill our promise of a comfortable environment. I can snail-mail you photographs, though—the cabins, the scenery, the farms."

"That's not the same," Martin said. "And it's a big decision to just take the plunge."

"You have to think of it like starting a new job," Nolan said. "You don't get to try it out while you keep your old job. It's a leap of faith, and if you don't like it, you quit. And like a new job, there's a probationary period. Six weeks. That's for us as well as you."

"I get it," Martin said, rubbing his chin. "But it's not just me. I have to consider my daughters, and I'm not sure how they'll feel about being without their phones or social media—being away from their friends. It's a huge ask. But maybe we need to step away from everything for a little while. And then there's the house. Jesus, do you sell, rent—"

"It's a lifestyle change, Martin, not a new pair of shoes. If you said you wanted to come now I'd refuse you on the spot. We don't accept people who make rash decisions." He started the truck, raising his voice to be heard over the rumbling engine. "You've got my card. Let me know."

They shook hands, then Nolan closed the door and peeled out of the parking lot. Martin watched his taillights until they floated from view, then went back inside Banjo McCoy's. He pushed his way to the bar, grabbed the same seat. The bartender brought him another water. He drank it and thought about Halcyon—imagined splitting firewood with a hefty axe, reading Hemingway by candlelight, watching his daughters collect eggs and pick strawberries and learn the names of plants.

It's a healing place, Nolan had said.

He'd slipped the business card into his back pocket, but took it out and looked at it in the glow of the bar lights.

"A better America," he said.

The band sang their sympathies for the devil.

In the cold light of morning, the idea of relocating to a peace-loving community off the grid—based on one conversation with a stranger—had less appeal. The business card was still in the back pocket of his jeans, slung over the arm of a chair in his bedroom. Martin took it out, considered it for a moment, then tossed it into the blue recycling bin in his office.

By noon—with the customary soul-ache firmly in place, and with the news of a young mother killed in a home invasion in nearby Jamesville—Martin dug through the recycling bin, found Nolan's business card, and placed it in the top drawer of his desk. He looked at it twice more that day.

On Sunday he googled *HALCYON COMMUNITY* and found several elderly care homes and a tree sanctuary. He tried *HALCYON A BETTER AMERICA* and *HALCYON NOLAN THORNE* and *HALCYON MOTHER MOON* but discovered nothing of relevance.

Nolan had said it wasn't a secret, but Martin wasn't so sure.

On Wednesday he broke down in Steadman's, aisle three, holding a can of Wolfgang Puck vegetable soup.

A stranger hugged him. It was nice.

Martin returned home from work the following day to find that Shirley had cut her hair spiky-short and dyed it black.

"You think we could have talked about this?" he snapped at her.

"Not really," she snapped back. "I'm nearly sixteen years old. I can do what I want."

"You're fifteen, and you can't."

She rolled her eyes and swept from the room, making sure she slammed the door extra hard.

Martin couldn't remember the last time he'd seen her smile.

13

Things got easier with Edith. They were still a long way from good, but she started to interact more often with the real world. By the tail end of the summer, she was down to fewer than two hours a day in her garden. Martin was hopeful she'd be ready for school when it started again in September.

Given Edith's history, the only people Martin could talk to about her were Shirley and Calm Dumas. Calm had given the Lovegroves her telephone number after her visit in May (a decidedly simpler method of contact than candlelight and telepathy). Martin had called several times since Laura's death.

"Edith says she can't remember the shooting," he said the last time they spoke. "But she streamed it—saw it happen. It's in her mind somewhere. I think that's why she's so withdrawn."

"Sheltering herself from wicked streams is one thing," Calm said. "She can't run away from reality, though. She has to confront her fears and deal with them. That's how we grow."

"How can I help her?"

"You make her feel as safe as possible. You show her love and happiness."

"I'm struggling with my own emotions," Martin said. "It's not easy showing happiness when I don't feel it myself."

"Love will lead you, Martin. And take comfort in knowing that Edith is spending less time in her garden. If she were going deeper, I'd be very concerned."

Flint Wood High reopened its doors on Tuesday, September 4. The press was there to mark the occasion, filming students as they ascended the front steps. The mother of one of the victims shouted, "*Leave us alone!*" into one of the cameras, and hit Autumn McKenzie from Fox 29 News with a bottle of water. A fracas broke out.

There were no news cameras at Frederick J. Sayles Elementary across town. The students arrived and went to their classes without incident. Edith Lovegrove was not one of them. She got out of bed on time, got washed and dressed, ate breakfast, but then froze at the kitchen table. Her eyes were glazed and unresponsive. "Hey, baby," Martin said, gently shaking her shoulder. "Come on out. It's time for school." When he spoke to Edith's principal an hour later, he explained that Edith needed more time. "She's incredibly fragile. Seeing her like that might upset the other students." Edith's principal said he understood completely, and gave Martin the name of two excellent counselors.

Shirley had gone willingly—if gloomily—to St. Mary's. By 11 a.m. she'd been sent home for telling one of the teachers to go fuck herself. She was sent home again at the end of the week, this time with a two-day suspension, for fighting. "I can't make any exceptions for Shirley because of what she's been through," her principal said when he met with Martin. "That would set a damaging precedent." Martin agreed that the correct course of action had been taken, and promised to have a serious talk with Shirley.

He did. It was a conversation that started out with raised voices and devolved into tears. They hugged desperately, with Martin, lost in darkness, trying to find some light to share with his daughter.

"It'll get easier," he said over and over. Such a bullshit, clichéd thing to say, and spoken with maybe 10 percent conviction. He hoped the strength in his arms compensated for the platitudes spewing helplessly from his mouth.

He woke early Saturday morning to find that Shirley wasn't home. He wondered if she'd snuck out late and hadn't come back. Fighting to maintain his composure, he called her cell phone. No answer. There was a list of names and numbers pinned to the refrigerator: Edith and Shirley's closest friends—the people they'd most likely be with when not at home or school. He started at the top and worked his way down. Nobody had seen Shirley, or knew where she was. Getting desperate, he broke into Shirley's email and searched for clues.

Nothing.

Edith was in the basement. The TV was on but she wasn't watching it. She sat on a beanbag eating a cold Pop-Tart, staring into space. Her skin was pale and her eyes lined with sleeplessness.

"I need you to call Shirley," Martin said to her.

"Call?"

"Whatever it is you do—when you contact her telepathically." Martin inhaled sharply. "Do it. Tell her to come home."

"Oh." Edith took a bite out of her Pop-Tart. "I haven't done that for a long time. I don't even know how anymore."

"What do you mean?"

"It's like a muscle." Her eyes rolled slowly toward him. "It gets weak if you don't use it."

Martin curled his hands into fists, counted to three, then relaxed them. "*Try*, Ede. Please . . . just try."

She placed her half-eaten Pop-Tart on the puffed-up side of the beanbag, closed her eyes, lowered her head. Martin shuffled his feet and waited. After a minute or so, she picked up her breakfast and continued eating.

"Well?" Martin asked.

"I can't do it," she said. "But it doesn't matter anyway."

"Why not?"

She looked at him blankly. "Because I know where she is."

Martin was familiar with Barrow Farm—the eyesore on the western edge of town that multiple land developers had unsuccessfully attempted to buy and turn into tract housing. It was owned by a retired Kentucky businessman who intended to sit on the property until he died, then bequeath it to his seven children and let them fight over the scraps. At ninety-four years of age, this was likely to happen sooner rather than later, and with the new Onondaga Mall offering retail and employment opportunities in the area, those scraps might be notably larger.

"Stay in the car," Martin said. "I mean it, Ede."

He'd parked deep in the yard, not far from the barn. Edith slunk all the way down in the backseat and assured him she wasn't going anywhere. Martin got out of the car and walked in the direction Edith had indicated, stepping around a rusted, overgrown trough, then over the desiccated corpse of some long-dead creature. High grass swayed in the field beyond. Martin pushed through it. A red-tailed hawk circled directly above, its wingspan dark and wide.

He had no trouble finding the well. It drew Martin forward, its darkness—and it *was* a dark place—like a center of gravity. It had obviously drawn Shirley, too; she sat to one side of the clearing, knees pulled to her chest, arms looped around her shins. Her new black hair shimmered in the clear morning light.

"Edith has her special place," she said by way of explanation, looking at the well's crumbling brickwork. "This is mine."

The cover—several weather-beaten boards—had been removed. Martin peered into the well. He didn't want to get too close; like any precipice, it had an inexplicable attraction.

"I miss you," he said, sitting close to Shirley, but not too close. It was important to give her space. "Both you and Edith. Even when you're home, you're not *really* home. It sometimes feels like I've lost all three of my girls."

She glanced at him. He saw the emotion in her eyes.

"Things will never go back the way they were." He shook his head. "But we have to believe they can be good again. Not just better than they are now, but *good*."

"Do you believe that?"

"I try to," he said honestly. "Some days it's not so easy. But I do believe this: that it's *not* the end of everything, and it *is* the beginning of something. Whatever that something is . . . that's up to us."

Shirley shrugged.

"And it *can* be good."

"But you can't stop your heart from aching," Shirley said. "I know that now. You can distract it for a while. Maybe even a *long* while. But twenty years from now—fifty years—the pain will still be there."

"And other pains," Martin added, scooching a touch closer. "Other pleasures, too. That's how we live, Shirl. The alternative is to give up. And that's really no alternative at all."

A warm breeze pushed through the clearing, making the tall grass dance and the blackberry bush rattle. Several small birds were stirred into flight. The elms marking the border of Barrow Farm showed yellow in their leaves. Fall was coming, and that was good, Martin thought. Summer had been hell.

"My therapist wants me to explore my darkness," Shirley said, wiping moisture from her cheeks. "You know—find the root of it. This place wants me to give it up." She leaned over her knees, her eyes locked on the well. "I think it's feeding on me. Like a vampire. It won't be happy until I throw myself in."

She reached out. Martin took her hand and held it like he'd never let go.

She said, "I have so much darkness to give."

Something Nolan had said at Banjo McCoy's stuck with Martin. It floated into his mind in his bleakest hours, and shimmered when he lay awake at three in the morning and everything else was dark: *Most people stay for a couple of years, then return to their old lives. They use Halcyon as a kind of reset, and that's fine.*

Martin picked up the phone several times over the next few days and twice dialed Nolan's number, but hung up before the connection was made. He kept waiting for the promise of Halcyon to fade, for it to appear more like a fantasy than a solution. This never happened, though. If anything, it intensified—became this glorious, healing utopia in his mind. And then one night, his heart aching and his eyes burning with tiredness, he crept into Shirley's room to find both girls sleeping together, Shirley with one hand placed on the small of Edith's back. And that was all it took—the sight of them together, his girls, his *life*, finding comfort in the most primal way.

I can do that, he thought. *I* need *to do that.*

If there'd been space in the bed, he would have crawled in beside them, folded his arms around them both, but there was not, so he huddled on the floor and slept awkwardly but somewhat peacefully, and woke close to dawn with a clear head and a knowing heart. He went downstairs, grabbed his cell phone from where it was charging on the kitchen counter. He dialed Nolan's number. It rang three times and went to voicemail.

"Hi, Nolan, it's Martin Lovegrove. We met a couple of months ago at Banjo McCoy's . . ."

He paused, but it wasn't hesitation. Quite the opposite. His mouth quivered, almost a smile.

Let's reset, he thought.

He took a deep breath and said very clearly, "Do you have room for three more?"

14

Valerie considered herself a people person. The islanders called her Mother Moon in part because she edified them with stories about the Glam, but mostly because she made them feel safe and special. Like any good mother, she offered comfort when they most needed it, and hope when it all seemed lost. "You truly live up to your name," Garrett Riley had once said to her, not long before he'd killed more than two hundred young Americans in the second-deadliest terrorist attack on US soil. She recalled how he'd sometimes frolic, like a lamb, in her company, and how he made mewling sounds, again, like a lamb, when he suckled on her breast.

The secret was to begin with their hearts—to offer compliments and kindnesses, make them feel exactly how they wanted to feel. The heart was a durable muscle, but gullible. Best of all, it provided a shortcut to the mind, which was where Valerie did her most notable work.

And of course, desperate people were the easiest to control. This was Halcyon's artifice: a community of broken, shapeable individuals, looking to tether themselves to something they could believe in. And for as long as she had these damaged souls at her disposal, she could scratch the Society's itch.

They could scratch hers.

She was not, however, superhuman; for every Garrett Riley or Glenn Burdock she was able to influence, there were three or four others she could not. It didn't matter how disillusioned they were, or how desperately in need of harbor, she just couldn't find a way in.

Case in point: Angela Byrne.

"We're returning to the mainland. To our Lord and Savior Jesus Christ."

Angela had come to Halcyon four years ago, a thirty-something church pianist, chubby as a piglet, broken down the middle. Nolan had found her praying in the True Light House of God after her husband had been killed in a Manhattan subway shooting. "She's lost faith in her country but not in her god?" Valerie had asked when Nolan gave her the rundown. "She's too religious. Potentially damaging. I'll never reshape her." And Nolan had admitted that yes, she was religious, but she was also wealthy. "You may not get her mind," he'd said. "But you might get her money."

Nolan, to his credit, had been absolutely right.

Angela stood in front of Valerie now, forty pounds lighter (that's what a daily dose of fresh air and not breakfasting at Applebee's five mornings a week did for you), hands knitted demurely beneath her bosom. Doris Travers stood just behind and to her left. Paula Wetlow was on the other side.

"He's calling us home." Angela unlinked and spread her hands, indicating herself and the other two women.

"I see," Valerie said. "That is unfortunate."

There had been a wall around Angela from the outset, with God perched atop it embodying salvation. Neither Valerie—at her most motherly—nor Glam Moon could compete. This was a problem, not because Valerie wanted Angela all to herself, but because religion wasn't welcome on Halcyon. "It engenders a passionate difference of opinion," Valerie offered by way of explanation. "Conflict, in other words, which is exactly what we've come here to escape." The main reason—although she couldn't tell Angela this, or anybody—was that she needed the islanders to share her belief in the Glam. A select few would be called on to do dark and terrible things, and they had to know there was something at the end of it for them. It was challenging enough to instill this level of faith, without God sticking His holy oar in.

Angela didn't outwardly defy her. She simply couldn't leave God behind. He was a part of her soul, just like the Glam was a part of Valerie's. She would've been gone long ago if not for her regular donations to the community. Halcyon was largely self-sustaining, but it had certain dark interests. There wasn't a black market in the world that would trade a crate of C-4 for a sack of turnips.

Valerie needed Angela's money.

"I know you're disappointed," Angela said. "But our minds are made up."

Valerie smiled even though all of her facial tissue was primed to rage. She put her hands behind her back so the women couldn't see how they trembled and flexed.

"Doris," she said. "Are you sure about this?"

Angela was a lost cause, but Doris Travers might not be. Valerie remembered how she'd arrived on Halcyon, empty of hope and soul. She'd found purpose, though, and strength. Halcyon had been good for her—a ladder when even the most meager of things seemed out of reach.

"Jesus came to me in a dream," Doris said. "He didn't say anything, but pointed south across the water, and a heavenly light shone from the tip of his finger."

"Amen," Angela said.

"Paula?" Valerie turned to the woman on Angela's right. "Are you ready to say goodbye to Halcyon? I believe you once called it your true Eden."

"I did," Paula agreed. "But as much as I love it here, I never believed in Glam Moon. I *do* believe in God, though—"

"Amen." Angela again.

"—and I'm ready to be His servant. Also, I miss my kids."

Valerie turned away from the women before the smile crashed from her face. She walked to the front window of her cabin and looked out. A beautiful view, with flickering trees to the east, their leaves beginning to turn, and the meadow directly ahead. She saw Jordan Little, the only child on the island, playing Frisbee. Ainsley Moore and Alyssa Prince carted produce to the storage barn north of the orchard. Alyssa was laughing about something, the sound carrying on the wind.

"It could be argued," Valerie said, "that you're doing God's work here. You live humbly, without sin or excess. You share your food and your warmth. If you believe in God, you have to believe He's here, not on the mainland, which still burns." She turned around, smiling again. "Seems to me that's where the other guy hangs out."

"All the more reason for us to spread God's love," Angela said.

Oh, Angela. An answer for everything.

"And where was God when your husband was shot on the train to City Hall?" Valerie couldn't resist this bitter retort. Not that it mattered; these dumb bitches had made up their minds. "Remember how close to suicide you were afterward? Did God put that bottle of sleeping pills in your hand? And Paula, this God you believe in . . . where was He when your daughter was raped and murdered? Absent, I suppose. Just like He was absent at the trial, when one of the perpetrators walked free."

Paula burst into tears.

"And Doris. Sweet Doris." Valerie's smile broadened—a grin now, teeth showing. "Jesus came to you in a dream. But did he come when you needed him most? Did a heavenly light shine from the tip of his finger when that thug put a bullet in your son's skull?"

"Stop it," Angela said.

"Did God take you in? Did He give you harbor?"

Doris started bawling as well. She and Paula supported one another while Angela looked on, her eyes narrow and hard. Valerie drew a deep breath, aware that the mask she'd worn so securely, and for so many years, had slipped just a little. From outside came the satisfying *thonk-thonk-thonk* of somebody chopping firewood.

"It's your life, ladies." Valerie said a moment later, when

the air had cooled by three or four degrees. She took a box of Kleenex—one of the small luxuries from the mainland that she couldn't do without—from the table next to the sofa and handed it to Doris, who took two and passed it on. "I would never stop you from following your heart, but I need to make sure your heart's in the right place."

"My heart is with God," Angela said.

"Amen," Paula said, and trumpeted a wad of snot into her Kleenex.

Valerie nodded. She took the box from Angela and walked it back to the table, also home to a small wooden lockbox. She tapped the top of it with one fingernail.

"When people tell me they want to return to their old lives, I always offer to show them the watch. A few of them have taken one look and been reminded of schedules, deadlines, and grind. They feel their blood pressure rising at the thought of being caught in traffic, or having to rush to make a meeting or catch a plane. They look at the watch and see the antithesis of freedom, and suddenly decide they don't want their old lives, after all. So I extend the same invitation to you now, ladies, in the hope you'll reconsider."

Paula and Doris looked at each other, clutching their Kleenex. Angela shook her head and stared at Valerie.

"I haven't seen a watch—or any timepiece other than the sun—for four years. But I know what one looks like, and I know what one represents. Not a prison, Valerie, but system, order, and continuity. It's all about perspective. Where you see restraints, I see possibility."

Again, an answer for everything. Valerie sneered.

"I want to thank you," Angela continued, "for everything you've done. You provided comfort when we were downtrodden and afraid. More importantly, you gave us the freedom and space to regain our Christian strength."

"A true Samaritan," Doris sobbed.

"Our appreciation is sincere, Valerie." Never Mother Moon—not with this one. "But we are being called by a higher power."

"Very well," Valerie said.

Angela lifted her chin and said, "I've been very generous over the years, but from this point forward my money will be shared with the True Light House of God."

"I'm sure they'll be very grateful," Valerie said. She had a stone caught in her throat that pinched when she swallowed. "And of course, I have to remind you—in order to protect the people here, and everything we've built—not to tell anybody about us. There are a lot of broken Americans out there, as you'll discover, and I fear we'll be overrun."

"We'll direct them to God's light," Angela said. "Which can shine on all, and has no maximum capacity."

"Similarly, we'll not talk about you when you're gone. One of our great successes is in embracing the present, not dwelling on the past. Your names will never be mentioned."

"It'll be like we were never here," Angela said. She turned to Paula and Doris. They nodded. "We can accept that."

"Nolan is off-community at the moment." Valerie stepped toward the three women, squaring her shoulders to appear undaunted. "As soon as he returns, I'll arrange for him take you home."

"Jesus will be glad to see us," Angela said.

Valerie said, "Yes, he will."

Nolan returned a week later, full of energy. He all but skipped up the pathway toward Valerie's cabin. *As if his shit don't stink,* she thought.

"Good news," he said by way of greeting, and with all the enthusiasm of a stage actor delivering his only line.

Valerie sat on her front step, glass of water in hand. She'd been watching her worker ants do their thing: gathering crops, chopping wood, moving supplies between the storage barn and the canteen. It was quite relaxing, in its way. Now she turned her attention to Nolan, one eyebrow raised skeptically.

"Are you okay?" he asked. They'd known each other a long time. It wasn't an intimate relationship, but he knew her as well as anybody ever had—including Pace, including her fuckwad parents—and could tell when she was in a shitty mood.

"I'm just peachy," she snapped. "Tell me the good news."

"Sure. Okay." He also knew when not to push. "We've got three new people coming in. A father and his two girls. Mommy dearest was a teacher at Flint Wood High. And yes, I know it's risky to recruit our own victims, but they were ripe for the picking."

"Children?" Valerie curled her lip. "How old?"

"Sixteen and ten," Nolan responded. "Minds like wet clay, I'll bet, and looking for a maternal influence in their lives."

"You don't know much about young girls, do you?"

"I . . ." Nolan had no more on the subject. He shut his mouth.

"And does the father have money?" Valerie asked. "A life insurance payout for the wife? Is he selling his house?"

"I'm not sure what his financial arrangement is, and it's usually not a good idea to ask too many questions." Nolan folded his arms. His nostrils flared. "Why do you ask?"

Valerie drank from her glass of water, wiped her mouth, and sighed. "We've gained three people, and that's great. Bravo, Nolan. But we've also lost three, and that's definitely *not* great."

"Who'd we lose?"

"Paula, Doris, and Angela."

"Well, fuck."

"And when Angela goes bye-bye, so does her money."

Nolan drew his hands down his pale, chiseled face. "Fuck," he said again. So much for his bouncy mood. "We'll get through this. We always lose numbers at this time of year. Winter's on the horizon. People freak out, they—"

"It feels like we're bleeding people," Valerie said. "But it's the money I'm most concerned about. Angela frequently signed over thousands of dollars. Every time I met with the Society, the transport to Engine City, the motels I stayed in . . . it was all on Angela's buck."

"Yeah, she's like a rich aunt," Nolan agreed. "And you can't . . . you know, *persuade* her to—"

"She's God's girl. I can't get close."

Nolan planted his fists on his hips and sighed. "We'll find a way, I promise you. We can sell the truck. I'll get a job on the mainland and come back weekends. I'll *commute*, at least until I've recruited people with money."

Valerie found a scrap of warmth inside her and used it first to smile, then to take Nolan's hand. "Yes, Nolan, if fate is kind, we'll scratch together the money to coordinate a few more events. I'll find the Skyway, and everything will be roses."

"I'll rob a goddamn bank if I have to."

"Such a faithful puppy." Her smile slipped. "I can only hope you get what you deserve. The one thing I know for certain is that something is coming. I can *feel* it. I just don't know if it's the beginning, or the end."

Nolan frowned. His hand dropped from hers and thumped limply against his thigh.

Valerie finished her water, got to her feet. "When do the new people arrive?"

"We have an arrangement for October third," Nolan replied blankly. "So, yeah . . . a week from today, unless you have any objections."

"I don't," she said, and nodded toward where Angela Byrne was loading pumpkins into a wheelbarrow. "You'll have three of God's little lambs on your outbound journey. He's calling them home, apparently."

"I understand," Nolan said. He pulled a whistling breath into his chest. His gray eyes flickered. "I'll make sure they get there."

15

It was easier for Martin to think of it as a temporary move, even though he had no idea how temporary it would be. He kept telling himself six weeks—that was the probationary period—but hoped it would be longer. On his own, he saw himself staying until his beard was long and white and he'd forgotten the Pledge of Allegiance. He was just one-third of the equation, though (and a minor third, at that). Their time on Halcyon would come down to how comfortably the girls settled.

"No phones?" Shirley had complained, and more than once, as if a world without cell phones was inconceivable. "No internet? And this is supposed to help us?"

"It *will* help," Martin promised. "We're going to refresh our pages, focus on what's important."

"By going back to prehistoric times? Jesus, will we have to bathe in the river? Kill our own food?"

"We're doing this, Shirl. It'll be good for us."

And maybe it was a blessing that he didn't know how

long they'd be gone. He could be vague about it with the girls and not have to lie. "Think of it as an extended vacation," he'd say. Or another favorite: "We're just taking a break from the real world." It didn't exactly silence their remonstrations. They were post-millennials being asked to live—albeit temporarily—like the Ingalls kids from *Little House on the Prairie*. An extreme change of pace, and tough for them to see the benefit, no matter how deeply they were hurting.

Jimmy and Felicity didn't understand, either. Martin gave them the car—a loaner, he insisted—and the house keys. He'd set Jimmy up as trustee with instructions to sell after six months, if they hadn't returned by then.

"Drop the money into my savings account," he said. "And put all our shit into storage. I'll make it up to you when I get back."

"Do you honestly think you'll be gone that long?" Jimmy asked.

"No, I don't. This is a precaution."

Felicity looked at Jimmy, then lowered her eyes. A sympathetic gesture. *He's lost his mind*, it said. She sat close enough that Martin could smell her perfume. It was jasmine-scented, more expensive than Curate.

"If you need to get something out of your system," she started, trying—and failing—to keep the patronizing tenor from her voice. "Then just do it. Go. Visit the Dalai Lama. Run across the country like Forrest Gump. Whatever it is, we *get it*. And you can leave the girls with us. We'll look after them until . . ."

She trailed off, but Jimmy finished for her: "Until you've found whatever it is you're looking for."

They were in Jimmy and Felicity's living room, all chrome and dark leather, with a huge 4K TV built into the wall and a stereo system that was worth more than Martin's car. It was the modern living space of a couple who valued their material possessions, and would surrender them for nothing.

"I'm doing this *for* the girls," Martin said. It was perhaps the fifth time he'd tried to explain it to them. "And okay. Sure. For me, too. This is an opportunity to take a deep breath and move forward in a different light. Because it's all shit right now, and I need to know—and need my girls to know—that there's still some good in the world."

"Can you at least tell me where this place is?" Jimmy asked. "You know, for when I need to come rescue you."

"I don't know where it is," Martin said. "I told you that. It's probably a gated community in the Adirondacks. Or maybe an island on a lake somewhere. It's close by, that's all I know."

"Jesus Christ, listen to yourself. You're shipping off to some secret location—cut off from the outside world, no phones, no fucking email—because some random guy in a bar showed you a business card." Jimmy ran his hands through what remained of his hair. "I'm worried about you, man."

"Well, shit, I *know* it sounds crazy, but do you know what's crazier? Sending my daughters to school in the morning and not knowing if they'll make it home. Checking for suspicious packages every time I use public transit. Going to the movie theater and worrying that some dickless psychopath is going to start shooting the place up." Martin ran his hands through his hair, too. His was fuller and darker than Jimmy's, but the expression was the same: total exasperation. "Halcyon may not seem very safe to you, but I have to believe it's one hell of a lot safer than being out here."

"Fear and paranoia." Jimmy shook his head. "*That's* why this country is on its knees. It's not damaged, it's *cowering*. And if you're not part of the solution, you're part of the problem."

"Shit, Jimmy, you've hit the nail on the head," Martin said sarcastically. "And I totally forgot that you volunteer at the Clear Conscience Soup Kitchen, and that you donate thirty percent of every paycheck to the lower classes."

"Hey, asshole, don't try to make me feel bad just because I choose to work my ass off. A few more Jimmy Lovegroves and this country is a better place."

"I'm not arguing with you." Martin held his hands up and sighed. They were coming at this from different ends and were never going to meet in the middle. "America's problems go beyond the size of your TV. And I don't want you thinking this is a protest move or political statement. I'm just taking my family out of the mix for a little while. We can heal quicker if we feel safe."

"You should move to Canada," Felicity said. "At least we can visit you there."

On the morning of October 3, Martin sat at his kitchen table and ran through a brief checklist. He'd taken a leave of absence from work and made a similar arrangement with the girls' schools. He'd set up direct payments with the bank to cover the bills—there was enough money to keep things ticking over for at least six months. He'd canceled his internet and cable subscription. Ditto Spotify, HBO Go, and Netflix. He'd arranged for Anthony Palazzo—Claudette's not-so-little brother—to rake the leaves every couple of weeks, and shovel the driveway if they hadn't returned before the snow blew in. He'd given his car and house keys to Jimmy and Felicity, who'd promised to drop in occasionally and make sure he still *had* a house, that it hadn't been ransacked or hit by a tornado. He'd packed one suitcase with clothes and toiletries, and another with towels and bedding. Edith and Shirley had done the same. They were also allowed to bring a few non-electronic personal items. Martin brought Laura's wedding ring, which he wore on a chain around his neck, a photograph of him and Laura in Rhode Island, and a copy of Kerouac's *On the Road*, both his and Laura's favorite novel, with little love notes scrawled into the margins for each to discover when rereading it. *You're MY girl, MY kind of girlsoul,* read one. *That's a GREAT idea: let's love each other madly,* read another.

Martin checked off the items one by one. The only thing he didn't have was his daughters.

Shirley was in her room, using her last moments of cellphone coverage to update her social media pages. He glimpsed what she'd posted to Instagram—a shot of the Hindenburg going down in a ball of flame, which she'd captioned: *MY LIFE IN ONE PICTURE.* This was followed by a string of emojis in various stages of distress, as if the burning zeppelin weren't graphic enough.

"We're leaving in ten minutes," Martin said.

She put down her phone. "I still think this is stupid."

"No. It's important. We're going back to good old American values: family, community, helping one another. It'll make you stronger. So when you come back here and see all the shit on the news, you'll know it's not like that everywhere. It'll give you hope. And if you're going to build any kind of future for yourself in this country, you *need* hope."

She looked at him, her eyes full of sadness, her hair standing in punky black jags. Seeing her like this—a dark outline of the bright girl that was tucked deep inside—he knew they were doing the right thing.

"It's not forever, right?" she asked.

"It's not forever," he said.

He found Edith in the backyard, sitting on the stoop, rocking to and fro with her hands linked behind her head. She didn't react when Martin sat beside her and placed one hand on her back, because she wasn't really there. It *looked* like Edith—a hunched, troubled version of her, at least—but her mind was somewhere far away.

"Hey," Martin said. "Come on out, babygirl."

These mental jaunts were still frequent enough to be concerning. The good news was that there'd been no more premonitions—none that had woken her screaming in the night, anyway. Martin wanted to believe they were a thing of the past, but even if they were, she still had problems. "Detached from reality," her teacher remarked on one of the few days Edith had made it to school. He'd heard similar expressions over the last few months. *Lost in her own world . . . Spaced out . . . Away with the fairies.* Jimmy had admonished him for not taking her to a child psychologist, but Jimmy didn't know about the streaming. Martin was afraid—as Laura had been—that after digging into Edith's mind, a shrink would place her on heavy meds, or worse, admit her into a psychiatric facility.

Halcyon would help.

He rubbed her back until she stopped rocking, recalling how she'd loved that as a baby. He'd place her belly-down on her blankie and sit beside her, his hand as wide as her back, rubbing ever so gently, and she'd lie there for however long, cooing and bright-eyed. Now she turned those same eyes toward him, frowning slightly, as if seeing him for the first time, or perhaps waking from a dream.

"You told me you wanted to be safe," Martin said, tucking strands of hair behind her ears. Her face was ash-colored, so delicate he thought it might break apart if the wind picked up. "It's time."

She blinked, then curled her arms around him, not emerging from her garden, but reaching from it. He held her as tightly as he could without hurting her, then lifted her into his arms and carried her away. She weighed nothing to him. She could have been a leaf or a flower. A ladybug sitting in his palm, wings open, ready to fly.

"Come on, babygirl," he said. "Come on."

16

Some seventy miles north, on a small island in the blue, blustery middle of Lake Ontario, Nolan Thorne was helping three jolly ladies make the opposite journey. He extended his hand and ushered them from the dock to the boat. They clucked and giggled as the deck pitched gently beneath them. "Safety first, ladies," Nolan insisted, fishing four bright lifejackets from one of the lockers. They clucked and giggled again as Nolan helped secure them, adjusting and tightening the straps. "The Lord is my true lifejacket," Doris said mirthfully. Both Paula and Angela laughed at that. So did Nolan. He thought it was very funny.

They took their seats behind the cockpit. Angela started humming, "A Mighty Fortress Is Our God," and the others joined in. Nolan fetched their luggage from the dock—not much, you never accumulate much on Halcyon—and stowed it securely.

There was no big send-off for the ladies. No fanfare. Mother Moon had numbers to protect, and she didn't want anybody thinking that returning to the mainland was cause for celebration. There were a few cursory goodbyes, but only Alyssa Prince accompanied them to the dock. She and Doris had a solid bond—an ethnic closeness, Nolan assumed, as if relationships were only determined by skin color.

They waved at each other now. Alyssa very sweetly made the heart symbol with her thumbs and forefingers. Doris—despite her obvious excitement at going home—had little tears in her eyes.

"It seems strange," she said, knuckling one of those tears away, "that no one here will mention us—that our names will be erased."

"Another of Valerie's silly rules," Angela remarked.

"It's to preserve the status quo," Nolan said, buckling his own lifejacket. He made a slight adjustment to accommodate the object he had strapped between his actual jacket and the left side of his ribcage. "If the people here talk about you, they'll invariably think about the mainland and if the grass is any greener over there. This creates doubt and turmoil, which can be damaging."

"To whom?" Angela asked.

"To Halcyon." Nolan fished the boat key from his pocket. "Like any society, it needs good, hardworking people in order to thrive. If everybody scampers off to the mainland because they believe it's all sweetness and light, then everything here is going to collapse."

"Then it'll just be you and Valerie," Angela said. "And won't that be sweet?"

"What's sweeter is providing a safe and comfortable

community where disillusioned Americans can restructure their lives." Nolan offered a beaming, disingenuous smile—a little something he'd picked up from Mother Moon over the years. "There's a reason for all of Valerie's 'silly' rules, you know."

This was true, but the reasons were not as altruistic as Nolan suggested. There were certain precarious pieces to consider—pieces like Garrett Riley and Glenn Burdock. Rules had to be implemented, and preventative measures taken, to keep Halcyon's past from bleeding into the present.

Now *that* would be damaging.

Nolan gave his lifejacket another tweak on the left side, then started the engine. It coughed twice and caught with a wet rumble. The blades chopped at the water, throwing up foam, and the ladies clucked again. Nolan applied a touch of throttle and eased away from the dock.

"Say goodbye to Halcyon, ladies."

The ladies said goodbye and waved. Alyssa Prince waved back. Behind her, Halcyon loomed green and gray. Its tall trees brushed the sky.

On clear days, on those rare occasions when the lake was blue glass, Nolan could get the center console up to forty-three miles per hour. He once made the mainland—dock to dock—in eighteen minutes. It usually took somewhere around half an hour, depending on the weather. An ideal cruising speed was twenty-five miles per hour, which made for an enjoyable run, and was easier on the gas. Today he hovered a little south of this, watching the mainland inflate in front of him, occasionally turning to see Halcyon *de*flate behind. After ten minutes or so, he throttled all the way down, shut off the engine, and slipped the key into his pocket. The boat bobbed silently on the waves.

"Is everything okay?" Angela asked. She was shivering a little—it was chilly back there—but still smiling.

"Absolutely," Nolan said, unfastening the clasps on his lifejacket. He then spread his arms and looked around, inhaling expansively. "The lake is incredibly deep here. About four hundred feet. Head a little farther west and it's almost twice as deep again. A true marvel of nature."

The ladies looked at one another, nodding appreciatively. Angela pointed at the sky, as if to say, *Hey, you up there . . . outstanding work!*

"I call this the point of no return," Nolan said. He inhaled again, his nostrils as round as nickels. "Before we continue, I need to be absolutely certain you've made up your minds. There's no going back from here."

The ladies, shivering, nodded as one.

"No going back," Angela echoed.

"Okay," Nolan said, and shot Paula in the face.

He'd pulled the pistol from the holster secured to the left side of his ribcage, a Glock 19 with an Osprey 9 suppressor, which made concealment problematic, but was necessary; they were five miles from the nearest shoreline but sound carried on the lake. He'd aimed for Paula's forehead, but the boat pitched as he pulled the trigger. The bullet smashed through her right cheekbone, tore through her skull, and exited at the back of her neck. She flopped. Her eyes were wide and rolling.

"Blurgh," she said, and Nolan shot her again, this time in the throat. She didn't say anything else.

Angela threw her hands into the air and leaped to her feet. "Goodness and blazes," she shrieked. "Goodness and blazes. Goodness and—" She was splattered with her friend's blood, her hair windswept, her feet tapping a crazy jig on the deck. It was only when Nolan leveled the gun at her that she stopped dancing and acknowledged her predicament.

"Blazes," she said.

Nolan pulled the trigger and one shot was enough. A small hole flowered between her eyes and her head snapped backward. She staggered for a second, then dropped to the deck. The lake wind rippled her clothes and hair, but that was the only movement.

Doris—likewise shocked—bolted from her seat and scuttled past the cockpit to the front of the boat, as if she might continue off the bow and hot-step it across the water like Jesus Christ himself. "Oh, sweet momma," she wailed, her hands trembling at the air. "Oh, Lord. Oh, mercy."

Nolan squeezed off a shot and damn if the boat didn't pitch again, sending the bullet skyward. He overbalanced and stumbled left. His foot came down in a puddle of blood and he hit the deck ass-first. The jolt caused his finger to jerk against the trigger and loose a shot. The bullet zinged past his face, warm as a kiss.

Too fucking close, he thought, staggering to his feet. He tipped right and almost went down again. Doris was on the other side of the cockpit, partially obscured from view. She'd run out of real estate, though—unless she wanted to go for a swim, of course. Nolan regained his balance and approached slowly, looking at her down the barrel of the gun.

Doris looked from the water to where her friends' bodies were sprawled across the deck. Her hands were linked in prayer, but it wasn't God she appealed to.

"Please, Nolan . . . please don't do this."

"You're a good woman, Doris. I wanted you to stay on the island, dammit." He aimed at her forehead. "This has to be done."

"But *why*?"

"No one makes it back to the mainland. With the exception of a few faithful foot soldiers, everybody you've said goodbye to is at the bottom of this lake. Nicole Little, Joel Sutherland, Christine Figgy, or Foggy—whatever her fucking name was . . ." He used his free hand to gesture over the side of the boat. "The point of no return."

"Garrett?" She looked at him with tear-filled eyes. Maybe she thought conversation was her only way out of this. It was a better option than swimming, but only just.

"He was one of our foot soldiers." Nolan shrugged. The wind gusted. Heavy waves slapped against the hull. "If we let you return to the mainland, you'd find out what he did, and we can't have that."

"I still don't understand."

"We've done some extreme things in pursuit of Glam Moon. Which doesn't make us all that different from Christianity, when you think about it. You people have been laying one another to waste since time out of mind."

Doris hugged herself and shivered. The tears rolled down her face. Some people were ugly criers, but not Doris. She was beautiful.

"We need to cover our bases. We can't have the mainland authorities finding out about us." Nolan sniffed, the sights still fixed on Doris's forehead. "And we can't have *you* finding out about Garrett, Glenn, or any number of other Halcyon alumni. I'm sorry, Doris, but preventative measures have to be taken."

"You're crazy," she said.

"It's all for the Glam," he said.

Doris took a trembling breath and looked at her fallen friends again. "They were good women. They were harmless." She pointed at them, and Nolan, stupidly, followed the tip of her finger. At that moment, a wave slapped the bow and the boat seesawed again. Doris seized her opportunity. She lowered her shoulder, threw herself at Nolan, and connected full force with his soft middle. She was fifty-one years old, maybe one-fifteen on the scales. He was three years younger and twice as heavy. Under any normal circumstance, she would have bounced off him like a ping-pong ball off a paddle. On a boat with a slippery deck—pitching this way and that—different physics applied; her diminutive mass, with all its forward momentum, was more than enough to knock him off balance. He stumbled backward with his arms flailing. If he'd been angled slightly to the right, he might have gone overboard. As it was, he tripped over one of the bait lockers and landed hard on his side. The Glock popped out of his hand, slid across the deck, and came to rest against Paula's left foot.

Doris's momentum was slowed by Nolan's bulk, but not enough to keep her from falling. She landed on top of Nolan, rolled clumsily over him, and thumped her head on the deck.

"Oh," she said.

"You fucking *bitch,*" Nolan said. He tried to get up but the boat swayed and he toppled backward, thumping the small of his back against the same locker he'd tripped over. He grimaced—shit, that *hurt*—but pushed the pain to one side. No time for pain, dammit—he had a situation to unfuck.

Doris, now, was on her knees and crawling toward the gun. Another wave pounded the hull and she fell into Angela, and for just a second it looked like the two ladies were snuggling to keep warm. *Spooning for the Lord,* Nolan thought, then Doris pushed herself up and clambered over her friend. The gun had skated midway down Paula's shin, almost within reach. "Oh," Doris said again, extending one hand . . .

"No you fucking don't," Nolan snapped. He lunged forward, grabbed one of Doris's ankles, and yanked her toward him. She twisted and kicked, but ineffectually. The distance between her hand and the gun lengthened, although she managed to snag something else—Paula's shoe. It was a slip-on, with a low, sensible heel hard enough to drive a nail into wood. Doris pulled it off Paula's foot as she was dragged past, then whipped around and cracked the heel against Nolan's jaw.

"Mother*fuck*."

Nolan stumbled backward. Doris lashed out with the shoe again but this time he caught her wrist. He squeezed and twisted, snapping the bone like a dry stick. Doris screamed. The shoe fell from her hand. Nolan picked it up and smashed the heel into her face several times. Blood and broken teeth leaked from her mouth. Her legs twitched.

"Oh," she said. "*Ooooohhhh*."

Nolan crawled over Doris. He retrieved his gun, propped himself on one knee, and shot her in the head. The force of the bullet turned her face away and that was good. Blood spread around her and made patterns on the deck as the boat bobbed and swayed.

He replaced their lifejackets with three large backpacks that he'd stowed in the rod lockers before leaving the island, making triply sure the clasps at the belt and shoulders were secure. He then arranged the corpses—belly down—over the gunwale, so that their feet trailed in the water and their hands touched the deck. One at a time, he loaded the backpacks with hefty chunks of granite (this stowed in a different locker) until the bodies were sufficiently weighed down. Then he tipped them overboard. They bubbled and sank, never to be seen again.

Their luggage followed. The suitcases floated for a while, then took on water and disappeared beneath the surface. He mopped up the blood using lake water and bleach, and found three of the six bullets he'd fired. Two were lodged into the deck. The one that had passed through Paula Wetlow's face was buried in the wooden lip of the transom, six feet behind where she'd been sitting. Nolan extracted them with a flathead screwdriver. The holes they left behind were shallow and didn't look like bullet holes at all. Still, he went over them with a medium-grade sandpaper and they all but disappeared.

After scrubbing the blood off the lifejackets, including his own, he took care of himself. His jacket, pants, and shoes were also covered in blood. Not good, but something he'd prepared for. This wasn't his first rodeo, after all. Over the years, he'd dropped seventy-six people into this lake and not all of them had gone quietly. He stripped to his underwear, washed himself from head to toe, then threw his clothes (along with Paula's shoe) into a Hefty bag with a good-sized rock and tossed it overboard. He always kept a set of dry clothes on the boat, which was sensible in an environment where it was easy to get wet. He dressed in them now. They were creased and smelled like the lake, but they were clean and dry and that was the important thing.

Nolan started the engine and rumbled south to the mainland. Once docked, he gave the boat a more thorough inspection. The gun and suppressor were stowed away. There were no stray drops of blood. No bullet or skull fragments. It wouldn't hold up to forensic scrutiny, but it didn't have to.

He walked to his truck. The clock in the dash read 11:43. He'd told Martin Lovegrove that he'd meet him at the RTC at midday. He was running about thirty minutes late, but that wasn't too bad, all things considered.

"Three out, three in," Nolan said.

He climbed behind the wheel, gunned the ignition, and went to meet Halcyon's newest family.

17

"No clocks, you say?" Jimmy made a show of looking at his expensive watch. It was 12:20 p.m. They'd made good time and arrived ten minutes early, which meant they'd been waiting in the RTC parking lot—granted, in Jimmy's comfortable Lexus—for half an hour. It felt twice as long, though. No thanks to Jimmy looking at his watch every two minutes (as if there wasn't a perfectly good clock in the dash), often tapping the face with one neatly clipped fingernail.

Shirley sighed in the backseat and said for at least the sixth time that she missed her phone, or Instagram, or some other bullshit that any person ten years older successfully grew up without. Edith tapped a drumbeat on the back of Martin's headrest. It annoyed the royal fuck out of him, but she wasn't in her garden, and she wasn't complaining, so he didn't say anything.

"You know," Jimmy said smugly. "The good thing about clocks is that they help you get to places on time."

"He'll be here," Martin said, but he sounded more

confident than he felt. They were waiting for a man he'd had one face-to-face conversation with. There'd been a brief phone call since, in which Martin had presented his questions and concerns, and Nolan had answered, perhaps not in great detail, but adequately. He'd also mailed out a starter pack of sorts—four brochure-style photographs and a list of guidelines titled *The Keys to Halcyon's Success*. The photos showed the layout of the cabins and the beautiful scenery. Martin shared them with the girls, who remained unimpressed.

The clock in the dash ticked to 12:25. Martin wondered how long they should wait before giving up and going home. It'd be tough—and unfair on the girls—to have to do this all again, though. If they went home now, they might just stay there.

On a similar wavelength, Jimmy said, "Perhaps it's a sign, Mart. You know, like the universe is trying to stop you from going."

"I'm with the universe," Shirley chimed in.

"He's twenty-five minutes late," Martin said. "Not three hours. Let's just chill."

"I vote we chill until twelve thirty," Shirley said. "Then go home."

"He'll *be* here."

And he was. Martin watched the clock tick over to 12:28, then looked up to see a white pickup truck roll into the RTC parking lot. Nolan was behind the wheel, his head scrolling from side to side, looking for Martin and the girls.

"Here we go." Martin opened the door and waved—got Nolan's attention. Nolan swung the truck around and parked two spaces to the left of Jimmy's Lexus.

"Your chariot awaits," Jimmy said.

Martin clapped his brother on the shoulder. "Take care, Jimmy. I'll see you soon."

"Hope so." Jimmy turned to the backseat. "*Adios,* girls. And remember, don't drink the Kool-Aid." He clasped Martin's arm before he could leave. All the smugness had gone from his tone and his eyes were serious. "I hope you find some peace, brother. And if it all begins to feel a little weird, get the hell out of there."

"Sure, Jimmy."

"I'm not kidding, man. There's a saying: *Better the devil you know*—"

"I got it."

Martin pulled their luggage—including Edith's cumbersome guitar case—from the Lexus's trunk as Nolan introduced himself to the girls. He was all smiles and bouncy handshakes. "You're going to love Halcyon," he promised. "Everyone's so excited to meet you." They climbed into the pickup and rumbled away, taking the 481 north out of Syracuse. Nolan apologized for being late but didn't give a reason why. Martin looked at the girls and smiled reassuringly. He was full of nervous excitement. Nolan sensed it—told him to relax.

"It'll be wonderful," he said. "I promise."

They drove forty-five minutes to the town of Fisherman's Point, perched—small and picturesque—on the edge of Lake Ontario. "So it *is* on an island," Martin said, and Nolan said nothing, only winked. They veered west and then north onto an unpaved road that cut between thick trees and arrived at a dilapidated summerhouse, crumbling into the earth and surrounding foliage. There was a boathouse beyond, its pale siding catching the steely light. Nolan parked in an overgrown driveway and shut off the truck.

"This isn't it," Shirley said, alarmed. "Tell me this isn't it."

Nolan chuckled and popped open the driver's door. "Heck, no," he said. "We're heading out there."

He pointed across the water. They saw nothing.

They carried their luggage to the boathouse, where the center console bobbed cheerfully in the slip. Now the girls brightened for the first time all day, both of them smiling. Nolan helped them aboard and they giggled as the boat rolled first one way, then the other.

"Safety first, ladies," Nolan said, handing them lifejackets.

"Ew, they're all *wet,*" Edith said.

Martin remained on the dock to hand Nolan the luggage, but paused before stepping aboard. He felt, then, the first pangs of uncertainty. He'd considered that Halcyon might be on an island, but never that it was so *far* off the mainland. They couldn't exactly walk away whenever they wanted to.

Nolan broke his train of thought. "Untie us there, friend," he said, indicating the line looped over the mooring post. And perhaps it was that Martin's caution had spiked, but he thought he saw something in Nolan's eyes—there and gone in a moment—that felt a little . . . *off,* somehow.

Martin untied but held on to the line. The boat bobbed and pulled as if willing him toward the island, but he held fast.

"You ready?" Nolan asked.

The girls looked at him, lifejackets fastened, their faces pale and trusting. Martin thought of Edith saying that she just wanted to be safe, and Laura—beautiful Laura—lying in a coffin for no other reason than that she turned up for work one morning. Yesterday's news printed headlines across his mind: an unexploded bomb found in New York City, a drunk truck driver killing twelve on the Massachusetts Turnpike, riots across the South after police shot an unarmed African-American youth in New Orleans.

Martin looked out through the boathouse and across the lake.

"I'm ready," he said, and stepped aboard.

18

The island came into view after only a moment, appearing to emerge from the lake, first a knuckle, then a fist. The finer details were filled in as they approached, as if it was being painted and all the depth and texture added last, from the bright fringe of wild flowers to the PRIVATE LAND and NO TRESPASSING signs. They pulled alongside a small dock, all of them shivering. They'd been almost half an hour on the water. It was exhilarating but cold. A small, thin man put down his fishing rod long enough to help them tie off.

Nolan introduced them as they disembarked. The man was Jake Door and his job was to fish off the dock and shoo away inquisitive boats.

"The signs do most of the work," Jake explained, smiling beneath an unkempt mustache. His cheeks had the ruddy, roughened look of a man who'd done some hard drinking in his time. "I just give 'em the beady eye."

Nolan chuckled and asked, "What's on the menu tonight, Jake?"

"We got some salmon. Some steelhead." Jake pointed at a large cooler that doubled as a stool. "Enough for everyone."

Small birds flitted and chirped ecstatically as Nolan led them through a patch of green woodland. Martin filled his lungs—it seemed he could breathe even deeper here—and smiled. The only sounds were the birds and the wind in the branches. No traffic hum. No cogs or grind. His uncertainty faded, leaving a residue of something not unlike a bad taste.

Nolan pointed out a few small farm plots, a storage barn, and a path that led toward one of the wells and the recreation hall. He promised a comprehensive orientation later. "I need to introduce you to someone *very* special first," he said. They followed a broader path past an open, grassy area—the meadow, Nolan called it—and numerous huts and cabins. Several people introduced themselves along the way, all with handshakes, smiling faces, and nothing but love for Halcyon and the lifestyle. "Every day is a gift," a woman named Gilda said. Like Jake Door, she had a broken-but-mended look, a suggestion that her ghosts were never far away. "Halcyon has done so much for me." Another woman—her name was Alyssa—pointed at Edith's guitar case and asked if she played.

"A little," Edith replied quietly.

"She's actually very good," Martin said.

"I play a little, too," Alyssa said. "Maybe we can start a band." Her smile was beautiful. No other word for it. She shared it first with Edith, shaking her hand warmly, then Martin. "Welcome," she said.

There were a number of larger cabins toward the end of the path, sheltered from the elements by a backdrop of swaying pines. Most were basic post-and-beam construction with wood siding. A few were sturdier log cabins, probably built before Halcyon was founded. They headed toward the largest of these, set back between the trees. Before reaching the front steps, Martin stopped and looked around. His lungs ballooned again, full of nothing but clean air. A huge smile stretched across his face.

He stopped the girls and had them look, too.

"Isn't it pretty?"

Leaves tumbled everywhere, brown and gold. Birds played in the wind and sang. The meadow was as inviting as a lagoon and the islanders busied themselves beneath a sky the color of old silver. Martin looked for the mainland but saw only glimpses of the lake where the tree cover was thinner. He felt the separation then, and it was greater than eleven miles of water. It was like closing a window on a loud noise. The idea of not seeing a car, or a computer screen, or a cell phone for at least six weeks filled him with bewilderment and awe.

I made the right decision, he thought. His uncertainty faded even more, and something in his chest—a tightness that had lived there for months, maybe even *decades*—let go, not all at once, but enough to draw a trembling sigh from him.

The door of the cabin opened before Nolan could knock and a woman stepped outside. She was in her fifties, with auburn hair, silver at the temples, swept back from her forehead, and perhaps the kindest face Martin had ever seen.

Her smile was as welcoming as an open fire in December, and her eyes—a deep, shining green—lifted Martin to the balls of his feet.

When she opened her arms, all three of them took an involuntary step forward.

"It's a beautiful day," she said.

The trees trembled in agreement and for just a moment the birdsong was deafening.

"For fifteen years I worked for a wonderful lady named Victoria Platt-Mellor. She and her husband bought this island from the Rockefeller family back in the 1950s, and spent many of their summer weekends here. After Bernard died in 1984, Victoria decided to live here permanently. She'd had her fill of the mainland—the devil's garden, she called it. Bernard was a wily businessman and I guess she saw enough of his dealings to know she wasn't far from the mark. Victoria hired me as cook and cleaner, my then-boyfriend Pace as groundskeeper, and the sweetest young girl—Peachie Pie, we called her, on account of her being from Georgia—as nurse. We all lived together for a few years, then Peachie Pie went back to Atlanta, and Pace . . . well, Pace died. So it was just me and Victoria. She was in her late seventies by this time, not bedridden but not exactly light on her feet. She needed a lot of taking care of and that all came down to me. I kept her clean and fed, kept her warm in the winter. Heck, I'd be out there splitting wood with the snow falling around me and my hands so cold I could barely hold the axe. I fetched her prescriptions from across the water, cleaned her sheets, read to her. I did it all. As the years wore on and Victoria became more infirm, I tried to persuade her to go back to the mainland. But she wouldn't hear of it. She wanted to die on the island, she said, and that's exactly what she did—the day before her ninetieth birthday, in fact. She was sitting up in bed, bright as a penny. I turned to put a log on the fire and when I turned back she was gone."

Martin, Shirley, and Edith sat together on a long, comfortable sofa. Mother Moon sat opposite in an armchair, speaking through her smile and regarding each of them in turn with her beautiful eyes. She had introduced herself as Valerie. "But most people call me Mother Moon." And Martin thought this moniker just perfect. She *was* motherly. *Grand*motherly, too. She effused warmth and grace. She smelled woody and strong.

"I returned to the mainland," Mother Moon continued. "Got a job arranging flowers, but I found it difficult to settle in after spending so much time away. That's when I heard from Victoria's lawyers. She'd left her children her money and mainland properties, but bequeathed the island to me. I was shocked, to say the least. But then I considered how we'd lived here for fifteen years together, and for twelve of those years it was just the two of us. We had a closeness to one another and to the island. It seemed only natural—and *right*—to leave it to me, and I had no problem seeing my name on the deed."

Martin sipped the homemade apple juice that Mother Moon had poured for him. It was cloudy but delicious. He thought that was how it would be with most things here—

rough around the edges but ultimately fulfilling. He looked around the cabin, comprised of three rooms: a living room–cum–kitchenette, a bedroom, and a bathroom. The walls were clad with pine, draped with warm artwork. There were thick rugs across the floor, plush pillows on all the seats. It was cozy and comfortable, the kind of place Martin had often thought about escaping to with Laura—a whole week of breathless sex, good books, and drinking wine by the open fire. Nothing plugged in but their souls.

"The early part of my life was extremely tough," Mother Moon said. Her smile faltered, but only for a moment. "No details necessary. Suffice to say the island provided an escape from all of that, and I wanted to give other people—other sufferers—the same opportunity. So I established Halcyon, a sanctuary of sorts, where people could get away from everything for a while, where they could feel safe and respected. We started out small. Just a handful of us, growing crops, building shelters. Then the towers came down and I was turning people away."

"I bet," Martin said. He recalled reading an article about how bunker and panic room sales had gone through the roof in the weeks after 9/11. A picturesque island in the middle of Lake Ontario—for those who knew about it, and who wanted to escape—would be an appealing alternative.

"We went from a few people picking berries and meditating to a *community,* and it soon became apparent that we needed structure . . . rules." Mother Moon hunched her shoulders and shuddered. "I do *not* like the R-word but there it is. Now, we have finessed those *rules* over the years—a lot of trial and error, let me tell you—and developed a system that protects Halcyon and everyone living here. It's been a community effort. We all respect the rules, and for as long as you're here we ask that you do the same."

"Of course," Martin said.

"Everywhere has rules," Shirley said. She finished her apple juice and leaned forward, elbows propped on her knees. "Schools. Libraries. The workplace. Without rules, everything collapses."

"What an amazing young woman," Mother Moon said, looking deep into Shirley's eyes. "And yes, you're absolutely right, but we pride ourselves on our free-spirited approach. So, in many ways, rules contradict what we stand for. Unfortunately, they're essential. It's a balancing act, and that's why it's taken so long to get right."

"Nolan ran through them with me," Martin said. "He also sent me a list: *The Keys to Halcyon's Success.* I showed the girls. I think we're good to go."

Shirley nodded. Edith slouched deep into the pillows and looked at Mother Moon over the rim of her glass.

"It's not a long list," Mother Moon said. "But I do want to draw your attention to one particular rule, or *key*—which, to Nolan's credit, is a much better word."

"Okay," Martin said, and took another sip of juice.

"We do not share our pains with others." The smile had dropped from Mother Moon's face but the warmth was still there. "You've all been through a terrible trauma. So has everybody else on this island. I would never expect—or want—you to keep your pain locked up. This is a healing place, after all. But please refrain from talking to others about it. There are a lot of fragile people here. Some of them are working very hard to keep themselves together, and it doesn't take much to break them."

"Sure," Martin said. "That's a straightforward request. And it's not like I was about to divulge my grief to a bunch of strangers."

"They won't be strangers for long, they'll be friends. But they'll always be fragile friends." Mother Moon looked to the window, where the clouds had broken up to show patches of cold blue sky. "I compare sharing your trauma to drinking in front of an alcoholic."

"We got it," Martin said.

"But isn't talking supposed to help?" Edith asked. It was the first thing she'd said since they'd all taken their seats. "That's what a support group is, right? Strangers talking about their sadness."

"*Another* amazing young woman," Mother Moon announced. She clapped her hands and looked at Martin. "My goodness, Dad, you must be *very* proud."

"I am."

"And yes, Edith, you're right. But a support group is a controlled environment with counselors and sponsors. I've been to many in my time and believe me, they can get out of hand in a hurry. We'd like to avoid that. You *will* need to talk about your sadness—about the incident. And when you do, I want you to know I'm right here. I am now and will always be someone who'll listen and offer comfort. There's a reason they call me Mother Moon."

"I wish I'd met you sooner," Shirley said. She looked at the older woman and in that second something passed between them. Martin couldn't say what, exactly, but it was there. Some kind of intuitive understanding, he thought.

Edith, still slouched, said, "Is your second name Moon?"

"No, sweetie." Mother Moon's eyes lingered a moment longer on Shirley, then drifted to Edith. "It's because I believe in a place—a special level of happiness—called Glam Moon. We'll talk more about that another time, but for now I'll just say that Halcyon is like the opening act."

There was a polite knock on the door, then it opened and Nolan came in. "Sorry to disturb you, Mother Moon. I just want to let our new friends know that their luggage is waiting for them in their cabin."

"Wonderful." Mother Moon beamed and turned her attention back to Martin and the girls. "Now, don't expect the Taj Mahal. It's basic, but comfortable. There's hot water and electricity, but we ask that you use it with consideration. Nolan will show you where the laundry facilities are—and again, be considerate. One full load once a week should be adequate."

"Okay," Martin said, thinking how the washing machine had run on a constant basis at their house. There would be many such adjustments, he was sure, and all of them steep.

"You have a kitchenette in your cabin, but everybody convenes in the canteen for their evening meal. It's usually served around sundown this time of year. Our chef, Joseph, does the most wonderful things with basic ingredients."

"Sounds great," Martin said.

"Nolan will give you a tour of the island and introduce you to anybody you meet along the way. Everybody is lovely here, without exception. We've had some bad apples in the past but they don't last long, do they, Nolan?"

"Not long at all."

"Take some time to settle in—to adjust to what will be a different, but rewarding, lifestyle. We'll get you working for your keep within a few days." She smiled magnetically. "Most non-skilled jobs are on a rotation basis, to keep it fair. Now, we recently lost one of our tutors, but Brooke is still here and she's excellent. We'll get you girls set up with her as soon as possible. And Martin, education isn't limited to our younger islanders; if you ever want to brush up on your math, or if you've a desire to learn French or Spanish, Brooke is fluent in both and she can teach you. We also have Alyssa, who plays guitar and piano, and loves to give lessons."

"Wow," Martin said.

"Shirley," Mother Moon continued. "I need a bright young person to help me with some small tasks. Not just yet, but in a few days, after you've settled in. What do you say?"

Shirley grinned. She looked at Martin and he saw her chest swell. Very different from the dark, damaged girl he'd found sitting by the well just a few weeks ago. It seemed Halcyon—or Mother Moon, to be more precise—had had an immediate effect.

"I'd be happy to help," she said.

"Excellent." Mother Moon's gaze lingered on Shirley again, then took in Martin and Edith, too. "Okay, I think we're good. Are there any questions?"

Shirley shook her head. Martin shrugged. "I don't . . . no . . . just, thank you, Mother Moon. Thank you for—"

Mother Moon waved him off, still smiling, then Edith emerged from the soft pillows and asked:

"Is it true there are no clocks on the island?"

There was a brief silence, during which Mother Moon's smile flickered and she narrowed her eyes—not unkindly, but as if she were trying to get a read on Edith, perhaps sensing some of the mystery that Martin and Shirley were all too familiar with.

"It's true," Mother Moon replied. "We're not governed by time. It's all part of that free-spirited approach I was talking about. There is, however, one watch, although it's more of a symbol than a timepiece."

She got to her feet and walked to a table beside the sofa that Martin and the girls occupied. On it was a plain mahogany box—a trinket box, perhaps. It was small but quite deep, with a brass-lined keyhole in the front. Mother Moon picked it up and drummed her fingernails across the lid.

"You keep it locked in there?" Martin asked.

"We keep it as a reminder of the mainland," Mother Moon said, not really replying. "All that tick and tock. All those busy little cogs working hard but getting nowhere. If you ever feel homesick, or if you just want to see it—"

"I want to see it," Edith said, and this time the silence was longer and edged with awkwardness. Nolan shuffled his feet and made a sound in his throat. Mother Moon frowned again.

"Most people are here a little longer before they ask," she said.

Edith's eyes were wide and innocent. Mother Moon looked from her to Martin, perhaps to see if he would step in, but Martin had always encouraged the girls' independence. He and Laura had never subscribed to the proverb about children being seen and not heard. Besides, he was curious to learn what kind of watch would be kept behind lock and key.

"I'll be right back." Mother Moon's frown disappeared and she smiled again. She set the box down, then walked from the living room into the bedroom. Martin heard a drawer open and close—it stuck a couple of times on closing, from the sound of it—and she returned holding a small key. She slotted this into the front of the box, turned it, and lifted the lid.

Martin and Edith leaned forward. The watch was the only thing in the box, which wasn't as deep as it looked from the outside. Mother Moon took it out, not the rare or antique timepiece that Martin had expected, but a basic, albeit handsome wristwatch with a gold-plated strap and zircon inserts at the numbers. The hands pointed to nine o'clock. It didn't even keep good time.

"Here it is," Mother Moon said. She turned her lower lip down, regarding it with disdain. "Around and around. Doing the same thing day after day. And here's a simple truth for you, Edith: the only people who mark off time are prisoners."

Edith said nothing, although her lips were pursed in a way that suggested she had some thoughts on the subject.

Mother Moon held up the watch a moment longer, then put it away. As she did, Martin noticed the bottom of the box wobble slightly. *A false bottom,* he thought, which explained why it was shallower than it appeared from the outside. It also explained the lock. There was something else in the box. Something Mother Moon didn't want anybody else to see.

She closed it, locked it, clutched the key as she walked over to the window. The blue sky framed her.

"You can leave whenever you want," she said. "But there's no coming back."

"We know that," Martin said.

"Of course, we hope you'll stay with us for a long time." She gazed out the window, and when she turned back she appeared to speak only to Shirley. "It's beautiful here."

19

Joe the chef really was terrific. He grilled the fish that Jake Door had caught and served it with sautéed garlic potatoes and green beans. It was the best meal Martin had had since before Laura died. Everybody in the canteen cleaned their plate and many—including Martin—indulged in a second helping. There were fresh fruit smoothies for dessert, cold and delicious, everything grown on the island.

The canteen was a large cabin with a spacious kitchen at one end and three long tables in the dining area. It comfortably sat thirty, although a third of the seats were empty. They looked hollow, somehow, the people who once occupied them gone forever, never to be discussed—one of the island's more rigid rules, Martin thought. He sat next to Jake and opposite Brooke, the tutor, a striking young woman with pale skin and hazel eyes. They talked about island life and seasonal fishing and the similarities in the French and Spanish languages. They never once discussed the traumas that had brought them here, although Martin could tell they were just beneath the surface. At one point, Brooke mentioned Glam Moon—how you could hold your hand beneath a tree's branches and the fruit just fall into it. Jake nodded and got a little misty-eyed.

"You'll learn all about the Glam," Brooke said to Martin. "It's *elevation,* and Halcyon is the ladder there." To which Martin smiled politely, but all he could think of was Jimmy saying to Edith and Shirley: Adios, *girls. And remember, don't drink the Kool-Aid.*

Edith sat to Martin's right and next to her was Jordan, a blithe, rose-faced girl two years younger than Edith. They responded to one another with broad smiles and lovely peals of laughter. "You've made a new friend," Martin whispered to Edith at one point, and she offered a kind of hopeful shrug. In that moment, her garden seemed a long way off.

Shirley sat at another table, opposite Mother Moon. Every time Martin looked over, the two were engaged in spirited conversation. Although, to be more accurate, Mother Moon appeared to be doing most of the talking.

After dinner, they all helped clean—a swift, industrious effort—and then went outside to watch the stars appear. There was a ridge of clouds to the north but it was otherwise clear. Fifteen of them lay on their backs in the meadow and absorbed the night sky. Miles from the nearest halogen bulb or sodium vapor streetlight, it was spectacular—the kind of cosmic vista that offered an intimidating sense of place. *You are insignificant,* the billions of stars said. *You and your problems mean nothing. Smile while you still can.*

"We do this a lot," a voice to Martin's left said. He looked and saw it was Alyssa, the music tutor. She'd introduced herself when they first arrived—asked Edith if she played guitar. Martin hadn't seen her at dinner. He'd been looking for her, too. He remembered her smile.

Jake pointed out constellations and somebody—Martin didn't recognize the voice—asked if there were stars in Glam Moon.

"There are," Mother Moon replied. "They're twice as bright, though. And the sky is wider."

Brooke—it sounded like Brooke—started singing James Taylor's "You've Got a Friend." Her voice had a raw but effortless tone, dusted with a growl. Everybody joined in on the chorus. Even Martin.

The stars winked and blurred. Here on the island, they appeared to hang lower.

Back at their cabin, the girls sorted through a pile of board games and chose Scrabble. They didn't know all the rules but Martin helped. He watched as they placed their tiles and passed a dictionary between them. Shirley kept score. She looked good flipping through the dictionary's pages, tapping a pencil against her teeth.

There was a bookcase in their living room half filled with a mix of fiction and non-fiction titles. Nothing *too* contemporary or potentially upsetting. No Dennis Lehane or Cormac McCarthy. Martin considered a Buddy Holly biography, but then took *On the Road* from his suitcase. He opened it at random and started reading the notes in the margins.

He sat in a soft, humming light and thought of Laura.

* * *

He dreamed about her every night, without fail. Some mornings he woke up happy and fulfilled. On others he dampened his pillow with tears. His first night sleeping on Halcyon, he dreamed she was there with him. They sat on an uncomfortable outcrop and watched a large bird circle above the water, even though there was no prey beneath. The mainland was a blur and the waves climbed and crashed, more like ocean waves. "He's going to eat," Martin said, pointing to the bird. Then they were in Mother Moon's cabin and the chairs were harder—*bonier*—and the fireplace was as black as a missing tooth. Laura stood with the mahogany lockbox in her hands and the flashlight expression on her face. "That has a false bottom," Martin said, pointing at the box. "She's hiding something." Laura opened the box, took out the watch, lifted the bottom. She showed Martin what was inside. It glimmered. He thought at first it was a piece of jewelry. A ring, perhaps, or a pendant. When he got closer he saw it was a bullet.

Three days passed before Edith disappeared into her garden. An improvement, no doubt, although she went deep. There were no clocks to tell how long she was gone, but it was hours. Maybe as many as five. Martin stroked her hand and brushed her hair, assuring her all the time that she was safe, that nothing could hurt her.

She and Martin went for a walk the following day. It was the kind of crisp fall morning that conjured images of hot, spiced drinks and pumpkin pie. Edith was bright-eyed, if a touch subdued. She wore a beanie and scarf that made her look oddly grown up, and a lot like her mom.

"Do you like it here so far?" Martin asked. They were in the woods north of the cabins, trying to identify leaves using a book—*A New York Fall*—they'd borrowed from the bookcase.

"I guess," Edith said.

"Jordan seems nice."

"She is, but we don't really have anything to talk about. She's never heard of Five Factor or Rihanna. She's never even seen a movie."

"It's good to meet people with different experiences," Martin said. "It broadens your outlook—makes *you* a better person."

"I guess." Edith picked up a leaf and showed it to Martin, who knew what it was but made a show of consulting the book, playing along.

"Northern red oak," he said, showing her the picture so that she could compare. Then he asked, "Is there anything you miss from home?"

"Lots of things," Edith replied at once. "YouTube. My bed. Netflix. Peanut butter." She smiled—looked even more like Laura. "But I've got you and Shirl. I'll be okay." And then she wrinkled her nose. "I'm already bored of Scrabble, though."

They kept walking, their breaths fogging the air and the leaves crackling beneath their feet. What Martin really wanted to ask—and perhaps the reason for going on this walk, just the two of them—was if she had a *feeling* about the island. Calm Dumas had said Edith was a streamer, and that she couldn't access psychic information on request. Even so, he wondered if she'd experienced any preternatural bad vibes.

"Do you have a good feeling about this place?" It was the look in Martin's eyes, more than his words, that conveyed his true meaning.

"It seems okay."

"Will you tell me if that changes?"

"Sure." Edith nodded. "But so far, there's only one thing I don't like."

"And what's that?"

"That Shirley has found a replacement for Mom."

There were things that Martin missed, too. Netflix and peanut butter, for sure, but also cold beer, his music collection, his favorite armchair. He wrote a list. It would help, he told himself, and he was right. Seeing everything scrawled down—two dozen largely inessential items—was both sad and satisfying. He thought of Buddhist monks abstaining from worldly pleasures to attain spiritual awareness. Asceticism, it was called—a lifetime practice. Martin was sure he could go without Budweiser and Led Zeppelin for a couple of months.

As the days rolled along, he became more comfortable with the Halcyon lifestyle. He learned his jobs and rotations, and adjusted to living without a clock. The faces around him became familiar, most of them webbed with kindness, despite their beneath-the-surface pains. They talked about themselves as much as the rules would allow—where they grew up and went to school, former jobs, favorite books and movies, their hobbies and interests. Some of them talked about Glam Moon as if it were a utopia they could sail to as easily as they had sailed to Halcyon. Martin never challenged them, but he believed that if Glam Moon could exist at all, it would be closer to Edith's garden than to a place where they could all run naked and feed each other grapes.

He went through waves of homesickness, but before long the mainland started to blur around the edges. Maybe it was from looking at the stars or listening to the others talk about the Glam, but the idea of surfing the internet or binge-watching *House of Cards* seemed vaporous, somehow. Ten days in, he wrote his list again and found it notably shorter.

But what he *really* discovered was a greater appreciation for the smaller things, which weren't small at all, but epic, wondrous things, everything from birdsong and star shine to the taste of real food and being able to take that extra half an hour in bed. He spent more time with his girls. They went for long walks, skipped stones across the lake, read books to one another. It was exactly the reset he'd hoped for.

On the evening of their thirteenth day, Martin stepped out of his cabin with his jacket buttoned against the cold. Leaves danced endlessly. Vague figures skimmed through the reddish dusk toward the canteen, where lights shimmered and the aroma of baking apples carried on the wind. Edith and Shirley were just ahead but he told them to go on without him. He was drawn, suddenly, to the colors in the west. They blazed through the trees, all but smoking. Because he was usually in the canteen, he hadn't seen a full sunset since he'd been out here.

He crossed the meadow and took the path north toward the recreation hall, then cut west through rust-colored sumac and a cluster of pines. On the other side, granite boulders formed a natural valley to an outlook, where the lake view opened all the way to the sky. The sunset was like burning oil.

"Wow," Martin said. A grin that felt as wide as the view spread across his face. He took three careful steps toward the edge of the outlook, which sloped thirty feet toward the water, then sat on the rocky ground with his knees drawn to his chest.

"Pretty impressive, huh?" a voice to his right said.

Martin jumped, looked toward the voice, and saw Alyssa standing fifteen feet away. She flashed her flawless smile.

"You scared the shit out of me," he said.

"Sorry," Alyssa said, but the smile suggested she wasn't *too* sorry. She stepped away from the bushes that had mostly hidden her from view and sat on the rocks beside Martin, shimmying her butt until she was comfortable.

"I guess we had the same idea." Martin gestured at the sunset. The sky was a psychedelic blend of red and orange, shot through with ribbons of blushing cloud. The lake reflected it all and shimmered.

"Great minds think alike," Alyssa said. She inhaled and her face glowed. "I come out here most evenings, unless it's too cloudy to see anything."

"That would explain why you're not always at dinner."

"The sunsets are more . . . fulfilling." She considered this adjective for a moment, then nodded. "They remind me of my husband. We used to drive out of the city, watch the sun sink into the Old Line Valley. 'It's like sharing a dream,' Jackie would say. The winter sunsets were the best, with the snow on the ground and the sky so pink."

"Beautiful," Martin said. He couldn't remember ever stealing ten minutes to watch a sunset with Laura. Such a small demand on his time. Such a huge return.

"He was shot by a policeman while reaching for his wallet," Alyssa said. Her eyes flickered momentarily, catching the colors. "It's never been easy for black people, but that was a particularly hard time. It seemed there were more folks than usual being shot or roughhoused by police. It got to be that the *good* cops feared recriminations and drew their firearms quicker than usual. So most of that bloodshed was fueled by fear—on *both* sides."

"That's usually how it works," Martin said.

"There was public outcry . . . riots. There were football players kneeling during the anthem, protesting the bodies in the street. Un-American or pro-American, you take your pick. All I know is that Jackie was one of the bodies."

"I'm so sorry to hear that," Martin said, and he was—he knew what it was like to lose a spouse so unfairly—but he was also taken aback by Alyssa's disregard for the rules. *We do not share our pains with others,* Mother Moon had said, making a point to single this rule out from the others. Nobody else on the island had even hinted at their pain. For Alyssa to do it, and so soon into their conversation, caught Martin off guard.

"So here I am," she continued. "I figured I'd come out here for a couple of months, find my inner calm, then go back home. That was nearly two years ago."

"You must like it here."

"I do. I have all the things I need and none of the things I don't. And let me tell you, it's a good feeling to put my head down at night and know that I'm safe."

Alyssa's skin was so smooth it was difficult to determine her age. Martin might have guessed late twenties, but the gray threads along her brow suggested she might be tucked into her forties. Not that it mattered. She was beautiful, and the sunset brought a blush to her face that made it difficult to turn away.

"So what brings you here?" she asked. Maybe it was the reflection of the red sky, but he thought he saw a touch of mischief in her eyes.

"You're just a rebel, huh?"

"You don't really know someone until you know their pains."

"Very true." A gull hooked overhead, its voice abrasive. Martin looked at it—watched it disappear into the sun-glare—and wondered where to start. "An accumulation of things: not feeling safe, worried about my girls' future, unfulfilled professionally, disillusioned emotionally. I felt these things for a long time, but they were really brought home when my wife was killed in a school shooting."

"Oh, hon." She touched his forearm lightly. It was a sweet, instinctive gesture. She knew his pain, after all.

"You don't recover," Martin said. "You don't heal. Not fully."

"Never," Alyssa agreed.

"But you arrive at a point where you know you have to move forward. There's no choice *but* to move forward, right?"

"Right."

"And I wanted to do that with a more solid foundation, to give my girls a hopeful look at life. But that's next to impossible when you turn on the TV or go online and see so much fear and anger everywhere. Then the opportunity to come here—to escape all of that—presented itself, and I decided to give it a shot."

"Recharge your batteries, huh?"

"Right. And it seems to be working. I mean, I *like* it here. It's basic but rewarding, and the girls are doing better than I could have hoped."

"Edith's great," Alyssa said, showing her beautiful smile again. "A little introverted at times, but such an adorable girl."

"Yeah, she can get lost in her own thoughts. And Shirley . . . hey, I was concerned for her back at home—she had some dark moments—but she's really broken out of her shell."

"I haven't spoken to her much," Alyssa said. "She's quite attached to Mother Moon."

"I wasn't sure what to make of that to begin with. But Mother Moon is having a positive effect on her, so I'm reluctant to intervene. I guess Shirley has found the strong female influence she was looking for, and that she *needs*."

"Everybody loves Mother Moon," Alyssa said. "But don't let Shirley drift too far. Every now and then Mother Moon has her 'pets'—people who latch onto her, and follow her like shadows. Then all of a sudden they leave the island. Never to be seen again. Has a kind of black-widow feel to it."

"Okay," Martin said. "That's worth bearing in mind."

"And sweet as she is, Mother Moon has her moments, for sure. I've known her to lock herself in her cabin for a whole week. And there are times she just disappears—goes back to the mainland. She can be gone for up to a month."

"Where does she go?"

"On a pilgrimage for Glam Moon," Alyssa replied. "That's what she says, although I have no idea what that actually means. She always comes back thin and pale, though, like she's been through some ordeal."

"It's her religion," Martin said. "Maybe she fasts, or wanders the land like Caine in *Kung Fu*."

"Who knows?" Alyssa smiled and looked at the fading sunset. The first stars glimmered in the darkness overhead. "I wouldn't deny a person their faith, but personally I've never bought into the Glam Moon thing. It sounds like an acid trip Mother Moon had when she was younger."

"I thought the same thing," Martin said. "A mental Shangri-La."

"Right. But it's given the people here something to believe in, even if it *is* only a state of mind."

Martin crossed his arms and looked at the waves chattering against the shore. Only the crests of them were visible in the gloom. "Each to their own, right? I have nothing against their beliefs other than a mild wariness that it might all go Jonestown. Or maybe I'm just determined to find a catch."

"What do you mean?"

"This place is too good to be true," Martin said. "There *has* to be a catch."

"Well, hon, I've been living here for nearly two years, and if there's a catch—other than Mother Moon being kind of odd from time to time, and the toilet seat being too damn cold in the winter—I haven't found it."

The sunset had darkened to a wine spill on the horizon. Martin looked at it a moment longer, then turned and surveyed the trees behind him, crowded with shadow and moving stiffly in the breeze.

"We should go back," Alyssa said, getting to her feet, brushing dust from the backside of her jeans.

"Right," Martin said, also standing. "If we can find the way. Jesus, it's dark."

"Stay close to me," Alyssa said, and squeezed his arm gently. "I have a flashlight."

20

"Stay there a moment. No . . . turn your face toward me . . . a little more . . . yes, just like that. Oh, my. If only I had a camera."

"Why?"

"I swear, my darling, in this light—in the glow from the fire—you look at least twenty years old. Such a beautiful woman."

"Oh—"

"Like a star."

Shirley blushed all over and felt a quiver in her chest that temporarily stole her breath. She blinked slowly, imagining her eyelashes long and curled—the lashes of a twenty-year-old *Vogue* or *Elle* model. Her lips felt plusher and pinker than usual.

"Beautiful," Mother Moon said again.

"Thank you."

"You'll be a queen in Glam Moon."

They had spent most of the day together. It was only

supposed to be an hour or so, but time mounted its wild horse and galloped away from them. Shirley had taken care of her few duties—making Mother Moon's bed, bringing the firewood in, reading from *The Breathing Verse* while Mother Moon reclined on her sofa—and then the two of them had gone for a stroll across the island. They talked about womanly fortitude, the dark mainland, and of course Glam Moon. When they reached the northwest edge of the island, where the rock face dropped seventy-five feet to the water below, Mother Moon threw her arms wide and cried out jubilantly. Her hair flew in the wind and her skin glowed. She looked primal. "You try," she said to Shirley, and Shirley did. She cried until her throat cracked and she thought the wind might get beneath her arms and lift her like a gull. It was invigorating.

"The island loves you," Mother Moon said as they walked back. "I can *feel* it. And here . . ." She dropped to her haunches, scooped up a palmful of cold dirt, and smeared it across Shirley's cheek. "Now its mark is on you."

"I feel stronger here," Shirley said.

Back at Mother Moon's cabin, Shirley had started a fire and they sat on the rug in front of it, very close beneath one blanket. They spent a long moment watching the flames crawl and curl. The first log had burned through before either of them spoke, and as usual the topic was Glam Moon.

"Can you really fly there?"

"Some of us can. Those who hold a special place, which you earn over time or by other means."

"Other means?"

"Glam Moon follows the basic principle of love: the more you sacrifice, the greater your reward."

"I'd want everything."

"The martyr earns her wings early." Mother Moon played with the black tufts of Shirley's hair, then trailed one finger to the dirt still streaked across her cheek. "You should know, sweetheart, that there's always a price to pay."

They watched the fire, huddling closer beneath the blanket. Shirley yawned and rested her head against Mother Moon's shoulder.

"It sounds like Edith's garden."

Mother Moon took a breath and held it. "What do you mean?"

"Edith has . . . psychological issues. She shelters herself by going to this place in her mind. She calls it her garden. It has warm rivers and silver flowers. She says she can breathe underwater there."

"And how does she get to this garden?"

"She just goes."

Mother Moon exhaled, but her body had stiffened and Shirley needed to adjust her head to get comfortable. Within minutes she was sleeping, and so the time galloped away. It was when she woke up and got to her feet that Mother Moon said she looked at least twenty years old.

Shirley turned from the fire, with its flattering glow, to the window and said, "I should probably go." The light had a softened quality. It was late afternoon. Her dad would be looking for her.

"Not yet," Mother Moon said. She took *The Breathing*

Verse from the side table and handed it to Shirley. "Another poem. One more."

Shirley read to Mother Moon every day, usually two or three chapters. They'd just finished Alice Walker's *The Color Purple* and now it was on to this book of selected poems—Mother Moon's favorite. She asked that Shirley open the book at random and begin reading, and if she read the same poem twice that was fine.

Shirley opened the book and read a free verse poem called "Little Bird," and when she finished there were tears on Mother Moon's cheeks.

"You read like small bells chiming. I feel it all the way deep. You bring happiness to everything, Shirley. Has anybody ever told you that?"

"I don't think so."

Mother Moon stepped toward her, removed the book from her hands, brushed black feathers of hair from her brow. "So pretty. Such a special young woman."

Shirley's heart trembled like something trapped.

"I should kiss you now," Mother Moon said.

"Yes," Shirley said. "You should."

Mother Moon leaned into Shirley and pressed her mouth to the girl's cheek where the dirt was smeared. She kissed her once there and again closer to the lips.

"I'm so happy you're here."

"I am, too."

Shirley left, stepping into the soft light with the island's mark faint on her face and the pressure of Mother Moon's kiss clearer and warmer.

* * *

Shirley spent more time with Mother Moon over the next week or so, to the point where Martin could go most of the day without seeing her. He asked her about it, not in a challenging way, but out of curiosity.

"She's my friend," Shirley said. "I enjoy spending time with her."

"What do you talk about?"

"All kinds of things. The island, the mainland . . ."

"You ever talk about Mom?"

"Never."

"Glam Moon?"

"Sometimes."

Martin suspected it was more often than *sometimes*. He frequently heard Shirley reference the Glam, not as passionately as some, but with enough conviction to make him think she was buying into Mother Moon's imaginary world. It bothered him more than it should. He wondered if he'd feel differently if Shirley announced that she'd found God and that heaven was her eternal reward. How was Glam Moon any different?

"It has more of a cult feel to it," Alyssa said when he'd posed the question to her. "Now there's a four-letter-word that'll strike fear into the heart of any reasonable-thinking person."

"But it's *not* a cult . . . right?"

"No, hon. It's a daydream."

Not unlike Edith, then, who still spent too much time in her own version of Glam Moon. Martin sometimes felt that the reality he was living in was so thin that he might fall right through.

Another week slipped behind them, full of lazy mornings, wholesome food, and poetic sunsets. Martin's list of the things he missed shrank to only four items, while his friendship with Alyssa deepened. Nothing romantic—he wasn't ready for that yet—although it'd be foolish to deny there wasn't a *little* romance in their meeting to watch the sun go down, and sometimes they did so holding hands.

Edith took Spanish lessons with Brooke and—as with everything else—excelled. Shirley amazed Martin by identifying not only the constellations but their prominent stars. Martin, for his part, took piano lessons. He told himself it was because he'd always wanted to play "Imagine" by John Lennon, and not because he wanted to spend more time with Alyssa.

Island life was good.

Mostly.

"Do you know what's inside the box?" Martin asked Alyssa one afternoon. They were playing Scrabble in his cabin. Edith had played for twenty minutes before getting bored and taking her guitar onto the front step. Shirley—no surprise—was with Mother Moon.

"The box?" Alyssa asked.

"The lockbox. In Mother Moon's cabin. The one with the watch inside it."

"Okay, gotcha," Alyssa said, rearranging the tiles on her

holder. "I'll take a wild guess and say . . . a watch?"

"Genius," Martin said, and smiled. "I mean *in addition to* the watch. The lockbox has a false bottom that she's using to hide something else. I just wondered if you knew what it was."

"I don't, but it's probably jewelry or something of sentimental value. We all have our little mementos." Alyssa gestured at Laura's ring dangling from the chain around Martin's neck, and at her own wedding ring, still on her finger.

"You're probably right," Martin said. He played the word *COVE,* added up the points, then said, "You know, we've been here almost a month, which means our six-week probationary period is coming to an end. If it was just me, that'd be fine, but I have to look out for my girls. I'm looking for reasons to leave as much as reasons to stay."

"Makes sense."

"And there are a few things that don't sit right with me. The whole Glam Moon thing, obviously. Then there's the weird little rules—the secrecy. I'm sure it's all about maintaining peace and order, but I can't help but think that something is being covered up."

Alyssa tacked a *D* onto *SHAPE,* logged a cool twenty-four points, and drew another tile. In the stillness they heard Edith playing her guitar on the front step—soft, melodic notes, the perfect accompaniment to the silver light streaming through the windows.

"And finally there's the lockbox," Martin said. "I keep thinking about it—wondering what Mother Moon is hiding. And sure, it could be some kind of memento or keepsake, but why lock it up? No one here is going to steal it."

“You know what I think: that you’re still looking for the catch.” Alyssa looked at him earnestly. “It’s okay to chill, you know.”

“I want to,” Martin said. “And hey, maybe my unease is fueled by the dream I had.”

“What dream?”

Martin sighed, rubbed his eyes, and said, “Laura was in it. She took me to Mother Moon’s cabin and opened the box for me to look inside. There was the watch and the false bottom . . . and underneath it was a bullet. So now I think—actually, I’m almost *certain*—there’s a gun inside. A small pistol. Which changes the complexion of everything this island stands for.”

“You’re going down a wild and wayward path here,” Alyssa said. “I’m sure that dream felt real and painful, hon, but it *was* only a dream, not a premonition.”

Martin’s eyes flicked to the window, where he could just see the back of Edith’s head as she played her guitar. He wondered what she would say about that.

“I like it here,” he said. “The girls like it here. We’re not ready to go home, but I’d feel so much better about everything—especially Shirley’s closeness to Mother Moon—if I knew what was inside that box.”

“She keeps it locked, though,” Alyssa said. “And if she’s hiding something, she isn’t likely to show you on request.”

“True, but the key is in a drawer in her bedroom. I bet I could find it in twenty seconds.”

“You’re going to break into her cabin?”

“There’s a difference between breaking in,” Martin said, “and taking a look around when she’s not there.”

"Jesus, that's risky." Alyssa looked at him with narrowed eyes. "That's a violation of her privacy. If she finds out, you're off the island. No coming back."

"I know that, but didn't you say that Mother Moon leaves the island every now and then—that she can be gone for up to a month at a time?"

"Yeah, but who knows when she'll leave next? And she always locks her cabin when she goes on those pilgrimages."

Edith changed tunes—something upbeat, strumming the strings and occasionally dampening them to add a percussive beat. Alyssa cocked her ear, smiling and nodding.

"Palm muting," she said. "I taught her that technique yesterday. Your daughter's a natural."

"She loses herself in whatever she turns her mind to," Martin said. "It can be hard to draw her out again."

They listened a moment longer, each placing a word on the board and tallying their score. Alyssa shuffled her tiles, then reached across the table and clasped Martin's hand.

"Listen, hon, if you're serious about this, you can always do it at dinnertime. Most everybody on the island is in the canteen, including Mother Moon. Also, it wouldn't be unusual if we weren't there because we occasionally watch the sunset together."

"We?"

"I'd be your lookout." Alyssa let go of his hand but held him with her gaze. "If for any reason Mother Moon leaves early, I'll knock on the window so you can get the hell out of there."

Martin frowned and sat back in his seat. "You'd do that?"

"Hey, if we *both* get thrown off the island, you're giving me a place to live." Alyssa smiled, then spread her hands. "If you really can't relax until you find out what's inside the box, this might be your best chance. But do me a favor: after you find it's a trinket or an old love letter, give yourself permission to chill out and enjoy the island."

"I will."

"Cross your heart?"

Martin drew an *X* on the left side of his chest. "So when do we do this?"

"The next beautiful sunset, I guess."

"Okay." Martin nodded. "It's on."

Edith stopped playing and for a moment the only sound was the breeze rushing around the cabin and the clicking of Scrabble tiles. Martin looked from the half-complete board to Alyssa. She tipped a wink and whispered, "I guess I'm not the only rebel, huh?"

Martin returned the wink, then added three letters to *COVE* and made *UNCOVER*.

21

They got their sunset three days later. An amazing purple and gold shock across the horizon. It would have been wonderful to watch the colors spread and melt into the lake, but Martin had no regrets.

"There'll be more sunsets," he said, "once my curiosity is settled."

They sat on the front steps of Alyssa's cabin and waited for Mother Moon to leave for dinner. She did so as the trees in the west flared with rich light. Shirley was with her.

"Hi, Dad," she said as they walked past. "Are you eating with us tonight?"

"We were just discussing that," Martin replied with a smile. "We're both hungry, but that sunset is very tempting."

"It *is* special," Mother Moon agreed, and her green eyes shone. "But it's eggplant parmesan tonight. One of Joseph's specialties."

Alyssa said, "Save some for us."

They waited until Shirley and Mother Moon were out of

sight, then Alyssa went to her position: in the deep shade of an oak that offered a view of the canteen. The pathway leading to it was illuminated by solar-powered lamps. If Alyssa saw Mother Moon returning down the pathway, she would cut through the trees and rap on the cabin's window, giving Martin two minutes—maybe—to get out.

Martin, meanwhile, had approached Mother Moon's cabin. There were a few islanders making their way toward the canteen, none of them paying him any attention. Nonetheless, he waited until the coast was clear before springing up Mother Moon's front steps. The door wasn't locked (Mother Moon only locked it when she went off-community). He opened it and slipped inside.

"Okay," he said, giving his eyes a moment to adjust to the gloom. It was warm. *Welcoming* was the word that came to mind, although Martin didn't think Mother Moon would be altogether welcoming if she discovered him there. Ashes glowed in the fireplace. There was a blanket on the floor in front of it. He had an uncomfortable vision of Shirley and Mother Moon huddled romantically beneath it but shut this quickly out of his mind. The whole point of this little adventure was to make him feel better about Mother Moon and the island, not to invent a scenario in which he felt worse.

He took Alyssa's flashlight from his jacket pocket (interior lights would alert other islanders; everybody flicked the switch when they walked out the door) but didn't turn it on until he'd navigated into the bedroom. He stepped carefully to avoid bumping into anything, assuming that Mother Moon would notice even the slightest thing out of place. It was dimmer still in the bedroom—the one window being smaller and east-facing. Martin muted the flashlight's glow by spreading his fingers over the lens, wanting to reduce the chance of it being seen from outside. He shone its meek light around the room, looking for anything with a drawer. The walls were mustard-yellow, hung with paintings of birds and trees. The dreamcatcher above the bed looked frayed and faded enough to have caught some of Victoria Platt-Mellor's dreams. Martin adjusted his fingers, allowing a little more light, and stepped deeper into the room. He saw two nightstands with a small drawer in each. There was an armoire with a heavy drawer in the bottom, and a three-drawer dresser beneath the window. The middle drawer was partly open, jutting like a crooked tooth.

Martin nodded. He recalled the sound of a drawer opening and sticking closed when Mother Moon had fetched the key. He stepped to the dresser, eased the middle drawer open, and shone the flashlight inside. It was full of neatly folded scarves and sweaters. Martin lifted the items carefully, searched the corners, but there was no key.

"Shit."

This was going to take longer than he'd hoped. Still, there was time: fifteen, maybe twenty minutes, depending on how quickly Mother Moon scarfed down Joe's eggplant parm. And hey, if she liked it so much, she might go for seconds.

He left the middle drawer exactly how he'd found it—jutting like a crooked tooth. The top drawer was home to dozens of pairs of balled-up socks and panties. Most were of the passion-killer variety, but there were a few negligees and lacy thongs, proving that Mother Moon still had a pulse into her fifties—and good on her, Martin thought. Again, he sorted through the contents carefully, telling himself that he was violating Mother Moon's privacy for all the right reasons.

He found nothing of interest in the top drawer, so moved down to the bottom. This had in it an assortment of items, including thick winter wear, an old pair of shoes, and a lace corset that matched some of Mother Moon's more risqué underwear.

No key, but beneath the corset—

"What the fuck?"

Of all the things he'd imagined discovering in Mother Moon's drawers—pornographic materials, illicit chocolate bars, a cell phone with internet access—a latex tiger mask was not on the list.

"Well, shit. That's . . . different."

It was incredibly detailed. Beautiful, even—a full over-the-head mask with two small eyeholes and a narrow slit to breathe through. Martin took it from the drawer and held it close to his face. The filtered light glimmered off its orange and black markings.

"You come out at Halloween?" Martin asked, then twisted his wrist to shake the tiger's head. No, Halloween had been and gone. There was no trick or treating on the island.

So what was it for? General high jinks? Or maybe some kind of sex thing? Was this what the man—or woman—wore when Mother Moon strapped herself into that lace corset?

Probably. And yes it was unusual. Yes it was kinky. But it wasn't a reason to leave the island.

"Back in your drawer, you bad ol' putty tat." Martin returned the mask face-up and placed the corset on top. He gently closed the drawer, then crept to the nightstand on the left side of the bed. He found some coins, an empty locket, three pens, a box of Tylenol, a tube of lubricant. He went around to the adjacent nightstand, opened the small drawer (it stuck a little—a good sign, he thought) and directed the flashlight inside. He saw the key at once. Its brass bow poked from between the pages of a fat paperback like a bookmark.

"Got you."

He made a mental note of the page number and slid the key out, then slunk back through the bedroom to the main living area. His heart had been running hard since he'd seen Mother Moon and Shirley leave for dinner, but now it really picked up the pace. He sneaked to where the lockbox sat on the side table. It was turned backward, he noted, with the keyhole facing the rear corner of the room. Martin swiveled it and slipped the key into the brass-lined hole. There was a split second where he wondered if he had the right key—he hadn't checked the drawer in the armoire, and there was every possibility Mother Moon had found a new hiding spot—then he heard the satisfying *snick* of the lock disengaging.

One glance toward the window, as if expecting Alyssa to rap her knuckles against it. A collar of sweat glistened on the back of his neck. He wiped it away and opened the box.

The watch didn't interest him, and it didn't matter that he hadn't seen one—or any kind of time display—for over a month. He removed it, placed it on the table, and focused the flashlight on the box's false bottom. He recalled how it had wobbled when Mother Moon put the watch back inside. He tapped against it and felt the give, then pressed against the edges until he found the sweet spot. One corner popped up enough for him to hook his finger beneath. He pulled the false bottom out and looked at what it had been hiding.

The flashlight caught a glimmer of metal and he thought for one heart-stopping moment that it *was* a bullet—that his dream had been a premonition after all. Furthermore, when he looked up he would see Laura standing over him with her dead face hanging and old leaves tangled in her hair. A chill rattled through him, then he noticed that it wasn't a bullet in the lockbox, and it wasn't a gun, either.

It was a ring.

"Okay," he said. He didn't know whether to be relieved or disappointed.

This was no dainty woman's ring, though. It didn't mark an engagement or marriage. It was a dull, unpolished gold, as clunky as a Super Bowl ring but without the showiness. Martin took it out and examined it in the flashlight's glare. Maybe it had belonged to Mother Moon's ex-boyfriend (*Pace,* Martin thought, the name drifting from the back of his mind), or even to Bernard Platt-Mellor. It had a menacing, *old* feel to it. There was a green eye on the front, not unlike the Eye of Providence. The inscription was dark with corrosion, making it easier to read.

"*Derevaun Seraun.*" He didn't know what that meant—he assumed it was Latin—but speaking the words out loud made him feel miserable inside. It brought to mind incantations, burning candles, pentagrams. He imagined a muscular man in a tiger's mask readying an altar for sacrifice.

Whatever the phrase meant, Martin didn't care for it at all. He didn't care for the ring, either; he dropped it back inside the lockbox with a mutter of distaste, as if he were flicking a booger from the tip of his finger. He had no idea why Mother Moon kept it locked away. As far as he was concerned, it should be at the bottom of the lake.

He shook his head and wiped more sweat from the back of his neck. As he picked up the false bottom to slip it back into position, Alyssa rapped her knuckles twice against the window—a crisp, no-nonsense warning that fired his heart into his throat like a cannonball.

"Oh, *shit*!"

Martin toppled onto his ass, dropped the false bottom. It took a moment to find it in the flashlight's meager glare. He had to widen his fingers over the lens to allow more light, then he saw it nestled in the shadow of the sofa. He snatched it up and jammed it into the box. He couldn't get it to fit at first, rotating it one way, then the other, until it dropped into position.

He looked at the door. How long would it take Mother Moon to make her way down the pathway to her cabin? They'd estimated two minutes, but what if she was in a hurry? She'd wolfed down her dinner quickly enough. No seconds for Mother Moon, not tonight.

"Don't even think about it," Martin hissed. "Just get the hell out."

He closed the box, locked it, swiveled it so that the keyhole faced the rear corner. All good, but shit *no*—he'd taken three steps toward the bedroom when he realized he'd forgotten to put the watch back inside. His heart lurched again and he stumbled back to the box. The key jittered around the hole for agonizing seconds before slotting in. He cranked it, flipped the lid, placed the watch inside. Then he locked the box again and rotated it into the correct position.

Okay, *now* it was all good. Martin looked at the door again, praying it didn't swing open, that he still had some time. He scampered across the living room, tripping on one of the rugs and rucking it up. He went back and straightened it out, then swept into the bedroom and over to the nightstand. The drawer was still open.

"Three sixty-eight," he gasped, riffling through the paperback's pages. He tried not to imagine what Mother Moon would do if she found him here. Kick him off the island, for sure, an embarrassment to everybody, especially his daughters. A dark corner of his mind provided a more austere punishment: laid across an altar while Mother Moon and the other islanders—Shirley among them—danced naked around him, chanting "*Derevaun Seraun*" and drinking rooster blood, their shadows long and wolf-shaped in the flickering candlelight.

Martin found page 368 and pushed the key inside, leaving the bow poking out like a bookmark. Then he closed the drawer. Or *tried* to close it. Of course it stuck. He jiggled it, gasping, sweat dripping off his jaw and onto his shirt.

"Come on, you bastard."

He heard the distinct thud of footfalls on the wooden steps, followed by the creak of the doorknob turning. *Caught,* he thought. *And so damn close.* Excuses raced through his mind. He felt like a child again, inventing a thousand elaborate fabrications to avoid being punished. Before the door opened, though, he heard Alyssa's voice—

"Mother Moon, I wonder if I could—"

More like the voice of an angel; she had stalled Mother Moon at the door, trying to buy Martin a little more time.

"Good girl," he whispered, finally working the drawer closed. He took one last look around to see that everything was more or less as he left it, then skipped around the bed to the window. He slid it open, hopped onto the sill, and all but fell outside. A deep throb of pain burst from his injured knee when he landed. Swearing under his breath, he reached up and pushed the window closed, then hobbled around the side of the cabin and melted into the gloom.

22

"Was it a gun?"

"No, it was a ring. A man's ring."

"Okay, then—"

"But it wasn't anything you'd ever want to wear. It felt *ancient*, somehow. And dirty. Like some kind of cult or secret society ring."

They were in Alyssa's cabin, which she'd once shared with a lady named Doris, but the second bedroom had remained empty since Doris returned to the mainland. There was no chance of them being interrupted or overheard, but they kept their voices low, just the same.

"It belonged to a man, though," Alyssa said, sitting back in her chair and folding her arms. "So it's not Mother Moon's ring."

"True, but she wouldn't keep it locked up if it didn't mean something to her." Martin sighed and ran his hands down his face. They were still trembling. "Honestly, I didn't get a good feeling from it. And there was an inscription:

Derevaun Seraun. Any idea what that means?"

"No."

"Me, either." He shook his head and gave Alyssa a weak smile. "Jesus, with Google I could find out in two seconds."

After stumbling away from Mother Moon's cabin, Martin had huddled in the woods until his heart rate dropped a couple of notches and his breathing evened out. By this time, some of the other islanders had returned from dinner and assumed their positions in the meadow. Martin joined them. He called out constellations and sang Cat Stevens songs. At some point, he felt a hand slide inside his own: Alyssa. He squeezed gratefully. Back at her cabin, he'd thanked her for saving his ass. She made him a hot drink with chamomile to help calm his nerves. He drank it quickly, with noisy slurps.

"It's fair to assume," he said now, looking down at the empty mug, "that Mother Moon is linked in some way to that ring. Do you agree?

"I agree."

"It could even be the reason for her odd behavior—why she disappears every now and then."

"Could be."

"If we can find out more about it—and about that inscription—then we'll know more about Mother Moon." Martin opened his hands and shrugged. "With her being so close to my daughter, that may not be a bad thing."

"Well, you have two choices," Alyssa said. "You can ask Mother Moon directly, which I don't recommend because she'll know you've been snooping—"

"Right."

"Or you can leave the island. But if you do that, there's no coming back."

"She's got her bases covered, huh?"

"There *is* a third choice."

"I'm listening."

"You can just let this go."

Martin recalled the dull weight of the ring, and how bleak he'd felt when he read the inscription. "I'm not sure I can do that."

"Then you need to ask yourself," Alyssa said, leaning forward, her shadow spreading across the wall. "Is this enough for you to want to leave?"

Martin sat silently while any number of images raced through his mind, from Shirley sitting beside the well—*It won't be happy until I throw myself in*—to a latex tiger mask staring at him in the gloom. He looked at Alyssa. She reached out. He took her hand.

"I don't know," he whispered, and in the next breath she was in his arms. Her closeness was the comfort he needed. "I really don't."

Martin had told Alyssa that he was looking for reasons to leave as much as reasons to stay. He imagined an old-fashioned balancing scale, with everything he loved about the island on one side, and the things he wasn't so jazzed about on the other. These were fewer, but heavier, with the ring being heaviest of all. Once added, the scale tipped one way, then the other. It vacillated for several days, causing Martin to lose both focus and sleep. Recalling Jimmy's warning finally settled it, though. *I hope you find some peace, brother. And if it all begins to feel a little weird, get the hell out of there.* And that was the key word: *weird.* The ring wasn't immediately dangerous, like a gun, or threatening, like a bullet (although that odd inscription sent a chill rushing through Martin whenever he thought of it), but it was unquestionably *weird.*

"I've decided to go home," he said to Alyssa. It was a chilly November evening, their faces turned to another fiery sunset. "I don't want to, but—"

"I understand," Alyssa said. She took his hand. "I'm going to miss you. Edith, too."

"I'll give you my address," Martin said. "If you ever decide you've had enough of these amazing sunsets, and that you want to get back into the grind—"

"I'll look you up," she said. "Count on it."

He spent the next twenty-four hours wondering how he would break it to Shirley, who, after only five weeks, was as much a part of the island as the trees and cabins. It was great that she had adapted so naturally, but taking her away could prove problematic. She was a sensitive young woman. The back and forth would be hard on her, not to mention unfair. She might never forgive Martin—a notion that broke his heart in every way.

But thinking about Shirley, another option occurred to him: to negotiate. All he needed was to leave the island for long enough to do a little investigative work—to learn about the ring and the meaning of that inscription, and in so doing learn more about Mother Moon. If everything checked out fine, they'd come back.

This meant Mother Moon bending the rules, which he wasn't sure she'd do. Not for *him*. But he was part of a three-way package that included Shirley, and for Shirley—her new "pet," to use Alyssa's expression—she might make an exception.

"My goodness, you're *radiant*. I don't mean to embarrass you, Martin, but you look like a different man."

"Thank you, Mother Moon."

"Leaner, healthier . . ."

"I feel great." He smiled, taking a seat beside the lockbox he'd deviously peeked inside. He imagined the ring in there, pulsing in the darkness like a fat spider beneath a floorboard, and moved over one seat. "I love the island—more than I expected to, if I'm being honest. The girls love it, too."

"And we love having you here." Mother Moon beamed, taking the seat opposite Martin. "You've brought, dare I say, a much-needed shot of exuberance to our community. Those girls . . . what bright lights they are."

"Thank you. I'm extremely proud of them."

Mother Moon nodded and poured him a glass of water, cold and delightful, drawn that morning from well number one. He'd drunk a lot of it since arriving on the island, which was one of the reasons he was leaner and healthier. He hadn't stepped on a scale, but he guessed he'd dropped at least fifteen pounds. The dad-bod was history.

"But you came to me for a reason," Mother Moon said, settling back into her seat and taking a sip from her own glass. "Let me guess: you love it here, but you've decided to go home anyway."

Martin fetched a deep breath and looked squarely at Mother Moon. Eye contact was critical here—a sign of honesty and trust. Fortunately, it was also easy. Mother Moon had such alluring eyes. Sometimes looking away was harder.

"Not exactly," he said.

She gestured for him to elaborate.

"I said from the beginning that we were only going to stay for six weeks. Maybe two months. That was our intention—to reset, then carry on. Obviously our thinking has changed, but I've left a lot of loose ends back at home."

"You and everybody else," Mother Moon said.

"I still have a house. My brother, who thinks I'll be home any day now, is dropping in a couple of times a week to make sure it hasn't burnt down." He had of course set Jimmy up as trustee on the house—an important detail that Mother Moon definitely didn't need to know. "My employers have kept my position open for me, and the girls are still enrolled at their respective schools, no doubt taking up places that could be filled by other children."

"So you want to go home and tie up those loose ends?"

"Right. They're hanging over me, and I'm finding it difficult to fully relax." He finished his water, set the empty glass down on the table, and fixed Mother Moon with a sincere expression. "All I need is four or five days. Maybe a week. I can quit my job, pull the girls out of school, put my house on the market—"

"Let me stop you right there." Mother Moon cut in. Her words had an edge but everything else about her was relaxed and appealing. "Everybody on this island, at some point, comes to me with the same request. They want a few days to sell their property or visit their loved one's grave for the last time. Or maybe they want to right some wrong with a sibling or friend. There's always something."

Martin nodded. He'd anticipated Mother Moon saying exactly this (he and Alyssa had improvised numerous scenarios) and it didn't faze him. He still had a couple of cards left to play.

"This is an all-or-nothing arrangement," Mother Moon continued. "I would never stop you from leaving. Go sell your house. Climb a mountain. Do whatever it is you've got to do. But there's no coming back. Not for anybody."

Except for you, Martin thought. *And Nolan.*

"We have rules for a reason." Her comfortable demeanor never faltered. "If I let you come back, then I'd have to do the same for Jake. Then Ainsley. Then Brooke. Before you know it, everything is coming apart at the seams. Trust me, Martin, I've been here before."

"You could say I left on a medical emergency," Martin suggested.

"That would be a lie. A deception." Mother Moon sat back in her seat, relaxed, in control. "We've no place for deception on Halcyon."

Martin's gaze flicked to the lockbox.

"I know you're worried about your house. But here's the thing: all those things you mentioned will sort themselves out. The bank will foreclose on your mortgage and sell your house for you, then your brother won't have to look after it anymore. Your employers will eventually realize you're not coming back and surrender your job to someone else. Same with the girls' schools. Everything you've mentioned will fix itself in time." Mother Moon leaned forward. If they were closer, she might have placed her hand on his knee, and he thought it would feel quite nice there. "The cold truth, Martin, is that everybody on the mainland is more concerned about their own lives than they are about yours."

"I know that," Martin said. "But I have a lot of money tied up in that house. My wife and I bought it after we were married, and we worked our asses off to pay the mortgage down. I don't want to lose it."

"I'm not asking you to," Mother Moon said. If she was at all concerned about the possibility of Shirley leaving, she didn't show it. "You've had your probationary period. This is where you ask yourself what's more important."

Martin poured himself another glass of water from the pitcher on the table. He wasn't as cool as Mother Moon, but he didn't spill a drop. Sitting back, he remembered something Nolan had said to him at Banjo McCoy's on the night they'd met. He couldn't recall it word for word, but it concerned Halcyon's income being supplemented by donations. Martin was no economist, but he knew that this way of life—the fuel, the mainland supplies, the building materials—couldn't be supported solely by selling vegetables, most of which they ate anyway. And with winter coming, the need for fuel and supplies—the need for money—would be greater.

It was time to play his first card.

"This is going to sound like a bribe," he said. He shrugged as if there was no way around that, then sipped his water and found Mother Moon's gaze again. "I want to make a monetary donation to the community, but I can't do that until I sell the house. Also, to be perfectly blunt, I'm not prepared to do that if I'm not living here."

Mother Moon narrowed her eyes and shifted in her seat—a subtle change in body language, but telling. He had her attention.

"A friend of mine is a lawyer," Martin continued. "I can set everything up with him, and get it done quickly."

"Are we negotiating, Martin?"

"I hope so."

"Even though my rules are nonnegotiable?"

"I believe we can benefit each other here."

She sipped her water, still incredibly cool, still in control. He thought she was going to say something, but she just held him with her eyes. If she were to roll her head from side to side, he'd probably follow, like a cat transfixed by a light.

"I'm hoping to find a way for us to stay," he said, breaking her gaze for long enough to set his glass down. "One that doesn't involve me losing tens of thousands of dollars on the house. We *want* to stay. We like it here." These things were true, as was the next thing: "Shirley is very fond of you."

There it was. His second card. The *Shirley* card.

"As I am of her." Mother Moon got to her feet and walked over to the window. The gray light emphasized the lines across her face, the auburn in her hair. She looked out at her island for a long time, lost in thought. When she spoke, her words had a distant, melancholic quality. "We sometimes get snow in November. That lake effect can come without warning. It unnerves people. Nobody wants to be stranded here like a character in a horror movie."

She smiled and looked at him. He got up, without being aware he was going to, and joined her at the window.

"We usually lose numbers around this time of year. Three or four people." She touched his arm gently. Her hair smelled of leaves and bark. "It's my favorite time, though. Those who stay come together. We eat steaming soups and drink spiced apple cider. We build great fires and huddle."

"Sounds wonderful," Martin said.

"Your timing is impeccable. We don't sell anything over the winter because we don't produce anything. To frustrate matters further, we burn through a lot more fuel. It's a financially challenging time. If Halcyon falls at all, it'll fall in the winter."

"So you depend on donations."

"Absolutely."

"Then let me help."

She looked at him, pouring light and sweetness from her face. He liked her, he really did—hoped like hell the ring meant nothing at all. *But why are you hiding it?* he thought. *Why the secrecy, Mother Moon?*

"I'll make you a deal," she said. "I think I can swing it because there are three of you."

"Go on."

"Take a few days. Go back to the mainland and tie up your loose ends. Then come back here and huddle with us."

Martin smiled. "I like the sound of that."

"We have a lawyer on the mainland who handles our donations. When you have the money, write a check, give it to Nolan, and he'll pass it on."

"I can do that."

"There's one condition."

The smile on Martin's face twitched. He raised one eyebrow.

"The girls stay here."

Martin stiffened, except for his jaw, which dropped an inch. He wanted to reply but his mind had flown into a dozen different directions.

"I don't think Shirley would go with you anyway," Mother Moon continued in a low voice, as if she didn't want to hurt his feelings. "And Edith will be fine. *More* than fine. It's only a few days, right? I'm sure Alyssa will happily take care of her." Her face suddenly lit from within. She touched Martin's arm again. "Oh, isn't she a *sweet* lady? I'm so happy you two have found a closeness in each other."

"We're just friends," Martin said distantly, then reined in his thoughts and brought the matter back to Edith and Shirley. "I'm not sure about this . . . they're my girls, it's—"

"Is it a trust thing?"

"No, it's—"

"Because if you don't trust us, why are we even having this conversation?"

She grinned to show that she was being playful, and Martin grinned to show that he understood that, but he didn't like the way it felt on his face—forced and desperate.

"No, it's not about trust. It's just . . . I haven't been away from them since their mother died." This was not true; they'd stayed with Jimmy and Felicity—several times, in fact—while he screamed at the sky and drank himself unconscious. "Edith is . . . sensitive. She suffers with night terrors. I'm just not—"

"She'll be fine. We can deal with this."

He nodded. Yes, they probably could. Edith hadn't had an incident since the school shooting, and Alyssa would happily take on a more parental role until he returned.

"I need to think about this," he said.

"We're negotiating, Martin. I'm meeting you in the middle."

"Right . . ."

"And this is the only way I can justify it to the others: that there are three of you, but only one third gets to leave and come back." She looked out the window again, nodding thoughtfully. "I can bend the rules here without setting a damaging precedent."

"I understand," Martin said. He scratched the back of his head. "Let me talk to the girls. See how they feel about this."

"That's a good idea." The coolness never left her voice. "Let me know what you want to do."

"Thank you for listening."

"I did more than listen; I acquiesced." She looked at him, still smiling. "You must have caught me in a good mood."

"When are you *not* in a good mood?"

"Oh, it happens." Her enticing eyes flared. "But most of the time I'm a ray of sunshine."

23

Nolan listened to Valerie while she explained the arrangement and her reasons for doing it. Yes, money was a powerful motivator—Martin was right to dangle *that* carrot, and his timing really was impeccable—but more importantly, him being off-community gave Valerie a window to get some one-on-one with the other daughter.

"She has something," Valerie said, but didn't elaborate.

Nolan nodded, faithful as ever, trusting that, when she finally walked across the Skyway to Glam Moon, he'd be right beside her.

"When do I take him back?" he asked.

"Soon. Your next supply run, maybe."

"You want me to . . . ?" He ran the edge of his thumb across his throat.

"No. I need the girls. Both of them. If anything happens to their father, we might lose them. Not physically, but emotionally."

"Copy that."

"We'll take care of him later, but for now it all needs to stay calm."

"Should I follow him?"

"What if he sees you?"

"He won't."

"He *might,*" Valerie said. She considered for a moment, then shook her head. "No. We have his daughters. He's not going to try anything foolish. Besides, he knows nothing."

"Okay. If you trust him, I trust him."

She walked to the open space in front of the hearth—the space where she had shared moments, intimate and otherwise, with so many islanders over the years. Their faces floated into her mind, all of them broken, but given hope at the end, from Robert Dander and Jeffrey Myles (only one hand, but he used it like a champ), all the way up to Garrett Riley, Glenn Burdock (he liked the back of his balls licked, that one), and now Shirley Lovegrove. Yes, sweet, young Shirley, who curled at the edges when Valerie touched her in just the right way, and who had that look in her eyes—that filmy, *anything* look, simultaneously deep and shallow, like a reflection in an inch of water.

Devotion.

"I feel such peace," Valerie stretched out her arms, threw back her head, and twirled once. "Can you feel it, puppy?"

"I can't." Nolan cleared his throat. "I'm happy for you, though."

"It may not be a good thing." Valerie shook her head, then stared at the ashes in the fireplace. "I've loved two people in my life: that vile cunt Pacifico, and my grandma on my mother's side, Grandma Lucy, such a kind and caring woman. One day she got a nosebleed going up three floors in an elevator and it wouldn't stop gushing. Turns out she hadn't been telling anyone about the partial loss of vision or the crippling headaches—didn't want to worry them, she said—and when they ran her lovely old noggin through the scanner, they found a tumor the size of a man's fist. They operated but the damage was done. She experienced a lot of pain, memory loss, disorientation. She pissed and shat herself. What a fucking mess. And then, for a couple of weeks before she died, she went all Zen. She smiled all the time. She had all her faculties, she was sharp and funny. 'I'm perfectly at peace,' she would say."

Nolan nodded. "You're saying this is the calm before the storm?"

"Who knows?" Valerie shrugged. "But I *can* tell you that Grandma Lucy's final days were spent in agony. Oh, she screamed and screamed. My mom told me she was bleeding out of her eyes. Can you *imagine*?"

"Christ."

"But for a while it was just like this." Valerie looked away from the ashes, spread her arms, and twirled again. "All peace. All buttercups."

Martin had barely started talking when Shirley cut across him, "I'm *not* going back." She folded her arms and looked at him determinedly. "We just got here."

"It's been six weeks," Martin held his hands up in a defensive manner, as if Shirley were throwing stones instead of words. "I want to make sure you're happy here."

"Yes."

"You're not missing anything from home? Your cell phone? Your friends—"

"I've got a friend here." Shirley sat back in her seat. The sunlight streaming through their cabin window threw one side of her face into shadow. "I'm not ready to go home."

Martin nodded and turned to Edith. "How about you, sweetie? You want to stay?"

Edith shrugged. "I wish there were more kids here. I get bored sometimes, but I got bored at home, so . . ."

"The bad things don't bother Edith here," Shirley added. "They stay away. Everything's calmer."

"We can stay a little longer, I guess," Edith said.

"Okay. Good. I want to stay, too." Martin looked at Shirley when he said this. "But listen, I have to go back to the mainland to tie up some loose ends. Just for a few days, then I'll be back. Are you guys okay with that?"

"On your own?" Edith asked.

"Yeah." Martin took Edith's hand and squeezed gently. "Alyssa is going to look after you. I think she's got some cool things planned. Your sister's going to help her. Right, Shirl?"

"Right."

"It'll be fine, I promise." Martin gave Edith his most reassuring smile. "But if you don't want me to go . . ."

"No. You go. I'll be okay."

"We got this," Shirley said.

Three days later, Martin and Nolan walked down to the dock, where the center console waited to take them to the mainland. Alyssa and Edith were a few paces behind. They came to say goodbye.

"Hey, it's just a few days," Martin said while Nolan prepared the boat.

"I know," Edith said, but she threw herself into his arms and gave him the tightest squeeze.

"Listen," he said. "I asked Shirley to keep an eye on you, but really I want *you* to keep an eye on *her*. You dig?"

"I dig," she said. There were small tears in her eyes. "Don't worry, Dad."

He kissed the tip of her nose. "I love you, sweetheart."

"Love you, too."

He looked at Alyssa. She found some space in his arms.

"I hope you find what you're looking for," she said. "Come back to us, okay?"

"You know it."

She surprised him with a kiss. Soft and warm and very close to his lips. Edith pretended not to notice but she was grinning.

The center console started with a wet bark and a snarl. "Let's go, loverboy," Nolan shouted. Martin rolled his eyes and smiled. He stepped aboard, strapped himself into his lifejacket, and grabbed a seat. The boat pulled away from the dock in a clamor of engine sound. Martin waved at Alyssa and Edith, then looked at the gray expanse of water ahead.

I hope you find what you're looking for, he thought, and touched where Alyssa had kissed him. She wasn't talking about information, but peace of mind, and that was exactly what he was looking for. He wanted nothing more than to learn that the ring hidden in Mother Moon's lockbox was an old fraternity ring, and that *Derevaun Seraun* was Latin for *Keep Your Pants On.* If that was the case, he would hand Nolan a check for ten thousand dollars and return to the island—likely stay there with a peaceful, easy feeling until Shirley went to college. Or perhaps beyond.

If not . . .

Well, he didn't want to think about that.

He blew into his hands. It was cold on the open water, with icy spray stinging his face. Some ten miles south, the mainland lined the horizon like the tail of a huge, sleeping alligator.

It was November 18. Four days until Thanksgiving.

Five until Black Friday.

PART III
DEREVAUN SERAUN

24

Shirley said goodbye to her dad at their cabin, then went to Mother Moon's. She took care of her duties quickly. Mother Moon watched her while eating slices of apple dipped in chocolate spread—a little treat Nolan had brought from the mainland. She occasionally poked her finger in and invited Shirley to lick it off.

"Shhh," Mother Moon whispered. "Our little secret."

Afterward, Shirley read two chapters of Hemingway's *The Sun Also Rises*. Mother Moon listened in a state of bliss, lying on the rug in front of the fireplace, twisting her fingers—still sticky with chocolate spread—through her hair. She wore a bathrobe, the belt strapped loosely so that the robe was open in front. Shirley could see her underwear and the tops of her thighs. They were darkly veined and scarred. "Some would say they're ugly legs but to me they're beautiful," she once told Shirley. "Every scar denotes fortitude. If I could stitch them into wings, I would."

By early afternoon the sun had run behind heavy cloud

and the inside of Mother Moon's cabin dimmed. A fine rain misted the windows.

"Light a fire," Mother Moon said.

Shirley did.

It blazed in the hearth and threw light that brought the room to life. Mother Moon stood. She lowered the bathrobe to her waist, turning her back to Shirley. More scars laddered her spine, crisscrossed her shoulders.

"Count them."

Shirley did.

"Thirty-six."

"Yes. Just on my back. I have eighty-two scars on my body, including the ones on my head. Here . . ." She lowered her head, separating her hair to show Shirley the several pinkish scars, one of which was very large. "There are dents, too. Here . . ." And she took Shirley's hand and ran her fingers over the dips and divots in her skull.

"I've felt them before," Shirley said.

"Every knock and blemish is a part of who I am. Experience is made up of two parts: education and tribulation." Mother Moon pulled the robe over her shoulders and tied the belt, tighter this time. She looked at Shirley. "Education develops a woman. Always. Tribulation is different. It can unravel her, or give her armor."

"Yes."

"I chose the armor."

Sometimes, when Mother Moon spoke, Shirley felt a flame inside her, beneath her soul, that lifted her like a balloon, so that her posture straightened and she raised her chin and looked at the world from a higher place.

"The island is made up of unraveled people," Mother Moon continued. "I'm helping them become stronger. But strength is exhibited in the things we do—how we choose to shine. Sadly, not everybody has a light. I think you do."

"I think so, too."

Mother Moon sat in front of the fire. It crackled and snapped. The light turned her eyes into reddish cigar burns that looked like they might start smoking.

"Do you have scars, Shirley?"

"One," Shirley replied. "On my knee. I fell off a swing when I was five years old."

"Show me."

Shirley showed her, rolling up the left leg of her pants. Mother Moon looked at it with her glowing eyes and smiled. "One scar. But oh, you're young. Sixteen. Your destiny is still a blank canvas. You'll add color, in time."

Shirley rolled down her pants leg. She straightened and looked at Mother Moon longingly, as if the color might come from her.

"I wasn't much older when it started for me," Mother Moon said. "The pain, I mean. And every wound . . . every bruise and fracture was like a waypoint on my journey to Glam Moon. By the age of twenty-two I had traveled an unknowable distance and seen more light than there is in a thousand sunrises."

The rain had picked up. It bounced against the window. Shirley liked the sound. Not the thunder, though. It muttered in the distance, then boomed.

"It exists, you know," Mother Moon said. "It's real."

"I believe you."

Mother Moon nodded and looked into the flames. Shirley considered the storm, wondering if she should go and keep an eye on Edith, who might be afraid. Instead she sat beside Mother Moon. Just for a little longer, she told herself, because she liked the warmth. Their bodies were years—and scars—apart, but in the flickering firelight their shadows were identical.

"Who are you?" the dog had asked.

"Your new girl," Valerie replied. Eighteen years old, her legs sprinkled with sweat, her heart galloping inside her chest. She looked around the room, at the colorful paintings and hanging scrolls, the windows with their view across the Hackensack River. There was a chest against one wall, large enough to climb inside. An oval lantern floated from the ceiling like the cocoon of some fabulous moth.

She registered all this within seconds, but her attention was primarily given to the room's occupants—these eight men in their expensive suits and detailed animal masks.

"She's too young," the snake said.

"She's perfect," the tiger said. He got out of his seat and stepped toward her, a tall man with large hands and a narrow middle. He touched her face, running his heavy ring across her cheekbone.

"Raven K. is dead," Valerie said. "You've got me instead."

The tiger clasped her jaw, angling her face from one side to the other. "How old are you?"

"Twenty-one," Valerie said, pulling away from him.

"Liar!" the ox snorted.

"It's not a lie."

"Do you know who we are?" the tiger snapped.

Valerie closed her mouth quickly. Her nostrils flared with heavy breaths. "No. And I don't care, as long as the money is good."

"Money," the tiger said, and roared with laughter. The other animals did likewise. Some stomped their feet and pounded their fists across the walls. The room trembled.

"What's so funny?"

"Before long," the tiger said, "every new breath you take will feel like a million dollars."

His fist came from nowhere. It connected with the top of Valerie's head and knocked her down. She moaned and tried to get up, but couldn't. When she touched her head, her fingers came away bloody.

"What . . . ?" She looked disbelievingly at the blood, then up at the animals. They loomed above her in a wild circle.

"We are the Society of Pain," the tiger said.

"What? I don't—"

"*Derevaun Seraun,*" the snake cried, and this odd expression echoed around the room from many animal mouths, building in ferocity, until it became an animal sound: a growl or a howl or something equally inhuman.

Valerie pushed herself to one knee, then with a great effort managed to stand. Blood trickled into her left eye. She blinked it away as she reeled toward the door. "To hell . . . with you crazy fuckers." But the rabbit blocked her path. He squealed something and pushed her back into the middle of the room. She nearly fell again but the ox caught her. He tossed her to the rooster, who bounced her along to the pig.

"Let me go. *Let me—*"

"You're not going anywhere." She was pushed to the tiger, who grabbed her by the shoulders and turned her around. The goat stood in front of her. He had a hypodermic syringe in his hand. He stepped forward and thrust the needle into her neck. Her feet went numb first, then her knees. She folded and everything went black.

The last thing she was aware of was the tiger's voice, dim and scratchy, as if he were speaking over a phone line with a bad reception: "Put her in the box. Let's go eat." And then, vaguely, someone grabbing her ankles and dragging her across the floor.

It was April 28, 1982. She was in the upstairs room of the White Lantern in Engine City, New Jersey, where she would stay for the next four years.

Valerie came to inside the box. She pushed against the lid but it was secured with a padlock, a hefty one judging by its clunky, rattling sound. She screamed for help but none came. She wept and kicked at the lid with the soles of her feet, then changed position and pushed at it with the dome of her back.

It was dark and silent everywhere. The restaurant was closed. The dead of morning, then. Confused and terrified, she started to pray, and was answered many hours later by the sound of the padlock clattering against the latch. The lid opened. Light flooded in. She was pulled from the box and collapsed onto the floor, fetal, covering her eyes.

She peered through the cracks of her fingers and saw the animals. The rooster held a knife.

"No, no, oh God no—"

She crawled toward the door. Her arms and legs felt limp and weak and her head throbbed. The ox grabbed her by the upper arm and yanked her back.

"What do you *want* with me?"

"We're fetishists," the tiger responded calmly. "Paraphiliacs, if you want to be all fancy about it. Our kink is pain. Specifically, the pain of others."

The rooster coolly stepped toward her and flashed the knife across her thigh. Her skin opened in a thin red ribbon. She screamed, slapped her hand over it, watched the blood ooze through her fingers.

"Please . . ."

The rabbit pushed one hand inside his pants and started to rub himself.

I'm not getting out of this alive, she thought.

"Take her clothes off," the tiger said. "Let's see how many times we can cut her before she passes out."

Valerie was way ahead of them. Her eyes rolled upward into her skull and she dropped into a cold faint where she felt nothing and saw no light.

She rose from her faint to find the goat stitching the gash on her leg with a curved suture needle and black thread. His fingers were bloody. There was another wound, already stitched, on her right hip. Another just below her left armpit.

"Goat," she said groggily.

"These will heal soon," he said.

"We can mend broken bones, too," the dog said, spinning the ring on his finger. "This will go on and on."

"And on," the pig said.

"And on," the snake said.

Food came every other day. She was let out of the box to eat it. Bland Chinese food. Noodles. Rice. Chicken. Sometimes fish. She wolfed it down with grunts and snarls.

A fat Chinese man—the restaurateur, she supposed—brought it to her. He had a key to the padlock, but wasn't one of the eight. He was too short and overweight.

She mostly ate with her fingers but sometimes he brought chopsticks.

"The end of pleasure is pain," the tiger said. It was just the two of them. Valerie guessed it was Sunday morning; there was an absence of traffic noise and she thought she'd heard church bells, although that might have been something she'd dreamed. Not that it mattered. Friday, Tuesday, Sunday . . . every day was the same in this room.

"Take away the pleasure, only pain remains."

"Fuck you."

The tiger lounged on one of the sofas, wearing an open-throated shirt and Levi's. Valerie lay on the floor. They had broken her leg with a hammer and set it with a splint. She could barely move.

"Pain shows us what we can do, how much we can endure,

physically and spiritually. It's also a gateway. Think about it. Self-flagellation, asceticism, fasting, perceptual isolation . . . all rooted in pain, and all practiced for the acquirement of purity, enlightenment, heightened awareness . . ." The tiger crossed his legs. He wore expensive loafers, no socks, and appeared incredibly relaxed. "When pleasure is denied, the channel to new possibilities, and alternate experiences, becomes broader."

"I don't know what you're talking about," Valerie groaned. She licked her dry lips and slumped against the wall. One of her wounds started to bleed through its ugly black stitching.

"We've traveled the world in pursuit of pain," the tiger continued. "We've spoken to people who've lost limbs, beaten cancer, survived plane crashes. We've heard stories about epiphanies, spiritual awakenings, hallucinations, astral projection, psychic development. Several people—from different parts of the world—claimed to have crossed into an alternate dimension, a place of warmth and healing."

Valerie's eyes rolled toward the tiger. She didn't believe him, but what he'd said filled her with a deep and longing ache. It sounded like a way out. Perhaps her *only* way out.

"A different world," she said.

"So we've heard. The common theory is that it's a hallucination brought on by the release of DMT in the pineal gland." The tiger stood up, walked over to Valerie, and placed the sole of his loafer against her throat. "But what if it's more than that? What if this alternate world truly exists, and the only way in is through the absence of pleasure?"

* * *

She lost track of time quickly. Even the seasons—long, hot summer days and icy white winters—lost their relevance. That was an *outside* thing, beyond the room, a world she didn't belong to and couldn't reach. It was an America that didn't realize she was missing.

Her internal clock failed. She'd always been regular with her menstrual cycles but the physical and emotional trauma knocked everything out of line. She cramped and bled for weeks—months?—and then everything shut down. Her body, as well as her country, had become a thing she didn't know. She never forgot her name, where she was born, or the hateful face of her father, but in every other way she lost her identity, even her humanness.

A set of bamboo wind chimes outside the door announced their arrival. It was a mockingly bright sound that paradoxically came to encompass everything dark. Valerie heard it most days, usually more than once. The animals sometimes came alone but more often in twos and threes. Rooster and pig. Dog and snake. Tiger, goat, and rabbit. She might go a long time without seeing one of them, then they'd reappear and continue their torment without missing a beat. She eventually stopped paying attention to the frequency and combination of their visits. It didn't matter. It just *was.* Only those occasions when they were all present really registered. They were the worst.

Sometimes they had hammers, tire irons, or good old-fashioned baseball bats. One strike with a blunt, heavy instrument would usually break a bone (or two), or at the very least crack it. On other occasions they came with sharper tools:

knives, razor blades, scissors, chisels. They brought a nail gun once, one of several power tools Valerie saw during her four years in that room. The picana was a favorite device: a copper-tipped prong wired up to a car battery, administering high voltage, low current shocks, usually to her most sensitive areas. Valerie wondered if they produced this terrible apparatus on special occasions. Birthdays, perhaps, or Thanksgiving.

Most of the time they waited for her to heal—usually courtesy of Dr. Goat—before using another heavy-duty tool. But they weren't averse to building hurt on top of hurt, wound on top of wound.

We're fetishists, the tiger had said to her at the beginning of this nightmare. *Our kink is pain.* Their fascination with the subject was terrifying, whether they were trying to unlock a parallel dimension or explore—and thus understand—their appalling darkness. They partook and observed with equal measures of euphoria. It was sexual, too, of course. They rarely touched her, but frequently indulged in one another—sucking, jerking, and fucking. Except for the tiger, who kept his clothes on. The tiger was a watcher.

Her spirit withered, then died. Eventually they stopped locking her in the box and chained her to a ringbolt in the floor, and they even stopped doing this after a while. She was too weak to do much more than groan and drag herself around the room. Mostly, she slumped against the wall, smeared with her own piss and feces—at least until the restaurateur scrubbed it away. She tried the door on occasion but it was always locked. She even—in a rare moment of fortitude and anger, perhaps proving that her spirit wasn't completely dead—threw a chair against the window. The glass was reinforced, though. Probably soundproof, too. The chair bounced back into the room. Heartbreaking. At that point, she hadn't been looking to escape, but to throw herself thirty feet to the concrete below. Death was a way out, after all, and certainly more attainable than crossing into an alternate world.

Or so she thought.

The Society kept her alive. They meted out the pain and torture, taking her to the brink and then letting her heal. The goat cleaned and dressed her wounds. Infections were fought with antibiotics. They crammed white rice into her mouth when she couldn't—or wouldn't—eat, and poured water down her throat until she choked.

She couldn't live forever, though; the damage to her spirit was beyond healing. Death was the only thing she prayed for—and *to*. It offered peace, escape, an end to her suffering . . .

"Take me, please . . ."

It became her god, her salvation.

"Take me now."

And it was while praying to this strange but certain god that she noticed the split in the air. She was lying on her back staring up at the ceiling—at the lantern, in fact, glowing softly above her. The split flashed like a coin catching light. Her dry lips stopped moving and she stared at it for a long time, thinking it must be a small tear in the lantern's paper skin. Only it couldn't be, because it was clearly *beyond* the lantern, in the same way that the stars were beyond the sky.

She reached with one trembling hand. The split grew

steadily, from one inch to two . . . to four. And soon it wasn't the split that fascinated her; it was the blue sky beyond.

It had pull and shine.

Two things happened as the split lengthened to a rift. The pull: Valerie felt herself being lifted clear off the floor, levitating in midair with her legs hanging limply. The shine: she felt her spirit being revitalized, like a wilted flower in sunlight.

She reached with both hands. Tears leaked from her eyes, rolled to her ears, and plinked three feet to the floorboards below.

"What are you?"

The edges of the rift billowed. A cleaner, *different* air wafted over her skin, filled with aromas of water and peach. She continued to ascend, but slowly, and thought that any moment she would hear the chimes on the other side of the door—that bright, jingle-jangle music. The animals would return with their hammers and knives. They'd grab her ankles and drag her down, only this time she would fight.

The feeling was similar to the hypnic jerks she sometimes experienced on the edge of sleep—a sudden falling sensation, only this time she fell *upward.* She passed through the rift and everything was brighter. It was, in fact, *too* much, a sensory overload. Valerie could only huddle and absorb her new environment in tiny, manageable increments. She trembled and wept, as much with happiness as fear.

I made it out.

Yes, she did. But this wasn't death. The grass beneath her

was full and green. It had a sweet, wine-like scent. The flowers nearby shimmered. She crawled through them, inhaling aromas she had no name for. Their coppery stems brushed against her skin and she couldn't shake the feeling that they were reaching for her, as if to check if she was real. She did likewise. She stroked them, tasted her fingers. Small, delighted sounds escaped her lips for the first time in years.

There was a bone-white forest on the other side of the flowers. The trees were tall and regal and their branches danced. Now Valerie got to her feet. Her legs were stronger. She didn't shuffle or stagger. She *walked.* It felt strange to be perfectly upright, like a human.

Don't let this be a dream, she thought. *I don't ever want to leave this place.*

She touched the trees' white bark, her fingers trailing from one trunk to the next. Tears continued to stream from her eyes and she slapped them away, almost laughing now. She scampered to the next tree and threw her arms around it. "I'm not leaving here. I'm never leaving." She kissed the bark, rested her tired head against it. "Never . . . never." Then she whirled from the forest to the edge of a river. It ran clear and shallow. She drank like a deer then washed her face. Given everything she'd endured, there was no way she should feel as good—as strong—as she did.

She swept downriver to where it was deeper and dived in.

Deep. There was a mild current and she let it carry her. When she opened her eyes she saw exotic river weed and flickering fish. She kicked her legs and followed them, tiny bubbles rippling from her nose. She opened her lungs and breathed.

The water washed the blood and grime from her body. She finally emerged close to a waterfall that reached to some dizzying height and fell as white as milk. Valerie swam beneath it into a cave where large-winged moths glowed brightly. She wept with happiness.

The sun was three times larger and offered a softer warmth. It didn't sink to the horizon but faded gradually, until it was almost transparent. Concurrently, the moon brightened like a slow lamp, so huge she could count the craters.

She slept beneath a tree with softly swaying fronds, and woke in the morning with birds all around her. They chirruped and warbled, then hit the sky as one, a terrific, colorful blur.

I can do that, too, Valerie thought.

She learned to fly.

Counting sunfades, it took six days to learn, and then she only managed short distances. On her first attempt, she leaped from a high ledge over the river, arms out, and hit the water with a delighted squeal. She tried again and again, and eventually the time between leaving the ledge and hitting the water grew longer, only by a second or two.

And then three. And then four . . .

At some point—maybe on her thousandth attempt—she went up, not down.

She tried from the ground, running with the wind, thinking she'd catch it like a kite. And she did. Her bare feet thumped over grass and soft earth, then they were pedaling at nothing but air. The wind grabbed her beneath the arms and lifted her. She soared over fields and streams and came down on her feet still running.

The fact that she had to *learn* how to fly, and that it took time, proved beyond all doubt that this strange and beautiful world was every bit as real as the America she had left behind. In a dream she would've flown without having to think about it.

"This is home now. It's home and it's God to me."

She was slumped over a boulder, enjoying its warmth and vibration. The land didn't speak to her, as such, but sometimes she felt its voice through the rocks and trees.

Home, the boulder agreed.

Nor was it a hallucination or state of mind. She was *here.* Her physical body had left the nightmarish room above the White Lantern, just as if she'd stepped out the door. Valerie sometimes wondered how long the animals had spent looking for her—if they'd shouted at or attacked one another, or perhaps taken their frustrations out on the fat little restaurateur. In the end, it didn't matter. She was here and she wasn't going back.

Valerie had been there at least a month but perhaps as many as three when she noticed the tiny split in the air. It didn't flash like a coin. It was dull, like a smudge. She treated it like she might a lump on her breast: ominous, potentially terrifying, but perhaps, if she ignored it, it would go away.

It didn't.

The split grew until she could see through it. There was no

blue sky on the other side, only yellowing sofas and bloodstained floorboards—things she was all too familiar with.

It started to pull.

Valerie tried to run, but it was like trying to run from the moon. She tried to fly, but that only put her closer to the split. She even dived into the lake and swam to the bottom, thinking it couldn't possibly get her there. The split followed, though. She looked up and there it was, hovering just beneath the surface.

It lengthened to a rift. She used a vine to tie herself to a tree—wrapped her arms around the trunk and held on.

"It's trying to take me. I won't let it."

Find your way back to us.

"I don't want to see the animals. I don't want to be back in that room. Hold me, tree. *Hold* me."

We'll always be here.

She fought with all her new strength—for days, it seemed—but to no avail. The rift had a gravity she could not defy. The vine frayed, then snapped. She clasped the tree until her fingernails split, pulling thin strips of bark away.

This is your world. We'll always be waiting.

"I don't know if I'll find my way back."

There's a way.

"Tell me." She snagged a branch and held it desperately. *"Please."*

That's for you to discover, the tree said. *But know this: there's always a price to pay.*

She experienced that hypnic jerk again, falling into the sky, in through the rift, and she screamed the whole way. The last she saw of her breathtaking world was the ivory trees and mountains beyond, then she was staring up at the lantern, swaying gently in a current of warm air.

She landed in a puddle of blood—from one of her wounds, she assumed. But no, it smeared the insides of her thighs. This was menstrual blood. Her first period in years.

I'm a woman again, she thought. *I am* me.

Valerie got to her feet and started looking for the split in the air. She checked the lantern, the walls, the gaps between the floorboards. She looked behind the pictures and underneath the sofas.

"Need . . . get back."

There's a way, the tree had said.

She believed this. One hundred percent. And she soon realized that she was wasting her time looking for a tiny split. What she wanted was an *entranceway*. Something arched and full of light.

It wasn't in this room.

She staggered to the window, threw her face against the glass, looked across the Hackensack to the Meadowlands and Manhattan skyline beyond. It was out there. Somewhere. It could be a portal on the ocean, like the Bermuda Triangle, or a gateway buried among ancient ruins.

"Where do I start?"

A voice in her head said, *At the end of pleasure*.

She fell to her knees and wailed, covering her eyes with both hands. And she might have convinced herself it *was* a dream, if only to save her sanity, except she still had fragments of bark beneath her fingernails and could smell the trees on her hands.

The wind chimes played their hollow music. A familiar horror rolled through Valerie. Would it be the ox with a baseball bat? The rabbit with the picana? *They don't know I'm here,* she thought. *I've been gone for months, they—*

The door opened and the restaurateur waddled in carrying a bowl of steaming noodles with two chopsticks pushed into them. He looked at her, saw the blood between her legs, and shouted something in Mandarin, perhaps outraged that he'd have to scrub it clean. Regular blood and piss and shit . . . that was all fine. But *menstrual* blood! He shouted again, pushed the bowl of noodles across the floor toward her, and walked out. The door slammed and locked behind him.

At no point did he appear surprised to see her. He'd brought her *food,* for God's sake.

"I didn't go anywhere," she whispered, then smelled her hands again. The aromas—pepper, citrus, bark—were distinct enough to bring more tears to her eyes. She examined her wounds. Her bruises had faded and many of her cuts had scarred over. Had they healed like this before she went away? Valerie didn't think so, but couldn't say for sure.

She huddled in the corner, trying to find a scrap of rationality in an irrational situation. In the end, she clung to the thin plausibility that time moved differently between the two worlds. A week over there could be ten minutes here.

And with this came the realization that it didn't matter anyway. The only thing she needed to focus on was finding a way back.

But first, she had to get out of this room, which wasn't a problem. Not anymore. She believed she could burst through the reinforced glass and land softly on the ground thirty feet below. But breaking out wasn't enough. She had to leave a mark on this world if she hoped to escape it. And she would start by making those fucking animals pay for what they'd done to her.

She grabbed the chopsticks from the bowl of noodles. Would the restaurateur remember that he'd brought them this time? Probably not. She crawled back to the corner, where a strip of the baseboard had come away from the wall, exposing rough brickwork beneath.

Valerie rubbed tip of the first chopstick back and forth against the bricks, turning it slowly.

She sharpened it to a point.

Pace had shared a theory at the end of his life that had stuck with Valerie, although she'd never bought into it: that the White Skyway might be accessible through a person, as opposed to an object or place. *People have incredible amounts of energy,* he'd said. *More than in any inanimate object or geographic location. It stands to reason that the way to Glam Moon exists in someone who has been torn apart, like you . . . or someone with an exceptional gift.*

"Tell me more about your sister's world."

Shirley sat up and blinked her wide blue eyes. She'd been resting her head on Valerie's shoulder, comfortable enough to drop into a light doze. Valerie had listened to her steady breathing while watching the fire burn.

"You mean her garden?" Shirley asked. Her hair was adorably mussed on one side.

"Yes, her garden."

"It's her fantasy world. She doesn't talk about it much. I *do* know that she built it herself. A tree here. A flower there. Like *Minecraft,* I guess—"

"I don't know what that is."

"Oh. Right." Shirley shrugged. "It's a videogame. You can create whatever you want. And Edith has created this world inside her mind. It's deep enough for her to disappear into for hours at a time."

"Is that so?"

"She's been working on it for . . . I don't know, six or seven months. Since before Mom died, anyway."

Valerie looked at the window, still streaked with rain. The sky beyond was a soup of dark clouds. The thunder had stopped, at least.

"Put another log on the fire."

"We're all out." Shirley got to her feet. "I'll bring some in." She crossed the living room, opened the front door, and stepped outside. Valerie whimpered and slipped one hand inside her robe. She cupped her breast and felt her heart drum through it. Shirley returned a moment later, her arms loaded with wet firewood. Rainwater glistened on her skin and her clothes were damp.

"Good girl."

Shirley dropped the firewood onto the hearth. "It might be too wet," she said, but Valerie said to go ahead, put a log on—it would burn. Shirley did what she was told.

"And take your clothes off. My goodness, you'll catch a cold."

Shirley peeled off her damp pants and T-shirt and lay them in front of the fire. She sat beside Valerie again. Valerie used the blanket they'd huddled beneath to wipe the rainwater from Shirley's face.

"There . . ."

"Thank you, Mother Moon."

"Is your underwear damp?"

"It's fine."

"Okay."

The log on the fire hissed and gushed a pearly white smoke. It caught soon enough, though. The flames were long and yellow.

"Six months," Valerie said. "I find that hard to believe."

"What?" Shirley looked perplexed.

"Nobody can build a world that quickly. Not even in their minds."

"Oh." Shirley nodded, catching up. "Edith."

"Yes . . . Edith." Valerie had removed her hand from her breast but still felt the thump of her heart. "Do you think she found a world that already exists, and that she thinks is her own?"

"Like Glam Moon?"

"Perhaps."

"I don't know. It's possible, I suppose."

"How often does she go there?"

"Most days."

"Why?"

"It's an escape." Shirley had taken the blanket and wrapped it around herself. Rainwater dripped from her hair and flashed down her face. "You probably won't believe this—it's totally weird, I know—but Edith was born with an unusual condition. It's kind of a family secret, and I'm pretty sure my dad—"

"Forget your dad. Tell me."

"She's psychic," Shirley said at once. "She has this . . . this *extra* energy inside her brain that is constantly tuned in to a psychic frequency. Most of the time it doesn't bother her because she filters the information, but when she's asleep and her brain is recharging . . . that's when the premonitions happen. Sometimes they're pretty bad."

Valerie stared at the fire, thinking that a girl—an exceptionally *gifted* girl—with access to the psychic universe could just as easily connect to a parallel world.

"Sometimes they're terrible," Shirley continued, lowering her eyes. "She saw the attack on my mom's school, but it was too late to save her."

"Poor little soul."

"She doesn't remember any of it." Shirley shook her head and wiped rainwater from her cheeks. "Anyway, before that, my parents had brought in this psychic lady. Calm Dubisch or Dubois. Something like that. She taught Edith the garden trick. And now Edith uses it as a shelter from the bad things, but also to escape a world without Mom."

"It's a place of healing."

"Maybe," Shirley said. "All I know is that she doesn't wake up screaming anymore. And she doesn't need me, either."

"What do you mean?"

"I used to be her shelter," Shirley replied. "She would climb inside my mind to hide from the bad things inside hers. It didn't bother me to begin with, but as I got older . . . well, I just didn't want her there anymore."

Valerie drew a deep breath into her lungs. "Let me get this straight: she created a pathway from her mind to yours . . ."

"A link, yeah. A telepathic link."

"A bridge."

"I guess."

"And did you ever . . ." Valerie trailed off. Her palms were sweating. Her heart was off the leash. "Did you ever climb into *her* mind?"

"No."

"But your minds were connected. A bridge goes both ways. Do you see what I'm getting at?"

"I think so."

Valerie stood up, wincing as the joints in her knees and ankles popped. She paced the living area, deep in thought, and settled in front of the fire.

"Your sister is obviously quite exceptional," she said, keeping the tremor from her voice. "A very special young lady."

This struck something inside Shirley. She sprang to her feet. "*I'm* special, too." Tears welled in her eyes, then ran down both sides of her face, bigger than the raindrops.

"Oh, sweet girl, I *know*." Valerie went to her, tugged the blanket away, and pulled her close. "I think you're amazing."

"Edith *always* gets the attention."

"Oh, baby."

They huddled like lovers in the fire's glow, Shirley with her wet face nestled in Valerie's neck, Valerie with one hand on the curve of Shirley's lower spine.

"It's okay." Valerie kissed the top of her head. This vulnerable, malleable girl. "I value you. Never forget that."

Shirley nodded and sniveled.

"And you know something: there may come a time when you need to show the world how special you are." Valerie fought back tears of her own. "You think you can do that?"

"Yes," Shirley replied. She looped her arms around Valerie's waist. "I know I can."

25

Martin had been away from the mainland for six weeks but it felt much longer. Everything was more abrasive than he remembered, beginning the moment he climbed into Nolan's truck. The fake-pine smell of the air freshener hit the back of his throat and lodged there, mingled with nauseating wafts of oil and gas. It was thirty-eight degrees outside and raining, but he opened the window a crack and didn't close it until they reached Syracuse.

"Today is Sunday," Nolan said. "I'll drop you at the RTC, and pick you up at two o'clock on Friday afternoon. Repeat that back to me."

"The RTC," Martin said. "Two o'clock, Friday afternoon."

"That's Black Friday, as in the day after Thanksgiving."

"Jesus. Thanksgiving." Martin shook his head. "That totally wasn't on my radar."

"You're in a Halcyon state of mind," Nolan said.

He was right, and it wasn't just the smell of the air freshener or the fact that a major public holiday had slipped his mind. Martin spent the drive to Syracuse with an agitated knot in his chest. There was more traffic than he remembered. The trucks were bigger and noisier, and they coughed thicker clouds of exhaust into the atmosphere. His unease didn't let up once Nolan had dropped him at the RTC. The suburban chorus—even on a Sunday—sounded like an orchestra warming up. People, like the vehicles they drove, moved faster. They stared straight ahead or down at their smartphones. There was nothing free about their range of movement; they could have been on treadmills.

Martin sat on a bench, trying to adjust to the noise and bustle. The fact that he felt this way—and after only six weeks—was as disconcerting as it was improbable. *A Halcyon state of mind,* Nolan had said, which was another way of saying a Mother Moon state of mind. She had indoctrinated him by way of her rules, methods, and language. A subtle and effective form of brainwashing.

He'd considered using Jimmy's internet to conduct his research, but that would only encourage questions he didn't want to answer. The library was a better option. It wouldn't take long to get the information he was looking for. Providing everything checked out, he could then gatecrash the family Thanksgiving, and assure them that life on Halcyon was everything he'd hoped it would be.

Time was on his side. Five full days. He burned the first hour walking to the downtown core, acclimating to the change of pace while trying not to look like he'd recently arrived from some alien planet. The rain picked up mid-afternoon, sheeting down in icy drops. Lightning crackled in the west and thunder rumbled. His stomach did, too. He ducked into the nearest bar to get out of the rain and grab a bite to eat. He had $112 in his wallet, untouched since arriving on the island.

The bar was called Ump's—a sports-themed establishment with more TVs than windows. Martin had lived in joints like this during his college days, but to his Halcyon state of mind it was uncomfortably overdone. He actually walked out, but the rain—hitting the sidewalk in ropes—drove him back inside.

He sat at the bar with the TVs flashing off his skin. Eight different football games and two news stations crowded his brain. The news stories could have been looped from the day he left: eighty dead following air strikes in Mosul; SCOTUS set to hear oral arguments in racial gerrymandering cases; three-year-old shoots his mom with a loaded gun; another high-profile PED scandal in major league baseball. Martin pulled his eyes away from the screens and looked at the menu. He was hungry, but the thought of rich food—greasy wings and loaded nachos—did nothing for him. He felt the same way about beer, even though beer had been number nine on his list of things he most missed from home. He ordered a Caesar salad with grilled chicken and a glass of water.

A clock behind the bar displayed 3:46 in glowing red digits. By the time he left—after he'd eaten and when the rain had eased up—it was 5:31 and dark outside. There was no point going to the library now; it would be closing its doors soon, if it hadn't already.

He checked into a hotel on East Genesee Street and went directly to his room, where he sat in a comfortable amount of light and thought about his girls. This was his third favorite moment of the day, bested only by Edith's goodbye hug and Alyssa's kiss. A smile touched his lips and remained there as he drifted off to sleep. He jerked awake some time later—he didn't bother to look at the clock—with a crick in his lower back and an old taste in his mouth. City lights glared though the window. Two sirens howled in the distance. Martin undressed, brushed his teeth, then stepped into the shower. His fourth favorite moment of the day. The water was hot and it soothed him. After toweling himself dry, he slipped between the cool bed sheets and slept until morning.

Derevaun Seraun wasn't Latin. It wasn't anything, really. The odd phrase originated in the short story "Eveline" by James Joyce, and had proved a source of debate among scholars. Many believed it was a reworking of Gaelic that loosely translated to "The end of pleasure is pain." Others suggested it was a corrupt take on the West Irish dialect, with "The end of song is raving madness" being a more accurate translation. Neither definition was particularly appealing, Martin thought. He defaulted, as he did throughout high school, to CliffsNotes, which interpreted the phrase "probably gibberish."

So what now? Martin thought. The phrase was not associated with any society or group, and Mother Moon's real name—Valerie something-or-other . . . *Keller,* perhaps?—didn't flash across the screen with red flags attached. An encouraging sign, of course, but he'd only scratched the surface so far.

"I have to keep looking," he murmured. "That's what now."

He opened a new window, went to Google, and typed

DEREVAUN SERAUN HALCYON into the search field. It brought back fewer than sixty hits. Martin scrolled through them all, clicked on a couple, but none were useful. He tried *DEREVAUN SERAUN VALERIE* and paused, his brain whirling. What *was* her surname? Both Alyssa and Nolan had told him at some point. Keller? Kemp? Kent? Something beginning with K. He tried all three and drew nothing of interest—a review of *Dubliners* written by a "Valerie Kent" in Arkansas, but that was all.

Martin sat back in his seat and brought the ring to mind. And it was the ring, more than the inscription, that had unsettled him. The fact that it was hidden beneath a false bottom, behind lock and key, sealed the deal. If Martin had discovered it in one of Mother Moon's drawers, or on top of the nightstand, it wouldn't have troubled him as much.

He googled *DEREVAUN SERAUN SECRET SOCIETY* and then *DEREVAUN SERAUN CULT* and spent the next forty minutes clicking, scrolling, and reading. All to no avail. Nearly every link pertained to Joyce or "Eveline" or the meaning of *Derevaun Seraun.* It eventually got to where he wasn't paying attention anymore. At one point a pop-up ad for the newly opened Onondaga Mall infiltrated the screen, promising unbeatable Black Friday deals, and he spent ten brainless minutes clicking through the links thinking, *I helped design that food court . . . That fountain was my idea . . . The back-painted glass really—*

He blinked hard, as if stirring from a vivid daydream. He'd been on the computer for three hours already and there was a mild throb in the center of his brow. It had the makings of decent headache—the kind that might force him into a mid-afternoon nap with a cold cloth draped across his forehead. It had been a while since he'd sat for any length of time in front of a computer. He had to acclimate to that just like everything else.

He stood up. Time for a break.

He ordered a sandwich from the deli across the street and ate it on a cold stone bench in Columbus Circle, using the time away from the computer screen to think things through. He'd discovered nothing, other than the speculative meaning of *Derevaun Seraun,* in three hours of online searching. Surely that meant there was nothing *to* discover, that he should abandon his shitty investigation. But Martin couldn't shake the sense that he wasn't digging deep enough—that there were stones left unturned. For that reason, he returned to the library, sat down at one of the available computers, and continued his research.

He googled *DEREVAUN SERAUN RING* even though *ring* was too generic a word. As he suspected, it produced 120 pages of links. He started scrolling, clicking on anything that appeared marginally hopeful. And maybe it was because he'd eaten, or because the fresh air had blown the cobwebs from his brain, but his eyes picked two words off the fourth page of searches that struck a curious note inside him.

. . . animal masks . . .

"Okay," he said. "That's something . . . maybe."

He clicked the link. It was a 2006 review of Joyce's *Dubliners,* written by a New Jersey "bookaholic" who called herself "wordslave0x9." Martin read the entire thing twice, but one passage stood out. He read this over and over:

> *Eveline's mother wailing "Derevaun Seraun" from her deathbed is supposed to be an emotional moment, but all I could think about was those seven guys getting whacked above a Chinese restaurant in Engine City, and how they were all wearing rings with that weird saying inscribed on it. They were wearing animal masks, too, which is some freaky stuff, when you think about it. I guess the story was covered up at the time (that's Engine City for you, folks!), but some old cop spilled the beans to the Sternbridge* Tribune *after he retired in the late nineties.*

Until that point, Martin's thought process could have been drawn with a pencil—a series of short, vague lines. Now it was more like a spray can with a partially clogged nozzle. His mind went everywhere with just the merest squeeze. After ten minutes of erratic conjecture, he closed out the internet, stepped away from the computer, and ambled around the library. Several circuits later, his thoughts had tapered into a somewhat manageable stream. He took them one at a time.

Mother Moon had in her possession (because it was too specific to be a coincidence) a ring and mask belonging to one of the victims of a mass murder—a crime damaging enough to be covered up.

How did she get those items? he thought. *They would've been zipped into evidence bags.*

Not if the murders had been swept under the rug. The evidence would have disappeared in a hurry. And besides, it didn't matter how she got them. The important thing was *why* she had them. Martin ruminated on this as he walked through the children's library. The juxtaposition between the colorful, playful items around him and the dark things tumbling through his mind was jarring, but it helped him focus.

"Macabre memorabilia," he whispered. A possibility. He recalled reading about certain morbid items selling over the internet: Osama bin Laden's tooth, Charles Manson's prison ID card, Lee Harvey Oswald's coffin. There was an underground market for such nasty curios. Maybe Mother Moon was a collector, or she had a particular fascination with this case.

Or she's connected to it in some other way.

Connected, okay, but that didn't mean she was *involved.* Mother Moon had told Martin more than once that she'd had a hard life. Maybe she'd been married to one of the victims, and kept his ring and creepy tiger mask for the same reason Martin kept his wife's ring on a chain around his neck.

This is different, he thought. *Laura was a sweet, gentle soul. The victims of this crime were obviously part of some fucked-up secret society.*

Right. Their motto was "The end of pleasure is pain," for the love of God. If Mother Moon was grieving, why not choose a less sinister keepsake?

Who said she was grieving? He was in the fiction section now, running his forefinger along the worn spines of titles, as if he had any interest in them at all. *Maybe those mask-wearing freaks did her wrong, and this is all part of why she founded Halcyon. She keeps the ring and mask as a reminder of the darkness she left behind.*

"They're symbols," he muttered. "Same as the watch."

Okay. That sounded plausible, but there was more to it. And although he'd read nothing to suggest Mother Moon was complicit in any wrongdoing, he couldn't ignore the uneasy feeling that had settled in the pit of his stomach.

Something's not right . . .

Or maybe that had more to do with the dream he'd had his first night on the island, when Laura revealed what was in the lockbox. It had been a bullet in the dream, of course, but it still felt like a warning—like his dead wife was trying to tell him something.

Alyssa had said it wasn't a premonition, but what if it was? What if that psychic mojo ran in the family?

He needed more information.

The Sternbridge *Tribune*'s online archives went back to January 2002, not far enough to uncover the retired cop's tell-all. Martin had more information now, though, and was able to dig in different directions. He eventually found the story on a site called *Engine City Spaghetti*, which dedicated itself to New Jersey's mob scene in the second half of the last century. Sternbridge's Warehouse District, aka Engine City, featured heavily.

It was a gaudy, gratuitous site that looked like it had been built in the early 2000s and not updated since. Martin would have taken everything he read with a pinch of salt, except it had a photograph of the actual *Tribune* article on screen. The quality was poor and not all of the text was legible, but he managed to extract the relevant information.

The retired cop was Sergeant Peter Baines, who hung up his badge in 1998 after thirty-three years of service, first in Newark, then Sternbridge. Most of the article focused on his dealings with the mob, how they all but ran the Warehouse District during Baines's time on the force. He recounted turning a blind eye to many a misdeed—even being made to falsify statements and hide evidence. "It's what you did," he said, "if you wanted to keep your job. And your life." Toward the end of the article, Baines got to what he called "the White Lantern Massacre." He didn't exactly spill the beans, as wordslave0x9 had suggested, but he revealed enough information for Martin to want to know more.

> *We were so used to making crimes disappear, but the White Lantern Massacre was something different altogether. It wasn't a mob job, to begin with. It was pure hack 'n' slash. And sure, a few crazy versions of this story have leaked out over the years, but the truth is nobody knows what went down in that room. The whole thing was cleaned up quickly. Very hush-hush. My guess is that the vics were important and respected members of society who were into something they* shouldn't *have been into. And no names were released because, hey, there was no crime, right? Anyway, that whole thing with them wearing animal masks was true. The rings, too. Like a championship ring but with a big green eye set into it. They were clearly into some messed-up stuff, but they met their match in that room. Must've raised the devil himself because, let me tell you, I've never seen anything like it.*

Engine City had cleaned up its act over the last twenty years, and was now a thriving riverfront community with million-dollar condos, Reiki practitioners, and organic coffee shops. The White Lantern was still open for business. It had a 4.1 Google review rating and apparently served the best Kung Pao chicken in New Jersey. Martin—clicking links fluidly now—discovered that Sergeant Peter Baines hadn't fared so well; he had died of prostate cancer in 2002.

With the help of specific search filters, Martin also nailed a date on the White Lantern Massacre: May 1986. Guesstimating Mother Moon to be in her mid-fifties, this meant she was in her early twenties at the time. It was difficult to associate someone so young with such a violent crime.

But the ring and mask in her possession suggested she *was* associated, either as a daughter or young wife of one of the victims. Or a victim herself.

Martin closed the open windows and sighed. He'd spent most of the day pinballing around the internet and all he had to show for it was more questions. Only one thing was certain: he couldn't return to the island with a partially uncovered story. Some unholy shit had transpired and he needed to determine Mother Moon's involvement. He'd taken it as far as he could online.

"It's time to get down and dirty," he said.

He was going to Jersey.

26

The dead woman lay on her side. Both her legs were missing and she was still burning.

No, Edith thought. *Not again.*

She pushed with her mind, looking for her garden. She'd become incredibly efficient at accessing it in the months since her mom had died. But not now. The window had opened with devastating force. It consumed her.

This can't—

Her head jerked backward. She saw a row of stores with their fronts blown inward and everything burning inside. Bodies were sprawled across the floor, dusted with ash. A wild-eyed woman sifted among the debris, crying out. Her voice was lost in the chaos.

A scream built on Edith's lips. She reached for her garden again.

Please . . .

But there was nothing. Not a single petal. Not a glimmer.

Fire trucks and police cars tore across a jammed parking lot.

Edith saw banks of shattered TVs and clothes burning on their racks. She saw checkouts with bodies draped over the conveyors and cash registers. More bodies littered the aisles and some were piled three and four deep.

No, please . . .

Edith got out of bed and stood slumped, coated in sweat. The room was dark but she knew Shirley's bed was empty. Shirley was in Mother Moon's cabin and would probably stay there all night. Desperate for shelter, Edith reached for her in the *other* way, the old way.

Shirley, I need you—

But her sister wasn't there. That door—that connection—was closed. Permanently, it seemed.

The stream shifted. She saw melted mannequins and shelves half-filled with blackened toys. A smoldering sign promised 50% OFF. Other signs read WHY PAY MORE? and BLACK FRIDAY SPECIAL. This latter—a long banner—had been draped over a row of corpses: a temporary shroud. Their legs poked out from beneath.

"Friday . . . pay," Edith said.

She made drawing motions with her right hand but it wasn't enough. The window pressed against her eyes and crushed her skull. She stumbled in the darkness, bumped into the nightstand. There was a glass of water on top and she knocked it to the floor.

"Pay."

The glass broke. Edith dropped to her knees and picked up one of the shards. The window dropped with her. There was no chronology in the things it displayed. One moment she was looking at a motionless escalator with a dead body slumped at the bottom, then the stream cut to crowds of bargain hunters pouring through open doors. Edith drew the piece of glass across her forearm. Her blood flowed. She saw smoke rolling through an empty food court, a news reporter in tears, and—from behind—a teenage boy in a bulky jacket pushing through waves of shoppers.

That's him, Edith thought. *He's the one. He's—*

But there was something about his punky black hair.

The stream switched. More horror. More death and smoke. Edith dipped two fingers into her blood and started to paint on the white bed sheets. First a *P,* then an *A.*

As she started to paint a *Y,* she saw the boy in the bulky jacket again. Except it wasn't a boy. The window focused on the teenager and Edith suddenly understood why the stream was so invasive, and why she couldn't escape to her garden. Like the shooting at Flint Wood High, this was too close to her. She was connected by blood, and couldn't turn away.

Shirley pushed through the crowds of shoppers. Her face was sick-pale. Sweat glistened on her throat. She stopped moving. People surrounded her, carrying boxes and packages, pushing carts.

Oh my God. Edith dropped the piece of glass and thrust out one hand, as if she could reach through the window and snatch her sister free.

Shirley, no—

Shirley lowered her head, muttered something, and pulled down the jacket's zipper. One moment she was there—whole and real, feeling and living—then the window filled with a burning light and when it faded she was gone. Everything was gone.

The scream that had been building inside Edith finally let loose. She fell backward, flailing on the floor, droplets of blood splashing from her arm. She was vaguely aware of a light switching on and arms reaching for her. A familiar voice—Alyssa's—whispered close to her ear.

"Ede, sweetie, it's okay now. It's—"

Edith fell again, but differently, not down or backward, but *into.* Her brain lit up as if someone had plugged it in. The window closed like a shutter slamming and Edith found her opening. She floated for a while and then emerged beneath the branches of a tree. A bird sang from high up and the sound calmed her.

She was in her garden. It stretched endlessly. All the color she could want.

Edith lay for a while in bliss before realizing that someone was trying to get in there with her.

27

They'll go away, Valerie thought after the first knock on the door, even though she knew it was late, and therefore urgent, but she struggled to even open her eyes let alone get up off the sofa. Besides, she had the girl snuggled in her arms, and the girl was warm.

Another knock, more insistent. Valerie made a discontented sound in her throat and rubbed her eyes.

"What's going on?" Shirley mumbled.

"We have a visitor."

Valerie eased herself away from Shirley and stood gingerly. Embers shimmered in the fireplace, offering a scant pink light. Valerie used this to pick her way across the living room. Whoever was out there knocked a third time and Valerie resisted the urge to yell at them. Instead she forced a smile onto her face and said, "I hear you," in the sweetest voice she could muster.

She flicked on the light, squinted at the sudden brightness, then opened the door.

"I'm sorry to bother you this late, Mother Moon," Alyssa said. Her eyes were wide but tired and she had blood daubed on her cheek. "I'm looking for Shirley."

Shirley came to the door a second later. "What is it?"

"Edith. She had a night terror, I think. Your dad told—"

"Is she okay?"

"Yes." Alyssa nodded. "She's resting, but you should probably be there when she wakes up."

"You've got blood on your face," Valerie said.

"Oh." Alyssa smeared one hand across her cheek, wiping the blood away. "Edith cut herself. Not deeply, but I don't think it was an accident."

"How can you be sure?" Valerie asked.

"It looks . . ." Alyssa paused, as if trying to make sense of what she was about to say. "It looks like she was using her blood to write something."

"She was purging," Shirley said.

Alyssa stared at her blankly.

"Something's going to happen." Shirley slipped into her sneakers and stepped past Alyssa, into the cold, damp night. "Something bad."

Edith lay in Martin's bed—where Alyssa had been sleeping—with her eyes closed, breathing steadily. Every now and then her nose would twitch or her brow would wrinkle, but other than that she was expressionless.

"She's deep," Shirley said to Valerie.

Alyssa had bandaged Edith's left forearm, and done a good job. Aiden Lythe—Halcyon's doctor—had removed it only to see if it needed anything more. It didn't. He bandaged it again and took Edith's temperature.

"She's fine," he declared, wiping the thermometer and placing it back in his medical bag. He looked at Shirley. "Does she have night terrors often?"

"She used to," Shirley replied. "She found a way to cope with them . . . mostly."

"Okay. That's good." Aiden zipped his bag. His hair stood in messy quills and he was still wearing his pajama pants. "I assume you know that night terrors are nothing to worry about. She'll probably sleep peacefully now, and won't remember any of this when she wakes up."

"She won't," Shirley agreed.

Valerie thanked Aiden for coming over. He waved it off, then suggested they all go back to bed and left. The front door closed behind him and there was a long stillness, broken only by the sound of Edith's steady breathing. Valerie sat on the bed beside her and smoothed the hair from her brow. Alyssa stood by the door with her arms folded. Shirley paced for a while, then sat on the other side of the bed.

"Is it possible to get word to Martin?" Alyssa asked. "Does anyone have contact information?"

"He's probably staying with my Uncle Jimmy," Shirley replied. "I don't know his number. And there's nothing Dad can do anyway."

"He should still be told."

"Nolan has a number," Valerie said, "in case of emergencies. I'm not sure this *is* an emergency; Aiden said she was fine. But we'll see how Edith feels when she wakes up."

Alyssa nodded. She unfolded her arms, shuffled her feet. Valerie regarded her briefly, but most of her attention was on Edith, looking at her closed eyes, wondering what was behind them.

Alyssa said, "I'll go take care of the other room. Sweep the broken glass. Change the bed—"

"Leave it for now," Valerie said without looking at her. "Go back to your own cabin, Alyssa. Get some sleep, for heaven's sake. And thank you for your help."

"I should stay," Alyssa said. "Martin asked me to look after Edith. I don't want to let him down."

"We're here now," Valerie said. "And you're not letting anyone down. You've been wonderful."

Alyssa hesitated, then offered a reluctant nod. "Sure . . . okay. Come get me if you need anything."

"We'll be fine."

Alyssa opened the bedroom door, but before leaving she asked Shirley, "What did you mean when you said something bad was going to happen?"

"Nothing," Shirley replied at once. "I'd just woken up. I was confused."

Alyssa paused a moment, as if she were waiting for a more truthful answer, then turned and left. The closing front door again signaled a protracted stillness, until Valerie, leaning close to Edith—almost close enough to kiss her—asked Shirley:

"How deep is she?"

"I don't know. Deep. I've seen her like this before. It could be a long time before she comes out."

"Sweetie, I don't care about her coming out." Valerie

peeled open Edith's eye and stared longingly into that crackling blue iris. "I just want to know how I get *in*."

Shirley stayed in the room for maybe an hour and then went to bed. Valerie didn't move from Edith's side. She kept looking into the girl's eyes, even into her mouth, as if she could crawl in and burrow all the way to Glam Moon. "What can you see?" she whispered, not just once but many times. "Show me, little girl. Let me in." Sunlight spilled through the window and painted long shadows across the room. Valerie heard blackbirds singing, a woodpecker knocking, Gilda Wynne brushing leaves from her front steps. The island slowly woke with its characterful little creaks and moments, but Edith remained deep in her own world, barely moving.

Exhaustion won out. Valerie slumped across the bed next to Edith and slept, but distractedly. She woke up to a brighter room. Edith hadn't moved a muscle. Valerie peeled her eyes open again and looked inside but saw nothing.

She shuffled into the girls' bedroom. Shirley was still asleep. Valerie shook her awake and pointed at the bloody letters scrawled across Edith's bed sheets.

"What does *pav* mean?"

"Whu? I don't—" Shirley blinked and shook her head.

"*P-A-V. Pav.*" Valerie jabbed a finger at each letter. "Your sister wrote it in blood. It must mean something."

"It's connected to the premonition. Could be anything."

Shirley got out of bed a short time later. She ate breakfast, then cleaned up the broken glass. Valerie had resumed her position at Edith's bedside, occasionally whispering to her—the same gently cajoling things. Her persuasive prowess had no effect, though. It was like trying to crack a safe using positive thoughts.

Alyssa came late morning, obviously expecting Edith to be awake and to look after her as promised. Shirley led her to Martin's room to show her that Edith was, in fact, still deep, except she said *asleep*, knowing it would prompt fewer questions.

"She doesn't normally sleep in this late," Alyssa said, touching Edith's brow with the back of her hand, perhaps to feel for a temperature. There was none, of course. "Are you sure she's okay?"

"You've never seen her after a night terror before," Shirley said. "She's always like this. It's like she . . . retreats."

"I think we should get Dr. Lythe to check her over again."

"He already did. She's fine."

Shirley sent Alyssa away. She said Edith would only want family around when she woke up, and there was no mistaking the hurt expression in Alyssa's eyes. Valerie watched from the window as she walked back to her cabin. If she returned later, Valerie was not aware of it; Edith emerged from her garden midafternoon and, for Valerie, the rest of the island disappeared. She gave the girl thirty seconds to orient herself, then swooped to the edge of her bed.

"Oh, Edith, you looked so pale and precious. I thought the slightest thing might break you." And how she hoped that was still the case.

28

Edith shut out the voices for a moment, and the faces—Shirley's and Mother Moon's—floating in and out of her vision. She focused on the far wall, on the dark knots in the pine paneling and a painting of two orioles. Gradually, she let the real world back in.

This was her dad's room. She couldn't remember how she got here.

"You were in your garden," Mother Moon said. Her eyes gleamed. They were usually so kind but now they just looked hungry. "You were deep."

Edith drank two glasses of icy water and felt better, more with it. A little later, she asked about the bandage on her arm and Shirley led her into their room, showed her the word she'd painted on the bed sheets. It stirred no memories.

"You obviously needed to get it out," Shirley said. "You cut yourself to write it."

"*Pav.*" Edith looked at the letters and frowned. "It doesn't mean anything to me now."

Back in the living room, Shirley placed two logs on the fire. They caught quickly and roared. She and Edith sat on the sofa. Mother Moon took the armchair closest to Edith and said to her:

"I'd like to see your garden."

Edith gathered her hands into her lap and looked down at them. She couldn't recall what she'd seen through the window, but she remembered being in her garden and hearing Mother Moon's voice. *Knock-knock, little girl. Let me in.* It was persuasive enough to reduce the distance between there and here, and Edith eventually poked her head out of her hole.

"Why?" she asked.

"We all need shelter," Mother Moon said. She displayed a warm smile but that hunger was still in her eyes. "A place to feel safe and secure. That's why I founded Halcyon: a refuge for the broken. But it hasn't been *my* refuge for a long time, perhaps because I unselfishly offered it to others, or because I'm just so used to it now. Either way, I need a place I can call my own, and where I can heal."

"Show her your garden," Shirley said.

"Are you broken?" Edith asked, looking at Mother Moon.

"Very."

"But you seem so . . . strong."

"That's one of the nicest things anyone has ever said to me." Mother Moon smiled again. "I wish it were true, but my ghosts . . . they never stop haunting me."

"You need to build your own garden." Edith stood and crossed to one of the house plants on the bookshelf, plucking a plush leaf from its stem. She returned to Mother Moon, placed it in her hand, and said, "One leaf at a time."

Mother Moon looked at the leaf for a moment, then dropped it on the floor. "Yes, I understand." She linked her fingers as if she were about to pray, but there was no reverence to her tone, only a slippery kind of coolness. "I need something to work from, though. You can't make a jigsaw puzzle without looking at the picture on the box."

"This isn't a jigsaw puzzle," Edith said. "There is no picture."

"You know what I mean." The smile reached Mother Moon's eyes and they shone. "Show me the garden."

"Do it, Ede."

"I don't know how."

"The same way you connected to my mind." Shirley drew an invisible line between her forehead and Edith's. "You make a bridge."

"It's not that easy," Edith said. "And I never built a bridge. I visualized. I *reached*."

"Then reach again. Reach for *me*, and pull me in."

Edith looked at Shirley, who nodded. *Everything's fine, Ede,* that nod said. *Trust me.* She recalled sitting beneath the willow tree in their backyard with Calm Dumas, and how Calm had opened a window into *her* world—her jungle. Edith had seen snow-capped mountains, a trickling stream, a couple of the odd creatures that lived there. *How are you doing that?* Edith had asked, and Calm explained that she used the electricity in her brain to power a connection, then projected onto the "place between"—the crossover, which was Dad's name for when two radio signals blended together.

That's where people like you and me are, Edith, Calm had said. *On the crossover. We're constantly picking up two receptions, and sometimes the voices are very loud.*

"Please," Mother Moon said.

Edith looked down at her hands again. She moved her palms four or five inches apart, as if they were holding an invisible grapefruit. "I don't even know if this will work."

"It will."

"I think you have to be able to see the place between."

"I *will* see it," Mother Moon said, and tears suddenly sprung from her eyes. She dragged a trembling breath into her lungs. "I've been training my mind for years."

Edith nodded and raised her hands, still cupping the invisible grapefruit. The fire crackled and the wind cut across the front of the cabin, making the door rattle. She shut all of this out and focused on the space between her hands.

It took almost no effort. She felt the flow of energy at once and had to spread her hands to contain it. Threads of light popped between her fingers. She smelled summer rain and saw the air separate.

"Okay," she said. "The window's open."

The branches of her tree nodded lazily and threw soft, spiraling blossoms into the sky. A hummingbird buzzed close to the window, as if it might venture through, but then zipped away in a sweet flash of blue.

"I don't see anything," Mother Moon said. Her eyes were wet. Her hands were tangled claws.

"You didn't see the hummingbird?"

"No. I don't see *anything.*"

"Keep looking," Edith said.

Valerie didn't move. She barely blinked. The rest of the cabin dwindled to a backdrop of washed color where nothing breathed and even less mattered. It was all about the window that Edith had opened, the size of a beach ball now.

The place between, she'd called it.

Valerie focused with everything she had. She looked not just with her eyes but with her mind. Her left eye watered with the effort. A cold pain needled the back of her skull. All she saw, though, was the girl's yellow T-shirt, her throat, strands of her hair. No flowers or trees. No goddamn hummingbird.

"I'm not getting it."

"Relax," Edith said. "Take deep breaths."

Valerie wiped the wetness from her left cheek and took several jerky breaths, each of which announced how fraught she was. The wise, composed mother figure was absent now. She imagined herself desperate and unseemly.

"Maybe we should take a break," Edith said.

"No. Keep going."

Time passed with the slow weight of a sinking anchor. Valerie felt every minute. Her vision blurred and doubled. She clenched her jaw and looked harder.

"These flowers are some of the first things I made," Edith said.

You didn't make any *of it, you little cunt.* Valerie forced a smile that ached and wiped more moisture from her cheeks. Both eyes were streaming now.

"What color are the flowers?"

"All colors."

"I'm not . . . I just . . ." Valerie adjusted her position, then she looked from Edith's side and still saw nothing.

"Maybe it just won't work for you," the girl said.

Maybe I should pry off the top of your skull and splash whatever's inside across the room. How about that? You think I'd see your precious fucking flowers then?

"It'll come," Valerie said. "I know it will."

She sent Shirley away just in case she was interfering with the signal. Edith insisted she wasn't but Valerie didn't want to take that chance. Shirley busied herself in one of the bedrooms and the sound of the light switching on sometime later informed Valerie that it was getting dark. How long had she been trying now? Two hours? Easily. She sighed, wiped her eyes, kept looking . . .

"I'm getting tired," Edith moaned. "My arms are aching. Can we rest for a little while?"

"I'm getting closer. I can feel it."

She felt no such thing. If anything, she was losing focus. And maybe that's what she needed to do, because that's when it happened. She blinked tiredly, thinking that when she finally got to bed she would sleep for days. Just the thought of—

Something flickered between Edith's hands. Valerie snapped her attention back to the window, then instinctively averted her gaze, as if she might scare it away by looking too hard. She caught the same flicker a moment later, then it bloomed into a seam of light that stretched from one of Edith's palms to the other.

Valerie whimpered, then covered her mouth.

"You see it?" Edith asked.

She nodded, but didn't want to move her head too much. Over the next several minutes, the seam flexed and widened, and the light from a different world shone in Valerie's eyes. She saw a huge yellow sun and magnificent trees. She watched a bear cub cuff at its reflection in the river. Any hint of tiredness—all thoughts of sleep and bed—vacated her mind.

Big tears spilled from her eyes.

I found you.

How could the girl think this was *her* world? There were too many perfect details to have been created by a ten-year-old: the way the birds bristled and pecked at their feathers, the exact shadows printed on the landscape, the tall flowers nodding their soft, colorful heads in the breeze.

This was not the Mother Moon that Edith knew—the kind, calm lady who'd welcomed them to her island, and whose smile felt like a warm towel after a cold swim. It was like she'd suffered a knock on the head and was mentally distanced from the woman she used to be. She mumbled and licked her lips. Her eyes were burning circles that should have sizzled with all the tears she cried. *Desperate,* Edith thought. *That's not quite right, but it's close.*

Maybe *crazy* would be closer.

How she looked was nothing compared to how she *felt*. Not content to simply see Edith's garden, she reached through the window with one trembling hand. The coldness was immediate. It felt like a blast of freezing air—an ugly, wicked wind that would wilt the flowers and kill the grass. Edith tightened inside. The fine hairs at the back of her neck lifted.

"My flowers," Mother Moon said, still with that mad, desperate look on her face.

"Mine," Edith corrected her, and slammed the window shut.

Pace had been right, Valerie thought later, when the girls were asleep and she was alone in the living room. The way to Glam Moon really *was* through a person's energy, one who'd been torn apart, or had an exceptional gift. Edith was that person. She could connect to the place between up and down. She could open the portal—the throat between worlds.

"But how," Valerie said, "do I *keep* it open?"

She imagined grabbing the axe from the woodshed, then coming back here and driving it through the little girl's skull. *Thonk!* One swift, hefty blow.

Hello, Glam Moon. Momma's home.

But what if that didn't work, and all she managed was to extinguish the source of the energy? That would be like shattering a flashlight when you were lost in the dark.

There had to be another way.

Pace came to mind again. She saw him in the kitchen of the house they'd all shared, explaining that the White Skyway was a gateway between dimensions. *In essence, a wormhole,* he'd said, *but with an exotic matter added, making it stable . . . traversable.*

"Exotic matter," Valerie mumbled.

Her mind ached. She went to bed. But not *her* bed. She dropped into the first one she came across, which happened to be Edith's bed with the bloody letters smeared across the sheets. She dreamed about the tiger and the ox and the rabbit and the snake and the pig and the dog and the rooster and the goat. She dreamed about hammers and picanas and nail guns, and also about what the Society had given her—*gifted* her: Glam Moon. *When pleasure is denied,* the tiger had said, *the channel to new possibilities, and alternate experiences, becomes broader.* She dreamed about fires and bombings and shootings and death and grief, the numerous acts of terror she'd orchestrated to bring about the end of pleasure. And why? To replicate the horror and desolation she'd experienced in the room above the White Lantern. Why? Because there was always a price to—

Valerie sat bolt upright and kicked back the covers. She scrambled from the bed, flicked on the light. Shirley was in her own bed but Valerie barely registered her; she was too preoccupied with the letters painted on the sheets. *P-A-V.* Except it *wasn't* a *V.* Edith had either run out of blood or been distracted by something else, but now Valerie could see that the crotch of the *V* had a very faint tail.

It was a *Y.*

"Pay," Valerie said.

This was a message. An *instruction. PAY.* In blood. *Edith's* blood. Valerie again imagined taking an axe to her skull. She even started toward the door, but then stopped and looked at Shirley.

Same blood.

Pain, she mumbled. *A gateway. A spotlight on the soul.*

The most exotic matter of all.

Valerie switched off the light but stood a moment longer, her skin tingling and her mind alive.

"There's always a price to pay," she whispered.

She crawled into bed with Shirley, kissed the back of her young, shapeable head, and held her close in the dark.

29

The White Lantern, Engine City. The vibe was friendly and relaxed, with Chinese folk music tinkling in the background and divine aromas wafting from the kitchen. Martin chose a seat by the window and ordered the famed Kung Pao chicken, but didn't enjoy it as much as he should have. It was impossible to shake the restaurant's history from his mind. He tried focusing on the lights glinting on the other side of the river, but his gaze kept drifting to the ceiling, as if expecting a pool of blood to form there and drip onto his plate.

He'd rented a car in Syracuse and arrived in Jersey early afternoon. His first stop was the Sternbridge Public Library, where he spent two hours digging through the *Tribune*'s archives, but found nothing new on the White Lantern Massacre. Reading the headlines from the 1970s and '80s, an outsider would believe Sternbridge was a run-of-the-mill Jersey town, when clearly that wasn't the case. Stories and truths emerged in later years, most of them centered around the Engine City mafia.

The library wasn't a total bust; Martin spoke to an older gentleman in the periodicals section who told him about the Cellar Bar downtown, where retired cops were known to share stories in exchange for booze. Martin went there and got talking to a grizzled old cop who could've walked right out of a TV show, and who indeed gestured at his empty glass every time Martin pressed for information. He said he wasn't part of the White Lantern cleanup crew, but he had friends who were. "Helluva goddamn mess. Triad hit, we think." And yeah, it was true the vics were all wearing animal masks and rings. He couldn't remember specifics; it was a long time ago, and besides, all the evidence was destroyed.

"All of it?"

"Every scrap."

"Is it possible," Martin asked, "that one ring and one mask made it out of there?"

"Anything's possible," the old cop replied. "Unlikely, though. The cleanup boys left nothing to chance."

Which meant that Mother Moon's mask and ring *were* a wild coincidence, or replicas, or had belonged to someone from a different, but perhaps connected, society.

Leaving the Cellar Bar, Martin was almost ready to call it quits. His verdict: Mother Moon had a darkness in her past that she couldn't let go of, but she'd never shown this darkness to Martin. Quite the opposite, in fact.

"Bottom line, Sherlock," he whispered to himself. "You've got zilch."

It was a cold evening, a light snow in the air. Martin imagined his cabin with a fire blazing in the hearth, curled up on the sofa with Alyssa while the girls read or played board games. The image was vivid, perfect, and he longed for it. But before he could journey back to the island, and to his girls, he had one stone left to turn.

"Is the owner in tonight?" Martin asked the waiter as he paid for his half-eaten meal.

The waiter nodded. "That's her at the bar."

Martin thanked him, put away his debit card, and walked over to the bar. It was late and there was only one other customer, who downed his shot and left. Martin grabbed a stool. The owner acknowledged him with a smile. She had a kind face and striking eyes, and was younger than Martin expected. Maybe midthirties. Martin returned her smile and ordered a ginger beer.

"You know," he said a moment later. "Your Google reviews rave about the Kung Pao chicken, and I have to say . . . it's pretty damn special."

"Thank you," the owner said, and smiled again. "The secret's in the peppercorns."

She had an accent, as charming as it was surprising. Martin couldn't place it, and while it might be delightful to listen to, he had to wonder—given her age and the fact that she'd likely grown up in a different country—how much she could tell him about what had happened at her restaurant thirty-two years ago.

"Martin," he said, extending his hand over the bar. She took it and shook. Her own hand was small, warm.

"Sasha. I'm the owner."

"I know that." Martin said, and sipped his ginger beer. "The chicken was good, but that's not the reason I came. I was hoping to speak to you."

"Oh?"

"About the history of your restaurant—specifically about what happened here in May of 1986."

Sasha had a small towel over one shoulder. She whipped it off and started drying glasses.

"You must be a writer," she ventured.

"What makes you say that?"

"Only two types of people ask about what happened here: weirdos and writers . . . and you don't look like a weirdo."

"Well, thank you." He raised his glass and smiled. "My daughters would likely disagree, but no, I'm not a weirdo. I'm not a writer, either. I'm an architect. A particularly boring one."

She cocked an eyebrow. Dimples appeared in her cheeks.

"Hey, I'm drinking ginger beer," he said. "Has there ever been a more unexciting drink?"

Sasha held the glass she'd been drying up to the light. "You have a point." Satisfied, she placed it on the rack, selected another. "So why the interest in my restaurant?"

"It's purely personal," he replied. "Whatever you tell me . . . you can rest assured I won't blog about it."

"A burning curiosity?"

"Something like that." Martin nodded. "But there's more: I know a lady, and I think she's connected in some way."

"Then you probably know more than I do." Sasha shrugged and started on another glass. "Honestly, I can't tell you anything that's not already out there. I was two years old in 1986 and living in a small village in Wales. My uncle owned this place. He was a horrible man, mixed up with a lot of bad people. When he died, he left this restaurant to his sister—my mum—the only family member who had any contact with him. We were on the other side of the ocean, but we came over and made a go of it. This was in 2000. We'd heard stories about what happened here, but it was difficult to know how much was true. Business wasn't affected, though, so we stayed, and I took the reins after Mum retired in 2012."

"So you don't know who the victims were?"

"Everything was covered up. No crime, no victims." Sasha flipped the towel back onto her shoulder and started wiping down the bar. "No victims, no names. Right?"

Martin ran his finger around the rim of his glass. "And your uncle didn't know who they were?"

"If he did, that was a secret he took to his grave. Along with many others. Most likely, he rented the room to a bunch of crooks—there were a lot of crooks in Engine City back then—and everything went tits up."

"Tits up," Martin echoed, and smiled. "That's a colorful understatement."

Sasha tossed the washcloth into the sink, folded her arms, and regarded Martin with her striking eyes. "The only thing I know is that some men were killed upstairs. I don't know who they were, or what they were into. I tried to find out more when we first arrived, but all I got were rumors and tall tales. You get to a point where you just have to scratch a line through it and carry on."

"I'm close to that point," Martin said. "But just for closure, you think I could take a look at the room?"

"Hmm, maybe you *are* a weirdo."

"Not me." He held up his right hand, fingers split. "Vulcan's honor."

Sasha grinned and said, "Follow me."

Martin brushed against a set of bamboo wind chimes in the upstairs hallway. Sasha explained that they'd been there since her uncle owned the place, and she'd take them down only they created a soothing music when the front doors were open and a breeze blew through. Martin thought they sounded like bones knocking together.

A door at the end of the hallway opened on a large room. Martin readied himself and stepped inside, as if expecting the victims to be scattered across the floor, or their tormented ghosts to howl the moment he set foot across the threshold. The room was colder, certainly, and smelled mustier, but there was no echo of yesteryear that he could detect. He walked around, looking at the pictures on the walls, at the two windows that, during the day, would offer views across the Meadowlands. A large white lantern hovered above a long table, the light inside glowing softly.

"No bloodstains," Sasha said. "No boogeymen."

"Just a room, huh?"

"Yup. One that needs a makeover. Badly."

"What do you use it for now?"

"Different things." Sasha ran her finger along the top of a picture frame and it came away dusty. "Storage. Private functions. Office space. We had a séance up here once—that was a whole *group* of weirdos, let me tell you."

"A séance?" Martin raised his eyebrows. "Did it . . . *reveal* anything?"

"Nah. The whole thing was a sham." Sasha smiled and rolled her eyes. "The medium called himself Dr. Hans Oculus. Thick European accent, *ja*? Except I overheard him talking on his cell phone outside, and his *real* accent was pure Joisey."

Martin nodded, recalling some of the mediums they'd used when trying to understand what Edith was going through.

Sasha drifted over to the windows, where the snow had picked up a little. Flakes brushed against the glass. "I also have this woman—another weirdo—who rents the room every three or four months. She stays here for a week, sometimes two. Sleeps on the floor. It's definitely odd, but she had an arrangement with my uncle, and my mum, and I try to honor that. Besides, she pays well and can be very persuasive."

Martin turned away from the hanging scroll he'd been examining and looked at Sasha through narrowed eyes. He recalled Alyssa telling him that Mother Moon sometimes left the island, that she could be gone for up to a month at a time. A pilgrimage for Glam Moon, Alyssa had guessed, but maybe Mother Moon was revisiting her past—her *ghosts*. And Martin knew firsthand just how persuasive she could be; he'd looked into her eyes many times and felt himself buckling.

"This woman," he said. "Fiftyish? Red hair?"

Sasha nodded.

"Valerie . . ."

"Kemp," Sasha finished, then snapped her fingers. "Okay,

got it. She's the lady you mentioned, who you think is connected to whatever happened here."

"We call her Mother Moon," Martin said. "She runs a retreat—an intentional community, of sorts. I live there with my daughters. It's all very easygoing and Zen. Only I found some items in her possession recently that got me wondering if she's the peace-loving altruist she appears to be."

"What items?"

"A tiger mask and a ring."

"Christ. Burn her at the stake."

"It's a distinctive ring," Martin added quickly, "set with a green eye and an unusual description: *Derevaun Seraun*. It led me here. All seven victims were wearing the same or similar rings."

"Animal masks, too." Sasha nodded. "Yes, I heard that. And whether it's true, or only partly true, it's fair to assume Valerie is connected."

"Maybe not to the murders," Martin said. "But to one of the victims."

They took a moment with their thoughts. Sasha pressed one hand to the window and gazed out at the snow. Martin walked around the table with his mind racing. He imagined Mother Moon sleeping on the floor in here, or huddled in the corner with her memories. But why? He shook his head. Could he live with never knowing the connection? Could he ask his girls to live with it?

"Does she ever ask about what happened here?" he asked Sasha.

"Never."

"And is she always alone?"

"Yes. For the most part." Sasha turned away from the window. "She has one visitor. He always comes at the beginning of her stay. Her dealer."

"Her *dealer*? You mean drugs?" Martin tried to imagine clean-living Mother Moon, who raved about the beauty of trees and the fresh lake air, tying a strap around her arm and shooting up. "Christ, what's she into? Coke? Heroin?"

"Jesus, no. I wouldn't stand for that." Sasha offered Martin a serious look, and he had a feeling she really *wouldn't* stand for that, no matter how persuasive Mother Moon could be. "I know the dealer. He's a nobody. Used to deal pot to schoolkids. He sells insurance now. Married with children. He doesn't deal anymore, except to Valerie, because, as we've established, she can be very persuasive."

"Weed?"

"DMT." Sasha folded her arms and stepped toward him. "It's a hallucinogen used in shamanic ceremonies. Valerie insists the dealer calls it Rhapsody. Her little thing, I guess."

Martin cupped his brow, thinking. Mind-altering drugs were definitely better than heroin, and more in keeping with Mother Moon's spiritual vibe. They also went most of the way toward explaining Glam Moon.

Still doesn't explain why she comes here, though, he thought. *The room of death.*

"She's harmless enough," Sasha continued. "Doesn't interfere with me or the restaurant. She's quiet, too. I hear her talking to herself occasionally, but that's about it."

"Do you check on her?"

"Of course. I bring her something to eat a couple of times a day. A salad or a sandwich. Never Chinese food. She *hates* Chinese food. Most of the time she doesn't even know I'm there. She's usually staring up at the lantern. Totally spaced out."

Sasha swatted the lantern and it moved in circles. Shadows glided around the room.

"Trippy," Martin said.

"I always assumed she was one of my uncle's exes—that they used to come up here and have wild, hallucinogenic sex romps together, and she's been trying, in her strange way, to reconnect with that. I never associated her with the murders. I mean, who *would*?"

"I guess we've given each other some new information today," Martin said.

"I know, right?" Sasha folded her arms and watched the lantern until it stopped swaying. "So now I'm thinking she's related to one of the victims, and that she comes up here to feel closer to him. Perhaps the DMT helps create a fantasy—an intimacy."

"I'm thinking along the same lines," Martin said. "Although the scene of a crime—and such a violent crime—is a strange place to create intimacy."

"I agree."

Martin looked at the walls, imagining them splashed with blood. Traces of it would still be there—under three or four layers of paint, perhaps, but still there. He looked at the floorboards and wondered how many times they'd been sanded and recoated to hide all the stains. *It was pure hack 'n' slash,* retired Sergeant Peter Baines had said in the *Tribune,* and the whiskey-soaked cop in the Cellar Bar had declared it a "helluva goddamn mess."

The end of pleasure is pain, Martin thought, and there was no doubt this room had seen its share of pain. Mother Moon coming here and tripping out . . . there was something undeniably unsettling about that.

"You still curious about what happened?" Martin asked, dragging his gaze from the floorboards. Sasha had moved back to the window, silent as a ghost.

"A little." She looked at his reflection in the glass. "But most of the properties along the waterfront have their own violent history. We're all doing our best to move forward and not think about the past."

They left the room together, Martin taking the lead, brushing against the bamboo chimes once again. The bone-music followed him to the bottom of the stairs.

"Thank you so much," he said at the front door, offering his hand again.

"I'm not sure I helped very much, but . . ."

Martin pushed open the door. Wind and snow gusted in and he heard the chimes again. His thoughts made a similar sound. Hollow, tuneless thoughts—that there was still so much he didn't know, and it seemed the only people who could answer his questions had been dead for thirty-two years. He might've fared better if he'd brought Dr. Hans Oculus with him.

This frivolous notion strummed an odd chord at back of his mind, and an idea quickly formed. He brought it to the fore, examined it, decided it was crazy, but also decided it just might work.

"If I were to come back with someone"—he used his body to shield most of the wind and snow—"who might be able to shine a light on what happened upstairs, would you be amenable to that?"

"Someone with a time machine?"

"I guess." Martin shrugged. "Kind of."

"Well, for the entertainment value, and provided they don't wreck my restaurant . . . I'll say definitely maybe."

"Good enough," Martin said, zipping his jacket. "I'll see you soon."

The snow was light enough that it blew across the sidewalk like dust. Martin lifted his collar and walked with his head low, breath pluming around him. He got into his rental car, cranked the heater to full, and drove the mostly empty streets until he found a hotel.

30

"I understand," Shirley said. Her eyes were huge and moist and her upper body trembled. "Doesn't mean I'm not scared."

"A bright light can be overwhelming." Valerie measured each word like a drop of medicine. "If sacrifice were easy, there'd be no achievement, no happiness, no love."

Her words hung on the air for a moment, then gradually soaked in. Shirley nodded and wiped her eyes. Valerie didn't cosset the girl, or soothe her; the strongest walls were built of stone.

"Did my mom die for this? So that I could be put onto this path?"

"She did."

"And Dad, coming here . . . ?"

"You see it now: your purpose." Valerie spread her arms, encompassing something bigger than them both. "Shirley, the Glam has chosen you. This is where you rise above."

Shirley wiped her eyes again and lifted her chin. Good.

"I was focusing on your sister for so long that I

underestimated your energy—a brighter, more breathtaking energy." Valerie stepped toward Shirley, still with her arms spread, deliberately treelike, a thing of great wisdom and strength. "She may be the doorway, but you're the key."

Valerie had spent most of the day alone, wandering around the island, thinking of ways to pay the price. It had been cold and demanding and a snow squall forced her to take shelter in a hollow tree. Looking out, she thought she saw the tiger standing in the swirling snow, watching her, but it was just her tired mind playing tricks. Even so, she cried out that she didn't need him—didn't need his animal friends, his Society, or his fucking drugs, then she wept for a long time, hoping this was true.

Finally, after the snow had stopped, and with the setting sun showing like a burn mark through rags of grayish cloud, Valerie knew what she had to do. She returned to her cabin and Shirley came a short time later. Valerie had already set the fire burning, and a warm, flickering light filled the room. Shirley started reading to her but Valerie soon held up her hand and said no, she couldn't concentrate, and when Shirley asked why, Valerie told her. She said, "I didn't think you'd be ready so quickly. You've amazed me." And then she explained to Shirley what was required of her—such a momentous, unselfish undertaking. Shirley listened, her eyes growing wider and wetter. There had been denial to begin with, of course, and then acceptance.

"I understand," Shirley said again.

"You are exceptional." Valerie spoke slowly and with a great weight to her words, like a steady, heavy drumbeat. "I am awed by you. *Over*awed."

"Thank you."

"You won't let us down. You're too strong. Too special."

She nodded at first, then uncertainty flickered across her face. This wasn't surprising, given all the thoughts and emotions barreling through her mind. Valerie thought it would pass, then Shirley slumped and buried her face in her hands. She sobbed from a deep, frightened place.

Valerie let her cry. She let her squeeze out every scared and doubting tear, and during this time she didn't move at all. She loomed, tree that she was—strong, wise force that she was. Shirley eventually looked up, the firelight reflected in her eyes. Valerie nodded once, then pushed herself deeper, laying herself across the girl's delicate brain. She felt it quivering beneath her and exerted the merest pressure in only the most critical places.

"All that bad energy you've carried. Those moments of anger and resentment at a world that has treated you pitifully. One moment of light can end it all."

"I know."

"It's godlike, in a way. Goddesslike."

"Yes."

"Show them, Shirley. Show them what you can do."

"I will."

"You will." Valerie broke her treelike stance. She walked to the fire and placed another log on. It burned beautifully. The glow shimmered off the walls and ceiling and painted her skin a fetching shade of red.

* * *

In her dream she took an axe to Edith's head, which was softer than she'd imagined, and there was smashed skull and brain all over, but worse, the energy was dead, the portal was dead. Valerie fell to her knees and tried to put the pieces back together but they slipped through her fingers and they were all black. She woke in an icy sweat and had to slap both hands over her mouth to keep the scream from breaking loose.

She clambered from her bed to her chest of drawers, opened the bottom one, took out the tiger mask. She lifted it to her face, smelled the latex, but smelled him, also—his expensive cologne, his skin. Valerie's eyes fluttered. She pulled the mask onto her head, returned to her bed, and fantasized about the end of pleasure. Her orgasm forced her to suppress another scream, using the pillow this time.

Shirley was still in the living room. She hadn't moved all night. Her expression was both familiar and strange, like a famous portrait with newly painted eyes.

"Did you sleep?" Valerie asked.

"No."

"Are you tired?"

"Yes. A little." She frowned, as if she didn't quite recognize her own voice.

"You should sleep. You have a great task ahead of you."

Shirley nodded and lay down on the sofa, one arm tucked beneath a pillow. She fell asleep within moments. A smoothness struck her face and her lips pulsed gently.

Valerie dressed and left the cabin. She greeted her followers with a beaming grin and a hearty "Good morning!" And it *was* a good morning. There was a skiff of snow on the ground and the sky was a cloudless, shiny blue. She walked swiftly, arms folded against the cold.

Nolan was in the storage barn, taking stock. Simon Song was with him, stacking hefty boxes, steam rising from his bald head. Valerie dismissed Simon and he left without saying a word.

"Everything okay?" Nolan asked.

"I know how to get to the White Skyway," Valerie said, speaking as if she knew how to get to the nearest 7-Eleven. "It's time."

Nolan dropped the notebook he'd been scribbling in. The pen, too. It trembled in his hand for a moment then fell to the ground. He looked at Valerie and his face took on a dumb countenance and Valerie wondered if she'd have to slap him—slap the fucker hard—just to bring him to his senses.

"Ruh . . . ruh . . ." he stammered. "Ruh . . ."

Valerie's hand twitched.

"Really?"

"Really. We have to create it, but I know how."

"Huh . . . huh . . . how?"

"It's complicated. You just have to trust me."

His mouth twitched, then his whole face crumpled and tears the size of buttons rolled from his eyes. He stammered something else, then dragged a sleeve across his cheeks and flopped his arms around Valerie.

"It's all just . . . I mean, it's . . ."

"I told you that something was coming, that I could feel it in the air." She pulled herself from his arms with a little mew of distaste. "I wasn't wrong."

"You're never wrong." He took a couple of robust breaths, wiped his face again, and managed to retrieve a shred of composure. "The Glam. I just . . ." He smiled pathetically. "I can come, right?"

"Of course. You've been loyal to me for many years." Valerie made a sweeping gesture with her right arm. "We're opening the Skyway right here on the island. It's a route in and out. You can come and go as you please."

"Skyway," he repeated moronically. His eyes glazed. "Wow. I mean . . . *wow.* I don't quite understand how it—"

"It's the girls, Nolan," Valerie said. "Edith and Shirley. Don't overload your brain, just think of it this way: one of them is the door, the other one is going to blow the door open."

"Ah, yes," Nolan said, as if that made perfect sense.

"Which leads me to my reason for coming down here . . ." Valerie placed a hand on Nolan's shoulder and urged him a little closer. "I'm going to need you to do something for me."

"Anything. I'll do anything," he said. "What is it?"

She told him.

31

Martin pulled into the White Lantern's parking lot and switched off the rental's engine. The restaurant was closed but Sasha had agreed to meet them there. She had an hour, she said, before she and her wife were due to join the in-laws for Thanksgiving drinks. Martin thought an hour would be long enough.

"This is the place," he said.

"I can tell," Calm Dumas responded.

He'd called her Wednesday morning, pulling her number from old cell phone information stored in the cloud. He had little doubt Calm would want to help, once he'd explained the situation, but whether or not she could do it over Thanksgiving, and before Nolan was scheduled to pick him up Friday, was another matter entirely.

Calm had stepped up, though. She had no family—only three dogs, which she could leave with a neighbor—and therefore no plans. She told Martin that if he could get her to Jersey, on his buck, then she would come. Booking a last-minute flight the day before Thanksgiving proved problematic, however, and he didn't want to put her on a bus. In the end, he decided the easiest way was to do the driving himself. So he made the seven-hour journey to Roanoke, Virginia, except it had been nine hours with the holiday traffic. He checked into a Holiday Inn for the night, then picked Calm up first thing Thanksgiving morning and headed back to Jersey.

They arrived in Sternbridge just after three p.m. and managed to find a restaurant that was open on the holiday. The food was good, but Martin had no appetite. He kept flashing back to last Thanksgiving: twelve of them, including Laura, sitting around Jimmy's huge dining table, food everywhere, the football game buzzing in the background, barely audible above the sound of good cheer. If someone had told *that* version of Martin that in one year he'd be sharing Thanksgiving dinner with an elderly psychic lady at some mom-and-pop restaurant on the outskirts of Rutherford, he would've laughed them out of the room.

Calm didn't have to read his mind to know what he was thinking. His expression, and the way he played around with his food, made it clear enough. She reached across the table, took his hand, and told him that she was thankful to be with a friend.

"I am, too," he said, and that was the truth.

Now, standing outside the White Lantern, he wondered if some of her thankfulness had ebbed. Her usual poise had slipped, and there was a wariness about her, a *watchfulness*, that sent chills racing through Martin's blood.

"Is it that bad?" he asked.

"It's ungodly."

"The restaurant?"

Calm drew her shoulders inward and scoped all around. The streetlights flashed off the lenses of her glasses. "It's the whole damn place."

Martin puffed out his cheeks and looked at Calm earnestly. "Are you sure you want to do this?"

She walked past him, heading for the front door. "Let's just get it over with."

"So close," Valerie whispered.

She was a journeywoman, a visionary—an astronomer who'd been watching the skies for the last thirty-two years, waiting for a certain rare star to go supernova. And now it was happening.

Valerie took deep, measured breaths. Every time she blinked she saw the "garden" in Edith's mind, every perfect detail, from the foliage and rock formations to the clear pools and waterfalls, all of which she knew so well, all—

"Mine," she whispered.

So close.

She had built a fire on the beach and it burned hungrily, sparks spiraling upward from the flames and fading into the air. Sitting beside it, feeling the heat it pushed out, she wondered if she'd ever be cold again. This time tomorrow, she could simply step across the Skyway and feel the sun on her skin—a sun that didn't sink beyond the horizon, but that gradually faded from the sky. Or she could swim in water that adapted to her mood: warm or cool, whatever she wanted.

"*My* water. *My* sun."

Valerie had brought a small bag with her. She opened it and took out the two items inside. The first was the tiger mask, devoid of all its threat and power. It didn't smell like him anymore, either. Her scent enveloped his; in the last twelve hours she'd masturbated six times while wearing the mask and urinated on it twice. The second item was the ring, as cold and heavy as it had always been, but duller . . . darker. She had removed it from the secret compartment in her lockbox earlier that day. The ghosts in her mind were clearer when she took the ring out, perhaps because it symbolized them as a group, or perhaps because her blood was still embedded in the inscription.

Sasha led them through the restaurant, weaving a path between the tables in the meek light. At the bottom of the stairs, Calm touched her elbow and said:

"It's kind of you to do this, particularly on the holiday."

"Not a problem," Sasha said. "I had to drop in anyway."

Calm smiled, although Martin noticed her eyes continuing to shift behind her glasses. Her hands were restless, too, making odd touching motions, occasionally reaching for things that weren't there—or at least not that Martin could see.

"If you're being honest, though," she said to Sasha, "you're only happy to do this because you don't think it will work. You'd pegged me as just another charlatan—or weirdo, isn't that your word?—before I'd even shown up."

"I, uh . . ."

"It's okay, sweetie. I get that all the time, but if you knew what I can *already* tell you about this place, you would never have allowed me through the front door."

Sasha closed her mouth and looked at Martin over the old lady's shoulder. He offered a shrug that conveyed very little of what he felt inside, but it was the best he could manage.

"We won't be long," Calm continued. "You can stay down here, if you don't want to know. You can stay, too, Martin, if you'd prefer to keep some distance, and I'll give you the details later. Your call."

"I'll be fine," he said.

"Me, too." Sasha said.

"Okay." Calm shuffled toward the staircase, then stopped and closed her eyes. "Your uncle kept her here. Against her will. Partly because they paid him, but mostly because he was afraid." Her eyes flashed open, fixed on Sasha. "A damn coward, your uncle."

"A proper arsehole, I'd say."

"That he was."

They made their way upstairs, pausing every second or third step while Calm made feeling gestures, sometimes touching the walls. This continued along the landing, until she reached the bamboo chimes, which she looked at for a second, then brushed with the back of one hand. They knocked and sang. Calm listened, eyes closed.

"This is how she knew they were coming."

When Calm had shown up at Martin and Laura's house in May, she told them that the psychic cosmos was vast and active, and that most people who connected to it were swept away.

Watching her now, Martin got the sense that she was navigating a dark and relentless energy, something that could fracture space and melt logic. She inched along the landing, then opened the door at the far end and was drawn into the room beyond.

"It's fast here," she said. "And deep."

She circled the table once, then unbuttoned her jacket and threw it on the floor. Martin picked it up cautiously, half expecting it to smell of sulfur, or to see smoke drifting from inside the sleeves. He looped it over the crook of his elbow and watched Calm as she worked, her hands sensing like antennae, her eyes constantly twitching.

"She was so young," Calm whispered.

"She?" Martin gasped. "Are you talking about Valerie?"

"They did bad things. But she made them pay."

Sasha had stepped into the room but remained close to the door, either trying to stay out of the way, or ready to bolt if the table and chairs started floating or ectoplasm oozed through the walls. Her face was a mosaic of amusement, bewilderment, and fear. Martin stood by her side. She looked at him with wide eyes and he shrugged vaguely again.

"This anything like Dr. Hans Oculus?" he whispered.

"Not . . . exactly."

Calm ran her hands along one wall, then took them away quickly, as if she'd touched something unpleasant. She stepped backward, shook her head. Her eyes cleared. She looked from Sasha to Martin and said:

"The pig bled first."

32

The lake was milky silver and the sound of it lapping the shore mirrored the calm she felt inside. It was a calm she knew would soon be spoiled, but that was okay. Her meeting with the animals was necessary. When it was over and they'd returned to whatever dark space they'd crawled from—forever, this time—the calm would return, and would never be spoiled again.

Valerie closed her eyes and clutched the ring tighter. She heard footsteps only moments later, descending from the bushes that fringed the cove. One set of footsteps, crunching first over leaves and cones, then scuffing through the sand.

"I knew you'd come," she said.

"We've never been far away."

It was the pig. She knew this before he even spoke—could tell from the wheezy, slobbery sound of his breathing. He lingered at the edge of the firelight, blending with the cheerless evening air.

"We're not at the Lantern?"

"You seem surprised." Valerie opened her hand, looked at the ring. She'd been clasping it for minutes now but it was still as cold as a pebble plucked from the lake. It would never be warm, she realized. She could hold it over the flames for an hour and it would remain a chip of icy darkness. "This meeting is on my terms, Pig. I'm in control now."

He squealed laughter and the sound carried through her. Ironically, he hadn't squealed when she'd killed him, which is when a pig *should* squeal. He'd screamed in a very human way. He'd groaned and gurgled, then he'd pleaded and died.

Wonderful sounds.

Valerie recalled waiting for the first of them to arrive, hunkered in the corner of the room, the sharpened chopsticks clutched to her breast. She was wound so tight with anticipation that she froze the first time the chimes jangled on the landing. It was only the fat restaurateur, though. He cleaned away her plate (didn't notice the missing chopsticks—good) and her poop, then grunted at her and left. An hour or so later the chimes rang again and this time it was the pig. She looked at him over her shoulder. A hefty man in a business suit and red power tie. He called her a worthless bitch and kicked her in the thigh. When he drew back his leg to kick her again, she whirled from her crouched position and drove one of the chopsticks into his balls.

He pulled away sharply and the chopstick snapped. Judging by the three-inch piece of wood in Valerie's hand, she surmised he had at least five inches buried in his groin. He hit the floor on his knees, pig-head thrashing, both hands cupping his dirty pig balls. She saw blood well brightly in the cracks between his fingers and it was the first blood she'd seen in four years that wasn't her own. He screamed in agony and Valerie hushed him by thrusting the second chopstick beneath the shelf of his jaw. It went in easily—and deep, too. He gurgled and fell, taking the chopstick with him. The back of his suit jacket had rucked up, though, and Valerie saw the knife strapped to his belt. She removed it from its sheath and stabbed him in the back of the neck. He groaned but didn't die. She stabbed him again and he *still* didn't die. She stabbed him twice in the face through his pig mask and blood spurted. "Please," he said. "*Pleeeaaa* . . ." He pissed himself and still wasn't dead—not quite—when she heard the chimes on the landing once again.

Knife in hand, Valerie reeled across the room and hid behind the door. It opened. The dog walked in. He stopped cold when he saw his fallen comrade. "What the fuck?" he said. Valerie came up behind him and thrust the knife into the top of his skull.

The dog had a meat cleaver strapped to a holster beneath his jacket. She hacked at him with it. His chest and arms and face. She dragged him behind one of the sofas where he wouldn't be seen from the doorway. She dragged the pig—dead at last—behind it, too.

Blood everywhere.

Knife in one hand, cleaver in the other, Valerie crouched behind the door.

She waited.

* * *

"I see the blood, of course. It's on the walls, on the floors. I can't *not* see it. But it's not the story. The pain is. A globe of pain that revolves and *e*volves. It's so colorful, so complex. Beautiful, in fact. And the girl . . . it's like she died a hundred times and each death made her stronger. She discovered something, some new belief, inside her, or *beyond* her, and then she rose. Not a broken girl but a blazing phoenix of a woman. A phoenix with blades. And I see her now, right here, where I'm standing, looking at this lantern and praying for . . . a flower? A tree? I'm not sure, but her heart is a bundle of glowing wires and the dead are scattered around her."

Calm snapped momentarily from her trance. She looked from the lantern to Martin and Sasha, both of whom took an involuntary step backward. Sasha shook her head. "No," she whispered, but Martin had seen it before—in the black and white photograph that he and Laura had used to call Calm back in May. He'd thought it a photographic aberration, but no, it was real: Calm had two irises in each eye. She blinked and they coalesced into one, like colored contact lenses sliding into position.

"Jesus," Sasha gasped.

Calm took a deep breath and said with chilling clarity, "She wanted the tiger most of all."

Valerie waited several hours. The light outside faded. She sat in the darkness listening to the flies gather on the corpses, the dim tinkle of Han folk music, and the thrum of conversation from the diners in the restaurant downstairs. She drifted into sleep but the bamboo chimes woke her. The door opened. A hand—the Society ring glimmering on the third finger—reached for the light switch and she used the cleaver to chop it off.

Her eyes had adjusted to the dark but the rabbit's had not. She dragged him into the room and slammed the door. "My hand," he whimpered. "What happened, what *happened*?" His rabbit shape—long quivering ears—stumbled in the gloom, and she hacked at it mercilessly from every direction, as if there were twelve of her. He went down and curled himself into a shuddering ball and she didn't stop until he was dead and had been for some time.

The ox and goat arrived together the following afternoon—two on one, but the element of surprise stacked the odds in Valerie's favor. She was able to weaken them both before they knew what was happening. Indeed, the goat fought for a period of time (only five seconds or so, but it felt much longer) with the cleaver lodged in his skull. It looked like a joke Halloween prop. Then he fell against the wall and the impact popped the cleaver loose. Blood jetted from the top of the mask and he died in spasms.

Valerie picked up the cleaver and wheeled on the ox. He had several knife wounds across his upper body but he also had the knife, which he'd pulled from a hole in his chest. "I'm going to kill you, bitch." His mask was comically askew. The knife trembled in his hand. "You're so fucking—" He took two swipes at her and the knife missed first time by four inches and second time by only one. His ox belly wobbled. A third swipe and this time the blade flashed across her left breast, cutting her close to the nipple. They circled each other for a time. The ox bled and weakened. Valerie waited for her moment and it came; his right leg wobbled and he slumped. She sprang forward, cleaver raised, and brought it down across his forearm. The ox shrieked and dropped the knife. He stumbled away from her, heading for the door, but his legs couldn't hold him. He hit the floor with a thud and Valerie—exhausted and hurting—was on him. She hacked as many times as she was able but the cleaver was blunt and it was tough work. She stopped for a rest. The ox snorted and bled and crawled toward her. *"Keelooh . . . fuggha beeeeeeesh."*

The chimes sounded.

Valerie groaned and staggered to her strike position behind the door, not sure if she had the strength for another fight. *This might be it,* she thought, looking at the blunt cleaver. *The best that I could do.* It was the restaurateur, though, who *never* came while the animals were here, doing their thing. Valerie could only assume the loud noises, not to mention the fact that five animals had shown up and none had left, had earned his interest. The door opened a crack and he poked his head inside.

"Glurrgh," the ox said from the floor, reaching with one bloody hand. "Geelp *neeee.*"

The restaurateur yelped twice with surprise—first when he saw the carnage, and again when Valerie lifted the cleaver to his throat. She slotted it firmly between two greasy folds and eased him into the room.

"I should cut your fucking throat, too."

His eyes were tiny glowing lanterns.

"Guilty by association."

"No. They *made* me. Please."

"Fuck you." Valerie kept the cleaver to his throat as she ushered him toward the large chest against the side wall. She flipped the lid open with her foot. The stench of her own sweat, piss, and suffering wafted out. "Get in."

He shook his head. He was sobbing now.

"Get *in*." She exerted pressure with the cleaver and pushed against the back of his head. "Don't make me ask you again. Get in the box, you fat fuck."

He got in the box and hunkered down. The lid closed, but only just. It would be very uncomfortable in there for him. Valerie dropped the latch but there was no padlock so she retrieved the knife from the floor and ran the blade through. The ox grabbed at her on the way back but she stepped over him as she might a spider. She then left the room for the first time in four years, pausing at the top of the stairs, listening for sounds from the kitchen or dining area. There were none. The restaurant was empty. She continued down. The front doors came into view and, like some long-ago dream, she recalled the eighteen-year-old girl who had stepped through them—a girl who was dead now, replaced by a raging demigod bound for the promised land.

She pushed through double doors into a large kitchen. There were two refrigerators, each the size of a walk-in closet. She found fresh fruit and slices of cooked meat and ate until her stomach throbbed. A large clock read 3:37 p.m. Kitchen staff would arrive for the evening shift soon. Valerie wiped away her bloody prints with a cloth, placed the blunt, sticky cleaver in the back of a huge dishwasher, then selected a replacement—

sharper than the first—from a knife rack on the counter. She passed through the dining area on her way back upstairs and paused at a display where two Chinese sabers hung either side of a ceremonial shield. They were dull and blunt, just for show, but Valerie thought she would appear all the more imposing if she were brandishing one when the last three animals arrived. Any edge, even a psychological one, was worth exploiting.

Valerie grabbed one of the sabers and went upstairs. The ox was still alive—he'd almost made it to the door. The saber had a blunt edge but a sharp tip and Valerie punched it through the ox's skull. It went deep enough that she had to wiggle the sword this way and that to pry it free. Blood poured out of the mask like water from a broken bucket. She grabbed the ox by the ankles and dragged him behind the sofa with the other animals.

Calm continued to circle the room but her movements were less erratic. She was *clearer,* more in the present than in whatever terrible history she was tracking.

"This place is sacred to her," she whispered, and looked at Sasha. "It's why she didn't kill your uncle. She *knew,* even back then. He's a link to this room, and this room is a link to . . ." She trailed off, one hand positioned in front of her face, as if shielding her eyes from a bright light. "To the *flowers* . . . ?"

"Glam Moon," Martin said.

Calm lowered her hand and frowned. He felt her inside his mind, gently picking, still deep enough in the psychic flow that her instinct was to reach for an answer rather than ask a question.

"Her version of Eden." Martin flipped Calm's jacket to his other arm and shrugged. "She claims to have been there once, many years ago. Her followers on the island believe Glam Moon is real and that she'll lead them there."

"Sounds like cult bullshit," Sasha said.

"But it always felt harmless to me, not so different from Christians believing in heaven." Martin sighed, a bitter hiss of air that leaked from deep inside him. "So that's why she comes here? Because it's her link to Glam Moon?"

"That explains the Rhapsody," Sasha said, then elaborated for Calm's benefit. "It's a drug. Valerie calls it Rhapsody, but it's actually DMT. A hallucinogen."

"I know what DMT is," Calm said. "Dimethyltryptamine. One of the most potent psychedelics on the planet. Some theories suggest it's produced in the brain—in the pineal gland—and that small amounts are released during sleep. It's what gives us our wacky dreams. Another theory claims that we get a massive shot of DMT when we're breathing our last, which accounts for the near-death experience phenomenon—the so-called light at the end of the tunnel."

"She nearly died here," Martin said.

"Or she *did* die, and came back." Calm nodded, as if she believed this to be the case, as if such a thing happened all the time. "Now she's using the drug, and the room's energy, to recreate the experience."

"Not anymore," Sasha said. "I won't allow it."

Calm touched the air again, then circled the table once more. Martin wondered what else she would reveal, although it didn't matter anymore. Mother Moon had survived an unthinkable ordeal, but she was still a confused, dangerous woman. He wanted nothing to do with her.

"She kept this so well hidden," he said. "If I hadn't found that ring . . ."

"It's messed up," Sasha said. The amusement had drained from her expression. Only fear and bewilderment remained. "One woman. She killed them all."

"Not all," Calm said. "The tiger got away."

She gathered more wood and fed the fire, aware of the silhouettes watching her. Five of them now. They stood at the edge of the firelight. Valerie tossed on the last piece of wood and sat with her back to them.

The ox: "What are we doing here?"

The rabbit: "Did she stage an event? Did I miss something?"

The pig: "She called a meeting. She says she's in control."

The fire swelled. Valerie wasn't concerned that one of the islanders might see the light, or the smoke, and mosey down for a look-see. Jake Door had made the mistake of interrupting her earlier, before the pig arrived. "This a weenie roast?" he'd asked jovially, and she'd barked at him like a dog with a toothache. "Oh my crows, sorry-sorry," he'd whimpered, hot-tailing it out of sight. Valerie knew he'd tell the others that Mother Moon was on the beach, and that they'd best give her a wide berth.

It was perhaps ill-advised to snap at him like that, but what difference did it make? Island life, as they all knew it, was history. She didn't need their faith anymore. Thinking about that filled her with a rush of excitement, but there was also disdain: that the islanders would follow her across the Skyway, despite doing nothing to earn their place in the Glam. Nolan was an exception; he'd been her faithful attendant for many years. She'd let him feel the sun on his face for a couple of hours a day. But to think of the others—those fucking freeloaders—swimming in *her* lake, eating *her* fruit . . .

Valerie picked up the tiger mask and ran her hand across its beautiful face. "We'll just have to see about that."

"What? What did she say?"

"Shhh, she might say something else."

"What are we even *doing* here?"

This last was the snake, who'd emerged from the shadows and joined the group. Valerie saw his thin silhouette from the corner of her eye and sneered. She recalled how he'd slithered into the deathroom all those years ago—took her by surprise because he'd slunk silently past the chimes. She'd been dozing on the sofa and suddenly the door opened and he was there, hammer in hand. It took him a moment to compute what had obviously transpired, and another to choose between fight or flight. He chose fight. Valerie was on her feet by this point, saber raised, the cleaver clutched in her other fist. "Let's fucking *do* this," the snake said, and they did it. They went back and forth, swinging wildly with their weapons, until Valerie realized that the snake's mask limited his peripheral vision. She adapted quickly—timed her strikes. The snake weakened and eventually fell. She drove the saber into his lower back.

"Crawl," she said.

He crawled.

He'd got some licks in, though. He broke several of her ribs with the hammer and maybe dislocated her jaw. Not serious injuries, but they made her fight against the rooster more challenging. He arrived after the snake died and she leaped at him from behind the door. Her opening attack was well-timed but she was weak and it irked more than hurt him. He deflected her second attack, then grabbed her by the throat and threw her to the floor. She crawled over bodies and through the blood until he grabbed her leg and yanked her backward. She flashed the saber but its blunt edge did no damage. The rooster whipped it from her hand, rolled her onto her stomach, and slapped the flat of the blade across her bare ass. "Naughty girl," he squawked. "Naughty *naughty*." The cleaver trembled in her hand but she didn't have the angle to strike. He slapped her ass again, then she managed to roll away from him. She threw the cleaver like a tomahawk and it caught him in the thigh. He yowled and hobbled backward. Valerie saw the hammer next to the snake's arm. She crawled toward it, grabbed the handle in both hands, and smashed it against the rooster's knee. His leg went out from under him and he hit the floor hard. Valerie retrieved the cleaver, and with one accurate strike the fight was all but over. Like the ox and pig before him, the rooster took a long time to die. But die he did.

Valerie waited two days for the tiger to arrive. The restaurant opened and closed its doors. The staff and diners came and went. She wondered how long it would be before the stench of the dead, or the fact that Mr. Fat Restaurateur hadn't been seen all week, prompted the more inquisitive staff members to venture upstairs. Or maybe they'd just call the cops. Whatever, Valerie knew she was running out of time.

He came when she was on the verge of giving up. It was early morning. The sound of a key rattling in the front door lifted her from a weak sleep. Moments later she heard footfalls on the stairs, then the hollow knocking of the chimes. Valerie sat up, alert, heart galloping. She picked up the cleaver and saber and started toward her strike position but the door opened before she reached it. The tiger swept into the room. He did not falter when he saw the bloodshed.

"This would explain why the pig hasn't returned my calls," he said. He uttered a dry laugh and stepped toward her, unafraid. "You're stronger."

"I found it," she said. "The healing place."

Valerie saw his eyes flash behind the mask, but didn't give him the opportunity to respond. She brought the cleaver down in a purring arc. He stepped to one side, avoiding the attack with ease. "Silly little girl," he said, and punched her in the eye. The strength flowed from Valerie's legs and she fell against the wall. The tiger struck her again. She saw the flash of his Society ring and then everything went dark.

She woke up some hours later. Kitchen sounds from downstairs. The chatter of happy diners. She waited until the restaurant closed its doors for the night, then ventured from the room. Her first stop, again, was the kitchen, where she drank water and absorbed proteins through cold meat and raw fish. She then washed herself in the sink, using a pot scrubber to get all the blood from her body. Afterward, she found some cook's whites and a jacket and left the restaurant.

"But I couldn't stay away," Valerie whispered, staring into the flames. "I *needed* you."

It was full dark now. The fire threw a dome of light but beyond was blackness. The lake ran against the beach and sighed. Behind her, the silhouettes shuffled and muttered. Eight of them now. The whole dirty gang.

She looked at the mask in her hands, as dead as the man who'd worn it, as threatening now as the sand, as the calm water. Her mind ran with memories of the streets—weeks spent digging through garbage cans, sleeping in a cardboard box beneath an overpass. The tiger had haunted every cold dream. He'd left her alive and walked away. She *hated* him. She wanted his teeth, his stripes, but she was certain she'd never see him again.

Valerie lifted the mask, turning it this way and that in the warm glow. It appeared to breathe.

"And then I found you," she said.

One of the silhouettes stepped forward—a confident, arrogant stride, even after all these years. He touched her hair and she let him.

"No," he said. "I found you."

Calm was so tired that she fell asleep on the drive from the restaurant to the hotel. Martin wasn't sure if it was because it had been an especially long day, with its early start and the journey from Virginia, or because of her efforts in the room.

It had taken her a full twenty minutes to detach herself from the psychic stream. They'd sat in the restaurant downstairs, sipping green tea to help calm their nerves. Sasha, meanwhile, had already removed the chimes from the upstairs landing, and tossed them directly into the garbage can. "Step one," she'd declared, dusting off her hands. "Step two might be to sell this joint, maybe buy a nice little place on the shore."

"I'm sorry to have revealed all of this," Calm had said. "I just say what I see—what I feel."

"I needed to know," Sasha had replied.

They'd left the restaurant and driven in silence, at least until Martin heard Calm's gentle snoozing sounds. He looked at her, the city lights passing over her lined, lovely face. She flinched every now and then, but her expression was mostly peaceful. He'd planned on taking her to the Sternbridge Holiday Inn, but kept driving until he found something more upmarket in Rutherford. She'd earned the extra stars.

"Hey, Calm." He nudged her arm gently. "Wake up, sweetie. Let's get you checked in."

She nodded, looking around, blinking her strange but wonderful eyes. "The Watermark. Oh, this looks expensive."

"Stay here until I come get you," Martin said. "Either tomorrow or Saturday. I'll be with the girls. We'll make the road trip to Virginia together."

She nodded and sat up. Martin was about to exit the car when she placed her hand on his arm.

"You were happy on the island."

"Very, but I always thought it was too good to be true."

Calm sighed. "It sounds pessimistic, but experience has taught me that few things are truly as they appear. Everything is layered, and the layers only get darker the deeper they go."

"So what do we do?"

"I don't know. There are no shortcuts. No easy roads." Calm smiled and drummed one finger against her temple. "I taught Edith how to build her own garden, but as a diversion from the bad streams, not as a permanent escape. We can't nurture our souls from a distance, Martin. We get stronger when we overcome."

"I just wanted my girls to see a different America. One where they didn't live in fear—and where I didn't have to be afraid *for* them."

"But fear has its merits. It's like pain. It can galvanize. It can show us who we really are. You looked for your own garden—really no different from what I told Edith to do. But I also told her not to go so deep that she couldn't find her way home. I think that's where you were. It's a good job you took a step backward when you did."

Martin nodded, remembering how bewildered he'd been when he returned to the mainland. Part of that was the six weeks he'd spent in the clean, open air. Most of it was Mother Moon getting into his brain with her talk of clocks and grind. Another six weeks and he might have been halfway up the ladder to Glam Moon.

Like Shirley, he thought, and shuddered.

"Maybe that's the real reason Valerie doesn't want people hopping on and off the island," he said. "They'd realize the hold she has on them and wouldn't *want* to hop back on. That doesn't apply to me, of course, because my girls are still there. She knows I'm coming back."

"Sounds plausible," Calm agreed. "Or maybe she has other secrets that are at risk if people come and go. There *is* more to this. I can feel it."

"Well, she found the tiger. Found him and killed him. Must have, because she has his mask. His ring, too, I assume."

"I don't know what happened when she left the restaurant," Calm said. "But yes, I think you're right. And she's holding on to the mask for the same reason she keeps returning to that room. She can't let go. Her ordeal, the animals, Glam Moon . . . it's all a part of who she is."

Martin shook his head. He wished he could hit the rewind button to that moment of uncertainty he'd felt before stepping onto Nolan's boat. Or better yet, to the last time he saw Laura, when he came close to pulling her between the bed sheets with him, keeping her there.

"You're leaving the island."

Martin looked at Calm. He wasn't sure if this was a question or a command, but his response was the same. "You're damn right. Nolan's picking me up tomorrow afternoon. Only reason I'm going back is to get my girls."

"Word of advice: keep what you know to yourself." Calm pointed a no-nonsense finger at him. "Don't ruffle any feathers. Just get the hell out of there."

"I'll play it cool," Martin assured her.

"Cool is good."

They got out of the car and walked toward the hotel's revolving doors. The light inside was copious and wonderful.

33

He sat down on the other side of the fire and she saw his face through the flames, as handsome as ever, a wisp of blond hair covering one eye, his smile all but indiscernible beneath a bushy brown mustache.

"Hey, sugargirl," he said.

"Hello, Pace."

The other animals shuffled closer. They didn't sit like Pace and their masks stayed on. All these years later, Pace's was still the only face she knew.

"My mask stinks," he complained, pointing at it in Valerie's hands. "Did you piss on it?"

"Twice," Valerie replied, holding it up like a hunter's trophy. "It holds no power over me."

There were snorts and growls among the animals. The dog stepped forward.

"What's this about?" he barked.

"It's about the end," Valerie said. "I don't need you anymore."

"Sugargirl," Pace said. "You couldn't get rid of us if you tried."

A few of the animals nodded in agreement, while the others appeared uncertain. They muttered and lowered their heads. The rooster scrunched his hands into fists.

"We *should* be at the Lantern," he said.

"The island has energy, too. And memories." Valerie looked at Pace. "Doesn't it?"

"It does."

The spiel that Valerie gave new islanders—how she'd looked after Victoria Platt-Mellor and inherited the island after the old lady died—was only partly true. Victoria did indeed move to the island following her husband's death, and lived out her days there, but she'd willed Halcyon—Gray Peaks Island, as it was officially called—to her youngest child, Pacifico, not knowing that he would only outlive her by five months.

Pace had told Valerie and the other girls about Gray Peaks over breakfast one morning. "How would you like to live in a place that very few people know exists?" he offered, and revealed how he'd summered on the island as a child—two hundred and seventy acres in the middle of Lake Ontario, accented by granite outcrops and towering pines. His mom lived there now, but her health had deteriorated in recent years and she needed looking after. Pace said he visited her once every couple of months, but it wasn't enough.

"We'll relocate there," he'd said, looking at Iris, Agnes, Amy, and then Valerie. "All of us. We'll look after my mother, and then, after she dies, the island will be ours. We can establish Halcyon, bring more people in. We'll harmonize and find the Glam."

The offer was met with great enthusiasm, and the group moved to Gray Peaks in the spring of 1991. It was the life that Pace promised, a new kind of freedom. They spent their days loving, swimming, fishing, and farming. They stored food for the winters. They built tall fires and huddled like bears. The only real work was the old lady, who became more demanding as her dementia deepened. Pace had expected her to live only a few months, six at the most, but she had no interest in meeting her maker so swiftly. She lived another three and a half years, and might have lived three and a half more if Pace hadn't finally smothered her with a pillow—the humane thing to do, he'd reasoned, and considering Mrs. Platt-Mellor had spent her final days smearing shit all over the walls and conversing with the ghost of Joan Crawford, it was a hard point to argue. Pace shipped her body back to the mainland, and from that point on the island was theirs. It became Halcyon.

It wasn't long before they tried DMT for the first time. They found peace through meditation, pleasure through sex, but Pace wanted to take it a step further. DMT, he said, would broaden their spiritual pathways. It wouldn't transport them to the Glam, but it would condition their minds to become more accepting.

Valerie's trips were sun-drenched. She never flew, but she walked on air. Sometimes her legs were vines with healthy leaves sprouting from the joints. It wasn't Glam Moon, though. Nothing like. The other thing she observed: Pace rarely took the drug himself. He was a watcher, and he usually watched *her*.

"What are you seeing, sugargirl?"

"Just . . . bright and . . . my legs feel . . ."

The other girls ran naked and sang. They danced and cried. Pace often carried Valerie to his bed. He was rough on those occasions. "Show me," he'd demand, one hand around her throat, banging into her body. "*Show me.*"

Until that point Valerie's life had been marked by a series of sudden, startling turns: running away from her home in Michigan to live in New York City; being held and tortured in a room for four years; escaping that room in a blaze of blood and glory; living on a remote island in the middle of Lake Ontario. It turned again after she overheard a conversation between Pace and Agnes. They'd been walking through the woods and didn't know that Valerie was gathering firewood nearby.

"The DMT is a trip," Agnes said. "But we should take Rhapsody. We should simulate the Glam."

"Rhap is extremely hard to come by," Pace replied. "It's available to only a select few—those in the upper echelons of society."

"Then we should make it ourselves. It's synthetic, right? Man-made?"

"Right, but the key ingredient . . . you need to be a goddamn quantum physicist to distill it."

"And what is the key ingredient?"

"Pain, and a lot of it."

They were silent for a moment. Valerie followed behind, keeping low and silent.

"Why pain?" Agnes asked.

"Because it's a gateway," Pace replied. "Always has been. When pleasure is denied, the channel to new possibilities, and alternate experiences, becomes broader."

Valerie had heard those words before, those *exact* words, but it was the way he spoke them—with a touch of arrogance, a tiger-like regality—that drove the air from her lungs and the strength from her legs. She fell with a soft thump and for a long time could not make a thought. When she could, her first was that Pace's hands appeared infinitely kinder without the ring on his finger.

A week later she and Iris traveled to the mainland for supplies. Once there, she "lost" Iris and took a Greyhound to Green Ridge, New Jersey, where Pace maintained a residence. She'd never been there, but had seen the address on various documents, including his driver's license. It was a small house with trash in the yard and dirty windows, one of which—the bathroom window, around back—slid open when she tried it. She stood on a crate, hoisted herself up, and wriggled inside. Dust coated everything. The rooms stank of mold and sourness. There was a different aroma in the bedroom, faint but familiar: of cologne, peppery, yet sweet. It induced a stream of nightmare memories. She found the bottle—it was called "Mountain" by Jaume Cadenas—in the top drawer of the dresser. The closet was full of dress shirts and zippered suits. Valerie recognized some of them. *Tiger clothes,* she thought. She found the mask in a shoebox in the attic. It took her longer to find the ring. It was in an inside pocket of one of the suit jackets, tucked into the corner. She'd missed it first time she checked.

Back on the island, the snow melted and spring whispered into the air—the buds showing green at their tips, peepers croaking in the woods. Pace returned from a short trip to the mainland to find Valerie waiting for him on the dock. She threw her arms around him when he stepped ashore and kissed his whiskery chin.

"Hey, sugargirl," he said.

"I've something to show you." Her eyes danced. She led him up the steps and through the burgeoning sumac and primrose, then through the evergreens. When Pace asked where the others were, she told him they were waiting. They cut through their orchard of saplings and past a half-built storage shed, and continued to the main cabin. Pace said he'd never known the island so quiet. He reached for her hand but she skipped away from him—dashed the last few yards, onto the porch and into the cabin.

"What are you playing at?" he called. His voice was full of mirth. Valerie heard his boots clomp up the porch steps, then the door creaked open. It was dim inside the cabin; Valerie had pulled all the blinds. Pace reached for the light switch, flicked it . . .

"For you," Valerie said.

She didn't know how he'd react. Would he be Pacifico, who'd shown ceaseless love, or would the tiger appear, with his dead soul and indifference to suffering? She watched his face as he absorbed the scene, knowing it didn't matter which version appeared; she'd kill him anyway. Twice, if she had to.

"My girls," he said, his jaw trembling.

Iris, Agnes, and Amy were tied to wooden chairs in the

kitchen area. Their throats had been cut and their eyes dug out. Each wore a sign written in blood. Iris's read THE. Agnes's read END OF. Amy's read PLEASURE.

"My girls."

Pacifico, then, meaning peace-loving. His throat worked, his penny-brown eyes swelled with tears. He ran his hand across them and looked at Valerie. She'd never seen him so frail. His body language announced some question she couldn't decipher. *Why did you do this?*, maybe, or *How did you know?* The answer to both—to any question he might ask—was the same: Valerie reached into the armchair beside her and pulled the mask and ring from behind one of the pillows. She held them up so he could see. Her hands were remarkably steady. Pace's were not. He wiped his face again and nodded stupidly.

"I told you once," she said, stepping toward him, "that if this isn't real—if *you're* not real—that I would break all over again."

"You did."

"You had fair warning. I mean, you *knew* what I could do."

"Yes."

"I loved you, Pace. I trusted you."

"Yes," he said. "I was counting on that."

Pace had joined his father's investment banking firm fresh out of college, and used his good looks and charm, rather than his family connection, to work his way up the corporate ladder. Money interested him, he said, but people interested him more. He spent his days underwriting deals and assisting acquisitions, and his nights hobnobbing with Wall Street high rollers. He claimed that 80 percent of new business came by way of the social scene.

As his reputation grew, his social scene narrowed—became more elitist. He was invited to private functions, and found himself drawn to the most debauched of them: the extreme kink and pain parties. "It started out with autoerotic asphyxiation and body suspension, and escalated from there. You wouldn't believe some of the things I've seen."

"Oh," Valerie replied. "I think I would."

Pace frequented this underground scene for a few years, then he and a small group of his "high society" associates started driving around the city, following a police radio to sites of shootings, car wrecks, fires, gas explosions, what*ever*—if there was pain, they were there. Members of this odd group came and went, but a core eight formed, and this eight became the Society of Pain.

"There are versions of the Society all over the world," Pace said. "They follow—and sometimes instigate—disasters to fulfill their . . . their *urges*. For some the pain is the focus, a source of arousal. Symphorophilia, it's called. A relatively new term. For others, it's that shot at Glam Moon."

"That's you," Valerie said. "You were different. You kept your clothes on."

"Oh, I hurt you plenty—"

"Yes."

"But it was never a sexual thing for me. It was always about what the pain might bring." Pace had made his way into the kitchen area and stood behind his girls. He played with their hair as if they could feel it. "Glam Moon. It's called Tukoko in Malaysia. Ukabu in Eastern Africa. In China, some people offer themselves as victims in the hope of catching a glimpse. That sounds hard to believe, until you draw comparisons to heaven, which requires its own sacrifice—ultimately your life. Did you know that seven out of ten Americans believe in heaven?"

Valerie shook her head. She wasn't sure why he was telling her all this. Perhaps he felt she was due an explanation. Or he was buying time, waiting for her to lower her guard. She kept her eye on him. She had a very sharp knife tucked into the back of her jeans.

"The other animals," Pace continued, "didn't buy into the spiritual side as much. They just wanted to see you bleed."

"Who were they?"

"Is it important?"

"No. But I always wondered why their deaths were covered up. I guess certain reputations had to be protected."

"You guess right," Pace said. "A former Republican governor. A property mogul. A federal judge. No, that story couldn't get out. Some wily reporter would have picked at it and eventually uncovered a trail of corruption that led all the way to the top."

Valerie thought of the pyramid on the reverse of the Great Seal of the United States, crowned with that shimmering, all-seeing eye. She looked at the ring still in her hand, at the very similar eye set within the inscription. Pace followed her trail of thought.

"Not the Eye of Providence, perhaps," he said. "But certainly the eye of governance."

"If they were all such powerful men," Valerie said. "How come you—a young investment banker—were in charge?"

"I wasn't supposed to be, but yes, that leadership role fell to me." Pace stroked the back of Amy's hair, then stepped around her chair. His boots made wet sounds in the blood. "I think because I was more interested in the process—in the Glam—so did most of the talking. Also, the others held positions of authority in their normal lives. They were happy to be led for a change. All part of the kink."

"And the masks," Valerie said, holding up the one in her hand. "Were they part of the kink, too?"

Pace looked at his old mask with a certain fondness. "We found them in a box at the restaurant. A Chinese New Year thing. Aside from concealing our identities in the event you escaped, we also thought they'd intensify the experience."

Valerie had spent the last few days mentally preparing for this confrontation, wanting to show no weakness, or even emotion. But something about this caught her off guard. The blunt truth of it, perhaps.

"Did it work?" Pace asked.

"Yes." She pushed the ring into her pocket and placed her hand on her hip, close to where the hilt of the knife jutted from the waistband of her jeans. "I still see you every time I close my eyes."

"We'll always be with you," Pace said.

"No."

"The other animals wanted to kill you. They grew bored of you. Of your lethargy—your lack of response." Pace stepped into the living room with Valerie. There was blood on the cuffs of his jeans. "But I saw something in your eyes. A rare depth. A boldness. I knew you could reach the Glam. Not only reach it, but uncover the Skyway. So I kept you alive."

"Uncover." Valerie spat the word. "Through torture, pain, and misery?"

"Any thug can cause pain." Pace spread his hands—hands that had beaten and babied her. "I consider it a more scientific process."

"People aren't science experiments."

"That's *exactly* what we are. All of us." He looked at her with hooded eyes, and it was hard for Valerie to imagine she'd ever seen love in them, or anything beyond malice. "People have incredible amounts of energy. More than in any inanimate object or geographic location. It stands to reason that the way to Glam Moon exists in someone who has been torn apart, like you . . . or someone with an exceptional gift."

Valerie shook her head. She'd endured a thousand hells and opened a tiny—and temporary—rift into Glam Moon. How much pain would be needed to uncover the White Skyway? Or how exceptional would a gift need to be?

"That's why I didn't kill you when I had the chance," Pace continued. "And why I pulled you from the streets, skinny-ass wretch that you were. I *saved* you, because I knew you were my way in."

"So what was the plan? To fill me with love and security, then tear me apart again?"

"A new experiment," Pace said. "Being systematically abused by eight strangers in animal masks is one thing, but to endure that same hell by way of someone you loved, and who you *thought* loved you . . . well, that's a different level of pain."

"And you've been planning this for what . . . eight years?"

"Eight and a half. But it's taken you a long time to develop trust, and to let yourself be loved. You're still not fully healed." Pace tapped his forehead again. "And of course I wanted to wait until we had Halcyon. It's harder to escape when you're on an island."

"Such an investment of time and effort," Valerie said. "And all for nothing."

"We had some fun along the way."

"You said I was set apart." She couldn't keep her voice from breaking. She felt herself weakening inside—she'd have to do this soon. "A gem, you said. An outrageous wonder."

"Not a lie," Pace replied. "You had something the other girls didn't. And I wanted it. I still do."

"Sorry to upset your plans." She threw the mask at him. "Put it on."

He didn't catch the mask. It bounced off his chest and fell to the floor, into a rill of blood that had trickled from the kitchen. When he picked it up, Valerie saw a red splash around the tiger's mouth, as if it had been eating.

"I'm a different man when I put this on," Pace warned. "Dangerous."

"You're more of an animal without it."

He smiled weakly and pulled the mask over his head. The composure that Valerie had been fighting for left her body in a whirl. The walls of the cabin closed in. The tiger appeared to grow a full foot and expand at the shoulders. Valerie pulled the knife from the waistband of her jeans. It had looked unreasonably large against the girls' throats, but seemed now too small, incapable of harming the tiger, who filled the space in front of her as he had filled her mind these past years.

He made claws out of his hands and roared, then jumped toward her. It was only the sight of that red splash around the tiger's mouth that snapped Valerie back into focus. That would be *her* blood soon, she realized. He would savage and devour her. She slashed the knife across the tiger's chest. It opened his jacket and T-shirt and the skin beneath but didn't slow him. He pushed her against the wall—laced his hands around her throat and squeezed. The room dimmed at the edges but not enough. She struck again. The knife plunged into the tiger's lower stomach. He said "*Blurrgh*," and buckled. His hold on her throat weakened. She pulled out the knife and stabbed him again. "*Bluuuuurgh.*" One hand dropped from her throat. His eyes blinked desperately through the little holes in the mask.

"Sugar . . . girl."

She stabbed him a third time, angling the blade so that it went up under his sternum and into his heart. He dropped to his knees with his head back and throat offered. She took it, whipping the blade across his Adam's apple. He died like that, on his knees. All told, it happened quickly.

She took a day to let her emotions out. Some of them had been tightly buttoned and they emerged in doglike howls and yelps. Some never fully emerged. She eventually calmed and slept that night on the sofa close to the tiger's kneeling corpse. In the morning she built a pyre and doused it with gasoline and dragged her old lovers on. They made bright flames. They warmed her again.

* * *

"But you kept the mask," Pace said. "The ring, too. You kept me alive."

"I kept *all* of you alive," Valerie replied, looking at the animals gathered around her. "No, alive isn't quite the right word. *Vital.* I kept you vital, and by extension, Glam Moon."

"The scars aren't enough?"

"I love my scars. Each one of them is an emblem of fortitude. They lead into my heart. Everything else—the mask, the memories—leads out to Glam Moon." Valerie considered this statement, then shook her head. "Or they *used* to. They're redundant now, of course."

"So we're redundant?" the goat said.

"Absolutely."

"Explain." This was the pig.

Valerie shrugged, as if the answer was self-explanatory. The ox and dog grunted impatiently, so she spelled it out for them. "It's simple: I kept you close until I found what I was looking for."

"That elusive Skyway," Pace said. He smiled, but there was an uncertain edge to his voice. "She's talking about the girl."

"Both girls. And myself, too."

"Explain." The pig again.

"It's a scientific process." Valerie looked at Pace as she said this, and couldn't keep the smirk from her face. "In layman's terms: you have the battery, you have the bulb, but you still need someone to flip the switch."

Stars peppered the darkness now. Valerie imagined the islanders gathering in the meadow, lying on the cold grass, joining hands and singing. Black hand, white hand.

Togetherness. The America they deserved. She imagined them walking across the Skyway—*her* Skyway—with that same peaceable approach. Her soul crackled like the fire and threw a similar light.

"Such anger," Pace noted. "Still."

"Soon," she replied, "there'll only be peace."

"But you can't get rid of us. We're everywhere. In your brainwaves and bloodstream."

"In the sound of the lake," the snake said.

"In the trees," the rabbit offered. "In the grass."

"We're the faces in the clouds," the dog said.

"And the shadows," the rooster added.

"Everywhere." Pace threw his arms wide. "You can open the Skyway, but we'll always be with you."

"You're dead to me," Valerie said. She got to her feet and walked to the edge of the lake. The ring had never felt heavier. She wasn't even sure she could raise her arm to throw it. But she managed, and the ring went far. It winked once, catching a bead of firelight, then was lost to the darkness. She heard the sound of it hitting the water. *Plink.* Such a diminutive sound for something so bound to misery.

Valerie closed her eyes for a moment. A wave broke and soaked her feet. She nodded and returned to the fire. The animals stood around it, but had lost substance. Only the mask in her hand was solid. She looked at it one final time, then threw it on the flames. It landed face-up and stared at her through its black eyeholes, then it shriveled and burned. The smoke it made was blacker.

"Done," she said.

She walked toward the edge of the cove. The first time she turned back, she saw that all of the animals had disappeared. Only Pace remained. He sat cross-legged beside the fire, staring forlornly into the flames. Valerie walked on, cutting through the shrubs and grasses, and turned back once again. The fire flickered and threw a blanket of bare light. There was no sign of Pace.

"Dead to me," she said again.

She walked through the trees using distant lights to guide her. Sound, too; the islanders had indeed gathered in the meadow, and were indeed singing.

34

Martin had checked out of his hotel in Sternbridge and was on the road by 6 a.m. It was a four-hour drive to Syracuse and he planned on doing it in one hit. Traffic wouldn't be an issue, not this early on Black Friday, but he wasn't taking any chances.

He kept to the speed limit even though everything inside him screamed rush. The sun was hinting at the eastern horizon by the time he made the Pennsylvania state line. The forecast promised clear skies across the region, but in upstate New York a storm was blowing in.

The girl had been silent on the boat to the mainland. She'd muttered, "Thank you," when Nolan helped her into his truck and shook her head when he asked if she wanted the radio on. Other than that, there'd been no interaction. This suited Nolan just fine, and besides, he was used to it. Driving south to their destination, he reflected how Mother Moon's subjects were often quiet at this time. Garrett Riley had stared out the passenger-side window the entire way—didn't utter a word until they'd reached the storage unit where the IED was parked. Barbara Chiltern had chewed her fingernails and sucked on the tips of her hair. The one time Nolan tried engaging in conversation, Barbara had burst into tears and started beating on the door, screaming, "*Let me out, let me out,*" and it took an hour to calm her down. Since then, Nolan had learned to mind his own affairs, and to give his passengers their moment of pensive silence.

They diverted from the Interstate east of Syracuse and followed dusty roads away from the city. "Scenic route," Nolan remarked a little later, steering around a dead deer spread across five yards of red pavement. They headed east then veered gradually southwest, through the rugged grays and greens of Madison and Onondaga Counties, until Nolan rolled in behind an abandoned gas station seven miles from the target location.

Shirley looked at him blankly.

"Instruction," he said.

They got out of the truck. Nolan opened the back door and took a cardboard box off the backseat. He set it on the ground but didn't open it yet. Shirley leaned against the truck's tailgate with her head down.

"You know what you have to do?" Nolan asked her.

She nodded.

"Okay." Nolan pulled a wristwatch from his pocket and handed it to her. "Put this on."

Shirley took the watch and looped it around her wrist.

"What time you got?"

"Nine twenty."

"You can tell the time. We're off to a good start."

"I'm sixteen, not six."

"Just making sure." Nolan tried a warm smile but warm smiles were not his thing. "Now, you got your doorbusters first thing—those crazy sons of bitches who camp out all night—but recent data suggests the busiest time for Black Friday shopping is the afternoon, peaking somewhere around three o'clock. Mother Moon says she won't wait that long, so you'll engage at one thirty. Repeat that back to me."

"One thirty."

"Electronics and department stores see the heaviest traffic, with checkout lanes being the most densely populated areas. This should be your focus, but use your judgment for maximum impact. Being one thirty, you might want to poke your head in the food court, too."

Nolan opened the box and took out a black puffer jacket, using both hands because it was heavy. He held it up for Shirley to see.

"This is your IED."

Shirley frowned.

"IED. Improvised explosive device." Nolan hoisted the jacket over the bed rail of his truck, like someone drying clothing in the sun. "Weighs about thirty pounds. Most of that is shrapnel—ball bearings and screws. The rest is an RDX-based plastic explosive called Kerna-H4. We wanted to use TATP because it's cheaper and easier to procure. It's also as volatile as hell. They don't call it 'Mother of Satan' for nothing."

Nolan paused to let this information sink in. The girl looked at the jacket with dead eyes. A vein in her throat jumped.

“With TATP, there’s a real risk of accidental detonation, especially in crowded places.” Nolan gave the jacket a couple of solid thumps. “Kerna-H4 can take the knocks. Heck, you can fire a bullet through it and it won’t go off. It needs a charge. A spark.”

“Why are you telling me all this?” Shirley asked.

“Because you need to know how the IED works. Knowledge enables you to adapt, and increases the chances of success. Moreover, I want you to understand how much effort has gone into making sure this *is* a success.”

“It will be.”

Nolan ran a hand across the back of his neck, damp with sweat despite the coolness of the morning. He looked from the girl to the jacket. “So. The charge I was talking about. The spark. You’ll notice the jacket is zipped up. That’s because it’s wired to a battery, which in turn is wired to a detonator. Unzipping the jacket—I’m talking all the way, so that the little pin pops out of the slider—will trigger the detonator. Allow me to stress the importance of this: *do not unzip the jacket until you are in position.* Repeat that back to me.”

“Leave the zipper alone.”

“Until . . .”

“I’m in position.”

“At what time?”

“One thirty.”

“Atta girl.” Nolan showed his teeth. It wasn’t a smile, but it was close.

“Thirty pounds,” Shirley said. “Might be too heavy for me.”

"The weight's distributed evenly. It won't feel like thirty pounds when you've got it on."

"Okay."

"All these puffy parts, across the shoulders, down the arms, they're packed with shrapnel. You can't even tell, huh?"

"Looks just like a regular jacket."

Nolan's chest swelled with pride. Mother Moon had told him to design a suicide belt—something that could be worn beneath regular clothes, but Nolan knew they often looked bulky and suspicious. It was his idea to modify a jacket. A puffer jacket, specifically, with all those little cavities for packing detritus. A snip here, a stitch there. *Voila!* It was also his idea to use plastic explosive instead of TATP. A couple of critical adjustments that could make all the difference. He'd waited a long time for the Glam, almost as long as Mother Moon. Everything had to be perfect.

"Okay, back in the truck," Nolan said. "We've got a little time to kill. Let's hit Dunkin' Donuts."

"I'm not hungry."

"We'll see."

Nolan laid the jacket on the backseat and kicked the empty box into the scrub at the edge of the lot. He got behind the wheel and they drove—in silence again—to a Dunkin' Donuts just off Interstate 81. He parked on a deserted side street a block away.

"Still not hungry?"

"You want to get a little closer? They have drive-thru, you know."

"This is as close as we get. By the end of the day, you'll be the most famous person in America. I don't want anybody seeing you in this truck."

"You've thought it all through, huh?"

"You want anything?"

"No."

"Fine. Keep your head down. If anybody walks past, don't make eye contact." Nolan got out of the truck and walked to the restaurant. He returned minutes later carrying a brown bag as heavily stuffed as the jacket on the backseat. He took out a large coffee, a breakfast sandwich, and a jelly donut for himself, and placed a hot chocolate and Boston Kreme on the dashboard in front of Shirley.

"In case you change your mind."

Shirley didn't touch her food to begin with, then she took a sip of the hot chocolate, then a bigger sip, and before long she was wiping sticky vanilla filling off her chin and brushing crumbs off her jacket.

"Usually at this time," Nolan said after he finished his sandwich, "I would offer instruction on what to say in the event you're compromised. But you're not going to be compromised. You're a sixteen-year-old white girl in a shopping mall. No one will look twice at you. That being said, you still have to be smart."

Shirley licked chocolate icing off her lips.

"Do not approach the mall until close to zero hour." Nolan pointed at Shirley's wristwatch. "By zero hour I mean one thirty: time of commencement. That way, there's less chance of running into someone you know. Also, the Onondaga Mall has only been open a few weeks, so security will still be bright-eyed and bushy-tailed. You're a sixteen-year-old white girl, but loitering will make them suspicious."

Shirley nodded.

"Don't make eye contact with anyone. Focus on the middle distance, and walk with a sense of purpose." Nolan took a huge bite out of his donut and jelly squirted onto his shirt. Still chewing, he said, "If you do see someone you know, act naturally and excuse yourself as quickly as possible."

"Dad," Shirley said.

Nolan rinsed his mouth with a gulp of coffee. "Dad? What do you—"

"My dad helped build that mall," Shirley said. Her eyes filmed over. "He's an architect. *Was* an architect, I guess."

"That's right. And a good man. A *damn* good man."

"I'm going to miss him."

"Let me tell you something," Nolan said, the last mouthful of donut poised an inch from his lips. "He's going to walk into the Glam, across the Skyway *you* open, and he's going to be incredibly proud of you."

This wasn't true at all. Nolan was scheduled to pick Martin up at two o'clock. Martin might think he was returning to Halcyon, but Nolan had something different planned: a bullet to the head and a trip to the bottom of Lake Ontario.

"I hope so," Shirley said.

Nolan finished his donut and coffee, then tossed the trash out the window, started the truck and drove toward the mall. He found a secluded spot a mile northwest, behind tangles of brushwood and a faded billboard that declared: THE GIFT OF GOD IS ETERNAL LIFE.

"This is the drop zone," Nolan said. "I have to leave soon. Mother Moon needs me for an urgent task. And I still have to pick up your father."

"You're leaving me here?"

"I have to, and I can't get any closer because of possible video surveillance around the mall." Nolan noticed the blob of jelly on his shirt. He wiped it off and sucked his finger clean. "You'll be fine. You've got this. Let me hear you say it."

"I've got this."

"Wait here until twelve thirty. I suggest you sit still and don't expend energy. Then start walking. Follow this road"—Nolan pointed through the brushwood—"until you hit Owen Street. Turn left on Owen and follow it all the way to the mall. It's about a mile. That's twenty minutes at a normal pace, but we'll allow thirty because of the jacket."

"Okay."

"Speaking of which, let's get it on."

They exited the truck. Nolan took the jacket off the backseat, unzipped it halfway, and helped Shirley pull it on like a sweater. She slumped, arms hanging. "Straighten your shoulders," Nolan said. "There, that's better." The sleeves were a little long but otherwise it was a good fit.

"So heavy," Shirley moaned.

"It's no heavier than a backpack."

She walked a little way and came back, rolling her shoulders to get a feel for the weight. The cold wind ruffled her hair, blonder at the roots. She shrugged and turned her lightless eyes to Nolan.

"I can't get her out of my head," she said.

"Mother Moon wants what's best for you. For all of us."

"What if she's wrong?"

"She's not."

Shirley turned away, her head low. Nolan shuffled his feet awkwardly. For fear of saying the wrong thing, he said nothing at all. The clouds moved in great pillows overhead and birds called. When Shirley turned back, he saw tears in her eyes.

"I'll see you in the Glam," he said.

She nodded vaguely. Nolan started toward his truck, but Shirley spoke his name very softly, very sweetly. He looked at her over his shoulder.

"Will it hurt?" she asked. A tear flashed down her cheek.

"You won't feel a thing," Nolan replied, and he believed this as much as everything else. "The moment you pull that zipper down, you're going to grow wings."

35

Valerie skipped from her cabin into the clear, cold air, kicking happily at the leaves and watching them flicker. Gilda Wynne greeted her with the broadest smile. "Oh my, Mother Moon, aren't *you* a ray of sunshine this morning!" Valerie looked at her and said nothing, only laughed—the shrill, unbalanced laugh of someone at the threshold of either madness or bliss. Gilda's smile faltered and she scurried away.

Valerie walked on, light of step and of soul. She ducked into the shelter of the trees, took the watch out of her pocket, and looked at it for perhaps the fiftieth time that morning. It was the same watch she'd kept locked in a box for so many years. Nolan had synchronized it with the watch he'd given to Shirley. Time: hours, minutes, and seconds, with meaning at last. At 1:30 the Skyway would explode from what Edith called the place between (and what a beautiful, poetic phrase that was: *the place between*), and Valerie would walk—no *swagger*—across it after all these years of searching.

Momma's coming home, she thought, and heard music in the air, a delicate plucking and plinking, not dissimilar to those bamboo wind chimes she'd heard over and over again. She followed the sound, wending gaily through the trees, and came to Alyssa's cabin. Alyssa was nowhere in sight. Inside, maybe, or attending to some island chore. Edith sat on the front step with a guitar across her knee.

"I was looking for you," Valerie said.

Edith put the guitar down. There were dark circles beneath her eyes.

"Where's my sister?" she asked.

"At the very edge of light," Valerie replied, and held out her hand. "Come with me."

A collision south of Scranton delayed Martin by almost an hour. He was sweating and irritable by the time traffic started moving again. Not only that, but a voice in his head—it sounded distinctly like Laura's—told him that time was running out. Paranoia, of course, due in part to being stuck in traffic, feeling helpless and far away, but due also to the many things he'd learned these past few days.

He'd fallen asleep the previous night with a box load of questions tumbling through his mind. The most pressing was whether or not to go straight to the police with what he knew. Ultimately, he decided against it. All he had was Calm's word, her *psychic* word, and that was hardly going to stand up. More decisively, it was impossible to implicate someone in a crime that, on record, never took place.

Be smart, he thought, and remembered Calm's advice:

Don't ruffle any feathers. He had a single objective: to get his daughters—and Alyssa, if she'd come—off the island. Once they were together and back on the mainland, he could decide the best course of action.

Martin hit Syracuse at 10:40 and kept going. He couldn't wait three hours for Nolan—he'd make his own way to Halcyon. That might arouse suspicion, but he had a solid excuse: to get back before the storm blew in, and to save Nolan a trip. Mother Moon might buy it, but if she didn't . . . well, no big deal. He was leaving the island anyway.

Most of the journey had been beneath blue skies. Heavier cloud rolled in as he drove north toward Fisherman's Point. He made it to the small lakeside town in good time, only to find the marina deserted. A few boats bobbed in their slips but that was all. Martin sat in the parking lot and pondered his next move. He could wait and hope someone showed up, he could try the larger marina in Oswego eleven miles east, or he could check Nolan's boathouse. Nolan might have made the trip already, and could be gassing up the center console or loading supplies.

Worth a shot, Martin thought.

He took Salmon Road out of Fisherman's Point and followed it six miles to Ridge Lane—the unpaved, unmarked track that led to the dilapidated summerhouse and water beyond. The rental bounced over the bumpy surface at a crawl. Martin tried to take comfort from the fact that he was close now, but paranoia crowded him from all sides.

Don't sweat it, he thought. *People have lived on Halcyon for years, safe and happy. It's all good, so just chill.*

Good advice, but impossible to follow. How could he chill with Laura persistently telling him that time was running out? He kept flashing back to that dream, too. That damn dream with the bullet, which had felt so much like a warning—a premonition.

Martin rounded the last bend and saw Nolan's truck in the summerhouse's driveway. He parked alongside and got out of the car. The smell of the lake hit him immediately. He inhaled greedily, listening to the wind through the branches and the distinct ticking of the rental's engine as it cooled. But not just the rental's engine. The truck's, too. Martin laid his hand on the broad white hood and felt the heat.

Nolan had arrived recently, probably within the last five minutes. He might be in the boathouse, after all. Martin followed the cracked path past the summerhouse. He was about to call Nolan's name when he heard an outboard motor rip into life.

"Shit."

Martin broke into a jog, feeling that old familiar pain niggling his left knee. He reached the boathouse just as Nolan pulled out of the slip.

"Nolan . . . Nolan!"

Shouting was pointless; there was no chance he'd be heard over the rumbling engine. Nolan zipped away, dragging a tail of white water.

"What the hell?" Martin said. Did he get the wrong time? No, Nolan *definitely* said two o'clock, and it was only 11:32 now. Which meant Nolan was either coming back within the next couple of hours, or he wanted to beat the storm. And if that was the case, when *would* he be back?

Martin's sense of foreboding deepened. He kicked at a mooring post, then looked up and down the shoreline.

He needed to find a boat.

A light snow started to fall.

Time of day was not a factor for people living on the island, but Nolan was not afforded that luxury. He too often made trips to the mainland, where minutes and hours ruled and everybody followed. In this regard he was still a prisoner, and he for damn sure was Mother Moon's prisoner, although he preferred to think of himself as her right-hand man. It wasn't so different from being in the military, but all he got for that was a head full of fuckery and a medal he ended up selling for food. At least with Mother Moon, the payoff would be more rewarding.

No clocks on Halcyon, of course, but Nolan kept an old wristwatch on the boat. He glanced at it as he approached the dock, where Jake Door sat with his rod in the water. It was 11:58. Mother Moon wanted him for some vital task. Which was fine, as long as it was quick; Nolan had a vital task of his own.

He shut off the center console's engine and coasted into the dock.

"How-do?" Jake put his rod down and stood to greet him. There were flecks of snow in his mustache.

"Tie me off," Nolan demanded, whipping the line at him.

"Well, shoot, a 'please' wouldn't hurt, fella."

"Please."

Nolan jumped ashore and hastened along the dock. Snow

blurred the air around him. It was still light—the heavier stuff wasn't rolling in until mid-afternoon, maybe early evening—but it was another reason to haul ass. If he were late collecting Martin, there was every chance they'd be stranded on the mainland together, a scenario that would call for some serious improvisation.

There were a few islanders doing chores—raking leaves, chopping firewood, stockpiling—but not many. Most were tucked up in their cabins, fires already blazing. Brooke Stone and Jordan Little were in the meadow, trying to catch snowflakes on their tongues. Brooke waved as he passed but he pretended not to see her. He marched directly to Mother Moon's cabin and rapped his fist against the door.

"Good, you're here," Mother Moon said, stepping onto the porch rather than inviting him inside. He caught a glimpse of the girl, Edith, sitting in an armchair eating one of the candy bars that Nolan had brought from the mainland on a recent trip.

"Snickers," Mother Moon whispered, following his gaze. "I'm trying to soften her up."

"Kids love candy," Nolan said.

"Well, this kid is tough to break," Mother Moon said, closing the door fully. "But I'll get her."

"You always do."

"She only has to open the window—the portal. Shirley will add the exotic matter." Mother Moon rubbed her hands together. "My little science experiment."

Nolan recalled the weight of the jacket, the ball bearings and screws packed into the sleeves and shoulders. "It's not going to be so little."

Mother Moon swept down the porch steps. The wind lifted her hair and peppered it with snow. "Where should we put the Skyway? I'm thinking that clearing in the north forest." She waved her hand in the general direction. "Very pretty there, with the pink lady's slipper blooming in the summer."

"Very."

"It'll be a place of power, like the Aramu Muru gateway. Or what's that other place, in Vermont? The Bennington Triangle!"

"I think the clearing is a perfect location for the Skyway," Nolan said in the calmest possible voice, but wanting desperately to hurry things along. "So . . . you wanted me to do something?"

Mother Moon nodded. She stepped back onto the porch and stood by the door, hugging herself against the cold. "Yes. Something very important."

"I'll do whatever you need," Nolan said. "You know that. But I don't have much time. I told the girls' father I'd collect him at two o'clock. It'll take a while for the dust to settle, but if I'm not there, and he's close to a news source when they identify—"

"You'll be there," Mother Moon said. "Besides, if he has any sense he'll meet you at the boathouse. He might even make his own way over to get ahead of the storm."

"That's a possibility," Nolan said, and it was one he'd considered. "I'll deal with him regardless."

"Yes, but first . . ." Mother Moon grabbed a fistful of his jacket and tugged him toward her. She lifted her face to his, almost close enough to kiss. "Not including me or the girl, or yourself, obviously . . . how many people are on the island?"

Nolan did the math quickly. "Fifteen."

"And how many bullets do you have?"

He took a step backward but she kept hold of his jacket. "What? I . . ." He shook his head. "Are you—"

"Do you really want these people striding to and fro across our Skyway, coming and going as they please?"

"Well . . ."

"They've done nothing to earn it. Fucking *nothing*. Those who have are already there."

"Right," Nolan said.

"We've kept Halcyon functional by introducing certain rules, and taking certain measures. The same applies here. If we lose control of the Skyway, we lose control of Glam Moon." She tugged him close once again. "Is that what you want?"

"No," he whispered. "Of course not."

"So I ask again: How many bullets do you have?"

"Enough."

"Good." She sneered. "Then get to it."

Nolan nodded but the uncertainty must have shown in his face, because Mother Moon pressed her body against his. He felt her hip bones, the softness of her breasts and belly, and she said in a voice that melted across his brain like butter:

"You can have everything, Nolan."

"Yes."

"Is that what you want?"

"Yes."

"Then you know what to do." She ran her tongue across his lips. It was as cold as the snow. "Kill them. Kill them all."

36

Shirley tried to recall a time in her life that she was happy—a moment of light to relieve the darkness inside her. There were memories, but they were all stained. Even memories of her mom—who was beautiful and kind and oh God Shirley *missed* her—were recalled through a gray mist. The only clear thing in her mind was Mother Moon's voice. It told her she was beautiful and strong, that she didn't need to be afraid.

We'll hover like hummingbirds, you and I, with our long beaks dipping and a warm rain in our feathers.

The clearing behind the billboard swayed one way then the other. Shirley staggered, dropped to her knees. She thought at first she could keep it down, then she vomited in a sour brown stream. Tears flooded her eyes. She coughed and wiped her mouth.

"I can't do this." The weight across her shoulders was terrible.

You can, Mother Moon replied, sharp and clear. *You will.*

"This isn't me."

One instant of selfless bravery is all it takes. One instant, and you'll forget how grief feels.

There was another option, a surefire way to forget grief, relieve darkness. Shirley wiped her mouth again, then got to her feet and grasped the puffer jacket's zipper. She felt Mother Moon recoil—it was like a twitch in her brain—then nuzzle closer. Shirley closed her eyes. She yanked the zipper down one inch, then three more.

No, girl. Not yet.

Shirley's hand trembled, then jerked away as if someone had tied a string to her wrist and pulled.

There's nothing we can't do. No light we can't reach.

"I'm so scared."

She started walking, dragging her feet. The jacket was *so* heavy. She managed only a hundred yards before having to stop and rest. Snow melted against the sweat on her face. She groaned and walked on.

She saw the mall a short time later.

As Nolan skimmed across the water to Halcyon and his meeting with Mother Moon, Martin raced east toward Fisherman's Point. He didn't plan on stopping—or even slowing down—until he reached the marina in Oswego. It wouldn't be buzzing with activity like it was in the summer, but he counted on there being at least one hardy fisherman willing to take him out. The snow had worsened, but the lake appeared calm enough. Scattered whitecaps, nothing more.

The one traffic light in Fisherman's Point turned red as Martin approached. He nearly ran it—heck, there were no other cars on the road—but caution got the better of him and he stepped on the brake. Waiting for the light to turn green, he looked from the deserted marina to the bar farther up the street. It was called The Hull, a surprisingly popular spot, judging by the number of cars in the parking lot. Martin looked at the marina again, at the few boats bobbing in their slips, and imagined the owner of one of those boats returning from a morning's fishing, then tying off to the dock and crossing the street for a cold beer.

"Good chance you'll find a fisherman," Martin muttered, "in a bar called The Hull, in a town called Fisherman's Point."

The light turned green. Martin drove sixty yards, then made a right into The Hull's parking lot. He found a space around back. His left knee throbbed again as he got out of the car and crossed the lot. The wind had picked up, skimming off the lake.

Hurry, the voice in his mind insisted. He imagined the flashlight expression that went along with that voice and quickened his step, despite the twinges in his knee.

The Hull was warm and smelled of good food. The dining tables were mostly full and a phalanx of broad bodies surrounded the bar. A single flat-screen TV flashed Quick Draw lottery numbers.

Martin checked his wallet. Sixty-three dollars. He found an ATM in the hallway leading to the restroom and withdrew one hundred and forty more. He returned to the bar with the money in his hand.

"I need to charter a boat," he announced in his clearest Dad Voice, which had been known to cut through sisterly caterwauling and other family clamor. A few diners looked up from their meals, and several of the bodies perched at the bar swiveled on their stools.

"In this weather?" one of them asked, an old-timer with whiskery jowls and a lazy eye. "Good luck, fella."

Martin flapped the money. "Two hundred dollars to whoever stops drinking and takes me to Gray Peaks Island."

His offer was met with amused mutterings and curious stares. Gradually, the clientele returned to their conversations, to their food and drinks. Martin stood for a moment, wondering if he had "crazy" written all over his face. He lowered the money and glanced around helplessly.

"Don't look like you got any takers," a voice said. It belonged to another old-timer sitting at the bar. He wore a battered baseball cap and military surplus jacket, looking for all the world like Quint from *Jaws*.

"Doesn't look like it," Martin agreed.

"I'll take you for three hundred," Quint said. He dropped a wink and held up a glass with two fingers of whiskey still inside it. "But I'm finishing this first."

Fifteen.

In the past there'd been as many as forty people on the island, and thank Jesus H. Christ that wasn't the case now. Fifteen was still a handful. Motherfuckers would scatter like lambs if he wasn't careful, but he could track them down. Fifteen was doable.

Nolan attached the suppressor to his Glock 19 pistol, adding seven inches to the barrel. Tricky to disguise a gun that length, but it wouldn't do to have gunshots ringing across the island. A suppressor wouldn't "silence" the report—that only happened in James Bond movies—but anyone within earshot would be close enough to take the next bullet.

"Fifteen."

He sighted down the barrel, then ran the magazine into the grip. A fifteen-round mag, and there was something very fucking propitious about that. Even so, Nolan wasn't foolish enough to believe he could make every shot count. He grabbed a fully loaded spare and tucked it into his jacket pocket.

"Corporal Nolan Thorne reporting for duty."

Mission time: twenty minutes, absolute max. Efficiency and accuracy were critical. He'd start at the dock—*adios,* Jake Door—and make his way north, checking the utility buildings and farms, the recreation hall and canteen, then bouncing from one cabin to the next. If it all went smoothly, he'd finish somewhere near his cabin, where he could replenish his ammo before going to get Martin.

"I've got this." Nolan closed his eyes for a second and drifted. *You can have everything,* Mother Moon had said to him. *Is that what you want?* He nodded, touched his mouth where she'd licked him—fucking *licked* him, like a goddamn popsicle. He wasn't sexually attracted to Mother Moon, never had been, but something about this gesture—the fucking *bizarreness* of it, perhaps—had given him a premium-grade boner. He'd probably jerk off later thinking about it, but right now he had work to do.

He lowered the pistol, stepped across his living room, and looked out the front window. Brooke and Jordan were still in the meadow, but had stopped playing and were heading back to their cabin. He couldn't see anyone else, although visibility was limited by the snow. This would affect his long-range accuracy, but that shouldn't be a factor. The main advantage of the weather was that it herded his targets inside, where they could be picked off point-blank.

"Got this," he said again, then tucked the pistol beneath his arm and stepped outside. He started down the path toward the orchard and dock beyond, walking swiftly and with the memory of Mother Moon's tongue on his mouth. He saw nobody on the path or in the orchard and didn't expect to. Jake Door would be the first person he saw. Jake fucking Door, who spent his days, rain or shine, fishing from the dock and shooting the stink eye at passing boats. A little snow flurry wouldn't faze Jake. No, sir.

Nolan passed through the woodland where the ground sloped to the water, moving with the surefootedness of a wild animal. He emerged from the trees and stepped onto the dock, pulling the gun from beneath his arm. Jake Door was in his accustomed place, not fishing, but pissing in the lake. He was side-on, so Nolan couldn't get a clean chest shot. He aimed for Jake's head, a smaller target. Nolan could *probably* hit it at this distance, even in the snow, but he wanted to be sure. He stepped closer.

Either the movement or the vibration along the boards alerted Jake. He looked up, dick in hand. "Whoa, shit," he said, and flinched just as Nolan pulled the trigger. No muzzle flash, just a deadened *pok* sound from the suppressor. The bullet scored Jake's right cheek and tore off his ear. If he hadn't flinched, it would have killed him instantly.

"Christ, man!" he said, letting go of his dick to touch the raw place on his head where his ear had been only seconds before. "I said, *Christ.*"

Nolan shot Jake in the chest. He flew off the dock and met the water with a foamy splash. *Two fucking bullets,* Nolan thought. He stepped to the edge of the dock. Jake was still alive, swimming lame, bleeding into the water. He looked at Nolan with frightened dog's eyes. "Fuck," he said. Nolan parked the third bullet into Jake's shoulder or maybe his arm and the fourth into his skull, which broke like an egg and leaked. Jake turned in the water and settled face-up. Waves rocked him.

Nolan grunted and marched back along the dock, through the woodland and orchard, toward their happy little community. The snow danced, spurred by the lake winds. Nolan wiped his eyes and saw the cabins in the distance. Some had lights burning, chimneys pouring smoke.

He touched his mouth.

"Everything."

37

"Are you cold?"

"A little. My face is cold. And my feet."

"We're almost there."

They walked through the woods, sheltered somewhat from the snow, but the wind was shrill and sharp. Valerie had wrapped them both in winter clothes. The girl's were too big, of course. She trudged with her head down.

"Is it warm where we're going?"

Valerie's eyes glazed momentarily. She thought of the slowly fading sun, how it touched the skin, and how the wind encouraged her to expand rather than huddle.

"Very."

They ducked beneath a half-fallen tree and pushed through yellowing ferns. To the left the woods thinned to marshland and the northwestern ridge, to the right they deepened. Valerie tapped Edith's shoulder and directed her that way.

"Where's my sister?" Edith asked a moment later, for perhaps the tenth time. "You said I could see her."

"I told you, she's doing something extremely important," Valerie replied. "Something amazing."

They walked on with breaths pluming. Valerie fished the watch from her pocket and glanced at it. Time was on their side, although she needed some of that time to persuade Edith to open the portal. Valerie didn't know if it would act like a lightning rod, or a magnifying glass in the sun, but this would be the focal point. This was where it would happen.

And not a ghost in sight, she thought. *No Rhapsody or Jesus or whatever the fuck else it's called.*

"Dead to me," she whispered.

"Huh?" Edith stopped, regarding her with deep eyes.

"Nothing. Keep going."

Valerie had been alone on the island for three years before the first ghost appeared. Not the tiger. The rooster. He came in the night, laid hands on her while she slept. He only disappeared when she screamed.

The goat was next. He stood at the edge of the woods and watched her work, saying nothing. She ignored him, but later, in her cabin, she saw his goat face at the window, breath fogging the glass.

"You're not real," she said.

"Have you found it yet?" he asked calmly, as if she hadn't buried a cleaver in his skull.

Locking her cabin door didn't stop them. She'd walk into the living room and the ox would be sitting on the sofa; the rabbit would be crouched in the corner of her bedroom, his ears poking up over the dresser; the pig and snake would hide behind doors or underneath her bed. She'd open her closet and see one of them in there.

"Have you found it yet?" Always the same question.

The tiger kept his distance to begin with, as if his pride had been hurt, but gradually edged closer. One night, he slipped into bed beside her, ran his hands through her hair.

"You don't even *want* to get rid of us."

"Maybe I'm just lonely."

"That's not it." He pressed against her, hard and cold. "You know."

"Know?"

"You can't find it without us."

Valerie feigned ignorance, and went about her life on the island as she always did. When she thought the animals weren't watching, she had what she called Skyway Ceremonies, in which she meditated by candlelight and touched her scars, hoping to open a seam between up and down. On her trips to the mainland, where she sold firewood and produce for money, she often traveled to the sites of recent tragedies and looked for a thinness in the air.

Nothing.

"One word," the tiger said to her, finding her at her most hungry, most desperate. "Rhapsody."

"It's a simulation," Valerie responded bitterly. "Besides, you said it was only available to the upper echelons of society."

"We are the upper echelons of society."

"You *were.*"

The tiger laughed. His stripes shimmered faintly. "Come see us. You know where we do business."

"I'm *not* going back there."

But she went back, of course. The fat restaurateur was still alive, fatter and wheezier. He looked at her as he might a revenant or vampire, and bowed to her every need. She went up to the room where the ghosts were waiting, where they were *strong*, and she revisited her pains.

It wasn't enough.

"You can't come empty handed," the dog said.

"There's always a price to pay," the rooster said. "And you know what the price is."

"Yes. The end of pleasure." Valerie regarded them hatefully. "What do you want me to do? Cut off my arm?"

"You can be more creative," the tiger said. "And it doesn't have to be *your* pain. Think scientifically: shifting energy signatures . . . the universal consciousness."

"We're distilling pain from the atmosphere," the goat said, spinning the ring on his finger. "The greater the pain, the more potent the drug."

"A mall shooting would work," the pig offered.

"A bus explosion," the rabbit said.

"You can bring down a plane."

"Set fire to a hospital."

"I *get* it," Valerie said, holding up her hands. "I just don't know if I can do it."

"Why?" the tiger asked. "Too many victims?"

"That's not it," Valerie replied, and it wasn't. Her country had done *nothing* for her—had turned its back on her, in fact, when she was down. As far as she was concerned, the whole goddamn shithouse could go up in flames. "It's a massive undertaking. I'd need money. *Lots* of money. And people."

"Then *get* people," the tiger said. "You have a preternatural talent for persuasion, not to mention an entire island to yourself. Bring in the lost and forlorn. Take their money and promise them heaven."

She did, and it proved easier than she could have expected, a succession of embittered Americans—victims of crime, of industry, of government. She brought in Nolan, who helped her recruit for and expand their community. Halcyon flourished. Valerie manipulated.

Robert Dander: car bomb, Hanover Street, Boston.

Jeffrey Myles: vehicular assault, Central Park West, New York City.

Jose Mazara: mass shooting, Riverside bus depot, Philadelphia.

On and on, and with every success she returned to the room above the White Lantern where the animals were waiting, growing in realness at the same rate as her addiction. The little pink capsule would be delivered to her, infused with pain.

"Can you feel it?" the tiger asked. "The shift in energy . . ."

"Yes."

"A nation hurting."

She took the drug.

"Fly away, sugargirl."

Thirty-one attacks over eighteen years, some big (Garrett's Buffalo bombing), and some small (Dana Jackson's Lombardo Museum fire, which killed only three), all engineered to satisfy her craving, although she never took her eye off the big prize.

"The White Skyway," Valerie muttered.

The wind knifed through the trees, pulling in more snow, making the leaves whirl. Edith stopped walking again. She looked at Valerie.

"The White Skyway?" She resembled her father when she frowned. "What's that?"

It's between here and there, Valerie thought. *Between up and down.*

She said, "Do you know what an Einstein-Rosen bridge is?" And then shook her head. "Of course you don't. You're ten years old."

"Ten and three-quarters."

"Do you know what a portal is?"

"I think so."

"A way of traveling vast distances instantly. A gateway between dimensions." Valerie wiped snow from her eyes. "The White Skyway is the same kind of thing."

Edith's breath plumed.

"The place you visit," Valerie said. "The garden you supposedly built in six months . . ."

"What about it?"

"It's Glam Moon. I know because I've been there. I recognize the mountains and trees. You connect to it by way of your psychic talent, but that doesn't make it yours."

Edith scowled at her. "I don't understand any of this."

"Silly girl! We're going to *create* the White Skyway: a portal between this world and Glam Moon, with an exotic matter—a certain secret ingredient—added to keep it stable."

"We?"

"We: me, you, and your sister."

Edith shook her head. "I won't help you. You're crazy if you think I will."

"I guess I'm crazy, then."

"Where's my sister? You said she—"

"Help me and your sister lives forever," Valerie cut across her, sharp as the wind. "She'll be immortalized in the Skyway."

Edith opened her mouth to say something, but only a little cloud of white air escaped.

"Do you know what immortalized means?"

Tears welled in the girl's eyes.

"It means that she'll always be remembered. Like Cleopatra or Joan of Arc. Isn't that beautiful?"

"What have you done with Shirley?"

"On the other hand, if you choose not to help, she'll die for nothing." Valerie sneered. "Is that what you want?"

Edith blinked and the tears spilled onto her cheeks.

"Keep walking."

The girl turned and trudged on. Valerie saw her thin shoulders shaking even through all the warm clothes.

They came to the clearing soon after, thirty feet across at its widest point. Snow speckled the ferns and branches of the surrounding trees. A cardinal—male, beautifully colored—took shelter in a cracked boulder. It stood out like blood.

38

His name wasn't Quint. It was, somewhat aptly, Sharky, a nicknamed he'd earned not from hunting great whites, but from the massive shark tattoo on his back.

"Its tail ends midway down my left ass cheek," Sharky said. "I'd show you if it wasn't so cold."

"I'm okay with not seeing it," Martin said. "Really, let's just go."

Sharky could kindly be described as meticulous—manually adding up his bar bill before paying, zipping and fastening all winter apparel before venturing outside, double checking his and Martin's lifejackets prior to departure. Martin opted for the less kind description: slow-as-fuck. It was 11:40 when he'd pulled in to The Hull's parking lot, and 12:18 by the time Sharky's trawler finally chugged out of the marina.

"How long before we're there?" Martin asked, shouting above the rumbling engine and rising wind.

"She'll go nineteen miles an hour when all's fine," Sharky

said, patting the boat's wheel. "But these conditions'll slow us up some. So I'll say . . . shit, maybe forty minutes."

Martin looked through the cabin windows. The heavy cloud that had been distant earlier was now dangerously close. Snow choked the air. Visibility was down to half a mile, maybe a little more.

"This is pretty bad, huh?" Martin asked.

"Seen worse."

What Sharky lacked in speed, he made up for in hardiness. His trawler was built for rough water, he said, and the GPS would lead him right back to the marina. "Biggest danger is another boat hitting us. That's why we got these." And he gestured at the navigation lights mounted on the cabin sides and masthead.

They rolled on, slow and steady, cutting an uneven white line across the gray water. Martin told himself that every minute on the boat was a minute closer to being with his girls, but the voice in his head wouldn't let him relax. He bunched his hands into fists, pressed them against his temples.

Sharky worked the wheel and whistled.

The SUV skidded across the sleety asphalt and missed Shirley by inches. The driver buzzed down his window and shouted. His voice was muffled, as if heard through a vat of water. Shirley saw his blustery face, his wife in the passenger seat looking alarmed, and two kids in the back with wide eyes and open mouths.

Shirley shook her head, rattling Mother Moon loose for just long enough to realize what had happened. She looked around the parking lot with a dazed expression, then raised one hand to the angry driver.

"Sorry."

"Watch where you're going," he snapped at her. "You're going to get yourself killed."

"I know . . . sorry."

The driver's wife leaned over. Shirley thought she might say something kinder, but she didn't. "Goddamn stoner," she yelled as the SUV pulled away. "Get your shit together."

Shirley watched the SUV's taillights fade into the falling snow. Some crowded part of her brain drew the parallel, where she was the taillight, and Mother Moon was the snow. If someone had asked her name at that moment, she would've struggled to tell them.

"I'm a nobody," she mumbled.

A muscle in her back throbbed. She straightened her shoulders, feeling every ounce of the jacket's weight.

You're not *a nobody,* Mother Moon said, crawling into her mind again. *Don't ever think that. You're a goddess. You're beautiful.*

Shirley continued across the parking lot. Cars zipped around her, looking for spaces. People flooded one way with empty arms, and the other with bags and boxes.

And we're so close now. Shirley pressed a knuckle to her forehead. Sometimes the voice hurt. It felt like a corkscrew, twisting deeper. *So close to the next world and all the light it will bring.*

The mall loomed ahead, new and bright. More people bustled around Shirley as she neared the main entrance. She heard excited chatter and Christmas music and the clear, adorable chime of children's laughter.

* * *

There was a period of time after her mom died that Edith felt incredibly alone. Her dad and Shirley were never far away, but were lost to their own grief. This, as much as the escape it offered, was the reason she'd spent so much time in her garden. It was a place of warmth, enhanced by her mom's memory. Edith often believed this was how she'd built it so quickly.

Standing in the clearing, Edith felt that loneliness again—a sense of being severed from the people who loved her. She had no idea what was going to happen. It was terrifying.

"We'll do it here," Mother Moon said, spreading her arms and turning her face to the snowy sky. "Isn't this a beautiful spot?"

Edith imagined her garden with its bright flora and soothing breeze. She could be there in a blink, and although she ached to be, she kept herself rooted in this world; Mother Moon had lost her mind—if she ever had a mind to begin with—and Shirley was in serious trouble. This wasn't the time to run away.

Edith closed her eyes. She *reached.*

Shirley, are you there?

Her brain ticked, working to find the connection—or *dis*connection—that linked her to Shirley's mind.

Shirley, talk to me . . .

There was a mild buzz but nothing more. Edith mostly found huge swaths of silence and darkness. That particular psychic muscle, which she'd used so effortlessly in the past, was weak now. Or perhaps it was because she was so cold and out of her element. She found it difficult to—

"I *said,* isn't this a beautiful spot?"

Edith opened her eyes. Mother Moon stood over her, arms still spread, hair flicking around her face in the wind.

"Yes," Edith managed. "It's beautiful."

"And a good energy, too." Mother Moon grinned, looking from one side of the clearing to the other. "It's perfect for the Skyway. Imagine it—that great bridge of light arcing directly into the Glam."

Shirley, where are you?

Mother Moon stepped into the center of the clearing. The cardinal was still there, sheltered in the cracked boulder. It riffled its bright feathers as Mother Moon approached, but didn't fly away.

"I need you to open the window," she said, looking at Edith. "The place between."

"I don't know if I can," Edith replied. "I'm cold and—"

"You can and you *will.*" Mother Moon plucked a watch from her pocket and pointed at it. "Your sister is almost in position. She'll make the connection at precisely one thirty. You need to give her something to connect *to.*"

"That doesn't even make sense."

"But *you* told me to do this." Mother Moon stepped toward her, lips peeled back from her teeth. "You told me to pay. You wrote it on your bed sheets. In blood."

Edith stepped backward. Tears gathered in her eyes again.

"Remember?"

"I don't . . . I can't . . ." She touched her arm where she'd cut herself—where she'd *purged.* And there was something about that. The stream, whatever terrible thing she'd seen . . . it bumped and nudged her mind but she couldn't make the connection. Her instinct—separate from her psychic ability, closer to her heart—told her it had something to do with Shirley.

She wiped her eyes and reached again.

Shirley, please—

This time her focus was broken by Mother Moon's hand. It whipped across her face in a pale blur. Edith's head jolted sideways. Her cheek throbbed in the cold.

"Ouch."

"Does it make sense now?"

Edith nodded.

"Stand in the middle of the clearing." Mother Moon pointed. "Open the window."

Edith shuffled past Mother Moon, stopping near the boulder where the cardinal still huddled. It brought to mind a memory of Calm Dumas, sitting in their backyard with a female cardinal hopping along her arm. This trickled into another memory: Calm twirling a willow leaf—the only leaf in the world—between her fingers, instructing Edith on how to build her shelter. *The beauty of a powerful mind,* she'd said. *But it can be dangerous, too.*

"Yes," Edith whispered. "It can."

Our power is real, Edith. This had been too broad for Edith to comprehend to begin with, but not anymore. *You don't want to go so deep that you can't find your way home.*

"No. That would be bad."

The cardinal flew away, disappearing quickly into the snowy sky. Edith couldn't shake the idea that it had stayed just long enough to deliver this memory.

Mother Moon edged toward the center of the clearing. Her eyes flashed.

"The window," she snapped. "*Now.*"

Edith recalled the last time she'd opened the window—how Mother Moon had reached in greedily, drawn by the light on the other side.

My flowers, she'd said. Her hand had felt so cold.

Mine, Edith had corrected her, slamming the window closed.

An idea formed. *A plan of attack,* her dad might have called it. Edith didn't know if it would work, but it was all she had.

Our power is real . . .

She'd built a garden in a matter of months.

How quickly could she build a bridge?

39

Something Shirley had said recurred to Nolan, and with new meaning: *I can't get her out of my head.* He pressed his palm against his forehead and growled. Yes, he knew exactly how that felt.

You can have everything, Nolan.

He found Simon Song in the storage barn, retrieving snow shovels from behind a pile of tools in the corner. Simon had his back to Nolan—didn't see him at all, didn't hear him, either. Nolan got to within two feet, leveled the pistol, pulled the trigger. A small hole appeared in the back of Simon's bald head. Blood and bone exited the front and hit the barn wall steaming. Simon fell with a snow shovel clutched in two hands, as if he meant to use it.

Wendy Noakes was in the recreation hall, dragging a mop across the floor. She looked up when Nolan walked in, saw the gun in his hand, and frowned. "Nolan, that's a gun," she said, and Nolan put a bullet in her chest. She flew backward, kicking her bucket over. Blood and water everywhere. Nolan left via the backdoor, checking for anyone else. There was no one. He cut through the trees and found Eliza Martino and Aiden Lythe in the canteen, cleaning tables. Good ol' Dr. Lythe, always willing to help out around the island when the clinic was slow. Nolan shot him point blank and he was dead before his knees buckled. Eliza screamed and ran. Nolan fired at her and missed—may have grazed her arm. He fired again, didn't miss. She hit the wall shoulder first and slumped there like a person resting. Joe the chef came out of the kitchen to see what in blazes was going on and Nolan shot him twice, first in the stomach, then in the throat.

Everything, Nolan. Is that what you want?

Six dead. Nolan checked the mag. Four rounds remaining, plus the loaded spare in his jacket pocket.

Alyssa had finished her duties and returned to her cabin, expecting to find Edith there. She'd been playing her guitar on the front porch when Alyssa had left, but that was before the weather turned. There was no sign of her now. Her guitar was just inside the door, though, propped against the wall. So she'd probably returned to her own cabin, and hadn't taken her guitar because of the snow. Or maybe she was at Mother Moon's with Shirley.

Alyssa showered quickly, then put on her winter clothes and went to find Edith. Martin was due back later that day, and she and Edith had planned a surprise party for him: good food, homemade party hats, live music. They had learned "Behind Blue Eyes"—one of Martin's favorite songs—for the occasion. Edith was excited to play it for him. She wouldn't have gone far.

Alyssa checked Edith's cabin first.

"Edith? Shirley?"

Silence.

"Anyone?"

She crossed the top of the meadow, then cut through the woods toward Mother Moon's cabin. As she approached, she noted no smoke pluming from the chimney. The windows were cold and dark. Alyssa climbed the front steps and knocked anyway.

No answer.

She peered through the window. No light or movement.

"Where'd you go, Ede?"

The rec hall? Maybe. Or the canteen for a lunchtime snack. Alyssa started down the steps, looking south across the meadow. She saw someone ghosting through the snow, moving determinedly. Not Edith, that was for sure. Alyssa was about to head west toward the canteen but then noticed the smoke billowing from Brooke's chimney. Brooke shared a cabin with Jordan Little—had become something of a big sister, or a mother even, after Jordan's real mom returned to the mainland and, true to the rules, never came back. Jordan had been a baby at the time. Mother Moon sometimes called her the island's child.

Jordan and Edith were friends. Not super tight or anything, but the closeness in their ages gave them a natural bond. Alyssa thought they'd probably been playing in the snow together, then had gone back to Brooke and Jordan's cabin for hot milk.

She'd try there first—it was closer—then she could scoot across to the canteen and rec hall.

Only so many places you can hide on an island, Alyssa thought.

She trudged past Gilda Wynne's cabin—also with its chimney pluming, a single warm light burning inside—and carried on past the woodshed to Brooke and Jordan's. She saw that figure ghosting through the snow again, then climbed Brooke's front steps and rapped on the door.

"You're right," Edith said.

"What do you mean?"

"My world. It *is* Glam Moon." Tiny snowflakes fell onto Edith's eyelashes. She blinked but didn't drop her gaze from Mother Moon's. "It's been calling to you for many years."

Mother Moon stood at the edge of the clearing, regarding Edith with an expression that appeared both suspicious and hopeful.

"It's why I'm here," Edith said.

"You're what . . . ten years old?" Mother Moon shook her head, her body curled against the cold. "I was there thirty-two years ago, before you were even born. If it's anybody's world, it's mine."

"My body is ten," Edith said, "but my psychic soul has been around a long time."

The wind scraped across the clearing and the snow circled, mixed with wet leaves and the crisp smell of the pines. Edith huddled, determined to hold her focus.

"You've earned your place," she said. "It's waiting for you."

"Yes. That's why we came here. To open the Skyway—"

"It's called the Crossover, and it's already open."

Edith spread her hands and pushed with every ounce of her psychic energy, channeling it—projecting it onto the place between. The window yawned with an electric thrum and that familiar smell of summer rain.

"What do you mean it's already open?" Mother Moon asked. "What are you doing?"

The tips of Edith's fingers glowed pale blue. She shuddered, fighting to contain the energy. *Imagine it,* Mother Moon had said, providing the blueprint—the single leaf—from which to work. *That great bridge of light arcing directly into the Glam.* The window offered a tempting glimpse, the first few steps, a shimmering light beyond . . .

"This is what you've been looking for," Edith said.

"I don't see anything."

Edith shifted position, taking two delicate steps toward Mother Moon. The window stretched, like a bubble filling with air.

"Focus on the place between," she said. "Like you did before. When you saw the Glam."

Mother Moon swept snow and hair from her eyes and looked harder, tilting her head this way and that. "But I have to wait for the price to be paid," she said. "For the bomb to go off."

The window flickered . . . faded. *Bomb,* Edith thought miserably, and remembered Mother Moon pointing at her watch. *Your sister is almost in position. She'll make the connection at precisely one thirty.* That déjà vu–like feeling bumped and nudged Edith's mind again. She saw Shirley (*. . . jacket, she's wearing a black jacket . . .*) and the word *PAY* but nothing more. Not that it mattered; everything she needed to know was in that single terrible word: *bomb.* Fear surged inside her, brighter than the light she had created. She used it like fuel and threw it at the window. It expanded beyond Edith's hands and towered into the snowy sky.

Mother Moon suddenly dropped to her knees. She opened her arms and a long moan escaped her. "I see it," she said, and shook her head as if she didn't dare believe it. "My God, I see it now."

A tear tracked down Edith's face. "We're waiting for you."

"We?"

"All of us. Your sky. Your flowers."

Maria Santos opened her cabin door with a towel wrapped around her head and another around her body. She'd just stepped out of the shower. "Oh, Nolan, could you come back after—" Nolan pressed the tip of the suppressor to her forehead and squeezed the trigger. *Pok.* Maria flew backward, over her sofa, then rolled and hit the floor. The towel around her head kept the blood from spreading.

Seven down.

Nolan's strategy—if it could be called a strategy; it was really just smarts—was to hit the cabins with smoking chimneys first. With any luck, the last eight islanders were tucked up inside, easy to pick off.

"Easy," he slurred.

Jesus, he might even have time for another Dunkin' Donuts before going to fetch Martin.

"Yum."

He trudged past empty cabins, looked up, and saw someone ahead of him—impossible to say who, and they were too far away to get off a clean shot. Oh well, he'd get them soon enough. He clomped up the steps of Ainsley and Franklin's cabin, firelight flickering in the window, looking all Christmassy in the snow.

Franklin opened the door. He was the older queer, swarthy and broad—the fucking *bear*, or whatever he called himself. He didn't put up a bearlike fight, though. One shot—*pok*—and down he went. Ainsley came in from the bedroom, shirtless, one hundred and twenty pounds of not fucking much.

Nolan took aim. Melted snow ran into his eye a split second before pulling the trigger and the shot went wide. Ainsley didn't run away or cower, didn't register any surprise or fear. He grabbed a knife off the kitchenette counter and ran at Nolan, one hundred and twenty pounds of ire.

Brooke and Jordan were on the sofa, wrapped in bathrobes, hot drinks in hand. They hadn't seen Edith, either.

"She's probably with her sister," Brooke said. "I bet they took a walk in the woods. It's cold but beautiful."

"Yeah," Alyssa said, nodding. "I'll check the rec hall and canteen. If she's not there, maybe I'll—"

She stopped, ear cocked, brow furrowed.

"What is it?" Jordan asked.

"Did you hear that?"

Brooke and Jordan shook their heads.

Alyssa said, "Sounded like screaming."

* * *

Nolan pulled the trigger again and hit Ainsley in the left shoulder. It slowed but didn't stop him. He stumbled toward Nolan and brought the knife down in a wild loop. Nolan managed a clumsy half step, avoiding serious—perhaps fatal—damage. The knife tore through his jacket, across his triceps and shoulder blade. Nolan shrieked, grabbed Ainsley by the throat, threw him against the wall.

"Dirty little bastard," he growled.

Ainsley raised the knife for another strike but his arm froze when Nolan jammed the pistol up under his jaw.

"What the fuck, Nolan?"

Nolan squeezed the trigger.

Click.

"Son of a *bitch*."

The knife came down. A silver flash. It ran through Nolan's forearm, out the other side. Ainsley pulled it free—giving it a little twist on the way—to attack again but Nolan wheeled away from him. He thumbed the mag release at the top of the Glock's grip. The empty slid out and clattered on the floor.

Ainsley came after him, hesitating only to look at the corpse on the living room floor. "Oh Jesus, Frank," he panted. "Jesus fucking Christ." The knife trembled in his hand. He lunged, but then slipped in Franklin's blood and fell on his ass. This gave Nolan the time he needed. He pulled the loaded spare from his pocket and rammed it into the pistol's grip.

* * *

"Stay here," Alyssa said, speaking to both but looking at Jordan.

She opened the door and stepped outside.

The knife wounds hindered Nolan's grip and it took three attempts to rack the slide. Ainsley was back on his feet by this time, and had finally decided that bringing a knife to a gun fight was not such a great idea. He scrambled for the door, managing one galumphing stride outside before Nolan put a bullet in his back.

"Fuck you," Nolan hissed. "Fucking crazy twink fuck."

Ainsley toppled down the front steps and landed on his knees. Blood poured from the holes in his shoulder and back. *"Help me,"* he screamed. *"Somebody please."* He started to crawl, raking his way through the snow. *"Somebody . . ."*

Nolan staggered onto the porch, doing his own share of bleeding. He took the steps slowly and limped after Ainsley.

"Help me."

The snow was heavy enough that Ainsley was just a vague shape but the blood he left behind was very bright. Nolan followed it. The gun trembled in his hand, but all he had to do was aim and pull the trigger. Easy enough. Of course, he had to do it six more times—at least—to get everybody on the island, but he'd faced bigger challenges in his life.

"Sure have," he mumbled. "Everything, right?"

He caught up to Ainsley, who'd pretty much stopped crawling by that point.

"Help me," he whimpered.

Nolan aimed. Pulled the trigger.

The back corner of Ainsley's skull disappeared and blood sprayed the snow. Ainsley dropped. Steam rose from his shirtless torso.

Yes, Mother Moon whispered. *Everything.*

Nolan touched his mouth where she'd licked him, then sighed and turned toward the other cabins. He took half a step and then stopped.

Alyssa Prince stood fewer than fifteen feet away, looking at him with shocked, frightened eyes. Her legs wobbled and he thought for one second she might faint.

"Hello, Alyssa," Nolan said, and aimed again.

40

Valerie rose to her feet. She didn't feel the snow that soaked her clothes and blew into her face. The cold didn't matter. A white archway had bloomed from between the girl's hands and announced itself in the clearing, as tall as the pines. Beyond: only light. Valerie couldn't see, but she imagined it stretching far and wide, all the way to Glam Moon.

Compare it to an Einstein-Rosen bridge, Pace spoke up in her mind. *In essence, a wormhole, but with an exotic matter added, making it stable . . . traversable.*

The son of a bitch was right—he knew what he was looking for. Kudos to him for that. He never found it, though.

Fuck you, tiger.

She found it. She alone.

Fuck all you animals.

Valerie took a teetering step toward the opening. It warmed her skin. It filled her eyes.

* * *

Alyssa had never had a gun pointed at her before, but she'd imagined it happening many times. More particularly, she'd *relived* it from her husband's point of view, those final few seconds before a Baltimore cop fired six rounds into him. What would she do differently? What should he, Jackie, have done to change the outcome? *I wouldn't have reached for my wallet, even if they asked me to. I would have put my hands even higher in the sky.* She'd run through dozens of scenarios, and always arrived at the same conclusion: it didn't matter what Jackie did or didn't do; the cop was going to shoot him anyway. Which always led to her final, desperate reaction: *I would have run.*

She watched Nolan shoot Ainsley, frozen to the spot, a thousand questions scattering through her shocked mind. When he said, "Hello, Alyssa," and aimed the gun at her, she thought of Jackie and all the things he might have done differently, and bypassed them all to settle on the one action that could have saved him.

She ran.

Nolan fired. Alyssa recognized the muffled clap of a silencer, although to her ears it sounded very loud and way too close. He didn't hit her, though. The snow provided good cover. Also, she'd noticed blood dripping from Nolan's right sleeve. His arm wavered when he pointed the gun at her and it took him a moment to steady it. She'd also noticed the deranged look in Nolan's eyes. He wasn't going to stop with her and Ainsley. He meant to kill everyone on the island.

Alyssa ran toward Brooke and Jordan's cabin. Her focus was not refuge, but rescue. She leaped the steps and barged through the front door, slammed it behind her. No key in the lock, of course. Islanders never locked their doors.

"Don't ask questions," Alyssa said to Brooke and Jordan. "Just trust me."

"What is—"

"*Trust me.* And help me with this thing." She gestured at the sofa they were sitting on. Brooke and Jordan sprang up and helped Alyssa push it against the door.

"It won't hold him," Alyssa said, running her hands through her hair. "Not for long, anyway. We've got to get out of here."

Jordan's eyes were huge. "What's going on?"

A thud as Nolan slammed into the door. He growled, thumped on it with either his shoulder or fist. The door bounced in the frame, butting against the sofa, which scraped a little way across the floor.

Follow me, Alyssa mouthed, gesturing with both hands. She tossed Brooke and Jordan their wet boots and stepped through to the bedroom. "We have to run," she whispered, crossing to the window. "Find somewhere to hide, until we can think what to do."

"Who is that?" Brooke asked, gesturing toward the living room.

"Nolan," Alyssa replied. "He . . . I don't know. He has a gun. We have to get out of here."

Another thud as Nolan bounced his weight against the front door. Alyssa slid the window open. "Out you go, hon. Keep quiet." She lifted Jordan and passed her through the window. Brooke was next. Alyssa hopped out and closed the window behind her.

"Go," she said. "Use the cabins to break his sightline. Head toward the woods."

They set out, moving quickly. Alyssa noticed they were leaving tracks in the snow, but they wouldn't in the woods—that's where they'd lose him, and Alyssa knew a few hiding spots. She looked behind her, saw nothing, but thought she heard the thud of Nolan striking the blocked cabin door again.

They weaved between one of the empty cabins and around back of the woodshed. Alyssa focused on Brooke and Jordan's bathrobes flowing out behind them, but then got an idea and stopped. Brooke stopped, too, looking anxiously over her shoulder.

"Keep going," Alyssa whispered. "I'll catch up."

She went back to the woodshed and grabbed the axe.

Nolan hit the door three more times, his shoulder throbbing, blood dripping onto his boots. Then realization struck, crisp as a slap. He stopped, listened, heard nothing from inside the cabin but the crackling fire.

"Fuck."

He staggered down the steps and went around back, and sure enough, beneath the bedroom window: fresh tracks in the snow. They led north.

Everything, Nolan. Is that what—

"Yes. It is. It fucking *is.* Just, please . . . shut the fuck up."

He followed the tracks, past darkened cabins where Jake Door, Wendy Noakes, and Joe the chef had lived. There were other islanders he hadn't got to; Jon Levy and Warren Dines had cabins near the power plant, and Gilda Wynne was not far from Mother Moon, but Alyssa was his priority. She'd *seen* him. As soon as he'd stopped her, he would take care of the others.

He grimaced, his left hand clamped over the knife wound in his right forearm. He passed the woodshed and saw the tracks veered in two directions, and it didn't take long to put the pieces together. One of them—probably Alyssa—had grabbed an axe. But that was fine. No fucking problemo. Bringing an axe to a gun fight was not so different from bringing a knife, and the last person to try that was ass-up in the snow with a hole in the back of his head.

Most of the cabins were dark, unoccupied, but Gilda Wynne's front window blazed with a cozy orange light. This made her a target, Alyssa realized. She had no idea how many islanders Nolan had already taken out (Edith, maybe—sweet little Ede, which explained why Alyssa couldn't find her, and Shirley, too), but she couldn't pass Gilda's cabin without at least warning her.

"Hold up," she said to Brooke and Jordan, her brain sorting through too many thoughts and emotions. She shook her head and focused on just one. "No. Go ahead. Wait for me behind Mother Moon's cabin. We'll head into the woods from there."

"What are you doing?" Brooke asked. She held Jordan's hand, who was crying. They were both so scared and confused.

"I have to warn Gilda," Alyssa said. "Go."

Brooke nodded. She and Jordan disappeared into the swirling snow. Alyssa looked back the way they'd come. All white. All silent. She took Gilda's front steps in two strides and thumped on the door.

"Gilda. Open up. It's Alyssa."

She thumped again. Looked behind her. Still nothing.

"Gilda."

The door creaked open and there was Gilda with her mousy hair bundled on top of her head and her inquisitive eyes shifting behind her glasses. She'd never been one of Alyssa's favorite people (she once called Alyssa a *darkie,* thinking it was a perfectly acceptable term, and Alyssa assured her in no uncertain terms that it was not), but Alyssa would hate for anything to happen to her—and hate herself if she didn't do everything in her power to prevent it.

"Listen to me carefully," she said, and maybe it was the urgency in her words, or the axe in her hands, but she had Gilda's full attention. "You have to come with me right now."

"Why?" Gilda asked. "What's going on?"

"It's Nolan. He has a gun. He's . . . it's bad, Gilda. Grab your jacket and boots as quickly as you can and come with me."

"But I—"

"*Please,* Gilda." Alyssa looked over her shoulder again. Still nothing . . . yet. "I know it's cold, but it'll be safer in the woods. More places to hide, and there's strength in numbers. It'll give us chance to come up with a strategy."

Gilda wavered, looking from Alyssa to the axe in her hands.

"Listen, I can't make you come," Alyssa said. "That's your call. But I suggest you find a very good hiding place."

"This is real," Gilda said.

"Very real." Alyssa looked over her shoulder once again. "You've got five seconds."

"I'm coming." Gilda grabbed her jacket from a hook by

the door and stepped into her boots. "Oh, I just put hot milk on and—"

She stopped, her eyes tracking past Alyssa, first narrowing, then widening. Alyssa swiveled and saw Nolan stumping toward them, raising the gun to eye-level.

"*Hello, ladies,*" he cried.

Alyssa felt the bullet before she realized Nolan had fired. It divided the five inches of air between her and Gilda and hit the cabin door with a nasty pop.

"Come *on,*" she said.

She grabbed Gilda's hand and ran.

Shit had gone south. In a big fucking way. He couldn't think about Martin. The storm was heavier than forecast (goddamn lake effect snow, always unpredictable). Only when it had passed, and when every islander lay dead around him, could he contemplate collecting Martin from the mainland—and only then if the Onondaga Mall bomber hadn't been identified. The situation was not irretrievable, but he'd need for everything to run baby's-ass smooth from this point on.

"Corporal Nolan Thorne," he groaned, wiping a bloody hand across his face, "dealing with shit. As fucking ever."

Nolan packed snow between his shirt and jacket sleeve to numb the pain and slow blood loss. He stepped into the woods, where fat flakes whipped between the trees but not as heavily. Visibility was improved. Good. But he'd lost the little lambs' tracks. Bad. He paused for a moment and listened. The wind roused the branches but also carried the sound of his quarry clattering through the understory.

"It's an island," Nolan said. "You can run, you can even fucking hide, but there's no escape."

He moved on, his eyes scanning for movement while his ears tracked every telltale sound. The knife wound across the back of his left arm and shoulder throbbed deeply. He paused to rest—to let his heart rate settle—then trudged on.

A crack here. A whisper there. He skulked toward the sounds, positive he was closing in. The woods darkened around him, but he didn't know if it was because of the storm or because he was getting lightheaded. At one point he saw blood on the ground—realized it was his own, that he'd walked in a circle. "Whafuck?" he gasped. He'd been tracking the sounds, but maybe Alyssa and company were walking in circles, too. That might be their strategy—to keep circling, leading him along, until he collapsed from blood loss. Pretty smart, but what if he were to stop and hide? What if—

Nolan froze, his thought process interrupted by a sound from the lake. A most beautiful sound. His mouth twitched into a cold smile.

It was an engine. A boat's engine, distorted by the wind but getting louder, approaching the island.

His thoughts kicked back into gear with Mother Moon's voice, not her pervading promise but something she'd said earlier: *If he has any sense he'll meet you at the boathouse. He might even make his own way over to get ahead of the storm.*

Martin.

Nolan's smile turned into a grin. One huge problem had sorted itself out. Maybe things were going to run baby's-ass smooth, after all.

He released the Glock's mag, counted the rounds through the witness holes. Ten, with one in the chamber. More than enough. He slapped the mag back into place, nodded, scoped between the trees. Alyssa and the other little lambs were hiding somewhere, but that was fine. Let them hide. They weren't going anywhere.

It was time to welcome Martin back to Halcyon.

Sharky throttled down and brought the trawler into dock, easing in behind Nolan's center console. Martin was already up, his lifejacket discarded, ready to spring ashore. The dock was empty, of course. It was strange not to see Jake Door in his usual position, but the storm had really picked up. Curiously, his fishing gear was still in place, draped in a blanket of snow.

"This shit turned nasty in a hurry," Sharky said, gesturing at the sky as he grabbed one of the mooring lines. "If it's all the same to you, I'm going to tie up here and wait for it to blow over."

"I don't see a problem with that," Martin said, stepping onto the dock. "But you'd better not come ashore. This is a private island. The natives get kind of cranky when . . ."

He'd been looking at Jake's fishing gear as he spoke, then his gaze trailed out to the water where he saw something floating midway between the dock and the shore. He might have dismissed it as a log or similar debris, but Jake's abandoned gear made him fear the worst. Jake could have slipped on the snow-covered boards, hit his head, toppled in.

"Shit," Martin said.

"Everything all right?" Sharky asked.

Jake had a landing net that extended maybe eight feet. It wasn't long enough. "Do you have a pole or hook?" Martin asked Sharky. "Something quite long?"

"Like a gaff?"

"I guess. Or a net."

Sharky had joined him on the dock and peered out, eyes narrowed beneath the peak of his baseball cap. "Well, shit. That's a body."

"A body? I'd hoped it was a log."

"Logs don't bleed."

Martin looked harder. "Are you sure? I don't see . . ."

Sharky returned to his trawler and came back with a gaff that telescoped to twenty feet. With his arm length and the hook on the end, he was able to snag the thing in the water and drag it closer.

"Oh shit, that's Jake," Martin said, turning away. He covered his mouth. Breath plumed between his fingers. "Jesus Christ. What the hell?"

"Can't be certain," Sharky said. "But I'd say that hole in his head was put there by a bullet."

"Jesus."

"I see multiple wounds. Head, chest, shoulder. I think we can rule out suicide."

Martin whipped around, heart galloping all the way into his throat. He looked at Jake again, then pointed at Sharky's boat.

"Your radio . . . Can you call the police on it?"

"Surely can. Coast guard, too." Sharky twirled one gnarled finger, indicating the storm. "But I'm not sure they'll come out in this."

"Try," Martin said. "Please try."

Sharky nodded. He started toward his boat while Martin picked his way along the dock.

"Hey, where're you going?" Sharky hollered. "Whoever did this is still out there."

"I'm going to find my daughters," Martin shouted without looking back. He reached the steps and started to run, managing only six or seven desperate paces before his left knee gave with a guitar-string twang of pain.

41

Valerie walked through the opening, into the glorious light.

Her first steps were tentative—baby steps, in every sense. She felt a childlike innocence, new to a life in which every experience would shape her. She cried like an infant, too. Big tears broke from her eyes. Tears of euphoria, mixed with trepidation. This was everything she wanted. It was beautiful, but overwhelming.

Another step, surer than the one before. But she paused afterward, her breath trembling in her chest.

"It's yours now," the girl urged. "You've earned this."

"Give me a moment."

Her nervous excitement ebbed when she realized she wasn't cold anymore. Her clothes were warm and dry. It wasn't snowing on the Crossover. She smiled, running this new name through her mind. It wasn't, perhaps, as poetic as the White Skyway, but it had a certain practical flavor, a realism that felt altogether *right*.

I'm here, she thought. *This is happening.*

She wondered what she'd do first—strip naked and run through her flowers, perhaps, or swim to the bottom of the nearest lake and huddle in the warm sand like a stingray. The Rhapsody had offered a taste of these things, but they were always dreamlike and over too soon. This was the real deal, and it was hers forever. The Crossover was traversable but Valerie doubted she would ever leave.

Why would I? she thought.

She squared her shoulders and walked with more confidence. The ground was solid beneath her feet, but the light had lifted and she got a sense of the Crossover's height. She eased toward the edge and dared to look. For all the light above and ahead of her, it was matched by the darkness below. *Pain and malady,* she thought, and shuddered. *The exotic matter.* She kept to the middle of the walkway, plenty of light on either side.

Another step, looking only forward. A breeze rushed at her, filled with the Glam's sweetness. It rippled her clothes and lifted her hair. She wanted to run but contained herself.

"You're almost there," the girl said. "So close."

Valerie nodded. She wasn't just warm now, she was positively hot. She loosened her scarf, unbuttoned her jacket.

"I'm coming," she said.

With her next step, she felt the Crossover wobble beneath her foot. Not by much, but enough. Valerie looked toward the edge again, a jolt of fear passing through her.

That was when the cracks started to appear.

Edith felt Mother Moon's coldness, but that was the least of it. She felt her disease, too—a wicked, destructive organism concerned only with its own survival. To have her so close was sickening, *violating.* Edith groaned and reached deep, struggling to hold the bridge together.

As much as she wanted to scream, she urged Mother Moon closer.

"Just a little farther," she said.

"But something doesn't feel right," Valerie said. The exotic matter churned beneath her. She took another hesitant step and watched two cracks zigzag to the edge. The light dimmed. Everything swayed.

"What's happening?"

"It's almost over," Edith said.

Valerie froze, her elation giving way to fear. The Crossover, it wasn't stable. She hadn't waited for the price to be paid, she should—

Another crack jagged between her feet. Valerie leaped to one side and looked up. The girl stood at the Glam-end of the Crossover, light flowing from the palms of her hands. The clearing loomed behind her, snow filling the air, trees bristling in the wind. *This isn't right,* Valerie thought, panicked. She turned around, stumbling as the Crossover rocked from side to side. More cracks raced in all directions. It wasn't this that made her scream, though. It was the sight of herself standing with her face drooping, eyes rolled back into her skull, an icicle hanging off her lower lip. That was when she realized that her body was still in the clearing, but her mind had been drawn into the place between.

* * *

Edith smiled despite the cold, despite the violation. She felt Mother Moon's horror—a miserable, twitching thing—as comprehension dawned. The light dulled and flickered around her. She looked at Edith with a broken expression. It was chilling.

"Light's out," Edith said.

She closed the window.

Valerie screamed again. She took three shaky steps toward the clearing before the Crossover shattered like ice. *Manipulative little bitch,* she thought. *I'm going to cut her in half. I'm going to feed her to the crows.* She lunged for her body but it was too far away.

The ground disappeared beneath her.

She fell a long way, into pain and malady.

Into darkness.

42

Martin staggered from the orchard, dragging his left leg. He passed the storage barn. Its wide door stood ajar, all dark inside.

"Shirley!"

The island was white and silent. Martin groaned. His fear was like a timber wolf that had sprung from the forest and clambered onto his shoulders. It breathed close to his ear.

"Edith!"

Cabin lights glimmered through the snow. Martin clamped his knee in one hand—just like he had when he'd raced to the school on the day Laura was killed—and limped toward them. He paused only once, to wipe snow from his eyes and listen for a response. There was nothing, only the wind and the trees shaking. He lumbered on and almost tripped over Ainsley Moore, partially buried in the snow. The hole in the back of his head was dark red and still warm. Martin backed away, stumbled, and fell. Pain blasted through his leg and he suppressed a cry.

This is bad. This is so fucking bad.

Laura was in his mind again, showing him the bullet in the box.

"What the hell is going on here?"

He recalled Sasha at the White Lantern saying, *One woman. She killed them all.* Was that what this was? Had Mother Moon gone postal—killed everybody on the island just like she'd killed everybody in that little room? Another thought occurred to Martin . . . that Mother Moon somehow found out he'd been snooping around behind her back, and this was the payback. One last massacre before the curtain came down.

No, he thought. *Please God, no. Not my babies. Please.*

Martin pushed himself to his feet. He ignored the cold, the pain—but couldn't ignore the timber wolf growling into his ear.

"Shirley . . . Edith. It's Dad. Where are you?"

Edith left Mother Moon slumped across the same cracked boulder the cardinal had taken shelter in. Snow fell into her open eyes.

"You've definitely gone somewhere," Edith said. "But I don't think it's Glam Moon."

Mother Moon said nothing. The corner of her mouth twitched.

Edith walked into the woods and crouched behind a fallen tree. She blew warmth into her hands, then closed her eyes and crossed once again into the place between. This time she distanced herself from fear and anger. They were present, but she held them at bay. She focused on love.

Shirley?

She reached for that connection . . .

Talk to me, Shirley.

Emptiness at first, then a response, but not what she expected. A voice called to her, so protective and familiar that warmth flowed through her and tears of relief burst from her eyes.

"Daddy," she said, her voice breaking with emotion. She got to her feet and started toward the sound. "Daddy . . . Daddy." The closer she got, the louder and more urgent her voice became, and soon she was flying between the trees, crying his name over and over, "*Daddy, Daddy, DADDY.*"

Cold, huddling for warmth, they'd heard the boat approaching, followed a short time later by voices. First Martin's, then Edith's. The relief Alyssa felt was painfully brief.

"He'll hear them," Brooke whispered, echoing Alyssa's thought.

She looked from their hiding spot: an old tree with its lower branches touching the ground. No sign of Nolan, only the gloomy, trembling woods.

"Brooke, stay on lookout," Alyssa said. "I don't think you'll see Nolan, but if you do, move from this spot quickly and quietly. If you don't, stay here until it gets too dark or too cold, then loop back to the cabins. Find an empty one. Hide inside. Stay there until you're sure this is over."

"You *can't* go out there," Brooke hissed. "Have you lost your mind? What are you thinking?"

"I'm not thinking," Alyssa said. "I'm doing."

* * *

Martin had checked their cabin—dark, empty—and had just stepped back outside when he heard Edith calling to him.

"Ede," he said.

Too many emotions. They combined to light a fire beneath him. He entered the woods north of the cabins and reeled toward the sound of his daughter's voice, stumbling from one tree to the next.

"Daddy," Edith called. She sounded so scared. *"Daddy."*

"Babygirl," Martin gasped, then called out to let her know that he was coming, he was close. *"I'm here, baby. Daddy's here."*

The questions, the fears . . . so *many,* and each tried to weaken him, drag him to the ground and feed on him. He shook his head—refused to give them light.

"Daddy."

"It's okay, sweetheart. Daddy's coming."

He saw movement ahead and to the right. It was difficult to tell who it was in the gloom, but he started that way, thinking it must be Edith, then she called out again—from a different direction—and he shifted course without a second thought.

"Edith!"

His knee felt as if someone had strapped a firecracker to it and set it off. At one point it gave beneath him and he fell. He picked himself up quickly and staggered on, pushing through the pain. He'd crawl if he had to.

"Daddy."

"I'm coming, babygirl."

Close now. So close. He peered through the trees, then saw a flash of her blond hair, a blue jacket that looked three sizes too big. He called her name and she looked up—saw him.

"Daddy," she said. "Oh, Daddy, Daddy."

"It's okay, Ede," Martin gasped. "I'm here now."

She threw her arms out, still thirty feet away, moving clumsily in her too-big clothes. It reminded Martin of how she used to raid Laura's side of the closet and play dress-up, a memory that filled him with melancholy and love. She'd looked so small, so *new*. Martin blinked at tears. She didn't look all that different now.

He might have carried this thought a moment longer—all the way into her arms, perhaps—but his attention was again snagged by that movement ahead and to the right. His eyes flicked in that direction.

Oh God, no—

Nolan emerged from the gloom, blood smeared across his face and dripping from his right sleeve. It trickled all the way down to the gun in his hand. He raised it and aimed at Edith.

She never saw him.

"Daddy," she cried, arms wide open.

"Ede," Martin whispered, then Nolan pulled the trigger. The report wasn't deafening. It didn't echo across the island or startle the birds from the trees. It was a muffled, unspectacular sound. Martin—in the split-second fashion such thoughts occur—wondered if it was even a real gun, or if it had somehow misfired, then the bullet struck Edith and blew her clean out of her boots.

43

Going to Edith was the wrong call. The moment he did so, Nolan would put a bullet in him, too, and if Edith was still alive, he wouldn't be able to help or comfort her.

This thread of logic flashed through Martin's mind, then rage took over—a screen of red so wide and bright that it blotted out the snow, the trees, the island, everything. He had no soul. He felt no fear or pain. He was a falling tree, a tumbling boulder. Nolan aimed the gun at him and fired. Martin didn't flinch. The bullet hit a tree to his left. Splinters flew. Nolan aimed again but either couldn't get off a clean shot or couldn't steady his hand. Martin half limped, half ran at him, using the trees for cover. He rose up on Nolan's left and caromed into him.

Nolan went one way—the gun popped from his fist, hit the ground, disappeared in the leaves and snow—and Martin went the other. Both men fell. Martin got up quickly. He grabbed a hefty branch and used it first to support his injured leg, then as a weapon. He raised it over his right shoulder and swung for the fences. Nolan was on one knee by this point. The end of the branch connected with his jaw and swiveled his head sharply. Teeth flew.

Martin drew breath and reestablished his grip on the branch. His second blow wasn't as ferocious for two reasons: the branch snapped when it met the back of Nolan's skull, and Martin's left knee gave out a split second before impact. He went down, his leg twisted beneath him. It should have hurt but didn't. He scrabbled around like a new animal, half got up, then fell again.

Snow flicked between the trees. The wind howled. It wasn't as cold or loud as whatever roared through Martin. He threw his weight against a mossy boulder and hoisted himself to his feet. Nolan was up, too. He'd lost a lot of blood. His mouth was a bright smear.

"Kill you," he said.

Martin recognized these as words but didn't know what they meant and had no reply; the red screen blanked everything. He and Nolan came together with a thud. They grappled. They threw punches. Nolan was the stronger man, but he was handicapped. His left arm drooped. His right spurted blood from the sleeve. Martin's rage compensated for their difference in ability, although he was injured, too. He was reminded of this every time he put weight on his left leg and it threatened to crumple beneath him.

"Kill you," Nolan said again. He swung his bloody right fist and it caught Martin—not hard, but square. His head filled with a bright, clear light, and he stumbled backward. Nolan rushed at him, shoulder first. Martin had no defense. He folded when Nolan hit him and they both thumped to the ground. They rolled down a shallow embankment, crashing through ferns, coming to rest at the base of an old yellow birch. Nolan grabbed Martin's hair and cracked the back of his head against the birch's surface roots. Four times . . . five. Nolan spat blood and laughed, then clambered off Martin and staggered up the embankment.

"Gun," he said, kicking through the foliage.

Martin rolled onto his side. Pain had broken through the red screen. He rose again, but slowly, shaking the bright spots from his field of vision. He started after Nolan but his leg buckled and he dropped. Nolan gave him a sideways glance and went back to looking for his gun. Martin pushed himself up, left hand in the dirt, right hand clutching a rock. It was the size of a baseball but shaped like a bird's skull, a dull point on one side. He came up behind Nolan with his arm swinging. The rock glanced off Nolan's head, grooving skin and bone—not the clean hit Martin had hoped for. Momentum sent him sprawling to the ground once again. The rock toppled from his hand and bounced out of reach. He felt something else underneath him, though. Another potential weapon, maybe. Groaning, Martin reached beneath his chest and pulled out one of Edith's boots.

"Oh," he said.

He turned and saw her lying facedown not fifteen feet away, blood blossoming through the hole in the back of her too-big jacket. But there was something else: her hand, it was moving . . . fingers spreading, then clenching.

"Hey, asshole," Nolan growled. A flap of scalp hung from the groove in his skull. It fluttered in the wind.

He'd found the gun.

Martin struggled to one knee but couldn't find his feet. He threw the boot at Nolan. It purred harmlessly wide. Nolan grinned and stepped toward Martin. He raised the gun. It wavered, but not enough.

He was too close to miss.

Shirley wiped sweat from her brow and tried to steady her breathing. The mall was suffocating, the air heavy with bright lights, body odor, and noise. She'd be agitated even without thirty pounds of shrapnel and explosive materials packed into her jacket.

A bald-headed man bumped into her but didn't apologize. He disappeared into Old Navy. More people streamed in and out of Forever 21, GameStop, Victoria's Secret . . . Everywhere she looked, they bustled and barged. Nolan had told her not to make eye contact with anyone, to walk with a sense of purpose, but it didn't matter. She could have ridden an elephant through and only those she trampled would have noticed. Nolan had also instructed her to detonate the bomb in the busiest location, but she could do it anywhere and cause staggering damage.

She looked at the watch. This would all be over soon.

A security guard patrolled nearby, his eyes flicking scrupulously from left to right. Shirley went the opposite direction. She walked into Gallagher's, a new department store with greeters dressed as dollar signs. Christmas music piped from a ceiling draped with twinkling lights. Shoppers droned through the aisles, programmed for one purpose. Shirley clasped the zipper, then took her hand away.

There was a water fountain in the middle of the store.

Children flipped coins in, making wishes. Shirley wondered if the fountain was her dad's idea. It was the kind of lovely, unnecessary thing he might come up with. A sad smile touched her lips. *I'm sorry,* she thought, and wiped a tear from her eye. It was in these wistful moments that Mother Moon's voice was loudest.

This is YOUR moment. NO ONE will shine brighter.

Shirley nudged her way toward the checkout lanes. They were plugged with people, herded by line barriers that snaked this way and that. Numbers flashed across cash registers. Scanners beeped continuously. The tall windows beyond looked out on another part of the mall, the stores there equally busy. Huge signs read 50% OFF and WHY PAY MORE?

Another person bumped into Shirley—a thirty-something lady with a kind face and a daughter Edith's age. She apologized and joined one of the lines. Shirley closed her eyes and tried bringing her own mom to mind. She saw her hair, hands, and body, but the face belonged to Mother Moon.

The Glam is waiting, sweet girl. We're ALL waiting.

Shirley looked at the watch again.

1:23.

She clasped the zipper and this time kept her hand there.

Snow billowed around Nolan. Blood ran from his wounds. All Martin saw was the tip of the suppressor—a tiny black hole that looked capable of swallowing everything.

Edith groaned behind him.

"Daddy," she said.

Nolan grinned. Martin waited. He stared at the suppressor

and wondered if he'd see the bullet come out—the first millisecond of combustion and then nothing ever again.

"She says I can have everything," Nolan said, spitting blood through the gaps where his teeth used to be. "I think I've earned it."

Martin realized these were supposed to be the last words he heard, some fucked up sendoff from a man who'd completely lost his mind. It didn't work out that way, though. Nolan's eyes suddenly shot wide and his arms flew open. The gun spun out of his hand. It landed in the ferns a short distance from Martin. "*Fuckamanfuck*," Nolan squealed nonsensically. His legs weakened but he didn't go down. When he turned, Martin saw the axe buried between his shoulder blades.

Alyssa came into view; she'd been standing behind Nolan. Her fists were bunched and her face was a storm. Nolan wheeled toward her, taking a couple of looping swipes with his damaged arms. She sidestepped them easily and kicked him flush in the balls.

Down he went.

"*Fuckaman.*"

Martin lunged for the gun, digging through the ferns, coming up with it quickly and aiming at Nolan.

"*Kill* him," Alyssa shrieked.

Nolan lurched toward him, still on his knees. One hand made limp grabbing motions at the axe in his back. He looked from the gun to Martin and shook his head.

"You don't have the—"

Martin shot him between the eyes.

44

Edith's world had shrunk to the size of a keyhole. She saw Alyssa through it, her face beautiful but troubled, and then she saw her daddy. He looked very concerned, too. Frightened, even. She didn't really know why.

"You're here," she mumbled. It seemed a silly thing to say.

"Shhh," he replied. "Don't speak, baby." And that seemed silly, too.

But maybe not; Edith moved to hug him—a dad-hug was exactly what she needed at that moment—but a white-hot pain flared through her left side, unlike any pain she'd ever experienced. She screamed and trembled. Her back arched.

"The clinic," her dad said. "Dr. Lythe—"

"She needs a hospital. And I don't know if Dr. Lythe . . . if he . . ." Alyssa trailed off. Edith felt a hand on her forehead. It was warm but it felt good. "But yes, the clinic first. We need clean bandages, gauzes, blankets—anything we can use to put pressure on the wound, stop the bleeding. And we'll need Nolan's boat key so we can get her to the mainland."

"The boat that brought me here is still at the dock."

"Let's not take any chances," Alyssa said. Edith looked at her through the keyhole, searching Nolan's pockets. Nolan lay in a bed of ferns and didn't move. He was covered in blood. Alyssa held up a set of keys a moment later. "Got 'em. Let's go."

"I don't think I can carry her quickly," her dad said.

"I can," Alyssa said.

Edith felt herself being lifted. More pain knifed through her stomach and ribs and all the way down her left leg. She tensed, crying out. "Okay, baby, everything's going to be okay." She couldn't tell if this was her dad or Alyssa, and it didn't matter; it was a soothing, floating voice that she held on to. Her eyelids fluttered. The keyhole—narrower now—showed snow falling through interlaced branches.

"Okay, baby, it's okay . . ."

Everything faded, then gradually came back. She heard someone crying. Her dad. The sound broke her heart and she tried reaching for him but didn't have the strength.

"Shirley?" he said a moment later.

"I don't know," Alyssa replied. She was short of breath but her arms remained strong. "I haven't seen her."

"Not here," Edith managed. "Gone . . . mainland." They had stepped out of the woods and into a storm that scraped and howled. It was nothing next to the pain. And the pain was nothing next to her fear. Mention of Shirley had brought everything bubbling to the surface. She relived her confrontation with Mother Moon—the crazy talk of Einstein portals and Shirley being immortalized. *But I have to wait for the price to be paid,* Mother Moon had said. *For the bomb to go off.*

The bomb.

"Shirley," Edith moaned.

The keyhole closed completely, peeped open, then closed again. Lying in the darkness, listening to Alyssa puff and pant, and to her father cry, Edith realized she had just enough energy to do one of two things: she could fight for her life, or she could try to reach her sister.

It was an easy decision.

Shirley . . . Shirley, where are—

Edith stopped. This wouldn't work. She wasn't reaching, she was *thinking.* The only way she could connect with Shirley was to rewire that old muscle. She had to start over.

Her hypnotherapist, Rafe Caine, drifted into her mind, with his mad beard and Star Wars toys. She heard his big brotherly voice at once, as if she was back in his office—which was how hypnosis worked; it was designed to be preloaded and recalled as needed. The suggestion was so strong that she even felt the soft couch beneath her, and saw the tranquil light floating in the darkness.

You are in control of your journey, he said to her. *You are aware of your surroundings.*

The storm raged. Alyssa walked stooped, curled protectively around her. Edith knew this even though her eyes were closed. Her father walked—no, limped—just behind.

"Hold on, baby," he said.

Edith positioned herself above these things. She saw the

deep space of everything below her, and everything *between*. The strange machinery inside her brain whirred. She took a fathomless step. Then another.

When the threat is near—when you feel *it within your airspace—you will visualize your alliance.*

Shirley.

Edith brought her face to mind. She didn't simply visualize it. She *built* it, just like she'd built her garden and the Crossover she'd whipped from beneath Mother Moon's feet.

See her hair and eyes, and the way she smiles.

Yes, every detail. Edith saw and recreated it all. She made it *real*—something she could reach out and touch.

Freckles like mine, she thought.

The wound in her back (or maybe it was in her stomach, or both) flared intensely. She screamed, faded, but held on. The pain sent a jolt to her brain. Edith felt that disorienting connect or disconnect sensation, then Shirley was there. Her sister. Her alliance.

Shirley . . .

Edith took another step across that deep space and reached with both hands.

Alyssa placed Edith on the cot in Dr. Lythe's clinic. She unzipped her jacket and removed it as quickly and gently as possible. The fabric surrounding the bullet hole was heavy with blood.

"We need to stop the bleeding," Alyssa said. "But we'll lose too much time trying to do it here, so we'll do it on the boat. Find me blankets, towels, gauze, anything that can be used as a compress. Also . . ." Alyssa grabbed two latex gloves and tossed them at Martin. "Fill them with snow. Tie a knot in the ends. They'll serve as icepacks."

Edith moaned. Her skin was pale, mottled with sweat.

"Okay, hon," Alyssa said, tilting Edith's head to keep her airway open. "You're going to be fine."

But she wasn't so sure; Edith was unresponsive. Her pulse was weak. While waiting for Martin, Alyssa found scissors and cut Edith's sweater and T-shirt down one side, exposing the wound. It was positioned on her lower back, a couple of inches to the left of her spine. She cut off Edith's jeans and found the exit wound in the top of her left thigh.

"The bullet came out," Alyssa said to Martin when he limped back into the clinic, both latex gloves packed with snow. "And it went down toward her leg, instead of up toward the major organs. That's good. But it traveled a long way, and that's not good."

"Is she going to make it?" Martin looked like he was going to pass out.

"I don't know, but we need to get her on that boat. Right now."

Alyssa wrapped Edith in a blanket and lifted her again, trying to keep the wounds elevated above her heart. She stepped into the storm and walked blindly south. Martin was right behind her with the gauzes, bandages—everything Alyssa had asked for—gathered in a sheet and bundled over one shoulder.

* * *

He scooped a handful of Advil on his way out the door, tore into the packets with his teeth, crunched four of them dry and shoved the rest into his pocket. A great grief had clambered onto his shoulders in place of the timber wolf. It was a familiar grief—an all-too-recent companion—and he hated it to the core. Questions and regrets raced through his mind but he had no time for them.

The wind rocked him. The snow crusted his face. Walking was difficult anyway, but his injured knee made it torturous. Martin gritted his teeth, put his head down, and hobbled on. His leg occasionally buckled but he didn't fall. By sheer will, he'd caught up to Alyssa by the time they reached the orchard, then pushed ahead.

"I'll tell Sharky to get the boat untied and started," he said. "That'll save us some time."

"Every second counts," Alyssa said. Edith, wrapped in a blanket, appeared very still in her arms.

Martin pushed on, fighting to hold it together. *Later,* he thought. *You can scream later. You can collapse and rage.* He wondered if Alyssa was carrying a corpse.

There was fading, then there was falling. The distance to her wounded body lengthened—she couldn't make a fist or lick her lips—but that didn't matter; Edith had sacrificed the physical to enhance the spiritual, to find her sister.

She saw Shirley's hair and eyes, the way she smiled, her freckles so like Edith's own. She saw her at once in a thousand ways, through the years. It was like riffling through a photo book. Most importantly, she saw Shirley *now,* with her shorter black hair and an equally black puffer jacket that Edith had never seen her wearing before. The connection was strong. Dying amped the psychic soul, apparently.

Shirley was in a department store. Surrounded by people. She was pallid and afraid, fingers clasping the zipper of her jacket. The combination of finding her in this environment, and the dreadful words Mother Moon had let slip about the bomb, recalled everything that Edith had seen through the window. For the first time ever, she remembered the bad things. She saw the bodies, the fire, the countless broken pieces. She heard the sirens and screams.

Her instinct was to run, find shelter. But that wouldn't stop the bad things from happening, and it wouldn't save Shirley.

There was no turning away. Not this time.

Edith opened her arms.

She *was* the shelter.

1:30.

Shirley lowered her head.

"I'm sorry."

She pulled the zipper down. Its teeth buzzed, a sound she likened to the hiss of a burning fuse. The jacket was three-quarters open when a voice bloomed inside her head. *Not* Mother Moon's. This was beautiful, full of love and power. It drowned Mother Moon's entirely. Shirley's breath caught in her throat and her teary eyes filled with light. She pulled her hand away from the jacket with less than two inches of closed zipper remaining.

"Edith," she said.

She didn't just hear her, she *felt* her. It was like her little sister had walked into the department store, burrowed her way through the crowd, and wrapped her arms around Shirley from behind. "Edith," she said again, warm tears spilling onto her cheeks. And then, in her mind: *You found me.*

Of course I did. I love you.

Oh, my goodness. I love you, too. Shirley smiled and ran the heel of her hand across her cheeks. *You feel so close.*

I am *so close.*

Shirley's joy was replaced by deep remorse. She looked around, at the packed aisles and checkout lanes, at the mothers and daughters, the brothers, sons, sisters, friends, lovers . . . all these people she was willing to—

She shook her head and looked at the zipper. Two inches away. That was all.

My God.

That wasn't you, Ede said, tuned in to her heart as well as her mind. *That was Mother Moon. She was using you. But she's not a problem anymore.*

Shirley pulled the zipper all the way up and stepped away from the checkout lanes. Her back throbbed under the weight of the jacket, but her mind, she realized, had lost its burden. She listened, but there was no whisper of Mother Moon. She'd fallen silent.

There was only Edith now.

You have to come with me, Shirl. Right now.

Where? I'm just . . . I'm so scared.

I know. But you held my hand for all those years. Now I'm going to hold yours.

No sooner had Edith said this than Shirley felt a small hand curl into hers. It tugged gently, led her back along the main aisle, through the cloud of Black Friday shoppers, into the mall proper. She walked in a daze past stores and kiosks, beneath the sale signs and bright lights, through waves of jolly Christmas music. When she stepped outside, the fresh, wintry air knocked her back on her heels. The world was startlingly white and wondrous, which only emphasized the terrible weight of what she carried.

The jacket . . . the bomb, Shirley screwed her eyes shut. It hurt to even *think* the word. *I don't know what to do.*

It's okay. Edith said. *I do.*

"Start the boat," Martin screamed, faltering along the dock. He had wondered if Sharky would still be there—if perhaps he'd decided that tackling a snowstorm was less perilous than docking on an island with a gunman on the loose. The idea of hauling ass *had* to have entered his mind, but he hadn't acted on it. And thank Christ.

"What the hell?" Sharky emerged from his cabin, flare gun in hand, clearly not taking any chances.

"Start the boat." Martin tossed the bundle he'd been lugging onto the trawler's snow-covered deck. "We have to go, Sharky."

"We're not going anywhere in this, mister."

"Yes, we are."

Martin looked over his shoulder as Alyssa emerged out of the snowy air. She shuffled carefully along the pathway and down the steps to the dock. The blanket covering Edith flapped around Alyssa's knees. As she got closer, Martin saw it was daubed with blood.

"Well, shit," Sharky said.

"It's my daughter," Martin said. "She's been shot. She needs—"

"Christ, man, get her in here."

Martin and Sharky helped Alyssa onto the boat. She went through to the cabin and lay Edith on one of the bench seats. Martin untied the mooring lines while Sharky started the engine. It rumbled faithfully.

"Did you radio the police?" Martin shouted. He freed the last line, then threw it and himself on board. His knee sang its misery, but the Advil had already taken the edge off the pain.

"I did. The coast guard, too. But it's like I said—they ain't coming out in this." Sharky hooked a thumb toward the other side of the dock, where Jake Door bobbed on the waves with snow in his eyes. "Not for one corpse floating belly-up in the water."

"Radio again. Tell them there are more on the island." Martin went to Alyssa. She'd taken the blanket off Edith, who lay with one arm hanging. Blood oozed from the wound in her thigh. She was still alive, but only just. "And tell them we need an ambulance waiting for us at the marina in Fisherman's Point."

Sharky turned the trawler around, already fighting the wheel. Heavy waves boomed against the hull. "You're assuming we'll *make* it to the marina at Fisherman's Point."

Martin looked at Edith again and said, "We have to."

* * *

Snow blew sideways across the parking lot. The traffic crawled, headlights blazing. Shirley walked with her hand out to the side, feeling Edith there. She passed a line of taxis and a longer line of people, and came soon after to a sign that read SHUTTLE. Two nearby shelters were crammed with shoppers. Shirley waited in the snow.

"I messed up," she whispered. "I'm such a bad person."

Don't say that, Shirl. You're beautiful.

"I need help."

The Syracuse shuttle pulled up. Its door yawned open. Most of the shoppers filed out of the shelters and onto the bus. It rolled away a moment later, throwing sleet from beneath its tires. Edith led Shirley into the nearest shelter. A small screen flashed ads for stores in the mall and a ticker along the bottom announced that the local shuttle was six minutes away. Shirley stood with her head low, trying not to cry.

I'm here, Shirl. I'm with you.

It took closer to fifteen minutes but the local shuttle finally arrived. Shirley asked the driver if he was going to Flint Wood.

"Second stop," he said. "Get on if you're gettin'; this'll be the last run until the storm's blown through."

Shirley boarded and took a seat toward the back. She smeared her hand across the fogged window so she could see out, get her bearings. They joined I-81 for one exit. It was a string of taillights. Shirley counted three cars in the ditch.

Not far now, Edith said.

First stop was Briarville, just off the Interstate, where four passengers got off and six got on. One of them sat next to Shirley, where she'd "felt" Edith sitting. She was about to say that the seat was occupied when Edith crawled into her lap, curled both arms around her neck.

I'm right here.

Good . . . that's good.

They passed another car ass-up in the ditch and the driver had a flare burning. It set the daylight an unholy pink and the snow looked more like ash. The sign for Flint Wood was just beyond this, then Judd's Gas Stop. Shirley wiped the window again, peering hard through the snow until she saw what she was looking for. She stood up and tugged the cord. The driver pulled over. Shirley stepped down the aisle, Edith one pace ahead.

"You sure 'bout this, girly?" the driver asked. "I can let you out, but there's nothin' here."

Shirley looked through the windshield, at the rusty gate collapsed on its hinges, the snow-covered driveway and derelict farmhouse beyond.

"Nothing good, anyway," she said.

Alyssa knelt beside Edith with a folded towel pressed to the entry wound in her lower back, and a gauze pad pressed to the exit wound in her thigh. When she looked and saw no red spots seeping through the material, she blew over her top lip and nodded at Martin.

"The bleeding has stopped, or at least slowed all the way down. Those icepacks helped." Both temporary "packs" had split under the pressure, but Sharky had a beer cooler with a couple of Freez Paks in that he willingly donated to the cause. "I don't think there's any damage to the major organs, based on the bullet's trajectory, but I can't account for shrapnel. I *am* certain it didn't hit the femoral artery on the way out, though. We'd know if it did."

"Right . . . thank you." Martin wiped his eyes with trembling hands and said it again. "Thank you, Alyssa."

"We're not out of the woods. Besides the blood she's already lost, there's risk of shock, sepsis, infection." A large wave hoisted the prow skyward and it came down with a thump. Alyssa rocked on her knees, maintaining pressure on Edith's wounds. "I've done all I can. Now we just hope."

Martin took a blanket, wrapped it around Alyssa, and kissed her cheek.

"You're amazing." He cupped her face in both hands. "I can't begin to . . . I mean, how do you even *know* this stuff? Are you a nurse? I thought you were a music teacher."

"I am," she replied, smiling sadly. "I learned about it after Jackie was killed. I think everybody in America should know how to treat gunshot wounds."

Another steep wave struck the hull. The trawler yawed alarmingly. Alyssa held Edith. Martin held Alyssa. Sharky worked the wheel and swore. He had to wait for the wind to dip to get them pointed in the right direction. A moment's calm followed. The GPS directed them to the next waypoint. Sharky radioed ahead and gave their ETA as approximately twenty minutes.

"We're over halfway," he shouted. "How's she doing?"

"Not good," Martin shouted back. "If you can go any faster . . ."

The lightest breaths escaped Edith's lips. Her eyelids

fluttered but didn't open. Martin took her hand. It was cold and small.

"I love you, baby," he whispered into her ear, certain that, even through the storm, and over whatever distance separated them, she could hear him. "Daddy loves you so much."

The wind rose again. Leaden waves, some ten feet tall, surged and bullied.

Edith curled her fingers around Martin's thumb and squeezed.

The barn appeared through the snow like some ghost ship out of the fog. Looking through Shirley's eyes, Edith experienced a familiar dread. Her recurring nightmare probed the edges of her mind. She saw the dead foal spilling from the well and hobbling after her on its moldering hooves. And Shirley—a horror-movie rendition of Shirley, at least—chasing her through the forest with splintered goat's horns curving from her forehead.

I'm coming for your soooooooul, she creaked.

Edith flinched. The connection to her sister weakened and she fought to hold on.

Shirley, I'm . . . I'm . . .

She felt pain again. Deep, unwavering pain. Her father's voice came to her from some faraway place.

I'm right here, baby. Daddy's here. Daddy loves you.

Shirley crossed the yard between the barn and farmhouse, stumbling under the weight of the jacket. Her hair flapped around her head, white with snow. Edith was now a step behind.

You can take my soul, she thought. *Just let me see this through.*

She was cold, though. So very cold.

Shirley stepped around the overgrown water trough. Edith looked but couldn't see the dead foal. It was there, though, covered by snow. A white hump like a small, newly filled grave.

Edith, are you still there?

The tall grass wasn't so tall; it was limp and brown, weighed down by snow. If not for the storm, she would have seen the old well long before she reached the clearing. As it was, she shambled to within inches of the crumbling brickwork before stopping. She threw her hands out, caught the edge. Had the cover not been in place, she might have fallen in.

Edith?

I'm here, Edith replied. *I'm . . . with you.*

Shirley was tired and cold. The muscles in her shoulders and back had knotted and her legs trembled. It was with considerable effort that she pushed the cover off the well. The exposed hole looked deeper and darker than it ever had. The pull was just the same.

My special place, she thought, and recalled what she'd told Edith on the day she brought her out here: *It's like extreme therapy, I guess. Unload your crap and go home.*

"Unload," Shirley mumbled, and screamed into the well until tiny dark spots buzzed in front of her eyes. She groaned, caught her breath, then screamed again. The anger was not new. Nor was the grief and self-doubt. The other feelings—regret, dismay, betrayal—were more recent additions to her complicated psyche.

They worked like accelerants, she thought. They could be handled individually, but were volatile when mixed with others.

Her throat burned. The exertion had started her nose bleeding.

She remembered the last time she came here, just after her mom had died, a period of such unutterable despair that she couldn't see a way through. She'd told herself she was there to unload, but couldn't deny that her intention may have been darker. Her dad had found her, so full of love and concern, but confused—broken—in his own way. *I think it's feeding on me,* she'd said to him, looking at the well. *Like a vampire. It won't be happy until I throw myself in.*

Blood dripped from her left nostril, swallowed by the well. It wanted more, she knew. She felt it pulling her, *willing* her. It was similar to Mother Moon, in many ways, offering itself as salvation, but really just a black, soulless hole.

"I have so much darkness to give," Shirley whispered. She'd said that to Dad, too, and it had scared him. It may have been the one thing she said that made him decide to take them to Halcyon.

Shirley . . .

Small arms looped around her middle. Edith. She didn't feel as real, or as strong, as she had at the mall, or even on the bus, but she was there, and Shirley was thankful.

You know what to do.

Shirley nodded. She unzipped the puffer jacket halfway and pulled it over her head, hefting and wriggling like an escapologist freeing herself from handcuffs and chains. The storm lashed her body. She gritted her teeth and looked down the well.

"Bad things belong in bad places," she said, and dropped the jacket into the darkness. She saw the flash of its lethal zipper, then it was gone. Three seconds later, it hit the water at the bottom with a heavy splash.

She would make her way to the barn soon and huddle there, wait for the storm to pass. There might be some dry hay in the loft or an old blanket she could wrap herself in. But first she needed to adjust to the feeling that had washed over her. It was sudden, uplifting, and powerful.

"Free," she said. And maybe she was. At the very least, she believed she was free enough to become a young woman who—one day—would have some light to give.

Shirley wiped the blood from her nose, the tears from her eyes. She dropped to her knees and cried.

"Thank you, Ede," she whispered. "I love you."

No response from Edith, only the wind purring across the mouth of the well.

"Ede?"

Her little sister was gone.

Shirley wiped her eyes again and remembered something her dad had said when he found her out here, and despite his brokenness his words had rung true then, and they rang true again now: that it wasn't the end of everything, and it *was* the beginning of something, and whatever that something was . . . that was up to them.

Shirley braced herself against the cold. She walked away.

The emotions pressed like unwanted guests against a door. Martin would open it soon enough, and they would pour in, smother him. Most would take up permanent residence. He would live alongside fear, share a bed with grief, clean up after anger. There'd be no escape.

That was to come, but for now he kept the door bolted.

His focus was Edith. She was pale and still. Every now and then a vein in her eyelid twitched or her tongue pressed against her upper lip. She was slipping, though . . . slipping away from him.

"Stay with me, baby." He lifted her hand to his lips and kissed it.

Like a dimly chiming bell, or some thin light glimpsed through the mist, Martin became aware that they were moving faster across the water. His gaze flicked away from Edith for a second. The waves still chopped and foamed, but not as severely, and he saw more of them; visibility had improved. The storm was passing.

"I see the mainland," Sharky heralded a moment later. "They're waiting for us."

"Ambulances?" Alyssa asked.

"Yup. Three or four, by the looks."

The trawler jounced and rumbled onward. Alyssa squeezed Martin's shoulder and whispered that they were nearly there.

Martin kissed Edith's hand again. Such small fingers. So delicate. He waited to see her eyelid twitch or her tongue touch her upper lip again but it didn't happen.

"Stay with me, baby."

Red and blue lights flashed on the mainland. They colored the falling snow.

"Stay with me."

45

She opened her eyes.

Nothing.

There would usually be something, she thought—a disparity in the darkness, a suggestion of texture or shape. She waited several minutes for her eyes to adjust, but they didn't.

The girl's voice puffed through her mind like smoke from a spent match. Two words, painfully accurate: *Lights out*.

Valerie made a discordant sound in her throat, somewhere between a groan and a cough. She pushed herself to her knees and started crawling. The floor beneath her was hard and cold, damp in places. She bumped into a wall, got to her feet, and felt her way along it. Its surface was nicked and scratched.

"Please," Valerie said, hating the vulnerability in her voice. She reached a corner and assessed the adjoining wall, then the wall after that. Around and around she went, until finally her fingers happened upon a switch. She flicked it with an excited gasp.

A light hanging from the ceiling buzzed and flickered.

Not a light. A lantern.

She saw her environment in ugly snapshots. No door, no windows, but four walls, familiar even without the hanging scrolls and discolored paintings of lotus blossoms. In their place was the same unsettling phrase scratched over and over, tattooing the walls from floor to ceiling.

DEREVAUN SERAUN.

The lantern sputtered, went out.

She smelled cologne a short time later—something sour and expensive. The lantern flashed once like the bulb on an old camera.

The rooster stood in the corner. He carried a long pipe with a piece of chain dangling from the end. His hands were larger than she remembered.

"You," Valerie mewled. Whatever strength she had in her legs drained quickly away. She spilled to her knees, and had barely caught her breath when, in the next brief burst of light, she saw the dog. His scissors made a terrible *snick-snick* sound.

The goat appeared next, armed with a suture needle and thread. "This will go on and on," he assured her, echoing words he'd spoken before.

"And on," the pig concurred. He'd brought the picana. It was wired to a car battery at his feet.

"And on," the snake said, sharpening his knives.

They surrounded her one by one.

He was the last to arrive, of course, and he came impeccably dressed, his stripes shimmering.

"Hey, sugargirl."

Valerie looked at him. Her scars itched. He dropped to his haunches in front of her and ran his powerful tiger hands through her hair.

"It's like I said . . . you can't get rid of us." The other animals snarled and grunted behind him. Their tools clanked heavily. "We'll always be with you."

The lantern flickered, then went out, and that was fine.

Valerie found she preferred the darkness.

EIGHT MONTHS LATER

GETTING CLOSER

Martin had watched *Smokey and the Bandit* four times and had paused the video throughout, but failed to recognize his therapist in any of the stunt scenes. It didn't help that the stuntwoman wore a Sally Fields wig, or that the video had that grainy, late seventies quality. The movie being forty-two years old was obviously a factor, but his therapist—comfortably into her sixties—had a clear, vibrant countenance. She had aged in the years since, of course, but kindly.

"The first thing I saw when you walked in," she said to Martin, "was your smile. Worth noting."

She would have noted this in her mind, Martin thought, because she never wrote anything down. She *used* to make notes, apparently, but found her patients became variations of scribbles (*doodles* was the word she used), rather than . . . well, people.

Martin nodded. "It happens. Usually when Saturn is in . . . I don't know, Aquarius, or something. I thought for sure you'd notice I'm not limping anymore."

"I did. The physical therapy is clearly paying off."

"It's going well. I finished at the clinic. Now it's just light stretching and reps at home." Martin touched his knee, but cautiously, the way he might touch a dog that had once bitten him. "I'm glad I got the surgery done. And I'll indulge in the metaphor, too: Something about moving forward. Blah-blah-blah."

"Most metaphors"—she smiled wonderfully—"are blah-blah-blah."

Her name was Daisy Drinkwater, a delicious name, worthy of everything from a Mark Twain novel to a Burt Reynolds movie. She was graceful and always calm, and her eyes . . . Martin would never forget Laura's flashlight expression, but Daisy had what he called a swimming pool expression. She could lift one eyebrow or wrinkle her nose and he'd be drawn in, and sometimes he'd doggy-paddle with his head above the water, and sometimes he'd dive deep.

As he did now:

"I *am* moving forward, but I have my moments, usually at night, lying in bed and staring into the darkness, thinking I should feel guilt, or forgiveness, but feeling nothing at all. I killed a man. Shot him through the brain. Snuffed him out like a candle. His thoughts, his joys, his dreams—however fucked up they may have been . . . I put an end to them all. And I feel no guilt. I keep thinking about what he did, not just to Edith but to everybody. The acts of terror, the victims, and for what? The whim of one crazy woman and her idea of salvation."

Martin looked at Daisy with a blank but honest expression. She returned his gaze, inviting him to keep swimming. He nodded, then glanced around her office, which was as methodized and comforting as Daisy herself. A window looked out on tall pines that swayed toward one another as if sharing secrets—not dissimilar to the view from his cabin window on Halcyon.

"I should feel something . . ." A bitter expression touched his face. "Right?"

"Because you haven't, doesn't mean you won't. You've been healing, in one form or another, since your wife died. It's not that you're not ready to deal with this. More a matter of priority."

The story broke, then escalated. What started out as a mass shooting on Gray Peaks Island developed into a cult saga with echoes of Heaven's Gate and Jonestown, but with its own demented ideology. It didn't take long for the surviving islanders to share their experiences, and when certain names came up (Garrett Riley, Glenn Burdock, etc.), the authorities put the pieces together with ease. Shirley's statement—procured over several careful sessions with FBI agents and psychologists—filled in numerous blanks, and suggested Jim Jones levels of manipulation and brainwashing.

In an interview with Anderson Cooper, forensic psychiatrist (and CNN go-to) Dr. Clyde Brisk said, "These people had already demonstrated a desire for utopia by abandoning everything they knew and beginning a new life on the island. Valerie Kemp—a pathological narcissist as well as a master manipulator—was able to use their disillusionment against them. Vulnerability, in the wrong hands, is a dangerous weapon."

Valerie had been rushed from the island to St. Joseph's in Syracuse, where she lay in a coma for eighteen days. She emerged, but barely. Her brain damage, doctors said, was likely due to severe hypothermia. By this time the story had exploded internationally and Valerie had achieved a level of fame reserved for movie stars and presidents. She became the new FACE OF EVIL, everyone's favorite boogeywoman.

Two books were already in the works. There was talk of a movie and an HBO special.

The press called her the Mind Witch.

She was moved from St. Joseph's to a secure psychiatric institution in Vermont. Much of her time was spent cowering in the corner, flinching at nothing. She frequently became "unreasonable" and on these occasions was placed—for her own safety, of course—in four-point restraints.

There were cries for blood (or at the very least, justice), but these went unanswered; Valerie was in no condition to answer for her crimes. This prompted extensive debate as to whether or not she was faking her mental deterioration. How could she go from being the Mind Witch, to having no real mind at all?

"*Tiger,*" she'd wail, her hands raised as if to ward someone off. *"Pig . . . rooster."*

She screamed a lot.

"I went to see her again," Martin said to Daisy, looking from the swaying trees to her inviting eyes. He splashed around for a moment, then swam. "They didn't want to let me in, but my lawyer pulled some strings."

"Once for closure," Daisy said. "That was my advice."

"I know. It was an impetuous decision, but I don't regret it." Martin shook his head. "The first time I went, I was angry; I needed to see the woman who killed my wife. I know she didn't pull the trigger, but she played her part. And yeah, seeing her helped. I don't know if it gave me closure—or if such a thing even exists—but it put me in a better position to move forward.

"The second time was . . . different. I'd had several months to evaluate my feelings, and I got thinking about the terrible ordeal Valerie went through as a young woman, and how that made her what she is."

"You needed to see her," Daisy said, "not as a monster, but as a victim."

"Being . . ." Martin reached for the right word, one finger pressed to his temple. "Being empathetic has given me some peace. I don't forgive Valerie, but I get that she has . . . grievances."

"Did you tell her as much?"

"No, but it was in my energy. I *projected* it." Martin looked at the whispering trees again. "Laura would be proud."

He'd told Daisy about the nightmarish events at the White Lantern, but not the authorities. This was one piece of information he kept to himself. Calm Dumas had an incredible mind that was tuned in to frequencies Martin couldn't fathom. He trusted her absolutely, but not everybody would. Most, in fact, would *not*, which could dilute his own and the other victims' credibility. In the end, he decided to let the shrinks and experts draw their own conclusions about Valerie Kemp, and her reasons for doing what she did.

Whatever they unearthed wouldn't change the diagnosis: the woman was batshit crazy.

Also, he had no desire to involve Calm in the investigation, not when he didn't have to. Or Sasha, either. Sasha had called him shortly after the story broke, and requested that, if possible, her name be left out of the mix. She'd recently put the restaurant up for sale and didn't want any complications. "I haven't opened the doors since you and your friend came," she said. "I can't stand to be in the place." She and her wife were relocating to Asbury Park, and she didn't want to be hounded by people thinking she had assisted or enabled Valerie Kemp.

Martin had wished Sasha well, and assured her that he'd already made the decision not to involve her. Eight months later, she had not been named, questioned, or implicated in any way.

Others were not so fortunate: three lawyers pinned to a reverse money laundering scheme using legitimate funds provided by islanders (this exposed after Angela Byrne's name emerged, and her bank activity was investigated). And an eyelash gummed to the plastic explosive they'd recovered from the well was tracked to a black-market weapons dealer who'd been on the FBI's watch list since 2012.

"Six weeks, you say?"

"I'm coming back . . . definitely." Martin sat up in his chair, hands folded across his chest. He wondered if Daisy had a name for *his* expression, which was warm, yet shadowed. A sunset expression, perhaps. "We need a moment to rediscover ourselves. It'll be good for us."

"Know where you're going?"

They'd discussed this, and decided to see where the road led them. The west coast, the Rockies, the deep south . . . it didn't matter; they'd run without rein or bridle, like manic horses.

"Anywhere and everywhere," Martin replied, and shrugged. "From the Redwood Forest to the Gulf Stream waters. And yeah, it's about rediscovering ourselves, but it's also about rediscovering America. I lost my way for a while there. I got scared—fell out of love with my country. But you don't fix things by running away. You have to integrate yourself, become a part of the structure. You have to get *closer*."

Martin's gaze tracked from a wasp tapping at the window to a painting on the wall—a Picasso-esque meeting of color and angles that could probably be interpreted a thousand different ways. There were several such curios in Daisy's office, all designed to encourage openness and conversation: bright plants, sculpture, odd little toys and trinkets . . . but not one lousy picture of Burt Reynolds.

Daisy blinked slowly. Martin took a deep breath, then stepped out of the pool. He experienced a moment's vulnerability—a nakedness, almost—then warmed to the air.

"A wise woman once told me," he said, "that you can't nurture your soul from a distance."

"Wise indeed. When do you leave?"

"How long do we have left?"

Daisy lifted her sleeve, peeked at her watch. "About three minutes."

Martin smiled again and said, "There's your answer."

* * *

A newish Ford Escape idled in the parking lot, its trunk loaded with bags and cases. Alyssa sat behind the wheel, her window down, singing along to the radio. Shirley was in the backseat looking at her phone.

"Excuse me," Martin said as he approached. "You think I could hitch a ride to love and absolution?"

"What a coincidence," Alyssa said, grinning. "That's exactly where we're going."

"Well, all right!" Martin jumped in on the passenger side. He leaned over and kissed Alyssa firmly on the lips. She placed her hand on his face. Her eyes shone.

"Cute," Shirley said from the backseat, looking up from her phone.

"We can go from cute to gross in zero-point-five seconds," Martin assured her. "No problem whatsoever."

Shirley rolled her eyes, but the corners of her mouth had perked upward.

The last few months had been easier, but Shirley's personal journey, since leaving the island, had been emotionally demanding. It didn't help that there had been confusion as to whether she should be treated as a victim or a suspect, at least until the investigation deepened and numerous psychoanalysts had the opportunity to spool through her brain. The fact that she volunteered information (she told the authorities what she'd been "programmed" to do and where she'd discarded the bomb) counted in her favor. Her silver-tongued Uncle Jimmy, who'd been present for questioning while Martin was at the hospital, demanded she be treated like a hero. She had resisted the Mind Witch's hoodoo, after all, where so many others had succumbed, and had nullified an act of terror that would have killed a lot of people.

But Shirley became neither hero nor villain. At no point was she placed under arrest, and her name was never released to the press. In regard to the attempted bombing of the Onondaga Mall on Black Friday, 2018, limited details were shared with the public.

She spent three months at a mental health care facility. Her behavior was monitored, with particular attention given to any "latent or subliminal influence" from Valerie Kemp. It was a campus-based facility in the Adirondacks, surrounded by natural beauty, with twenty-four-hour crisis support, art and education services, and various interactions designed to encourage behavioral and emotional growth. It was a good facility (paid for by Jimmy—bless him), where Shirley was able to continue the healing she'd started when she dumped the bomb down the well.

"Because it wasn't *just* the bomb," she'd said to Martin during one of his visits. "It was every bad thing."

She still had dark episodes: mood swings, nightmares, bouts of anxiety . . . These grew less frequent as the weeks turned to months, and Martin knew they would never heal completely. Her commitment never waned, though. She showed new strength every day.

The road trip had been her idea—to go wherever, to find peace and remedy in their environment. "I want to snowboard in the Rockies, catch a tube in Malibu, eat peyote buttons in the desert." Her eyes had been wide, daring, and totally serious. "I'll benefit more from *living* than I will from sitting at home popping antidepressants."

"We all will," Martin had said. "Let's do it. Let's just go."

The Escape cruised through town. Alyssa drove with her sunglasses on, tapping her hands on the wheel in time with the music. Martin watched the buildings scroll by—the post office, Chase bank, Starbucks. They were all familiar to him, a part of the everyday fabric, but soon he'd be looking at farmland, rivers, and vistas he'd never seen before. Every view would be a new experience. He smiled and looked over his left shoulder. The sunlight flashed across Shirley's face, highlighting her freckles, making her hair shimmer—blond again now, shoulder length. She glanced at him. Her expression was every bit as illuminating and searching as her mom's. That was a good thing.

"Check out this restaurant," she said, turning her phone to Martin. "It's in New Jersey. The owner is this crazy lady who thinks her cat is a reincarnation of Michael Jackson."

"We're totally going," Alyssa said. "We can be there for dinner."

"What kind of restaurant?" Martin asked, recalling a certain establishment in Engine City, where he had no wish to go, not yet and not ever.

"Homestyle," Shirley replied. "It's in Green Ridge, wherever that is."

"Sounds good," Martin said. "Can you call ahead, make a reservation?"

Shirley nodded eagerly, already dialing. Alyssa smiled and placed her hand on Martin's thigh. He saw himself reflected in her sunglasses. Older, trimmer, altogether happier than the man who'd set out for Halcyon almost ten months before. His life had been a blur since then—really since Laura died. There'd been no easy days, but he was learning to manage his pain more effectively.

They drove across Makers Bridge, then east on Sparrow Road. A short time later, Alyssa made a right turn into the Heritage Home parking lot. She found a space within view of the south garden and main entrance.

"Booked," Shirley said, hanging up. "Table for four. Seven o'clock."

"Great," Martin said. "Now call your sister. Tell her we're waiting."

"No need," Alyssa said. "Here she comes."

An eleven-year-old girl, tall for her age, with flowing blond hair and clear eyes, walked across the south garden, her face turned to the sky. She moved unsteadily, in part because of the injury, but also because of the guitar case she carried. Every two weeks, she played for the old folks at Heritage Home—classic (but cool) songs from a golden era: The Beatles, Patsy Cline, Johnny Cash. She had quite the fan club, apparently.

Edith stepped out of the shade of a sprawling willow tree. She saw them and waved.

"Edith suffered thirty-four percent blood loss. During such trauma, the body adopts numerous defense mechanisms—a kind of 'red alert' to preserve vital functions. Blood pressure drops, hormones and neurotransmitters are released, and the heart rate increases. In the case of a class-three hemorrhage, it can increase to a hundred and twenty beats per minute." Dr. Johnny Pride—Edith's trauma surgeon—made an elevator out of his right hand and had it ride to an imaginary upper floor. He was a stocky man, but with long, thin fingers that appeared designed for exact work. "This was not the case with Edith. Her heart rate was abnormally slow when she arrived—I'm talking one beat every five or six seconds. She was breathing, but slowly, like someone meditating. Now, I've been doing this eighteen years and have seen pretty much everything, but I've never seen *that*. One of our nurses described her as 'not present,' and I'd say that's a perfect description."

Martin had spoken with Shirley and found out what had happened, so knew exactly why Edith wasn't present. There was no reasonable way to explain this to Dr. Pride, though, so he didn't try. Instead, he asked if Edith's atypical state had presented a complication.

"On the contrary," Dr. Pride replied. "With Edith's body—improbably—on pause, we were able to administer fluids and stabilize her quickly. I mean, she still lost a lot of blood, but not nearly as much as she might have. I will add that your friend's intervention was critical."

Martin had looked at Alyssa, who sat in the waiting room with her head down and her hands between her knees. She looked up and their eyes met. Their matching smiles were weary but warm.

"Make no mistake," Dr. Pride said. "She saved your daughter's life."

The bullet had deflected twice, first off the thick wing of Edith's left hip bone—causing numerous fractures—and again off her left femur, exiting her thigh an inch from her femoral artery. Dr. Pride told Martin that wound ballistics was a fascinating science, because bullets had a tendency to do their own thing. "I once removed a bullet from a patient's small intestine after he'd been shot in the *knee*," he said colorfully. "And I've seen numerous non-lethal shots to the head, including a close-range effort where the bullet skated *around* the skull, leaving nothing but a headache and a nasty scratch." He avoided the word *luck.* Taking a bullet was never lucky, he said, but for Edith, it could have been much worse. Along with muscle, tissue, and ligament damage, she'd suffered extensive (but reparable) nerve trauma, as well as multiple fractures to the ilium and femur. Definitely *not* lucky, but the same bullet could easily have shattered her pelvis and sent bone fragments through her abdominal cavity and reproductive organs—*or* deflected to her heart and killed her almost instantly. It was also worth noting that had the bullet entered two inches to the right she would almost certainly have been paralyzed, and had it exited an inch to the left she would have bled to death.

"Studies suggest," Dr. Pride had said, "that women feel pain more acutely than men, but they're also more likely to survive a traumatic injury."

"Just goes to show how strong they are," Martin said.

"Strong, yes, although in my professional medical opinion"—he couldn't keep the smile from his lips—"your daughter is a total badass."

"Tell me something I don't know," Martin said.

* * *

Edith hoisted her guitar into the trunk—she didn't need any help—then hopped in beside Shirley.

"Do we know where we're going yet?" she asked, fastening her seatbelt.

"First stop: New Jersey," Shirley said. "To meet Michael Jackson."

"Right," Martin said. "After that . . . everywhere else."

Alyssa cranked the ignition. "Let's hit the road."

Two hundred miles that first day with many more to go, bopping along to the radio as the scenery changed and the sun crept west. Every now and then the signal would fade, or another radio station would ghost in, but they didn't touch the dial. On those occasions they sat in a content, thoughtful silence and listened to the crossover—the place between—knowing that, with time and distance, it would clear.

ACKNOWLEDGMENTS

First and foremost, my thanks to the people who made Halcyon possible, perhaps without knowing it: Jaime Levine, who acquired it (unwritten) as part of a two-book-deal for Thomas Dunne Books in the United States, and the late Mickey Choate, who agented said deal. I owe them both so much, and will never forget what they have done for me. Thanks also to Will Anderson, formerly of Thomas Dunne Books, who helped me develop the pitch, and to Pete Wolverton and Thomas Dunne for giving me a shot to begin with.

The team at St. Martin's Press deserve a standing ovation. No doubt about it: Joe Brosnan, Justin Velella, my US editor, Michael Homler, who is always professional and kind, and the seriously awesome Lauren Jablonski. Thank you all so much. Working with you has been a pleasure and an honor. Equally, thanks to my brilliant UK editor, Cat Camacho, the wondrously talented Julia Lloyd, and the whole crew at Titan Books who have done such an amazing job bringing *Halcyon* to readers across the pond.

To the agents: Laurel Choate, for whom I have nothing but gratitude and admiration. Howard Morhaim, who has demonstrated such patience, wisdom, and generosity. Sean Daily at Hotchkiss & Associates, whose enthusiasm has never waned. Deepest thanks to you all.

My thanks to the friends, family, and members of the community—too many to mention—who have shown their love and support in myriad ways. To the nameless thousands, in books, in person, and online, whose photographs, stories, and articles helped in the (extensive and sometimes heartbreaking) research for this novel.

And as always, my love and thanks to my wife Emily, and our children Lily and Charlie, who give me all the light and healing I need.

ABOUT THE AUTHOR

Rio Youers is a British Fantasy Award-nominated author whose short fiction has been published in many notable anthologies, and his novel, *Westlake Soul*, was nominated for Canada's prestigious Sunburst Award. Rio lives in southwestern Ontario with his wife, Emily, and their children.